LUCKY STIFF

"Annelise Ryan has done it again! Her heroine Mattie Winston has a way with a crime scene that will keep you reading, laughing and wondering just what can possibly happen next in this entertaining romp. Wisconsin's engaging assistant coroner brings readers another winning mystery!"

—Leann Sweeney, author of the Cats in Trouble Mysteries

"*Lucky Stiff* is a roller coaster ride of stomach clenching action, sizzling attraction, belly laughs, and a puzzler of a mystery. Annelise Ryan has created a smart and saucy heroine in Mattie Winston, who you just can't help but like especially as she endures what is possibly the worst road trip ever. What a thrill ride!"

—Jenn McKinlay, author of the Cupcake Bakery Mysteries and the Library Lover's Mysteries

FROZEN STIFF

"Ryan mixes science and great storytelling in this cozy series . . . The forensic details ring true and add substance to this fast-paced and funny mystery. Good plotting and relationship drama keep the mystery rolling, while Mattie's humorous take on life provides many comedic moments."

—*Romantic Times Book Reviews*

"[Mattie's] competence as a former ER nurse, plus a quirky supporting cast, makes the series intriguing. Ryan has a good eye for forensic and medical detail, and Mattie gets to be the woman of the hour in her third outing."

—*Library Journal*

"Absorbing . . . Ryan smoothly blends humor, distinctive characters, and authentic forensic detail."

—*Publishers Weekly*

SCARED STIFF

"An appealing series on multiple fronts: the forensic details will interest Patricia Cornwell readers, though the tone here is lighter, while the often slapstick humor and the blossoming romance between Mattie and Hurley will draw Evanovich fans who don't object to the cozier mood."

—*Booklist*

"Ryan's sharp second mystery . . . shows growing skill at mixing humor with CSI-style crime."

—*Publishers Weekly*

WORKING STIFF

"Sassy, sexy, and suspenseful, Annelise Ryan knocks 'em dead in her wry and original *Working Stiff*."

—Carolyn Hart, author of *Dare to Die*

"Move over, Stephanie Plum. Make way for Mattie Winston, the funniest deputy coroner to cut up a corpse since, well, ever. I loved every minute I spent with her in this sharp and sassy debut mystery."

—Laura Levine, author of *Killer Cruise*

"Mattie Winston, RN, wasn't looking for excitement when she became a morgue assistant—quite the contrary—but she got plenty and so will readers who won't be able to put this book down."

—Leslie Meier, author of *Mother's Day Murder*

"*Working Stiff* has it all: suspense, laughter, a spicy dash of romance—and a heroine who's guaranteed to walk off with your heart. Mattie Winston is an unforgettable character who has me begging for a sequel. Annelise Ryan, are you listening?"

—Tess Gerritsen, *New York Times* best-selling author of *The Keepsake*

"Mattie is klutzy and endearing, and there are plenty of laugh-out-loud moments . . . her foibles are still fun and entertaining."

—*Romantic Times Book Reviews*

"Ryan, the pseudonym of a Wisconsin emergency nurse, brings her professional expertise to her crisp debut . . . Mattie wisecracks her way through an increasingly complex plot."

—*Publishers Weekly*

Books by Annelise Ryan

WORKING STIFF

SCARED STIFF

FROZEN STIFF

LUCKY STIFF

BOARD STIFF

Published by Kensington Publishing Corp.

Board
Stiff

Annelise
Ryan

KENSINGTON BOOKS
http://www.kensingtonbooks.com

KENSINGTON BOOKS are published by

Kensington Publishing Corp.
119 West 40th Street
New York, NY 10018

All Kensington titles, imprints and distributed lines are available at special quantity discounts for bulk purchases for sales promotion, premiums, fund-raising, educational or institutional use. Special book excerpts or customized printings can also be created to fit specific needs. For details, write or phone the office of the Kensington Special Sales Manager: Kensington Publishing Corp., 119 West 40th Street, New York, NY 10018. Attn.: Special Sales Department. Phone: 1-800-221-2647.

Kensington and the K logo Reg. U.S. Pat. & TM Off.

ISBN-13: 978-0-7582-7276-8
ISBN-10: 0-7582-7276-6
First Kensington Mass Market Edition: March 2014

eISBN-13: 978-1-61773-031-3
eISBN-10: 1-61773-031-9
First Kensington Electronic Edition: March 2014

10 9 8 7 6 5 4 3

Printed in the United States of America

Chapter 1

I can't tell if the shrink sitting across from me, a psychiatrist by the name of Maggie Baldwin, is disturbed or intrigued by my fascination with dead bodies. She is sitting in her chair, leaning forward, pen poised over the tablet she has on her lap. The eager expression on her face reminds me of the one my cat, Rubbish, gets whenever he spies a bug he's about to pounce on. I wonder if the doctor is about to have me hauled off by the cops on a 51-15, the part of the Wisconsin state code that deals with the emergency detention and involuntary commitment of people who are deemed mentally unstable, a euphemism for what we used to call "bat shit crazy" back when I was a nurse working in the ER.

"So tell me, just what is it about dead bodies that fascinates you?" Dr. Maggie asks.

At the very least, I fear she's envisioning some fame-garnering write-up in a psych journal highlighting the exciting yet disturbing mental case she's just discovered, so I try to explain myself better.

"I'm not fascinated by dead bodies per se. Well, not exactly." I sigh, frustrated by my inability to express what I mean. "You see, this is why I didn't want to come here. I tell you I'm fascinated by my work and the next thing I know you're making me out to be some kind of weird necrophiliac or something. You people aren't happy unless you can come up with a fancy psychiatric diagnosis on everyone you see, and if one doesn't present itself, you'll make one up. I'm sorry to disappoint you, but you won't be filing your Mattie Winston chart under psycho."

"I see," she says, scribbling something on her pad.

"No, I don't think you do." I'm feeling a bit irritated and try to see what she just wrote down.

"You're angry."

"Did your fancy degree help you figure that out, or is it the snippy tone in my voice that cued you in?"

She sighs, shifts a bit in her chair, and puts the pen down on top of the tablet. Then she folds her hands in her lap, her fingers interlaced.

I note she has an expensive French manicure and several rings—three with diamonds and one with a giant blue sapphire—the combined worth of which is probably more than I'll make this year. She's a tiny woman, the kind who can wear pencil skirts and fashionable shoes, the kind who can eat whatever she wants and not worry about it, the kind who can realistically expect to be carried over the threshold someday. Psychiatrist or not, she has no understanding of what it's like to be me—six feet tall with size twelve feet and living on the wrong side of the two-hundred mark on the scale.

"I'm not your enemy, Mattie," she says. "I'm here to help you."

"I don't need any help."

"Apparently, Izzy felt otherwise," she says softly.

Yes, he did, damn it. And her reminder of this fact is like a slow dagger penetrating my flesh one centimeter at a time. Izzy is my friend, my landlord, and my on-again, off-again boss. I trust him and would do almost anything for him. That's the only reason I'm here now with Naggy Maggie, who sighs again, picks up her pen, and lifts the front page of her tablet. Underneath that page is a sheet of paper with stuff typed on it. I want to ask her what it says, but her next words give me a pretty good idea.

"My understanding from Izzy is he's concerned about the emotional trauma you've been through recently. He told me that you're a nurse and that you and your husband, David, who is a surgeon, both worked at the local hospital here in Sorenson. Some months ago, you discovered your husband was having an affair with one of your coworkers at the hospital, and this particular coworker was then murdered. When Izzy did the autopsy, it was discovered she was pregnant and tests proved that the baby was your husband's. You and your husband—"

"Ex-husband," I correct.

"I'm sorry. You and your ex-husband were suspects at one point, though you were both eventually cleared. You have now divorced him, undergone some financial ups and downs, and met a new man you have—or had—a romantic interest in. I believe Izzy said he's a local homicide detective, is that correct?"

"Yes. His name is Steve Hurley."

"Izzy said a non-fraternization rule meant you had to choose between a working relationship and a romantic one with this man. Is that correct?"

I nod.

"And you chose the latter," she says, driving that knife forward another centimeter or two.

"I tried to, but it didn't work out."

"Izzy said you resigned your position with him because you thought you were getting hired back at the hospital, but your ex-husband did some kind of political wrangling and the job fell through."

"Yes it did," I say, feeling my anger build again. "What David did was totally unnecessary. He'd already moved on. He's dating our insurance agent. The job I was going for was a night shift position in the emergency room. It's not like I was going back to my position as an OR nurse. David and I would have hardly ever crossed paths. But apparently the risk of it happening even once was too much for him. He told the director of nursing that it would be too awkward. Since he's the only general surgeon on staff right now, the administration can't afford to piss him off."

"Izzy said you got a decent settlement in the divorce, so the unemployment wasn't a financial stressor for you."

"It wasn't the money that was the problem with not having a job. In fact, I was fine with it as long as I could be with Hurley. But that didn't work out, either."

"What happened?"

"Well, after several months of flirtation, Hurley and I finally consummated our relationship."

"You had sex."

I nod, smiling at the memory.

"I take it from the expression on your face that the sex was satisfactory."

"Very."

"So what went wrong?"

"Everything. We were still in bed when his door-bell rang. When he answered it, there was a woman and a teenage girl standing on his front porch. Turns out they were his ex-wife, who isn't really an ex because she never filed the divorce papers, and the daughter he never knew he had. Needless to say, it was a bit of a shocker. Since things haven't gone well for them lately, they moved in with Hurley."

"That must have been painful."

"You're a master of understatement."

"So what does Hurley plan to do from here on out? What are his plans? Where does this leave the two of you?"

I shrug, and look away from her.

"What does Hurley say?"

"I don't know. I haven't talked to him since it happened."

"Which was when again?"

"A couple months ago, right after the new year."

"Hurley hasn't tried to speak to you in all that time?"

"Oh, he's tried," I say. "Several people have tried, but I haven't wanted to talk with anyone."

"Yes, Izzy mentioned that he felt like you were avoiding him and everyone else. So what have you been doing all this time?"

"This and that," I say with a shrug. "I spend a lot of time at the casino. I discovered I like to play black-jack, and occasionally some poker. It relaxes me."

"When was the last time you were at the casino?"

I hesitate a beat too long and I know she knows I am considering a lie. "Last night," I admit.

"Do you go there every night?"

Again I hesitate, and again I realize it's pointless. "Lately I have, yes. But that will be changing. Now that I'm back working with Izzy, I have to be available to take call."

"Are you okay with that?"

"Very much so." I quickly add, "I mean, I do feel bad that Jonas Kriedeman couldn't keep the job. I know he wanted it as much as I do. Unfortunately, he discovered he has allergies to formaldehyde and sodium fluoride that are so severe, he was having trouble breathing even when he wore protective equipment. It worked out okay for him though, because his job as an evidence tech at the police department was still open. They tried to eliminate the position and pass off the evidence collection duties onto the detectives and officers to save money, but it proved to be too much and too many things were getting missed. When they heard that Jonas was interested in coming back, they were more than happy to let him step back into his old position. In the end, it worked out well for both of us."

"When I asked if you were okay with that, I was referring to the fact that you will no longer be able to go to the casino every night."

"Oh," I say, feeling totally stupid. "Sure, why wouldn't I be?"

"How much time have you spent there in the past two months?"

"You think I'm an addict, don't you?"

"Do you think you're an addict?"

I wag a finger at her. "No no no," I say with a sly smile. "I know that answer-a-question-with-another-question trick. I used to use the same technique on my patients all the time when I worked in the ER. And I used it when I was working with Izzy, too, whenever I had to question someone."

"Are you planning on going to the casino tonight?"

Once again, I find myself hesitating because the truth is I *had* planned on going. Friday nights are my favorite. It's busier than during the week and the blackjack tables are generally full, which makes for a more interesting evening most of the time. But I know that admitting to this will only fuel the fire Naggy Maggie has already kindled so I opt for an indirect and far more virtuous answer instead.

"Actually, I'm meeting someone I know at a local gym for a workout session tonight."

"And what friend is this?"

"Sheesh," I say with what I hope is a disarming and distracting chuckle. "You make me feel like I'm back in high school being interrogated by my mother."

Maggie arches her brows and starts scribbling on her tablet. "So, who is the friend?" she asks again.

As I cuss under my breath for mentioning my mother, my heart skips a beat, and I wonder what psychological flaw I've just revealed. I know there must be some pathological skeletons hanging in my closet of a brain because of my mother.

"I'm going with Bob Richmond, a semiretired detective on the police force," I tell Maggie. "We worked a case together awhile back, and he ended up getting shot. Turns out that may have been the best thing that could've happened to him. He was grossly overweight, hanging in somewhere around four hundred pounds. After his surgery, he lost a bunch of weight and he's been working out at the gym. He looks pretty good and he's lost nearly a hundred pounds. I had agreed to be his workout buddy back before he got shot, so he's calling in that chit again. I figure I can use the exercise. I tend to eat more when I'm stressed, so I'm sure I've gained a few pounds over the last couple months." This last comment proves that I, too, am a master of understatement.

Maggie doesn't say anything for twenty or thirty seconds. She just sits there in her chair looking at me with this enigmatic Mona Lisa smile that makes me nervous and pisses me off. When she finally does say something, I realize she wasn't at all fooled by my attempt to divert her attention. "And after your workout, will you be going to the casino?"

"Fine. Yes," I say irritably, sagging in my chair. "I might go for a little while, but if I do, it won't be for long. My on call hours start at seven o'clock tomorrow morning, assuming you approve me for duty."

"That's not my job. Izzy already rehired you."

"Yeah, but he made the offer contingent upon my seeing you. Why is he doing this to me?"

"Because he cares about you and he's concerned. As am I."

"I'm fine." Even I know this is a lie. I'm far from being the equivalent of a psychiatric code blue, but my mental state isn't exactly stable, either. My life over the past two months has been a hot mess of frustration, confusion, and self-loathing.

"I think you're okay for the moment, but the fact remains you haven't seen Hurley yet, correct?"

I sigh. "That is correct."

"And whether or not you're willing to admit it, this gambling thing has me concerned. So here's what we're going to do." She gets out of her chair, walks over to her desk, and sets her notebook and pen down. Then she picks up another notebook. It's one of those black and white composition books, the kind that I used to have in middle school. She walks over and hands it to me.

"I want you to start keeping a diary. At least once a day, I want you to sit down with this notebook and jot down what you did for the day, and what your thoughts and feelings were at the time. It doesn't have to be very detailed as far as activities are concerned, but I do want you to be honest in recording your thoughts and feelings. No one will see what you write unless you want to share them with me, and what you decide to share with me is up to you. I think it will help you zero in on some key emotions and feelings that will help us over the long term."

"The long term? I have to come back?"

"At least once more," Maggie says. "Let's plan on meeting again on Monday after your weekend on call and we'll see how things have gone. Then we'll figure out where to go from there."

Great. It's not bad enough that Izzy has forced me to see a counselor when he knows how much I hate shrinks, he's also managed to hook me up with one who's giving me homework. This can't end soon enough for me, but first I know I'm going to have to convince Maggie that I'm not addicted to gambling. It won't be easy; in my mind's eye I see the weekend stretching out before me, sitting in my cottage, twiddling my thumbs, aching to hit up the casino, but unable to go. The very thought of it makes my palms start to sweat.

That's when I realize that if I'm going to make it through the weekend and get rid of Maggie, someone will have to die.

Chapter 2

Saturday, March 1

Dear Diary,

    This is the first of my entries, dictated not only by the shrink Izzy made me see, but also by my new personal trainer, Gunther, who I'm convinced is a throwback to the era of Medieval torture chambers. Both Dr. Maggie and Gunther want me to record my feelings, emotions, and activities each day, though Gunther also wants me to track what I eat. He says it's part of what he calls my new life plan, which I find ironic since I'm pretty sure the end result of the "exercise circuit" he ran me through last night will be my death. First he strapped me into some contraption that looked like a birthing chair and kept pulling my legs apart like I was the wishbone on a turkey. Then he put me on another machine where I had to pull on a bunch of bars with weights connected to them. It made my boobs bounce like beach balls in an ocean surf. Then I had to ride a bicycle to nowhere while sitting on a seat about as wide as the average thong, which gave me a severe case of 'rhoid rage. I think I must have blacked out after that because I don't remember the rest of my "circuit."

This morning when I tried to get out of bed, my muscles screamed at me and I ended up walking like a ninety-year-old woman. My arms hurt so bad I couldn't hold my coffee cup and when I tried to brush my teeth, the pain made me want to rip my arm off my body and beat Gunther over the head with it. I was so tired by the time I finished with the machines that I flat out refused to get on the treadmill, which should be called a dreadmill. I kind of wish I had one here now, though, so I could walk Hoover on it instead of having to leash him up and take him outside.

I was surprised how fast the stiffness set in. By the time I got home, I was already walking as if I had a broomstick up my ass and the hot shower I had hoped would help, only made me more tired. I didn't sleep much, though. Every time I moved, it hurt so much it would wake me up. And it's hard to sleep without breathing. The worst part of it all was watching Bob Richmond run through his circuit, which included some of the same torture devices Gunther made me use. Richmond, who was the fattest person I knew three months ago, breezed through the circuit with only a tiny pant to show for his efforts. I, on the other hand, was wheezing like a broken accordion and vacillating between fearing I was dying and wishing I was dead. It took four ibuprofen and two extra-strength acetaminophen tablets this morning to get me to where I could pull my own pants up.

The good news is my utter exhaustion and near-death experience with Gunther kept me from going to the casino last night. I didn't even miss it. This should make Dr. Naggy happy and maybe get me paroled soon.

Before starting my note this morning, I thought about what I should write to comply with her assignment. That's when I realized how diabolical it was of her to give me a notebook with the pages sewn into place. I know she said she wouldn't ask to look at or read what I wrote, and it is up to me if I want to share, but I don't believe her. If I commit something to these pages that I later want to delete, I'll have to tear the page out or scribble over it. With this composition style notebook, I can't do either of those things without leaving evidence, and I'm afraid of what conclusions she might draw from my second guessing. So I've done the next best thing, instead. I'm using a pencil to write everything down. At least then I can erase the evidence if I think it's too damning.

This is the start of my first weekend on call since I got my old job back. Since Dr. Naggy wants me to record my activities and feelings, I will say that I'm happy to be back at a job I love doing. But I also find myself longing for a call because the weekend is stretching out before me bereft of anything fun to do.

Not that someone dying is fun, but it is something to keep me busy. Right now I need that to distract me mentally and because if I stop moving for very long, I may not be able to talk my protesting muscles into starting again. Of course, work will mean seeing Hurley again and I'm not sure how I feel about that.

Gunther's request that I record what I eat isn't off to a great start. I've been eating out a lot lately, grabbing stuff on my way to and from the casino, so my cupboards are looking a little bare. For breakfast this morning, I finished off half a pint of Ben & Jerry's Chunky Monkey ice cream. I would have behaved better, but aside from pet food and a can of peach slices that I didn't have the strength to open—it hurt too much when I tried to pull the tab—it was all I could find. As it was, I had to let the ice cream sit out for a bit and soften up so I could get it out of the container.

I'm bored, I don't want to sit still, and I don't want Gunther's tortures to be for naught, so I suppose the smart thing to do at this point is to go grocery shopping. Since I'm turning over a new leaf, I'm making up a list of healthy crap to stock up on.

Maybe this diary thing isn't such a bad idea after all.

Chapter 3

It's strange how life works out, and sometimes, like today, death is even stranger. It is the ultimate equalizer, eliminating the barriers that separate the Haves from the Have-Nots, the blacks from the whites, or the young from the old. It can be feared or revered, expected or surprising, welcomed or shunned. But it cannot be avoided. It is the one thing we all have in common: some day we are going to die.

That day has arrived for the man I'm staring at and I'm not sure which part of this scenario is stranger: the fact that I'm standing in a men's room with another woman, the fact that there is a corpse on the floor, or the fact that the woman standing beside me is alive, but looks deader than the body at our feet.

Since I live in a small town of about 11,000 souls and the odds of me knowing any one of them are pretty good, I should probably feel guilty that someone is dead since I was sort of wishing for exactly that less than an hour ago. But I don't. God is punishing me enough as it is by making every movement feel like the bite of a Taser.

It all began with my decision to go grocery shopping. I loaded myself and my dog, Hoover, into my car, a midnight blue, slightly used hearse. Inconspicuous it is not, but it's reliable, has relatively low mileage, and most important, it was what I could afford back when I bought it.

It's a beautiful spring day—forty-eight degrees outside already—atypically warm and sunny for early March in Wisconsin. But then the whole winter has been kind of wonky, with warmer temperatures and much less snow than usual. Because of the warm temperature, I cracked the windows in the hearse and Hoover forwent his usual spot in the back where the smells keep him in sniffing heaven, and settled into the front passenger seat, instead.

I got out of the hearse and shut the door, leaving Hoover inside with the windows half down. I didn't bother to lock the doors. Sorenson is a small, Midwestern town with Midwestern values, and unlocked doors on cars and even houses are fairly common. Not that we don't have our share of crime. But I'm not too worried about my car since most people, thieves included, are reluctant to look or search around inside a hearse.

I turned to head into the grocery store and nearly got run over by a big white car that braked at the last second. Had it been going any faster, I'm sure it would have hit me, but it was moving so slow I hadn't realized it was moving at all. The car was a large, mostly white Cadillac, circa 1980-something. One of the perks of living in a small, self-sustaining town is the low mileage on many of the cars. There are plenty of vehicles on the roads in Sorenson that are older than I am. Between the winter salt, the spring-time potholes, and the summer and fall collisions with drunken tractor and combine drivers, most of the cars around here have had more body work than an aging Hollywood star.

Behind the wheel was Irene Keller, who is eighty-something years old and the owner of the Keller Funeral Home. She leaned out her side window. "Oh, Mattie! Thank goodness I caught you!"

This struck me as an odd thing for her to say considering that she doesn't know me all that well and has never been overly friendly toward me unless she's trying to sell me a casket. Our main connection is Bjorn, an elderly gent who taxied me around for a week or so after I wrecked my car and before I bought the hearse. Bjorn is Irene's husband. They tied the knot almost two months ago after a very hasty courtship. Then again, when you're both past eighty, the definition of hasty when referring to courtships is likely not what it is for the rest of us. My only other connection to Irene is Barbara, Irene's hair and makeup artist to the dead. Barbara is also my hairdresser, and a very talented one. The fact that she works in the basement of a funeral home, makes me lie down on an embalming table, and always smells faintly of formaldehyde are minor transgressions I've learned to overlook in exchange for her wizardry. Seeing Irene reminded me that I was long overdue for a visit to Barbara.

"I was on my way to your house when I saw you pull out," Irene said, wringing her arthritic, veiny hands. "I didn't think I'd ever catch up to you. Thank goodness you pulled in here."

I've seen Irene drive. She'd have trouble catching

a cripple on crutches as slow as she goes. But since I suspect she can't see all that well anymore, it's probably just as well. She looked genuinely upset and I'm certain she would have been pale if she'd ever had any color to begin with. But she's had skin as flimsy and transparent as one-ply toilet paper for as long as I've known her.

"What's wrong, Irene?"

"It's Bjorn," she said, and for a second I was certain she was going to tell me he had died. But then she shocked me by saying, "I think he killed someone."

"You think Bjorn killed someone?" I was certain I must have misheard her because the Bjorn I know can hardly figure out how to get his pants on each morning and forgets who he is each night after sundown. Then I remembered that up until a few weeks ago he was driving a cab for the local service. Had he run over someone? "Did he have an accident with the taxi?" I asked her.

"No no. He quit that job right after we got married."

"Then why do you think he killed someone?"

Irene shook her head and the skin beneath her chin flapped like a turkey wattle. "Not here, not in public," she says in a whispery voice. "I need to show you."

"Show me what?"

"The biggest mess you'll ever see."

That was saying a lot because I've seen some pretty big messes in my time. A smart person would have run as fast as possible in the opposite direction. A smart person would have written Irene off as a nut job with an overactive imagination. But curiosity is my third biggest vice, right behind food and gambling, and today *smart* was taking a holiday. I was already trying to figure out how to spin this for my diary.

I got back in the hearse and followed Irene out of the parking lot and toward the east side of town at a snail's pace. Several minutes later, she pulled into the lot of the Twilight Nursing Home and parked. I found a space near the end of a row, realizing that a hearse out front was probably less likely to attract attention here than it would in other places. I again cracked the windows and told Hoover to stay.

When we reached the main entrance, which took longer than it should have since neither of our bodies were moving very well, Irene grabbed my arm and leaned in close, speaking in a conspiratorial whisper. "I don't think the staff knows yet so just pretend you're here to see someone."

"Who?"

"I don't know. Pick someone. Don't you know someone who lives here from your days working at the hospital?"

There were several someones who fit the bill, and I picked a name at random. "Okay, I'll say I'm here to see Gladys Stumper."

Irene had her hand on the door handle. Instead of pulling the door open, her head whipped around so fast her neck made a loud snapping sound.

I waited, wondering if her head would fall off, or if she'd fall to the ground paralyzed. Neither happened.

"Hell, no, Winston," she sneered. "Gladys died a month ago. Had the big one during the night. They found her cold and dead in bed the next morning, the lucky bitch."

I was a bit appalled by both the news of Gladys's death and Irene's comment.

"What?" Irene said, seeing my expression. "You don't know what hell it is, getting old. Wait until you get to be my age. You develop furniture disease, your farts turn to dust, and your face starts looking like a prune, which by the way, will become one of your favorite fruits. Every time you move, your bones creak like a haunted house . . . assuming you *can* move, since your joints work about as well as a rusted hinge. If you're lucky, you won't end up like Bjorn, who is so senile most of the time he could hide his own Easter eggs. As if that's not enough, you watch all your friends die these long, painful deaths and hope you'll be one of the lucky ones, like Gladys, and go quick, painless, and in your sleep."

Though I should have known better, I had to ask. "What is furniture disease?"

She looked at me like I had the IQ of a grape. "It's when your chest falls into your drawers. Get ready for it, honey, because with that rack of yours, you'll be using them as knee pads before you know it."

I straightened up and pulled back my shoulders to prove to myself that I was a long way away from furniture disease. "Okay, how about George Cummings?" I offered. "Is he still here and kicking?"

Irene shook her head sadly. From behind us, we heard the sound of Hoover barking and Irene's eyes lit up. "I have an idea. Go get that dog of yours and we'll take him in like he's one of those therapy dogs."

"I don't know, Irene. He's well behaved and all, but he's never been around a lot of people."

Irene dismissed my concerns with a wave of her hand. "He'll be fine. Go get him."

Since Irene was clearly determined, I did as she said and fetched Hoover from the car. Fortunately, I carry a leash in the car at all times so I hooked him up and headed back to Irene.

"Perfect," she said, giving Hoover a tentative pat on the head. "Now follow me and try to act like you don't know what's going on."

"That shouldn't be a problem since I don't," I reminded her.

We entered the facility and any semblance of normal living intended to be implied by the tasteful, homey decor and warm wall colors was immediately undermined by the faint but distinctive smell of stale urine. There was a small sitting room to our right and a door with a sign that told us it led to an administrative wing. To the left was a very long hallway with rooms on both sides, and I could see another hallway that broke off halfway down and ran to the right.

A heavyset woman with short, gray hair was sitting behind an enclosed area with a sliding glass window straight ahead of us. She was dressed in a white nurse's uniform and a name pin on her left breast identified her as CONNIE LANE, LPN.

"Back already?" Connie said to Irene.

"I have a lot of friends here," Irene said as she picked up a pen and signed her name in a logbook labeled *GUEST REGISTRY*.

"Not to mention potential customers," Connie said with a sly laugh.

"Really, Connie?" Irene said, setting the pen down and staring at the woman with a distasteful look that made Connie cough and flush bright pink in her cheeks. "Funeral humor? In this place?"

"Sorry," Connie muttered. She looked over at me

then and said, "Sorry, but we don't allow dogs in the facility."

"This isn't any old dog," Irene said. She slid the book over to me and I signed my name on the next line. "He's one of those therapy dogs. You know, the ones that go into hospitals and such to cheer up the patients. We set it up with Bernie like two weeks ago."

Though I knew Irene was lying, she was good enough at it that she had me convinced. Connie still looked doubtful and she stood up and peered over the desk at Hoover, who was busy sniffing every square inch of the floor.

"I don't know," Connie said.

"Oh, for Pete's sake," Irene said, clearly exasperated. She took out her cell phone. "I'll call Bernie and let him tell you."

"No no, that won't be necessary," Connie said, sitting back down. "I'm sure it will be fine."

"Come on," Irene said, tugging at my shirtsleeve. "Let's go."

We headed down the hallway to our left, past some offices, a large cafeteria-style dining room filled with empty tables, some public restrooms, an activity room, and a therapy room. At the intersection of the next hallway was a nurse's station that wrapped around the corner of the intersection. There wasn't a soul in sight.

"Where is everyone?" I asked Irene.

"Most of the nurses are either on break or in the wing that runs off the end of the hall down there," she said, nodding straight ahead. "That's where the bedbound patients are, and some of them have to be fed. This wing is for the walkers and wheelers. Those are the folks that can get around on their own either on foot or with a wheelchair. There are a lot of Alzheimer's patients and other types of senile dementia in the mix. Physically, they are in decent shape, but mentally, they require a living situation where they can be monitored more closely. You can tell which ones they are because they all have ankle alarms on, like they're some housebound prisoner. That's so the current administration can keep an eye on them, but still cut back on staffing."

The rooms we passed were all set up with the same basic layout of hospital-type furniture: adjustable beds, over-bed tables, bedside cabinets, and handicapped-friendly bathrooms with plenty of grab bars. Each room also had plenty of personal items, things that belonged to the individual patients, tiny touches intended to make the room seem more like home. It didn't work. The place reeked with the sad scent of institution.

We passed a staff break room where I saw another woman in a white uniform and two nursing assistants—identifiable by their youth, their colorful scrubs, and their ID tags—sitting around a table drinking coffees and sodas.

"After lunch is afternoon free time," Irene said. "That's when everyone gets herded into the TV room to watch a soap opera, or work on a jigsaw puzzle so the staff can take a break."

We reached the end of the hallway and entered a large dayroom with two big-screen TVs—one at each end—and French doors that led to an outside garden and patio area. There were a couple dozen residents here: some in wheelchairs, some seated at one of the four circular tables in the room, and some standing around conversing.

I also saw a group of people out in the garden

area. Despite the unusually warm weather, which typically will have a lot of hearty Wisconsinites running around outside with nothing more than long-sleeved shirts on, here in the land of old-age metabolisms and thin skin, the dress was a bit warmer. There was a faint haze hovering above the heads of the people outside and when I saw thin contrails of smoke circling upward, I realize they weren't out there just to enjoy the weather; they were smoking.

Everyone um the dayroom turned to stare at us as we entered and the murmur of conversation quickly faded into an uncomfortable silence. I saw Bjorn sitting at the end of a couch, his expression forlorn, and I scanned the room looking for the dead person. Everyone looked alive, though over in one corner there was a drooling guy in a wheelchair who gave me a moment's pause.

"Look at the cute dog," said a lady working on a jigsaw puzzle. "Come here, boy."

Hoover looked up at me as if he was asking permission, so I reached down and unhooked his leash. He padded over to the woman who had called him.

"What's she doing here?" grumbled a man who was glaring at me. He was wearing a plaid flannel shirt and suspenders to hold up his blue jeans, the waist of which was riding just beneath a huge girth of gut. He was standing against the wall, holding on to a walker that had a drop-down seat. "She works with the cops, doesn't she?"

"She's okay," Irene said. "She's smart. She'll be able to figure this out and she'll know what to do so we can decide how to present this to the cops."

Whoa! "Um, present what to the cops, Irene?" I asked, my stomach churning nervously. "What exactly is going on here?"

"Might as well show her," an elderly woman in a wheelchair said. She had a terrible palsy that made her look like one of those bobble-head dolls.

"Come on." Irene headed for the door that led outside. "I don't want to go past that desk Nazi again, so I'm taking you in through a back door."

I handed the leash off to a man who was also sitting at the puzzle table and, after getting assurances from him and others that they would keep an eye on Hoover, I followed Irene.

We wound around the enclosed garden area to the right and slipped through a gate in the six-foot-high fence surrounding the back area. "Normally this gate is locked on the other side with a simple slide bolt, but I unlocked it earlier," Irene explained, closing the gate behind us but leaving the bolt lock open.

She headed for a door, stuck a key in the lock, and led me inside. Based on the layout of the building, I guessed that we were at the back end of the administrative wing. This was confirmed once we paused to let our eyes adjust after the bright sunlight outside. Just ahead to my left was an open door to an office, and I eventually made out other offices with closed doors that were marked EXECUTIVE ASSISTANT, VICE PRESIDENT, CHIEF FINANCIAL OFFICER, VOLUNTEER DIRECTOR, and NURSING DIRECTOR.

"Are you glad to be back with Izzy?" Irene asked me as she started down the hallway.

We passed an open office, which was quite spacious. The sign on the door said PRESIDENT.

"I am."

"Why did you leave?"

"Because I'm an idiot."

Irene stopped so suddenly I almost ran into her.

She turned and stared at me, eyeing my hair with what I can only describe as a look of disgust. "Barbara says you haven't been in lately. You know that keeping up your appearance is important to your state of mind and your mental health, don't you?" She palmed a sadly thin curl of hair beneath her ear, pressing it into place. "Take it from someone who works hard at it, your appearance is everything."

It was hard to take her too seriously given that I have dust bunnies at home with more hair than she has on her whole head. Her comments about mental health made me wonder if she knew things about me that she shouldn't, but I decided I was just being paranoid and wondered what Dr. Naggy would make of that whole train of thought.

"I've been busy," I said in my defense. "And my mental health is just fine, thank you."

"Humph."

"Where is the dead person?" I asked impatiently. We had passed all the offices and were nearly at the end of the hallway. All I could see up ahead were restrooms, a small copy and mail room, and the doorway that led to the reception area at the front of the building.

"He's in here," Irene said.

I was only mildly surprised when she strolled into the men's restroom. I sensed early on that this whole situation was going to be weird and this proved me right. I followed her in, and stopped short when I saw the dead man slumped on the floor by the sink. His bald head was wedged between the wall and cabinet, his blue eyes wide and staring out of a face the color of a ripe plum. His legs were splayed, but his arms were bent and his hands were frozen into claw-like shapes that were resting on his chest. There was a white powder of some sort sprinkled on his face, and inside his mouth, which was gaping open, I saw a large, white mass. He was of average height, reasonably well built, and looked to be in his mid- to late forties rather than in his golden years, so I was pretty sure he wasn't a resident of the place. He looked vaguely familiar, but the white powder all over his face made it hard for me to figure it out. Out of habit, I squatted beside him to probe for a carotid pulse. It was a stupid move, one born of years working at the hospital. It was unnecessary for two reasons: one, this guy was clearly dead, and two, the act of squatting made my body scream out in pain when I used muscles that were still in shock after last night. Once the agony abated and I got a closer look at the victim's face, it hit me who he was.

"Oh my God," I said. "Is this Bernie Chase?"

"It sure is," Irene said.

Bernard Chase was the current CEO and owner of the Twilight Home. He bought it six or seven years ago when the guy who used to own it died and his family put the place up for sale as part of the estate settlement.

"What the hell happened to him?" I asked Irene.

"That's the problem," Irene said. "Nobody knows for sure, except maybe Bjorn, and he isn't telling . . . if he remembers."

I pulled my hand back from Bernie's neck and wiped it on my pants. "Do you think that stuff on his face is cocaine?"

"Pretty sure it's not," Irene said, and then she pointed toward Bernie's feet. Hiding under one of his pant legs was an empty plastic container that once contained isolyser powder, a substance that when sprinkled on anything wet, quickly turns the liquid into a solid. It's used to make it easier to clean up hazardous spills, or solidify body fluids that are being disposed of. The thought of someone ingesting or inhaling the stuff as it appeared Bernie had done, made my skin crawl, though the sensation might have also been my muscles staging a mini coup. I imagined how it must have felt for him, as all the fluid in his mouth, throat, lungs, and stomach expanded into a hard solid mass, making it impossible for him to breathe, compressing the blood supply in his neck. I prayed that the latter caused a quick loss of consciousness for him, because it was simply too horrifying to imagine anyone dying slowly that way.

"We need to call the police," I told Irene.

"Not yet. Something isn't right here and I don't want Bjorn getting into trouble for something he didn't do."

"Why do you think Bjorn had anything to do with this?"

"Because he was in here with Bernard. He came in after lunch to empty his catheter bag and he had that powder stuff with him. Even with those newfangled bags you got him, he often has trouble emptying them, so he carries that powder with him all the time, ever since you showed him how well it cleans up urine spills."

I grimaced, recalling how I'd done just that the first time Bjorn taxied me. His leg bag was bulging with urine and while he was showing me how hard it was for him to manage the drainage valve, he emptied the bag all over the floor of his cab. Since we were at the hospital at the time, I ran inside and grabbed some of the isolyser powder to help me clean up the urine.

"Even if Bjorn had the powder, why would he kill Bernard? Or anyone, for that matter?"

"Because he wanted him dead," Irene said matter-of-factly. "Everyone here wanted Bernard dead. And frankly, no one will be sorry he is."

I felt like I'd just walked into the Twilight Zone and just when I thought the situation couldn't get any more bizarre, Irene delivered her coup de grâce.

"Bernard Chase needed to die. He's been killing off patients ever since he bought the place."

Chapter 4

That's how I came to be squatting in a men's room with a dead guy who has just been declared a serial killer. I stare at Irene, completely at a loss for words.

"It's true," she says. "At first we thought we were imagining things, but once we started watching more closely, it became clear. When someone here has a setback and becomes bedbound, they die within weeks. Their daily cost of upkeep erodes Bernie's bottom line, so he gets rid of them. Didn't you notice how many of the patients here are up and about? The wing he has reserved for the bedridden patients only has twenty beds in it and there are sixty beds in the whole place. Those twenty beds are his breaking point to make money."

Now that she is pointing it out to me, it does strike me as odd. Most nursing homes are filled with bedridden patients. Still, murder is a big leap from manipulating a patient population. "What evidence do you have that he's been killing people?" I ask her.

"Unfortunately it's just a gut feeling at this point. I've had my boys look for clues when patients from here come to our funeral home, but short of doing a full autopsy, we haven't been able to come up with anything. Bernard probably changed his methods each time to keep anyone from getting suspicious. You know, smother one person with a pillow, poison someone else . . . that sort of thing."

I'm starting to think Irene might need Dr. Maggie's services for her paranoid delusions. It's not that unusual for people to die from one or more of the many complications that can come from being immobile or bedbound, not to mention the effects of whatever accident or illness got them that way in the first place. "Have you told anyone?"

"I told the police chief, Greg Hanson. I thought I had him convinced at one point, but he was only humoring me. He thinks I'm some dotty old lady like his alcoholic grandmother. I may have myself a tiny tipple now and then, but I'm nowhere near old lady Hanson's level of consumption. Hell, that woman was such a drunk, when we cremated her it took two days for the fire to go out."

I frown. I have to agree with Greg Hanson. Irene sounds dotty and paranoid. "And you think Bjorn killed Bernie by pouring that powder down his throat?" The skepticism is clear in my tone.

Irene rolls her eyes and lets out an exasperated sigh. "Good Lord, girl, have you been listening to anything I've been saying? We think Bernie is killing people. Bjorn wouldn't want that to go on. He was in here with Bernie. And that"—she points to Bernie's face—"is Bjorn's powder stuff."

I shake my head. "I'm not buying it, Irene. For one thing, I don't think Bjorn has the strength necessary to overpower Bernie and force that powder down his throat. Sure, Bjorn has several inches on Bernie height-wise, but Bjorn also has severe crippling arthritis, fading eyesight, and the reaction time of a snail. I can't see him besting Bernard in any sort of physical encounter. Two, I don't think Bjorn has the personality necessary to kill someone. Every time I've been with him he's been sweet, kind, and gentle."

Irene says nothing, but she looks doubtful.

"What did Bjorn tell you happened in here?"

"That's the problem. He doesn't know. When he gets stressed his dementia worsens. He doesn't remember anything about being in this bathroom. It might come back to him later, or it might not."

"Irene, we need to call the cops now, regardless of what you think Bjorn did or didn't do. Let them sort it out."

"Should I get him a lawyer?" Before I can say anything, Irene answers her own question with a vigorous nod that makes her neck crack. "Of course, I should. I need your brother-in-law, Mattie. Can you call him for me? Call him before we call the cops? That way we can ask him what we should do."

Calling my brother-in-law Lucien is not something I ever look forward to doing. He is crass, obtuse, offensive, and a general pain in the ass. But he's also a darned good lawyer who happens to be married to my sister Desi, which at least shows he has good taste.

"I suppose it can't hurt to consult with him," I say, wondering if it's true. Talking to Lucien can hurt in so many ways. I grab hold of the sink edge and stand, the pain it triggers nearly making me pass out. When the little floating stars disappear, I take out my cell phone and dial Lucien's cell, but I get a message saying the number is no longer in service. I start to dial his office, but remember it's Saturday and decide to call his home instead. It's not a call I look forward to for reasons other than wanting to avoid Lucien. I haven't spoken to my sister in weeks.

Desi answers on the second ring.

"Hi Desi, it's Mattie."

"Oh my God, Mattie! It's about time. Are you okay? I've been so worried about you. I've been by your place a couple times, but you're never home."

"I'm fine. I've been busy. I'm sorry if I worried you."

"Busy with what? We heard you weren't working for Izzy anymore."

"I wasn't for a while, but I started back with him a few days ago."

"Oh, good. Mom was worried, too. She even came with me one of the times when I stopped by your place."

This is surprising news. My mother is not the most caring of parents. She is also a hypochondriac and a germophobe who rarely leaves her house. The fact that she would risk exposure to come to my place is touching . . . and scary. I wonder if she was dressed in a Level Four Biohazard suit.

"I'm sorry I worried you guys," I say. "I promise to stop by either today or tomorrow and catch you up. Right now, I'm in a bit of a time crunch and I need to talk to Lucien. I've got an urgent problem and I need his help."

There is a long pause, long enough that I start to think the call dropped. "Lucien isn't here," Desi says finally in a sad voice. "We're separated and he's living at the Sorenson Motel for now."

"Separated? I didn't know."

"How could you? You've been impossible to find or talk to for weeks and weeks."

Guilt washes over me as I realize how selfish I've been, too wrapped up in my own misery to realize that other people might be suffering, too. That's probably what Dr. Naggy Know-it-all wrote down on her little tablet. "I know, Desi. Again, I'm sorry. I was . . . going through some stuff myself. When did this happen? And why?"

"It's been a couple weeks now. It's a long story."

"Are the kids okay?"

Irene folds her arms over her chest and starts tapping a foot.

"Ethan seems to be handling it with his usual indifference to anything that doesn't have multiple legs or an exoskeleton. But Erika is another story."

Ethan is ten, soon to turn eleven, and a bug fanatic. He has a collection at home that would give most people a lifetime of nightmares . . . and that's if you only see the dead, mounted ones. He also has a few live specimens: a tarantula tagged with the incongruous name of Fluffy and a three-inch-long, Madagascar hissing cockroach. Erika is thirteen and struggling with her identity, a battle that has recently left her with a dark, Goth-like appearance and a rather morbid fascination with death.

"Listen, Desi, I promise I'll stop by and see you. Tonight if I can, tomorrow at the latest, okay? But right now I have something very serious to deal with and I need Lucien."

"Okay."

"I tried calling his cell, but I got a recording saying it was disconnected. Did he get a new number?"

"He doesn't have a cell right now. None of us do."

There is a bitter tone in her voice that tells me there is more to this story, but in the interest of time I let it go.

"Can you give me the number for the motel then?" I ask.

She does so and I commit it to memory, hang up, and redial. I'm expecting to get the main office, but Desi must have given me a direct line to a room because Lucien answers.

"Lucien, it's Mattie."

"Mattiekins," he says, but the exuberance I'm used to hearing whenever he greets me with this nickname is missing. His flat, dead tone frightens me; I've never heard him so down before. "Have you talked to your sister? Is she willing to take me back?"

"I'll be happy to talk with you about Desi a little later, but right now I need your help." I explain what the situation is and he agrees to come over to the nursing home right away.

"In the meantime, call the police and get them started," he says. "Just don't let anyone talk to them until I get there."

"Will do, and thanks."

As soon as I disconnect the call Irene says, "You didn't know about your sister's separation?" She looks at me with disbelief, shaking her head. "I guess the rumors I heard about you were true."

"What rumors?" I ask, cursing the free flow of information that seems to permeate this town.

"That you dug yourself into a hole and never climbed out of it."

"I'm fine," I insist, and before she can take the time to determine the veracity of my statement I tell her, "Get out your cell phone and call 911."

"Why do I have to call? Can't you do it?"

"They might have questions that only you will

know the answers to," I tell her. "Just remember that you are being recorded so don't say anything that you don't want to have come back to haunt you."

"Okay, but if I'm going to call the cops, you have to go outside and let the others know."

"Why?"

"Just do it, okay?"

"Fine." With that I head out of the bathroom, down the hall, and back outside. When I come back through the gate in the fence, the people in the garden area who are smoking look at me with suspicion, as if they think I'm the cigarette police. I get an idea of why Irene wanted me to warn them when a whiff of their smoke reaches me. It isn't an ordinary cigarette smell; it's spicy and aromatic. I look closer at the cigarettes they are holding and see they are hand-rolled. Were the old folks smoking doobies?

"We're calling the cops," I say to no one in particular.

They exchange looks and a couple of them shrug. But then everyone moves to extinguish what they're smoking—some in the birdbath, some in the fresh mulch of a flower bed where a few crocuses and daffodils are braving the early spring, and one thin-haired lady pinches her smoke off and stuffs it inside her bra.

A tall, gangly old man hanging out by the door to the dayroom turns to head inside, but he stops when a portly fellow with a full head of gray hair says, "That's right. Run and hide because the cops are coming, Herb."

"At least I *can* run, Ed," Herb says. "With that gut of yours, it's a wonder you can even stand up."

Ed shrugs and grabs his gut in both hands, giving it a little shake. "Hey, when you have a big tool you need a large shed to store it in. At least I don't have a fake tan that looks like I rolled around in a tub full of Cheetos."

Ed's description is spot on and Herb seems to realize it. His eyes narrow and his hands clench.

One of the women standing nearby reaches over and puts a hand on Ed's shoulder. "Back down, you two. Now is not the time to wage your battles. Save it for the Op-Ed page."

When she says this, I realize who Ed and Herb are. For years, Ed Turner and Herb Patterson have waged a battle of wits and words through letters to the editor of our local paper. Their debates have ranged from such weighty topics as health care reform and gun rights to more picayune matters like how many tractors should be allowed to park at the local VFW and what hours the liquor stores can be open.

I leave them to their debate and head back to the administrative wing. I have to knock on the outside door—it's locked—and wait for Irene to let me in. Once inside, I halt for a few seconds like Irene and I did earlier so my eyes can adjust to the light. I'm about to ask Irene how the call went when the door behind her opens and a group of people stroll in. Two uniformed police officers enter and Connie, the nurse who was manning the desk out front, is close on their heels. I start to head toward them, but I'm stopped in my tracks when a fourth person walks in.

It's my first sight of Hurley in over two months and it takes my breath away.

Chapter 5

Connie Lane stops and stares at us with a confused and panicked expression. "What are you people doing back here? And why are the cops here? They said someone is dead? I'm the charge nurse. I should know what's going on."

I ignore her, unable to take my eyes off Hurley. My chest hurts, and for a moment I'm afraid I'm having a heart attack. Hurley looks back at me and our eyes lock. For a few brief seconds, it's as if we are the only two people in the room.

"Hey, Mattie. Good to see you," says a voice that's not Hurley's.

I finally tear my eyes away from Hurley and shift my attention to Junior Feller, one of the local uniformed cops. I've known Junior since grade school.

"Can you tell us what's going on here? The 911 center said some woman called to report a murder."

"Yeah, can you tell us what's going on here?" Connie echoes. The words seem to register with her and she pales. "Murder? There's been a murder?"

It takes every iota of strength I have not to look back at Hurley. I want to stare at him, to drink him in, to lock that vision in my mind forever so I can torture myself with it for months or years to come. Instead, I try to focus on Junior and the situation at hand. "It appears someone killed Bernard Chase, the owner and administrator here. He's in the bathroom." I gesture toward the men's room.

Connie gasps and clutches a hand to her chest. "That can't be. Mr. Chase isn't even here today. It's Saturday. He would have let us know if he was here."

"Trust me, he's here." I walk over and open the bathroom door. Junior and the other uniformed cop, a new guy I don't know whose name tag reads P. FOSTER, push past me to enter the bathroom. Hurley starts to follow and I finally risk another look at him. Our eyes meet again and I feel a pressure in my chest . . . and an odd heat in my loins. My mind briefly flashes on the last time we were together and I feel my entire body flush hot. Then he turns away from me and focuses on the body of Bernard Chase.

Irene is standing close to me and she looks shaken. I slip an arm over her shoulders, as much for my support as hers. My legs still feel like jelly after last night's S&M session with Gunther, and even the act of raising my arm causes a grabbing pain in my mid-back region.

Connie follows close on the heels of the cops and stops just inside the doorway with a gasp, staring at Bernie's body on the floor. "Oh my God!" she says, her eyes huge. She looks over at Hurley. "I knew something like this would happen," she adds, her voice decisive.

"Why is that?" Hurley asks, and just the sound of his voice makes my legs start to quiver.

"Because I had lunch with him yesterday and we ordered Chinese takeout. I was there when Bernard opened his fortune cookie." Her voice drops to an ominous level. "The fortune was blank."

There is a pause and then Junior says, "And?"

"And what?" Connie says, looking confused.

"What made you think something was going to happen to Mr. Chase?"

She stares agape at him, and then looks at the rest of us. "Really?" she says finally, with an expression of disbelief. "Come on, people. His cookie had a blank fortune in it for heaven's sake. I mean, that pretty much says it all, doesn't it?"

That it does, I think, though it says more about Connie's mental status than it does Bernard's victimhood.

"You had takeout?" Irene snaps. "Why is that? You didn't want to eat the same crap that gets served to the patients here?"

Connie shoots Irene a menacing glare that makes me slip my arm off Irene's shoulders and back away a step, fearing she might burst into flames.

"You should see what passes for food around here," Irene says. "They're constantly doling out all kinds of ground-up mystery meat that they hide under gravy so no one will notice the weird taste. The bread they use in their sandwiches is always stale. Plus they overcook everything. The vegetables they serve are limper than most of the wangers in this place."

Connie and Irene engage in a stare-down that lasts an uncomfortable length of time. It's obvious there is history and no love lost between the two women.

Hurley turns suddenly and exits the bathroom. He takes me by the arm and pulls me a little way down the hall, making my aching muscles protest. "I've been trying to reach you."

"I've been busy."

"So it would seem. Why haven't you called me?"

"I needed some time." I look away.

"And now you've had it. We need to talk. Don't go anywhere." With that, he heads back into the bathroom.

Irene has apparently released Connie from her dark-side death glare because the woman is scurrying off to the main part of the building, no doubt to act as the town crier. Irene walks over to me and says, "What's going on with you and Hurley?"

"Nothing."

"The hell you say." She narrows her eyes at me. "Anyone can feel the sparks coming off the two of you. What's up?"

I sigh. "Not now, Irene. I'll tell you later." I step over to hold the bathroom door open so I can watch and get a little more eye time with Hurley.

Junior Feller says, "How is it you're involved with this, Mattie?"

"Irene nabbed me and had me come by."

"Why did she do that?" Hurley asks, looking from Bernard to me.

"We just happened to run into one another," Irene says.

Hurley narrows his eyes at her. "You just happened to run into Mattie here at the nursing home?"

"Not exactly," I say. "It's a long story. I'll fill you in later."

Hurley opens his mouth as if to say something more, but after a moment he apparently decides otherwise.

He turns his focus to Bernard's body and cocks his head to one side as he studies it. "What is that in his mouth?" he asks of no one in particular, squatting beside Bernard's head.

"I think it's isolyser powder," I say. "It's that stuff that turns a liquid into a solid."

Hurley looks at me with a grimace. "You mean that stuff we use in the back of the squad cars if someone pees or pukes in there?"

"Probably," I say with a shrug. I'm not sure what the cops use for those purposes, but since health care facilities use it the way Hurley just described, I imagine it's all the same stuff.

"Eww," Junior says with a shudder. "Is that what killed him? If it was, it couldn't have been a nice way to go."

"I'm not sure if that's what killed him, but it looks like it might have been," I say.

"Who found him?" Hurley asks.

Irene shoots me a panicked look and after a moment's hesitation I say, "Irene did." Technically it's the truth as far as I know since we don't know if Bernie was dead when Bjorn fled the restroom.

Hurley doesn't miss the exchange of looks. "So Irene, what reason did you have to enter the men's bathroom?"

Crap! Clearly I hadn't thought my answer through. But Irene is saved from having to answer by the arrival of several more people who enter the administrative wing from the front inside doorway: Izzy, another uniformed cop named Brenda Joiner, and my brother-in-law Lucien.

Lucien's arrival, as usual, is problematic. I know there will be awkward explanations of how he knew to come here at all. Plus, because of my history with him, I'm always nervous whenever he's around, anticipating some obnoxious comment or leering look. His appearance usually adds to the level of discomfiture because it's never what anyone would call professional. His clothes are always wrinkled, stained, and frayed-looking, and his strawberry blond hair has a vigorous natural wave that Lucien tries to tame with enough grease to deep fry cheese curds for the entire town.

Today he looks worse than I've ever seen him. His clothes are messier than usual, his hair is weeks past the need for a cut, and his chin is covered with several days' worth of stubble. Plus his face looks haggard and tired. There are large, dark circles under his eyes, and his skin has a pale, sagging look to it. He looks ill and that frightens me. Lucien may be a big pain in my ass much of the time, but he is my brother-in-law and in some small part of my heart, I feel affection for him. I've long suspected that his obnoxious behavior and apparent misogynistic attitudes are nothing more than a cover he uses to protect his true feelings and to scare the bejesus out of everyone he meets. It's part of what makes him such an effective and successful lawyer, and such an annoying human being.

Hurley, not surprisingly, moans in frustration at the sight of Lucien. "What are you doing here, Colter?"

"Mattie called me to represent certain folks here who feel they need someone to look out for their best interests."

Hurley shoots me a venomous look, to which I shrug.

"All I did was track him down for Irene," I say. "It was her idea and at her request."

Izzy looks in the bathroom and then at me. "How did you get here already?"

"Irene got a hold of me. Long story."

"Have you done anything yet to process the scene?"

I shake my head. "I didn't know what I was walking into," I explain, "so I had Irene call the cops first thing when I saw the body."

Izzy sets down his scene kit, opens, takes out a camera, and hands it to me. "Why don't you start shooting pictures while I do the preliminary exam."

I step into the bathroom and quickly fire off several shots of Bernie's body and the bathroom. When I'm done, Izzy gloves up and kneels next to Bernie to begin his exam. I'm about to join him, but Hurley grabs me by the arm and hauls me out into the hallway again, letting the bathroom door close. He drags me closer to the outside exit and away from the huddle of Irene and Lucien.

"Hey," I protest, shaking my arm loose. "What the heck?"

"Exactly my thoughts," Hurley says. "What the heck has been going on with you? I've been trying to get a hold of you for weeks. The only phone number I had was your work cell phone and Jonas Kriedeman ended up with that. I came by a couple times, but you were never home and I haven't seen you anywhere around town."

"Well, now that I'm back on the job, you'll be seeing me plenty."

"What about us?"

"There isn't any *us*."

"How can you say that after our . . . after we . . . you know." An exasperated breath practically explodes out of him. "Come on, Mattie, you can't tell me that our time together wasn't magical and amazing."

"That it was," I admit, "at least up until the moment where your wife and kid showed up."

Hurley sighs and his shoulders sag. "I told you, I had no idea Kate didn't go through with our divorce. That was almost fifteen years ago. I don't have any feelings for her anymore. Nor did I know we had a kid together. I promise you, this was as much of a shock to me as it was to you."

Somehow I doubt that. "Are they still staying with you?" I ask, though I know the answer already. I've done my share of spying on Hurley's house over the past couple months.

"Yes," Hurley admits. "But only until Kate gets back on her feet. I can't just throw her and Emily out on the street. That's where they'd be if they weren't staying with me."

"That's very kind of you." I turn away to head back to the men's room, but Hurley stops me by grabbing my arm again and hauling me into Bernard's office. He shuts the door behind us, and whirls me around so that my back is against the door. He leans toward me, one arm on either side of me.

I'm vaguely aware of my aching body screaming at me, but something about Hurley's body coming in full frontal contact with mine makes it seem vague and distant. "That was a bit rough," I tell him, trying to sound angry though the truth is I'm rather titillated. "And this is a crime scene."

"We're not disturbing anything and I need to talk to you. I can't take this anymore, Mattie. I've been going crazy, thinking that you're so angry about what happened that you'll never see me again. Please tell me that isn't the case."

"Obviously not, since we're going to be working together again."

"You know what I mean," he says, his voice rife with frustration. "Why have you been avoiding me?"

"I've been avoiding everybody, Hurley, not just you."

"Where have you been all this time? Every time I went by your place your car was gone."

"I've been spending a lot of time at the North Woods Casino."

Hurley frowns and I anticipate a lecture about the evils of gambling. Instead, he moves his body in closer to mine. "Are you seeing someone else? Is that it? Are you and Joe Whitehorse an item?"

Joe Whitehorse is an investigator for the Indian Gaming Commission. Hurley and I met him during the last case we worked together and Hurley's suspicion that Whitehorse and I might be an item is understandable since there was some serious flirting going on. I did try to get something going there, but after one short, awkward date during which Whitehorse told me, "I'm really not that into tall women," I knew it was a bust. I later found out from some of the staff at the casino, some of whom now know more about me than my family does, that Whitehorse is a compulsive flirter and a serial dater.

"Oh, yeah, that's it," I say to Hurley, my tone thick with sarcasm. "I jumped right out of your bed and into his. Yep, Whitehorse and I are an item all right. We're so much an item, everyone is calling us MatJoe." I stop, take a breath, and shake my head. "Geez, Hurley, just what kind of slut do you think I am?"

"The kind I like," he says, and before I know what's happening, his lips are on mine. In a flash, two months of anger and confusion disappear. There is nothing in my head except the delicious sensations Hurley is triggering all over my body. I reach up and pull him to me; his hands run through my hair.

Then I hear a voice call out on the other side of the door, from out in the hall. "Hurley?" It was followed by, "Where the hell did he go?"

It's Junior's voice and Hurley and I spring apart like a fake-snake-in-a-can gag. I wince and freeze for a second as my body recovers from the sudden movement.

"Are you okay?" Hurley whispers.

I nod, and wince again as a lightning bolt of pain races down the back of my neck. "Gym workout last night," I whisper. "I'm a little sore."

The two of us take a few seconds to smooth our clothing and hair, and Hurley swipes a hand across his mouth and whispers, "Any lipstick?"

I whisper back. "I'm not wearing any. Does my hair look okay?"

His eyes rove over my head in a way that makes me weak in the knees. "It's beautiful."

This, to me, is proof that Hurley must be blinded by love, though I suppose lust can alter one's vision, as well. But to call my hair beautiful when it has an inch of dark roots showing and enough static frizz to attract every stray sock within a ten-mile radius, shows just how clueless Hurley is to the realities of the moment. I couldn't be happier.

With a deep, slow sigh and a quick glance at the front of his pants, Hurley turns and opens the office door. "In here, Junior. Mattie and I were just checking out Bernard's office."

I take a good look at the office for the first time. It's very spacious with an average size desk positioned in front of the back wall where a large bookcase is sandwiched between two big windows. On the right side of the room is an oblong table with eight chairs around it that I assume is used for meetings; on the other side there is a leather sofa and chair, a Tiffany floor lamp, and a coffee station. The walls are adorned with modernistic art, and large potted ficus trees are growing in front of each of the two windows. The top of Bernard's desk is organized clutter, with several distinct piles of papers, magazines, notebooks, and books. There is evidence of Bernard's recent presence: his desk chair is pushed back and turned sideways as if he just got out of it; a set of keys, including one for his car, is on one corner of the desk; and a jacket and hat are on the leather chair. On the left side of the desk is a landline phone—one of those multi-button things—and the handset is lying on the desktop on its side rather than in the cradle where it belongs. Beside it is a cell phone. I pick up the phone and try to turn it on, but the battery is dead.

On the right side of his desk is a half-filled coffee mug, and several papers are spread out over the desk blotter. I walk over to take a look at the papers, wondering what was important enough to drag Bernie in here on a Saturday, and see that they are tax forms for the Twilight Home. I snap dozens of pictures of the room, the desktop, the phones, the coffee mug, the position of the chair, even the tax records, then I pull open the desk drawers and take pictures of the contents without moving anything.

When I'm done I head back out into the hallway intending to check back in with Izzy. I see Hurley standing outside the bathroom door with Irene and Lucien, and as I approach, Hurley says, "This case just got a lot more interesting."

"Why is that?" I ask.

Hurley cocks his head and smiles at me. "Somehow I think you know already. Or are you going to tell me that Irene didn't mention to you that everyone here at the Twilight Home thinks Bernard Chase was a serial killer?"

Chapter 6

I decide to take a page from Dr. Naggy's playbook and avoid answering Hurley's question by tossing out one of my own. "Do you believe her?"

"It doesn't matter if I believe her. What matters is whether or not the other patients here believe it, because if they do, we have a very long list of suspects."

"So no quick and easy resolution for this one," I say. "Though I'm guessing most of the folks who are residents here wouldn't have the physical wherewithal to overpower Bernie."

"Not alone," Hurley says.

"Ah, interesting idea," I say.

Irene and Lucien are a few feet away, whispering back and forth. Hurley turns to them and says, "When are you going to tell me the full story, Irene? Why would anyone here think Bernard Chase is a serial killer?"

Irene looks at Lucien, who nods. "You're going to think I'm crazy or senile, but I'm not," she says.

"Just tell me," Hurley says with amazing patience.

"Promise me you'll keep an open mind."

Hurley nods and makes a circular motion with his hand, a signal for Irene to get on with it, so she does.

"While we don't have any real proof, we're all pretty sure that Bernard has been bumping off some of the patients here, the ones who become bedridden and require more expensive care. It seems like every time someone around here takes a turn for the worse, they end up dead."

"First of all, why does that seem unusual?" Hurley asks. "I mean some of the folks here aren't in the best of health anyway or they wouldn't be here, right?"

"Not necessarily," Irene says. "Some of them are physically healthy, but they have mental issues that make it unsafe for them to live alone, and either they have no family or their families can't be bothered taking them in. There are plenty of folks living here who don't have any life-threatening problems, but they either don't have a place to stay because they can't afford a home, or they're disabled enough that they can't live alone. Some folks are lucky enough to have families who care and take them in. But let's face it; a lot of us old folks are considered little more than a pain in the ass to our children."

There is a tone of bitterness in Irene's voice that makes me wonder if her own family has had similar issues with her recently. Overall, she seems to be doing well for her age, but she looks like one of those dried apple dolls and my nursing gut tells me she is one good sneeze away from a rapid response team.

Hurley says, "I get that, Irene, but I don't think old people dying when their health worsens is so unusual. Nor does it mean Bernard Chase was killing them off. That takes me to my second question. Who is this *we* you're referring to? Who besides you thinks this?"

Irene scoffs. "Pretty near everyone in this place. They've all been on edge lately, afraid of that one fall that causes a broken hip, or that little cough that leads to pneumonia, because around here, that's a guaranteed death sentence."

"Irene, Hurley's right," I say. "Those things happen everywhere, not just here. It's part of aging. It's how we die. It isn't pretty and it isn't nice, but it is what it is."

"Humph! Easy for you to say," Irene snaps. "You're still young yet. Just wait. One day, you'll have more pills than the neighborhood pharmacy, and your mind will start to slip so that the only thing you can retain with any regularity is water. Get back to me when you start gauging your attraction to the opposite sex on whether or not they can still drive. Then tell me how it is what it is."

I don't respond, mainly because I know Irene well enough to know it'd be a waste of time and breath, and also because I sense her fear and feel sorry for her. It can't be easy knowing death is lurking around the next corner.

Lucien, who has been uncharacteristically quiet through all of this, a fact that makes my inner alarms clang even louder, finally speaks up. "Is anyone under arrest?"

"Not yet," Hurley says. "It seems I have an entire facility of people to talk to."

Lucien looks at Irene. "If everyone here thinks Bernard Chase was a killer, why are you the only one who called a lawyer?"

"It wasn't for me," Irene says.

Before she can explain herself, Connie Lane bursts through the front entrance to the wing. "I need all of you to stop what you're doing." She might as well have told us to dance a jig. "The board is on the way."

"The board?" Lucien says. "What are you going to do, paddle us?"

"I'm referring to the board of directors," Connie says with a reverent tone. "I called to let them know what's going on. With Mr. Chase's death, our vice president is now in charge and she said no one is to do anything until she gets here."

Hurley shakes his head and sighs. "No, this is a crime scene and as such, I am the one in charge."

"Dorothy isn't going to like that," Connie says.

"Dorothy Granger?" I ask, and Connie nods. I let out a low whistle and tell Hurley, "You might have met your match. Dorothy was one of the hospital supervisors back when I first started working the ER. She pretty much ran things her way, something the existing director of nursing was happy to allow. No one complained because it turned out that Dorothy's way worked well and the DON at the time was an idiot. Unfortunately, the hospital CEO figured out that the existing DON was an idiot and fired her, hiring Nancy Molinaro to take her place. Both management and the hospital's general culture underwent a drastic overhaul, and when Dorothy and Nancy came together, it was like trying to bring together like poles on two different magnets. The resulting repellent force became part of hospital lore mainly because Dorothy is one of the few people Molinaro ever fired who didn't disappear altogether. We all figured it was because Molinaro was new to the area and hadn't had time yet to set up her body disposal process.

"Anyway, Dorothy got snatched up by Twilight Home's previous owner and hired on as the director of nursing. If rumor has it right, over the past decade she helped turn this place into a decent, clean, and profitable venture. Plus she got to run things her way again. It was a win-win for all. But I have to tell you, Dorothy is a force to be reckoned with."

Hurley doesn't look the least bit intimidated. He looks at Connie and says, "Do you know who Bernard's next of kin is?"

"His wife Vonda."

"I'll need an address. Can you tell me why Bernard was here on a Saturday?"

"I have no idea," Connie says. "I didn't even know he was in the building. He parks out back in the side employee lot and comes in through the rear entrance on his workdays, so I assume he does the same if he comes in on an off day. He can be back here without anyone knowing."

"Does he typically come in on the weekends? Or other off hours?"

Connie closes her mouth, and swallows hard. After the slightest hesitation—enough to let me think that she's hiding something—she shakes her head. "Not that I'm aware of." She quickly adds, "But I always work the day shift. I don't know what happens at night." She shoots me a worried look and I'm guessing that even if Hurley wasn't intimidated by my description of Dorothy Granger, Connie is. "Is the place going to have to close down? Am I going to lose my job?"

I shrug, unsure why she directed her question to me. "I don't think the place will shut down. It's home to a lot of people. As to whether or not you'll lose your job . . ." I shrug again.

Connie rears back as if I slapped her in the face. Her expression shifts from fearful, to stunned, to angry in a matter of seconds, and she directs her menacing gaze at Irene. "This is all your fault. You're always sticking your nose in where it doesn't belong. And now look what you've done!"

"Be quiet!" Hurley says to Connie, who looks put out but says nothing more. "Go get me Bernard Chase's address." Connie scurries off and Hurley shifts his attention back to Irene. "Why do I get the feeling you're not telling me everything?"

Irene looks at me, then at Lucien.

Lucien says, "It seems Bjorn might have been the last person to see Bernard Chase alive."

"Really?" Hurley says. "And when were you going to tell me this?"

"We just did," Lucien says with dead calm.

"Where is Bjorn now?"

"In the dayroom," Irene says.

"Fine. Go get him and bring him here, please."

Lucien nods and starts to steer Irene toward the front entrance to the hallway, but Connie has just returned with a slip of paper in hand—Bernard Chase's address I presume—so Irene does a quick about-face and heads for the outside exit, instead.

Hurley takes the paper from Connie and watches Irene and Lucien leave. As soon as they are out the door he turns to me with a puzzled expression. "What's wrong with Lucien? He looks like hell and he's behaving like a normal person, all polite and crap. Is he okay?"

"I don't know. I just found out he and Desi are separated, so maybe that's playing into things."

"Ouch. That's rough," Hurley says in a low voice. "It's no fun when you can't be with the one you love." An awkward silence fills the space between us until Hurley says, "We really need to talk later."

I nod, but don't say anything. Instead, I open the door to the men's room and ask Izzy if he needs my help.

"I'm ready to bag Bernard," he says, and I go in to help him while Hurley gets out his cell phone and starts making calls.

Junior stands by the door, propping it open, while Izzy and I tuck Bernard away inside the body bag. We are zipping it up when Lucien and Irene return with Bjorn in tow. They walk up to Hurley and Lucien says, "We need to show you something."

"Go ahead," Irene says to Bjorn.

Bjorn bends over and rolls up first one pant leg, then the other. On both of his lower legs are lines of fresh, red scratches. Next, he undoes his pants at the waist and pulls them down over his right hip, revealing more scratches.

Hurley looks at the marks. "Did you scratch yourself, Bjorn?"

Irene answers for him. "Bjorn didn't make those scratches, Bernie Chase did. He did it to him here in the men's room."

"Is that true, Bjorn?" Hurley asks.

He nods, looking frightened.

I start to get up from my kneeling position on the floor with the intent of walking over to Bjorn to offer him a friendly touch, but my muscles have other ideas. When I try to stand, my leg starts trembling and a stabbing pain shoots up my back. It's severe enough to make me suck in a breath and cuss to myself, and I even experience a brief wave of nausea. I clamp a hand over my mouth to keep my bile and my profane utterances where they belong. Izzy has picked up on my distress and I sense his eyes on me. Eager to appear shipshape for the job, I swallow down my pain and talk to Bjorn from where I am on the floor. "Bjorn, can you remember what happened? Irene said you have trouble remembering things sometimes."

"I do. I couldn't remember what happened before when she asked me, but I think I can now," he says.

"He does this," Irene explains. "His mind wanders a lot and sometimes it comes back and sometimes it doesn't. Stress makes it worse. The other day he was supposed to pick me up at one o'clock and he forgot. He took himself out for lunch to Dairy Airs instead. When I finally caught up to him and reminded him that he was supposed to pick me up, he had no recollection of us ever discussing the matter. But the next day he not only remembered the entire conversation, he remembered that he had forgotten to come and that he had gone to Dairy Airs instead."

"Tell us what you remember," Hurley says.

Bjorn wrings his hands and shifts nervously from one foot to the other. "I-I remember being in the bathroom to empty my bag and—"

"Empty your bag?" Hurley interrupts. "You mean a garbage bag or something?"

"No, he means his urinary catheter," I say.

"Oh."

Bjorn continues. "I was trying to get the lid off that powder stuff because I always seem to spill some urine on the floor no matter how careful I am. The lid was really tight and my arthritis was flaring up, so it was a struggle to unscrew that top. But I finally got it and that's when Bernard came into the bathroom. He was behind me and he banged the door really loud when he came in. It startled me because of the noise . . . and because he was acting funny, like he was drunk or something."

"Drunk?" Hurley echoes to no one in particular.

"Yeah," Bjorn says. "It was like he was drunk, but I don't think he was. At least, I couldn't smell it on him. He stumbled over to me, and he was trying to talk, but he wasn't making any sense. And then he just sank to the floor. He looked terrible, all sweaty and pale, and as he was going down he started grabbing at me. One of his hands got caught in the waist of my pants and the weight of him going down pulled them half off. That's how I got the scratches on my hip. He started grabbing at my lower legs and it almost made me fall. I still had the open bottle of powder in my hand and when I tried to catch myself it spilled all over Bernard's face. He started to gag and choke and it scared me. I dropped the bottle and I ran."

"When you say Bernard wasn't making any sense, what do you mean? What was he saying?"

"It wasn't words," Bjorn says. "He just kept making this weird gurgling sound."

"Did you try to help him at all?"

Bjorn hangs his head, looking miserable. "I didn't know how. He was acting so strange, I got scared and ran out of here to find Irene."

It hits me then, the question that should have come up earlier, but I hadn't thought of it. "Why were you in this particular bathroom? How did you get to it? Isn't this administrative wing locked on the weekends when there's no one here?"

"The back door is locked all the time," says Connie. "You can go out, but you can't get in without a key. The front door to this wing is locked in the evening and night hours during the week, and all day on the weekends. Plus there's someone at the front sign-in desk most of the time to make sure no one comes back here who shouldn't."

"The back door was locked," Irene says. "But we were outside enjoying the nice weather in the garden area. Bjorn forgot to empty his leg bag before we left the house and it was getting really full. He was afraid it might break or leak, but the closest public toilet is out front in the main hallway. That's a long way to walk when you've got a full bag of urine on your leg, so I let him in through the outside administrative door knowing that this bathroom was much closer."

"How did you get in if the back door was locked?" Hurley asks.

"I have a key."

We all register surprise at her answer.

"You have a key?" Hurley says. "Why? How?"

Irene shrugs. "I've had one for years. The previous owner gave it to me to use when we came here for pickups. They didn't want us taking dead bodies out through the front door. It looks bad for business, you know. So we would always come in through the back door and leave that way, as well. Now we call in and the nursing supervisor on duty lets us in the back door, but no one ever asked me for the key back. I don't even know if Bernard knew I had it. To be honest, I never really thought about it. I've been through that administrative wing so many times and I knew where the bathroom was." She shrugs again. "It just seemed like the most logical and simple solution for Bjorn."

Hurley shakes his head and lets out a perturbed sigh. "It may have seemed so at the time, but it's ended up with Bjorn being implicated in Bernard Chase's death."

Izzy has been standing by listening. "If what Bjorn says is true, Bernard might have died from natural causes. Pale and sweaty sounds like a classic cardiac presentation. The powder could be incidental." He pauses and frowns. "Although . . ."

"Although what?" Hurley asks.

"Well, based on my exam of the body it looks like the isolyser powder got into Bernard's airway. That, plus the dark coloring of his face, suggests he died from asphyxiation. So if he did have a heart attack, or a stroke, or some other natural event, it's possible he could have survived if not for the isolyser powder."

"Oh no," Bjorn says, and he hangs his head.

"It's also possible he might have died anyway," Izzy says. "I won't know for sure until I open him up."

Bjorn refastens the waist of his pants and looks at Hurley. "Are you going to arrest me?"

"Not at this time," Hurley says. "Let's see what the autopsy shows. Did you see anyone else back here when you came in to use the bathroom?"

Bjorn shakes his head. "The only person I saw was Bernie. After what happened in the bathroom, I went straight out the back door. I even forgot to empty my urine bag."

"Okay," Hurley says, giving Bjorn a reassuring pat on the shoulder. "That's all for now. You can go home if you want, but I might come and talk to you more later if that's okay."

Bjorn nods.

Izzy says, "I've got Johnson's funeral home coming by to pick up the body. I figure it's best if the Keller Funeral Home isn't involved at all in this one."

We all nod; this is a no-brainer since Irene owns the Keller Funeral Home and no one is sure just how involved Bjorn is at this point.

Izzy turns to me. "Mattie, can I talk to you in private for a minute?"

"Sure." We walk off down the hall toward Bernard's office, leaving the others by the bathroom.

"How is everything going?" Izzy asks me once we are out of earshot. "Are you okay with working around Steve again?"

I try not to look guilty as I flash back on what Hurley and I did a little while ago on the other side of the door Izzy and I are standing next to. "Everything is fine. We picked up where we left off with our working relationship."

"Oh, good. I thought it might be awkward for you."

"Maybe a little at first, but we got past it pretty quickly."

"I noticed you were limping earlier, and when you got up from the bathroom floor you had some trouble. Is everything okay?"

"Yeah, it's fine," I say with a dismissive wave of my hand. "I went to the gym last night for the first time in months and now my muscles are staging a protest. It's nothing a handful of ibuprofen can't cure."

"How did things go with Maggie?"

I want to tell him it went horrible, that I hate shrinks, and that the damned woman gave me homework. I want to tell him that I'm scared I'm going to reveal some innermost thought that isn't fit for public consumption, and then Maggie will have me declared nuttier than squirrel poop. Instead I say, "It went well. I'm glad you made me see her. I think it will be therapeutic."

"Good, good. I'm really happy you're back on the job."

"Me, too. Are you going to do Bernard's autopsy today?"

"I feel like I should since we don't know yet if this is a criminal case."

I'm hit with a wave of nausea all of a sudden and I clamp a hand over my mouth.

"Are you sure you're okay?" Izzy asks.

"I'll be fine. I'm just sore from my workout last night, and I haven't eaten anything today." This isn't true, but I'm not going to undo the good of telling him I worked out by admitting I had ice cream for breakfast. "I was at the grocery store when Irene nabbed me and brought me here."

"There's a stomach bug making the rounds. Maybe you're coming down with that."

"I hope not. I'm sure I'll feel better once I eat."

"Go get something to eat. Arnie's in the office today catching up on some stuff, and he's been assisting me a lot lately with the autopsies because of Jonas's sickness. He can help me do Bernard and you can stick with Hurley and finish up here."

"Okay." I get a flushed, hot feeling just thinking about sticking with Hurley. This isn't going to be as easy as I thought. I foresee a lot of cold showers in my future. Or many nights snuggled up with a dog-eared copy of *Fifty Shades of Grey*.

Izzy starts to head back to the bathroom, but stops and looks back at me. "Hey, what's up with Lucien? He doesn't seem his usual self."

"He and Desi are separated, though I don't know any specifics."

Izzy shakes his head in commiseration. "That's rough. I hope they work things out. I can't imagine what Lucien would be like without the calming influence of your sister."

That's something I hadn't thought about. If Lucien with Desi was calm, one can only imagine how horrifying he would be without her. The possibilities are heart-stoppingly scary, and I make a mental note to look into helping them reconcile as soon as possible.

Chapter 7

The door at the front end of the hallway opens and a nursing assistant pokes her head in. "The Johnson funeral home is here." She turns and disappears back to wherever she came from.

Junior shudders and mumbles, "Yikes, the Johnson sisters."

It's not an unusual or unexpected response. The Johnson sisters are twins who are being groomed to take over the family business and they take their responsibilities very seriously. This attitude might be, in part, due to their parents' determination and odd sense of humor, which became apparent early in the girls' lives when they were adorned with the names Cass and Kit. In addition to their names, the sisters look the part with Morticia Addams-like hair, complexions, and clothing, though instead of tight black dresses they wear tight black shirts and pants. My niece Erika thinks they're the coolest thing since smartphones.

Lucien takes the arrival of the funeral home as his cue to leave, and he takes Irene and Bjorn with him, exiting through the outside door at the other end of the hallway. When the door to the front opens again, I expect to see Cass and Kit coming through with their stretcher. Instead, three people march in: two women and one man. One of the women is Dorothy Granger so I guess that the other two are also administrative honchos of some sort.

Dorothy doesn't look any different from the last time I saw her, which is amazing considering that it was nearly ten years ago. She is tall with an otherwise average build, and dressed in gray slacks, a lavender blouse, and sensible gray flats. She has a black wool coat draped over one arm and her brown hair, which is streaked with steel-gray—an appropriate color given that I'm pretty sure her spine is made of steel—is pinned back in a neat little bun. She's one of those women whose age is a mystery as she never seems to change.

"Hi, Dorothy. Long time, no see," I say. All three people stop and stare at me.

Dorothy opens her mouth to speak, but the man in the group beats her to it. "Where's this cop who says he's in charge?" he grumbles. "Some cop out front told us the administrative wing is off limits. We need to get into our offices."

"That's not going to happen right now, sir," Hurley says, stepping in front of me and showing the three his badge. "I'm Steve Hurley, the detective in charge. Who are you?"

"I'm Al Hubbard, the CFO for the Twilight Home. This is Dorothy Granger, our director of nursing and the vice president."

Vice president? Dorothy has done well for herself.

"And this," Al says, pointing to the second woman, a thirtyish, brown-haired woman wearing thick eyeglasses, a midi skirt, and a simple white blouse, "is Jeanette Throckmorton, Bernard's administrative assistant."

Jeanette looks at us from beneath lowered lids and when she sees me watching her, she quickly turns away. She shifts her weight from one foot to the other and her hands keep opening, closing, opening, and closing. The woman is obviously nervous and I want to know why. Something tells me it's more than just the fact that her boss might have been murdered. I add her to my mental list of people to talk to soon.

"Is it true?" Al asks Hurley. "Is Bernard dead? Did someone kill him?"

"It is true that he's dead," Hurley says. "As to how he died, we aren't sure at this point. But until we can rule out foul play, this section of your facility is to be considered a crime scene and therefore off limits."

"That's unacceptable," Al says. "We need to initiate our emergency protocols right away. And we need to contact our lawyers."

"You can do whatever your protocols dictate as long as it doesn't involve access to this administrative wing, or otherwise interfere with my investigation." Hurley's tone makes it clear who's in charge, though Al squares his shoulders and puffs himself up like he wants to challenge him. Hurley ignores Al's posturing and continues with his instructions. "I'm glad you're here. You can help us with our investigation and the sooner we figure out exactly what happened, the sooner you can have your offices back. There are certain things I'll need access to and questions I'll need answered. I assume you will cooperate?"

"Of course. We want to help," Al says. "But before we provide you with anything, we need to consult with our lawyers."

"I suggest you do so quickly," Hurley says, pinning the CFO with those steel blue eyes. "Have any of you notified Mrs. Chase yet?"

Dorothy, who has been standing by quietly throughout this exchange, finally speaks up. "I tried to call her, but she isn't home. She had a show in Madison last night so she might have spent the night there."

"A show?" I say. "What is she, some sort of actress?"

"No," Dorothy says. "She's an artist and a fairly successful one from what I hear. She's been selling her stuff at this gallery in Madison for years. It's some kind of environmentally themed stuff that's very avant-garde and trendy with the rich set. Vonda is all about the environment. That's why I wasn't able to reach her. She doesn't have a cell phone. She thinks they're a bane on society, polluting the air waves and the landfills. And she's convinced they cause brain tumors. She's a bit dotty if you ask me, but then most of the artists I know fit that description."

"Has anyone gone by her house to see if she's home?" Hurley asks.

Al, Dorothy, and Jeanette all look at one another, and then back at Hurley. They shake their heads in unison.

"Can you give us some idea of how long this is going to take, Detective?" Dorothy asks.

Izzy steps up and says, "I'm Dr. Rybarceski, the medical examiner. I plan on doing an autopsy on Mr. Chase this afternoon so we can determine all the causes of death. Once we know the results of that, we'll have a better idea of where we stand."

"All the causes of death?" Al says. "What does that mean?"

"It means there is an obvious cause of death that may be an incidental finding," Izzy explains. "Based on what our witness described, I'm not convinced that there wasn't something else going on as well."

"There was a witness?" Dorothy says. "Are you saying someone saw Bernard die?"

"In a way," Izzy says. "But I'm not at liberty to say anything more right now."

"That reminds me," Hurley says, scanning the walls and ceiling. "Do you have any security cameras in this place?"

"No," Al says. "We considered putting some in, but in the end the idea was tabled."

"Mr. Chase didn't want to spring for the expense," Dorothy says, with a tight-lipped look of disapproval.

"Do you think this witness killed Bernard?" Al asks, handily changing the subject.

Hurley answers this one, leaving Izzy looking relieved. "No, we don't. However, he may have caused certain events that ultimately contributed to Mr. Chase's demise, though we believe it was accidental."

"If you believe his death was accidental, then why all the police tape across the door out front?" Al grumbles. "Why bar us from our offices?"

"We have reason to believe Mr. Chase was dying before our witness ran into him," Hurley says.

"You mean from natural causes, like a heart attack?" Dorothy asks.

I recall the tax forms I saw on Bernie's desk and figure that alone might have been enough of a shock to give him a heart attack.

"Possibly," Hurley says. "Or it could have been

something unnatural, like a poison, which is why we are declaring this a crime scene for now. If his death wasn't natural, we need to preserve the scene and any evidence that it might contain."

The board members' inquisition is interrupted when the door at the end of the hallway opens and one of the Johnson sisters comes strolling in, pulling a gurney behind her. She stops and stares at the small crowd in front of her, all of whom look to be very much alive. "Where is my pickup?"

"He's in here," Izzy says, pointing toward the closed men's room door. "Are you alone?"

"I am. Cass has that stomach flu that's been going around. I was going to bring Dad along, but I figured there'd be folks here to help me so I wouldn't need him."

Al, Dorothy, and Jeanette move down the hall toward the outside exit to make room for Kit and her stretcher. Because the bathroom door closes automatically, and because the stretcher won't fit inside the bathroom with the door closed, getting Bernard's body loaded for transport proves to be something of a challenge. Izzy holds the door open while Hurley, Junior, and I help Kit lift the body off the floor. Bernard Chase isn't a big man; I estimate he stood about five-ten and weighed somewhere in the neighborhood of a buck sixty. But dead weight feels like double the real weight and halfway to the stretcher my back seizes up and I lose my grip. Hurley's quick reflexes and strength are the only things that keep us from dropping Bernard's body on the floor.

Izzy follows Kit out the door. He needs to maintain custody of the body and that means watching her load it into her van and following her to the ME's office.

I step out of the bathroom and look down the hall

for the board group, but to my surprise they are gone. "Where did they go?"

Hurley walks down the hall toward the exit, looking into each office as he goes. "They must have gone outside," he says when he reaches the end of the hall. He walks back to us with a worried expression on his face. "Junior, I want an officer posted in this wing twenty-four-seven until we know how Chase died. I don't trust that bunch to stay away like I told them."

"No problem," Junior says. "I can stay here for now and I'll make some calls to cover it later. I know some guys who are looking for some overtime. I'll run it by Chief Hanson first, but given how broad this investigation might be, I don't think he'll mind."

"Thanks. I guess our next step is to find and notify Bernard's wife. We should check on their house to make sure someone didn't do her in, too." Hurley looks at me. "Are you up for it?"

I nod, remembering that the delivery of sad news is one of the aspects of this job that I don't miss. "Can I ride with you? I'm thinking the hearse won't be a good vehicle to show up in. And I need to run home first because I have Hoover here."

"You're bringing him to death scenes now?"

"I didn't know I was going to a death scene. Irene nabbed me in the grocery store parking lot and brought me here."

"No problem. I'll follow you out to your place."

We head back to the recreation room where I find Hoover in the middle of a circle of people in chairs and wheelchairs. A man is rubbing Hoover's ears while Hoover rests his head in the man's lap, looking happy and content.

"It's my turn," the man next to him says. "Come on, Ted, quit hogging the dog."

"Sorry folks," I say, "but it's time for the dog to go home."

This announcement is met by a series of moans and groans.

"Are you going to bring him back?" a woman in a wheelchair asks. "He is the sweetest thing."

"Sure," I say with a shrug. "I don't see why not."

After hooking Hoover back up to his leash, I lead him down the halls. I fully expect to run into one of the board members or Connie, and have some more explaining to do, but fortunately they are all gathered in the dining room and if any one of them saw a dog go by in the hallway, they apparently opted not to question it.

After exiting out the front door and climbing into the hearse, I decide to do a quick swing through McDonald's and order Hoover a hamburger for his good behavior. I consider ordering something for myself, but my stomach still feels unsettled so I decide to wait.

My stop at the drive-through takes enough time for Hurley to beat me to my house. He is waiting for me when I pull up, standing on the front porch, leaning against a post. "Did you get lost?" he says as I get out.

"I did a quick drive-through at McDonald's to get Hoover a treat."

Hoover bounds out of the car and runs over to him, whining and wagging his tail as if he is greeting some long lost lover. I kind of know how he feels. As I look at Hurley, all tall and lanky leaning against my porch post with that blue-eyed smile, I want to wag my tail, too.

After letting Hoover water a tree, I head inside and Hurley follows. Before I know what's happening, he closes the door and grabs my arm, spinning me back toward him. He pulls me in close so that my chest is against his. "Can we talk before we go see this woman?"

I'm not sure I'm physically capable of speech at the moment so I simply nod.

"I am so sorry about this mess with Kate. Believe me, I had no idea she never filed the divorce papers. Nor did I know she was pregnant. Her reasons for keeping all that to herself are a bit sketchy. Every time I ask her about it, she shrugs vaguely and mumbles something about how she was worried I'd make her give the kid up. Believe me, there is absolutely nothing between us, anymore. To be honest, there never really was. That's why we decided to divorce."

"That's all fine and dandy, but it doesn't change the fact that you're a married man, Hurley. And you have a kid."

"The marriage part I'm taking care of. That should be finalized in another week or so. The kid I can't do anything about." His eyes soften and he lets out a tiny sigh. "Not that I'd want to. Emily is great. She's smart, funny, sweet tempered. . . . I'm a little pissed that Kate kept her from me all these years. But the whole fatherhood thing takes some getting used to. I'm not sure I'm cut out for the job."

I see genuine affection in his eyes and find it touching . . . as well as worrisome. Some silly part of me wonders if his feelings for his daughter will somehow roll over into renewed feelings for a woman he once cared about enough to marry. Then I remind myself that Hurley isn't mine to be jealous over.

"I get that you didn't plan any of this, Hurley," I

say, pushing away from him. "But it doesn't change the reality of it. And now that I'm back at my old job, we have the issue of our conflict of interest problem to deal with again, too." I shake my head and squeeze my eyes closed. "I don't know, Hurley. It seems like everything in the universe is working against us. It's as if we aren't meant to be together."

Hurley closes the distance I created between us and pulls me to him. Before I can object or say another word, he kisses me. And then his hands start going places that turn my mind to mush. It's only a matter of seconds before the universe starts playing a different tune.

"Still think we don't belong together?" Hurley says as we lay side by side on my bed, stark naked, happily fulfilled, and utterly exhausted.

"That wasn't a fair test."

"I'd say it was a pretty good test."

"Just because you know how to make me crazy doesn't mean the universe wants us together. I can't give up my job again, Hurley. And I hate to sound like a broken record, but technically you're a married man."

"It's too late not to break that commandment if that's your worry. Besides, it's not like Kate and I had a viable marriage of any sort. Hell, I haven't spoken to or seen her in nearly fifteen years. As for the job, let's just keep this little tryst between you and me."

"I'm not much into that ménage à trois stuff, anyway." I say it in a half joking tone, because I'm seriously concerned about the future of my job and our relationship.

Hurley seems to sense this. "We can do this, Winston. We just need to be careful and avoid suspicion by not spending any time alone together in places where others will notice."

"You mean like here, now?" As if my words prompted the Fates to screw with us, there is a knock at my door. Hurley and I fly out of bed and start rounding up our clothes, which look like debris from a laundry bomb. I holler out, "Just a second," as I hop on one foot, my muscles screaming in agony as I try to get my pants back on. Hurley grabs all his clothes and dashes into the bathroom, shutting the door behind him. As soon as I have myself decently covered, I head for the door, though in the interest of time I forgo my bra and stuff it under a pillow. I smooth my hair before opening the door and paste a friendly smile on my face. The smile quickly disappears when I see who's standing on the other side.

Chapter 8

"Lucien? What are you doing here?"

He steps inside, not bothering to wait for an invitation, and heads for the couch, plopping himself down like a ragdoll. "Mattie, you have to help me. I miss my family. I miss Desi. I need them back."

"This isn't the best time, Lucien," I say, shooting a wary glance toward the bathroom door. What will Hurley do? I know he's on the other side of the door listening. He has to know it won't take Lucien long to figure out Hurley is here given that his car is parked outside. Lucien may be annoying, but he isn't stupid.

"You have to help me, Mattie. I can't go on."

I've never seen Lucien like this. He's always been confident and self-assured despite being irritating as hell. Now he looks like a man defeated, ready to give up. It makes my heart ache. If I have any doubts about how down he really is, they are eliminated when Hurley steps out of the bathroom and Lucien simply acknowledges him with a nod and a "Hey, Hurley."

I'm really worried. The Lucien I know would never let a moment like this go by without making a crass remark. I close the door and go sit on the couch beside him; Hurley settles into a chair on Lucien's other side.

"Shouldn't you be with your clients?" I ask Lucien.

"Irene and Bjorn went home. They know not to talk to the cops unless I'm there." He shoots a glance at Hurley. "No offense."

"None taken."

"Irene seems to think I need to represent all the patients in that place, but unless they contact me and ask for representation, they're on their own. I don't think any of them need a lawyer, anyway. It's just as well if they don't. I can't seem to focus with all this stuff that's going on between me and Desi."

"What exactly is going on?" I ask.

"I screwed up," Lucien says. "I've been working a lot, picking up any case I can get. It's kept me at the office late and forced me to go in on the weekends. I haven't been getting much sleep and then I forgot our anniversary. Desi might have forgiven me that one transgression, but then I missed Erika's play, and Ethan got some award at school and I missed that, too. Hell, I don't even know what the award was for." He shakes his head in dismay, stares at the floor, and sighs.

I'm puzzled because based on what I know of my sister, none of this sounds like separation material.

Lucien clarifies things by adding, "Your sister thought I missed all those events because I was having an affair."

"Were you? Are you?" I ask.

He scoffs. "Like I could ever love anyone else the way I love her."

His words come across with surprising sincerity and I'm touched and a little envious.

Lucien raises his head and looks at me. There are tears forming in the corners of his eyes. "I know what everyone else thinks of me. That whole boorish act with the sleazy banter, and the offensive attitude, that's my thing, my shtick. It keeps people on edge and off balance."

He's right about that.

"It distracts people from what I'm really up to and it enables me to move in for the kill before anyone even knows there's a viable threat. It's part of why I'm so successful. Desi has always been able to see through all that. She knows me deep down inside. She knows a part of me that no one else does. And that knowledge, that security of knowing I have Desi at home waiting for me every night is another key to my success. I can't bear the thought of disappointing her and that's why I've been working so much extra, and staying in the office late at night. That's what had Desi thinking I might be stepping out on her, but I never have and never would do that to her."

"Tell her that," I say.

"I did. And I think she knows now that I'm not cheating on her. But it's the other stuff. She's just so angry with me. You have to help me, Mattie. Help her understand how much I need her and love her. I didn't mean to hurt her."

"Lucien, I'll do what I can, but I'm still confused as to exactly what the problem is. And you have to understand that my allegiance will always be first and foremost to my sister."

He nods. "I wouldn't expect anything less of you, Mattie."

"Is it all the hours you're working that's the problem? Can you cut back some?"

"Cutting back isn't an option right now, and anyway, it's not the extra hours that have her upset."

"Then what is it?" I ask, thoroughly confused.

Lucien gives me a sheepish look. "It's embarrassing. I can't believe I was so stupid."

The possibilities are mind-boggling, knowing Lucien as I do. I use that fact to try to reassure him. "Lucien, I promise you that whatever you did, I am imagining things that are a whole lot worse." I pray that this is true. "So just tell me."

He considers this, looks from me to Hurley and back to me again, and then hangs his head. "It started a couple years ago. I was doing pretty well investing on my own in the stock market and when some of my clients found out about it, they asked me to invest some money for them, too. I agreed to do it, charged a nominal fee, made them a decent profit, and word spread. Before I knew it, I had a couple dozen people who were giving me money to invest and the sums were getting bigger and bigger. It was a nice little side business for a while. Then the stock market turned on me and I started losing."

Hurley wrinkles his brow and scratches his head. "Well, aside from functioning as a financial investor without a license, which may or may not be a crime, what's the problem? Lots of people lose money in the stock market."

Lucien grimaces. "It wasn't a lot at first and I felt pretty bad about betraying the trust of the people who had faith in me. So instead of telling them about the losses, I covered them."

"Covered them with what?" I ask.

"Our savings."

With that answer, I begin to see the light of Lucien's darkness.

"I also put more of my own money into the market thinking that if I could just find the right mix, I'd be able to make up my clients' losses as well as my own. Desi and I had quite a bit saved up so I figured we could afford it, and sooner or later I'd be able to replace it and then some, once I got a better handle on the current whims of the market. But it seemed like every strategy I tried was doomed and the losses just kept piling up. Eventually, they got so big I couldn't tell my investors because I'd all but wiped them out. For some of those folks, it's all they have. It's money they're counting on for their retirement."

"How much of your own money did you spend, Lucien?" Hurley asks.

Lucien looks down at the floor and shakes his head again. "Between losing investments of my own and covering those of my clients . . . all of it," he says, looking glum. "There's nothing left. Plus my business hit a slump for a few months so there wasn't much coming in and I fell behind on all the bills. Desi found out when she took Erika and some of her friends out for an afternoon at the movies and the car got repo'd right in front of them. After Desi got herself and all the kids home, she went to the bank and found out all our money was gone. She confronted me that night when I got home and I told her what happened. She threw me out of the house and she's still so angry she won't speak to me. Erika won't either. She says I humiliated her in front of all her friends."

"Well, hell, Lucien, can you blame them?" I ask

him. "Why on earth didn't you tell Desi what was going on in the beginning?"

Lucien slumps into a sad, pathetic ball of crushed human being. "I didn't think I'd have to. I was sure the losses were temporary and that I'd be able to make them back. Desi has always trusted me with that stuff. She's always admired my ability to make money, through work and through investing. I didn't want to let her down." He looks away from me and wipes at the tears welling in his eyes. "I didn't think I could bear to see the disappointment on her face when she looked at me. And I was right."

My heart squeezes in sympathy with Lucien's pain. I now have a better understanding of just what it was my sister saw in Lucien all those years ago and likely still sees in him today. His love for her couldn't be more obvious.

"Do your clients know?" Hurley's tone is gentle. Much as he hates Lucien, even he can see the man is utterly defeated.

Lucien shakes his head. There follows a silence of perhaps twenty seconds' duration, and Hurley and I are aware that on a normal day, Lucien would have managed to squeeze in at least two, maybe three crass remarks in that period of time. Instead, he is just sitting there staring forlornly at his feet.

The silence is finally broken by the buzz of Hurley's phone.

"Give me some time and I'll see what I can do," I tell Lucien as Hurley takes out his phone. He doesn't take the call, however.

"Will you talk to your sister?" Lucien pleads. "Tell her I'm lost without her? I love that woman more than anything in the world. I don't know what I'll do if she doesn't take me back. I can't eat, I can't focus;

I haven't slept more than a wink in days. I just lay there night after night, staring at the ceiling."

"Maybe you should try counting sheep," Hurley offers.

I shoot him a look of horror and shake my head. Even with this toned-down version of Lucien, I don't think the inclusion of farm animals in his bedtime rituals is a good idea.

"I'll talk to Desi," I tell Lucien. "But I can't make any promises. Desi has always been her own person and she's entitled to be extremely pissed off with you right now. I can't guess how long it will take for her to get over it, assuming she ever does."

"I know that," Lucien says with a sniffle. Then he does a classic Lucien move by wiping his nose on his sleeve. "I just thank you for trying."

"In the meantime, what's the situation on your bills? I can help you out."

I'm excited that I have the financial means to help my family, but I'm also cursing myself for my gambling fetish. I've managed to lose more than half of my divorce settlement. I realize my gambling problem isn't any better than what Lucien did except that the only money I lost was my own. Still, I have my job back and close to two hundred grand still in the bank, which ought to be enough to buy Desi and Lucien some time.

Lucien stares at me blankly, and I'm not sure if he doesn't know the answer to my question or if he just doesn't want to say it. So I dig my checkbook out of my purse and write him out a check for twenty grand. "Will this be enough for you to get by on for now?" I ask him, tearing the check out and walking over to hand it to him.

He takes the check and stares at it for several long

seconds. Then he lunges up from his seat and grabs me before I know what he's doing. "Mattiekins, you are the best!" He gives me several pumping squeezes that I guess are meant to be hugs and kisses me on the cheek. It's all I can do not to reach up and wipe it off with my hand. When Lucien finally releases me and dashes out the door, I give in to the urge and swipe a hand across my cheek.

I look over at Hurley. "Interesting."

"Yes."

"You don't suppose he realized there was anything going on with us, do you?"

"I doubt it. He seemed pretty caught up in his own problems."

"I hope so. We dodged a bullet here, Hurley. We can't let that happen again."

He rises from his chair and starts walking toward me. "No, we can't."

"We have to be careful not to let our hormones call the shots," I say as he closes in.

"Yes, we do," he agrees, so close that I can feel his breath warm on my face.

"So, no more hanky-panky, right?" I'm barely able to get the words out because I'm suddenly breathless.

"None at all." Hurley bends forward and gives me a light kiss on the lips.

Chapter 9

Fifteen minutes later, we are again lying on my bed in a state of exhausted pleasure and dishabille. So much for convictions.

"What are we doing, Hurley?"

"Something that feels really, really good," he says with a dumb-assed grin.

"You know what I mean."

"Let's not analyze it. I say we just put it behind us and move on. Deal?"

"Deal."

I don't think either one of us truly believes this. We reassemble our clothing and actually make it out of the house and into Hurley's car. Our drive is made in silence, but it's a comfortable one, reminiscent of the old days before our lives got so tangled.

Bernard Chase's address is a few miles outside of town, five acres of land that was once part of a farm that was sold off in chunks, some of which became private property, and some of which became a new golf course. Bernard's house is a pretentious spread with stone facades, solar panels, professional landscaping as far as the eye can see, and a hammered copper roof atop an out-of-place cupola perched on one corner of a humongous wraparound porch. There is an attached three-car garage and while I can see the upper part of a boat through the window of one bay, I can't tell from the front drive if there is a car in either bay. Hurley parks us right in front of the mansion-style, crescent-shaped concrete stairs going up to the porch. As we get out of his car, an overweight hound dog whose ears drag on the ground comes waddling around the far right corner of the house. He lets out one baying woof that might be a warning or a greeting and then he stops to stare at us.

"Hey, pup," Hurley says, extending a hand. With that, the dog wags his tail and waddles over to us.

As Hurley gives me a glimpse of his backside by bending down to pet the dog, I'm thinking I'll be the next one in line to wag and waddle. Those thoughts are cut short when the front door to the house opens. I look and see a jeans and sweatshirt–clad woman with long, straight, dark hair standing there.

"Are you Mrs. Chase?" I ask.

"Who the hell are you?"

Ah, a friendly sort. I let Hurley take it from here, figuring his manly attributes might make more headway with the woman than I can.

I hear a vibrating noise and Hurley straightens up from the dog and takes his phone out. He looks at the screen, frowns, and sticks the thing back in his pocket. The two of us climb the stairs, Hurley speaking as we go. "I'm Detective Steve Hurley from the

Sorenson Police Department and this is Mattie Winston, a deputy coroner with the Medical Examiner's Office."

"So who died?" the woman snaps, clearly unimpressed and, one hopes, uninformed of our reason for being here.

Hurley, never one to mince words, says, "Your husband Bernard."

There is the faintest hint of a flinch in her expression and then she smiles. "No, really, why are you here? Is this some practical joke my sister set up?"

"This is no joke, Mrs. Chase," Hurley says. "Your husband Bernard was found dead this morning."

The smile is gone, replaced with an expression of concern and confusion. Then she rapid-fires questions at us. "What happened? Did he have a heart attack? Was he in a car accident or something?"

"We won't know exactly what the cause of death is until an autopsy is performed, but there are some suspicious circumstances surrounding his death. His body was found in one of the bathrooms at the Twilight Home, which I understand your husband owned and ran."

Mrs. Chase nods slowly, her eyes gazing off in thought. Then she says, "A bathroom? Did he die on the toilet?"

"Not exactly," I say, and she looks at me with such sudden sharpness, I suspect she hasn't fully registered my presence until now.

"May we come in?" Hurley asks.

Mrs. Chase stares at him as if the words he uttered were some foreign language. After a few beats, she nods and steps aside, so Hurley and I head through the door. What I can see of the inside of the house is as ostentatious as the outside, but I'm starting to notice a trend. The floors are bamboo wood, and a good portion of the decor, including most of the furniture, is also made of natural objects such as stone, plant materials, and wood. The lighting at the moment is mostly natural sunlight streaming in through windows, skylights, and sun tubes, and the light fixtures I can see are all fitted with fluorescent bulbs.

"Your house looks to be very eco-friendly," I say.

For a moment, Mrs. Chase's demeanor changes. Her face lights up and breaks into a huge smile. "Yes, I do try to minimize my footprint on our planet." She gazes around at the interior and sighs. "It's a challenge given Bernie's tastes. He could care less about saving the planet, but I try." She seems to realize how inappropriate her tone is under the circumstances and looks away with a wince. "Anyway, please tell me what happened to Bernie. Did he suffer? What do I need to do?"

Her matter-of-fact tone and apparent lack of concern for the death of her husband confuses me at first. I can't tell if she's simply in shock or truly indifferent. But her next comment clarifies things.

"I suppose I'll need an alibi as I'm certain to be a suspect, right?"

"Why do you say that?" Hurley asks.

"Well, it's obvious, isn't it? The spouse is always one of the first people you cops look at when someone is murdered. I watch enough TV to know that much."

"No one said your husband was murdered," I say.

She shoots me a look of impatience. "All right, if you want to play word games, we can do that. I believe you said it was suspicious circumstances. That sort of implies murder, doesn't it? It won't be a secret that Bernie and I weren't on the best of terms with our marriage. We've been undergoing counseling and we divided the house up into separate suites for each of us months ago. The closest thing we've had to sex over the past year is when we occasionally meet at the coffeepot in the morning and one of us says, 'screw you' to the other."

Hurley bites back a smile. "When's the last time you saw your husband, Mrs. Chase?"

She gives him an annoyed look. "Don't call me that. My name is Vonda Lincoln. Lincoln is my maiden name and I kept it. None of that traditional name-change bull crap for me, thank you very much. As to the last time I saw Bernie . . . to be honest, I'm not sure. I think it's been several days. That gas hog of a BMW he drives was in the garage last night when I got back from my workout session and it was gone this morning when I went to the grocery store— which reminds me"—she turns and opens a drawer in a small table against the wall, removing paper and pen—"I need to write myself a note so I'll remember to speak to the manager of the grocery store here. There isn't enough organic stuff available. I spoke to him last year and he ordered some organic veggies for a while, but now it's back to the same old crap. He never did get any of the other organic foods I asked for, or the organic cleaners I asked him to stock."

"Wow, you're quite dedicated to this stuff," I say.

"I'm just being responsible. That's the main reason Bernard and I are splitting up. He told me he was green when we met and started dating. He made an effort for a while, but it became clear to me once we were married that he's just a resource-consuming hog like everyone else. I think he only pretended to be green to win me over. I mean, look at this house. Do you know how hard I had to fight to get the solar panels put in, and the special rain water collection system? But Bernard is all about the money. Screw the earth!! All that matters to him is his wallet and bottom line.

"I mean really, why can't he change over from those plastic disposable diapers he buys for patients at the Twilight Home to cloth ones that are laundered? Do you have any idea how much room those diapers take up in the landfills? Or how long it takes for them to decompose?"

"Laundering the diapers uses resources, too," I say, and I'm rewarded with another dirty look for my effort.

"Bernie doesn't care about the environment at all," Vonda goes on. "I tried to convince him to cut back on the lighting in that place, but he wouldn't do it. Hell, so many of those old folks can't see worth a damn even when the lighting is good, so why have everything lit up so brightly all the time? And don't even get me started on the water consumption issue. I mean, come on, do those old folks really have to flush every single time they use a toilet? Some of them have bladders the size of a pea and they go twenty times a day."

I realize I'm staring at Vonda with my mouth hanging open and I snap it shut. The woman is clearly on a roll; it's as if someone flipped a switch and turned her on, like some Disneyland animatronic spokesperson for green living. She has grown so animated with her speech that small beads of sweat have broken out on her brow. I don't know about Hurley, but I don't have any idea what to say to this woman. Then, as I take in the designer jeans she's wearing, I metaphorically perform a circus act by sticking my foot way into my mouth.

"Do you know that those jeans you're wearing are made in China, a country with a *huge* carbon footprint, and that they have a formaldehyde coating on them when they're first made?"

Hurley and Vonda stare at me like I'm the star attraction at the freak show. Vonda's expression turns into something scary. It makes it easy for me to imagine her killing her husband and any costly or eco-unfriendly patients at the Twilight Home.

"I'm just saying that sometimes it's easier to talk about living green than it is to actually do it," I say, wincing at the nervous tremor I can hear in my voice.

Hurley's phone buzzes again and after a quick glance at the screen, he hits the IGNORE button and returns the phone to his pocket. He turns his attention back to the Green Menace and breaks the silence. "Can you vouch for your whereabouts this morning?"

"I'm sure the folks at the grocery store will remember me," Vonda says.

And not fondly, I imagine.

"Other than that, I've been here at the house all morning. When did Bernie die?"

"I'm not at liberty to share that information at this time," Hurley says, which I know is a dodge since we don't really know yet. "When were you at the grocery store?"

Vonda's mouth morphs into a sardonic grin that gives me a chill. "I'm not at liberty to share that information at this time."

I'm impressed that Hurley's expression doesn't

alter one whit. Still stone-faced he asks, "Do you mind if we take a look around?"

"As a matter of fact, I do." Vonda tilts her head to the side and folds her arms over her chest. Her body language is clear.

I'm not sure at what point she decided we were the enemy, but that line has definitely been drawn. I suspect it happened when I turned fashion police on her, and as such, I'm going to hear it from Hurley later.

"Since Bernard didn't die here and this is my home as well as his, I believe I have the right to refuse you entry without a search warrant, don't I?"

"Yes, you do, for now," Hurley says. "But I assure you I'll return with one later. In the meantime, don't leave town. Good day, Mrs. Chase."

Hurley whirls around and leaves the house so fast it takes me a few seconds to realize I should be leaving with him. I'm tickled and smiling at the nasty little jibe he made by calling Vonda Mrs. Chase, but when I glance over at her and see her glaring at me, my smile evaporates. I make a hasty retreat, flinching and nearly falling down the stairs when I hear the front door of the house slam closed behind me. Hurley is already in his car with the engine running when I hop into the front seat. He revs the engine and tears out before I can get my seatbelt on, leaving a blue cloud of smoke behind us. I suspect this is no accident. Hurley's cloud of smog is one last flip of the finger to Vonda.

His face is tight and he looks mad, but I'm not sure if it's at me or Vonda. "Boy, she's a piece of work, isn't she?" I say, finally securing my seatbelt as he turns onto the county road and eases up to highway speed. He says nothing, so I try again. "I'm glad we got out of there when we did. If we'd stayed much longer, I suspect she would have had me rolling my own tampons."

Hurley's face twitches and then he breaks into a grin. He glances over at me and shakes his head.

"What?" I say.

"That's one of the things I love about you, Winston. You can always make me laugh."

Oh. My. God. He said he loves me. Well, sort of.

"What's your take?" Hurley asks.

My take is it's ass-kicking, mind-boggling, heart-thumping awesome!

"Do you think she killed him?" Hurley says.

Okay, he didn't exactly say he loves me, but he did say he loves something about me. That still counts, doesn't it? I wonder what Dr. Maggie's take on it will be?

"Mattie?"

Back down to earth . . . "Um, I don't know. Maybe."

"Maybe? Since when are you one to equivocate?"

"We should wait and see what the time of death turns out to be and then check out her alibi. No doubt the store manager will remember her if her story of taking him to task is true, so that part should be easy to check. Maybe that will rule her out. It's too early to say, I think."

Hurley shoots me a quizzical look, like he thinks maybe I've turned into a pod person.

"Do *you* think she did it?" I ask him.

"To be honest, no, I don't, not that she couldn't have, though. If the level of animosity she has toward Bernard is any indication, she's got motive aplenty. She isn't a large woman, but she is tall and solidly built and I think she could take the guy. They're about the same height and while he outweighs her, he looked kind of soft, whereas it's obvious she's serious about working out; her arms are muscular, and those legs may be slender, but I'm betting they're powerful."

There's a hint of admiration in Hurley's voice when he mentions Vonda's legs. I make a mental note about my own commitment to continue working out, and one of my thigh muscles twitches in protest at the thought. "So why don't you think she did it?"

"Because she seems a little too eager to have us think she did. I suspect she has an ulterior motive. She wants a chance to get some free publicity to push her green platform."

"Ah." I see how that could work and give a grudging nod of respect to Vonda. She might be smarter than she looks. "Does that mean you aren't going to go back there with a search warrant?"

"Oh, I'm going back there all right. And I plan to tear through every bit of that place—hers and his—if for no other reason than to piss her off. I don't like that woman."

Good. Legs aren't everything. "So where do we go from here?" To me it's a loaded question that can apply to our case, our relationship, our lives, and our jobs. But Hurley jumps straight to the case.

"Are you hungry? I need to get a bite to eat, then we should head for your office to see what Izzy has come up with on the autopsy."

"Food sounds good to me." The nausea from earlier has dissipated for the moment and now all I feel is hungry. I'm hoping it was hunger that caused the nausea in the first place. "Where do you want to go?"

"Does Chinese sound okay?"

It does, and a few minutes later we are seated in a

booth at the Peking Palace. I don't bother to look at the menu. I have it and practically every other menu in town memorized. Hurley doesn't look at it either; we just snag a passing waitress and give her our order.

As I sit in the afterglow of Hurley's love comment on top of the gleeful anticipation of finally getting some food, the Fates decide to screw with me yet again. I see Hurley focus on something over my shoulder toward the main entrance, and his expression changes to something I can't quite interpret. Then I hear a voice I've heard before, on the night that broke my heart.

Chapter 10

"**S**teve, you haven't been answering your cell phone. What's up with that?"

It's Kate, Hurley's wife from fifteen years ago, the one he said he thought he had divorced after only a few months of marriage. Standing beside her is the daughter the two of them apparently had. I wonder if Hurley had a DNA test done, though even without a test, it's not hard to believe that Emily is his. She has the same tall build, dark complexion, jet black hair, and brilliant blue eyes Hurley has, whereas Kate is medium height, mousy complected, reed thin, and has brown hair and eyes. In fact, if one were to go on physical appearances alone, it's easier to believe Emily is Hurley's daughter than it is to believe she's Kate's.

My understanding of the situation two months ago when Kate and Emily first appeared on the scene was that Kate was broke and had nowhere else to go. She'd lost her job and her house, and she needed to mooch off Hurley for a while. The idea of a daughter certainly made that an easier sell, so, physical resemblances aside, I hope Hurley checks the veracity of Kate's claim if he hasn't already.

"I've been busy," Hurley says, sounding annoyed. "I'm working a case."

"Yes," Kate says with a brittle smile and a sideways glance toward me. "I see how hard you're working. If I hadn't seen your car pull in here, who knows how long you could have been working here with your . . . your . . . ." She pauses and cocks her head at me. "Just what is your relationship these days?"

"Actually, Mattie recently took back her old job so we're working partners again."

"Really?" Kate flashes that brittle smile again.

Emily, who is standing beside her mother looking embarrassed and extremely uncomfortable, glances around us to see who might be watching or listening in on our awkward exchange.

"What do you want, Kate?"

"Something urgent has come up and I need to go out of town for a few days. I want to leave Emily here with you, but I didn't want to do so without asking first."

Having Kate's butt as far away from here as possible sounds good to me, so I'm a little annoyed when Hurley starts giving her the third degree.

"What's so urgent that you need to leave now? Why is it going to take a few days? And why can't you take Emily?" He seems to sense that his words might have come across harsher than he meant and he turns to Emily. "Not that you aren't welcome to stay, Em. You are. You're welcome in my home any time and for as long as you want. I just want to know what your mother is up to."

His words hit me hard. I realize that any relationship I have with Hurley in the future will, out of necessity, also include Kate and Emily. I'm not sure I like the idea, at least the Kate part. Then I again remind myself that I can't have that kind of relationship with Hurley, anyway, so it shouldn't matter. It shouldn't. So why does it? Damn.

"I found Brent," Kate says.

Hurley, who looks puzzled, shakes his head and shrugs.

"Brent," she repeats. "My brother?"

"I thought you said he was dead."

"I said I thought he might be dead for all I knew because I hadn't heard from or seen him for so long. The last time I did, he was heavy into drugs and hanging with a bad crowd."

"Then why would you want to hook up with him?" Hurley asks. "That's the last thing you and Emily need in your life right now."

"Brent swears he's clean and has been for the past year," Kate says. "He went through a detox program and was staying at a halfway house in Cincinnati."

Hurley frowns. "And you need to see him right away because . . ."

Kate looks around to see who might be listening and then she ticks me off by sliding onto Hurley's seat and sidling up to him. Emily, who looks even more uncomfortable than before now that she's standing there alone, starts to fidget. I feel sorry for her so I slide over on my side of the booth and pat the seat beside me. With a grateful smile, she settles in, sitting bolt upright, her hands folded demurely in her lap.

In a low voice Kate says, "Brent told me he owed some money to his dealers when he went into his court-ordered rehab and now that he's out, they want it back. He doesn't have it because he used the stuff he was supposed to sell. He says they'll kill him if he can't pay them back so he left the halfway house and he's been in hiding."

"Kate, you need to stay out of this," Hurley says. "Let your brother fix his own problems."

Kate pouts, and to my dismay, she looks adorably cute and vulnerable when she does it.

"He's the only real family I have left other than Emily," she whines. "My mother is still alive, but she's so far gone mentally, the last time I visited her she thought I was the queen of Persia. As messed up as Brent may be, he is my brother and I can't just abandon him. Given the situation, I don't think it's safe to take Emily with me."

"Just what do you intend to do with Brent once you find him?" Hurley asks.

Kate gives him a funny little grin, implying an apology as yet unmade. "I was hoping you could help me with that. He needs a place to hide out for a little while. It won't be for very long," she adds hurriedly as Hurley opens his mouth, presumably to object.

"Are you crazy?" Hurley says. "Your brother has thugs who are out to get him and you want to bring him here to my house?"

Kate pouts again, smiling prettily, and I can sense Hurley weakening.

"The thugs are in Cincinnati," Kate argues. "They'd have no reason to look for him here as long as he doesn't leave a trail of any sort."

Hurley sighs heavily and rolls his eyes. "Can't he just come here? Why do you need to go and get him? That seems unnecessarily dangerous to me."

"He doesn't have any way to get here," Kate says.

"He has no car, nor does he have money for a bus or train. As it is, he's relying on friends to loan him a couch to sleep on and to feed him. He had to quit his job because the dealers would have found him there easily. I could send him bus or train tickets, but I figure the less of a trail there is, the better."

"I suppose you're right," Hurley says with a begrudging nod. "But it still sounds dangerous. Maybe I should go with you."

Kate and Hurley on a road trip together? I don't like the sound of that at all. "How can you leave now with the case we have going?"

"I can't," Hurley admits. "But we don't have to go right now."

"Yes, we do," Kate says. "Brent says every day he stays in Cincinnati brings him closer to getting found. His dealers have a lot of connections and it's only a matter of time."

"How are you communicating with him?" I ask.

"I got one of those throw-away cells when Emily and I left Chicago and I gave the number to the nursing home where my mom is. I told them they couldn't give the number out to anyone except my brother and I gave them a test question to ask any callers, a question only Brent would know the answer to. Brent was smart enough to contact the nursing home to see if they knew how to find me. From there it was pretty simple."

"I'm scared for you, Mom," Emily says to Kate. "I don't think you should go. Steve is right. It's too dangerous. We should find another way to get Uncle Brent here."

"I'll be okay," Kate tells her. "Brent says the friends he's staying with are friends of people he met in rehab so he had no prior connection to them.

There's no reason the drug dealers would find him there without a lot of searching and questioning. Even then they might never find him, but Brent doesn't want to take that risk, or put the people he's staying with in any jeopardy. Since I haven't seen him in years, there's no reason for anyone to be looking for me. I doubt half the people who know Brent even know he has a sister, so it should be pretty simple. Two days, three at the most. We'll be back here in no time."

"Why don't you let me call someone in the Cincinnati police department to see if they can expedite things for you and keep Brent safe?"

Kate winces and gives him an apologetic look. "I'd rather not get the cops involved. Brent's detox and stay at the halfway house are conditions of his probation, so technically he's in violation. Plus the cops don't know he was dealing. They busted him for using. If he tells the cops some kingpin dealer is after him for a debt, they might lock him up and hit him with new charges."

"I doubt that," Hurley says, his brow furrowed in thought. "But the probation thing is a problem. I'm a cop. I can't have him staying at my place if he's in violation of his probation."

"Then I'll take him to Madison and he can stay in a homeless shelter, or at the Y until I can afford my own place," Kate argues.

The waitress arrives with our food and Hurley and I offer to share with Kate and Emily. Emily takes us up on it, but Kate says she isn't hungry—an utterly foreign concept to me—and asks for a drink of water, instead.

"Thanks to you letting us stay at your place, I've got almost enough saved for a deposit on an apartment," Kate says as she watches us eat. "I only need another month or two. And Brent can get a job, too."

"Where are you working?" I ask, liking the direction this is going. I had assumed Kate and Emily were freeloading off Hurley all this time.

"I'm clerking at the Quik-E-Mart," she says. "Night shift. It's not great money, but it's enough to get by on if we rent one of those cheap condos on the other side of town."

I know the place she is referring to. It was some investor's idea of affordable condo living that was built back in 2007. Right after that, the housing market crumpled and the poor saps who bought condos found themselves owning something worth half what they paid for it. A lot of people just walked away and took the hit on their credit. A few stayed. Others moved elsewhere, but petitioned the condo board to allow for rentals. It was approved and now the place is almost solely occupied by renters. It's not a bad section of town, but the rent is so cheap that a lot of the people who live there aren't your upper crust of society. A fair amount of drug activity goes on there and the cops visit for domestic violence complaints a lot.

I can't imagine Hurley letting Kate and Emily live there, but Brent would be another story. It's a viable option and Hurley seems to sense this.

"Okay," he says with a resigned sigh. "Keep your cell phone with you at all times, and I want you to check in with me every twelve hours." As Hurley runs through a few more safety precautions, Kate nods her agreement, looking relieved.

Emily, on the other hand, looks scared.

When Hurley is done with his speech, Kate reaches across the table and takes her daughter's hand. "It will be okay, Em. Don't worry."

I'm not sure I agree with her, but I keep my thoughts to myself.

Kate departs a few minutes later, leaving Emily with us. When we are finished eating, Hurley asks Emily if she would prefer to go home or hang with him at the police station.

Much to my surprise, Emily turns to me. "I don't suppose I could go with you to your office? I'd kind of like to see what you do."

"I don't think you're ready for that," Hurley says. "Some of the stuff Mattie deals with can be pretty gruesome. Besides, I don't want you getting under foot."

Emily's shoulders sag and her disappointment is palpable. I sense something in her that I've seen in Erika, who also has a keen interest in anything bloody, gory, and having to do with death. I'm sure Dr. Maggie would have a field day with both of them.

"Actually, I don't mind giving Emily a quick tour of the office and showing her some of the basics," I say, hoping Hurley isn't upset that I'm butting in. "She can hang in the library for a while. Arnie's in today. I'm sure he wouldn't mind bragging on what he does."

"Who's Arnie?" Emily asks. "Does he cut people open?"

"Not usually," I tell her. "Although, he does assist the medical examiner from time to time if we are busy, or if the regular assistant, like me, isn't available for some reason. Most of what Arnie does is process evidence and conduct lab tests. Oftentimes, it's his results that end up solving the crime."

"Will I be able to see an autopsy?" asks Emily.

"Probably not. But maybe we can set something

up for a future date if it's okay with your mom." I see Hurley make a face at me. "What?" I ask with a shrug.

"I don't think that's an appropriate environment for a young girl."

"How old are you, anyway?" I ask Emily.

"Fourteen. I'll be fifteen this summer."

"That's older than Erika, and she's handled the stuff in my office just fine."

Hurley frowns and rubs his fingers across his brow. "I wish your mom had given me an owner's manual, or some kind of guidelines before she left."

"She's always telling me I should explore new things. As long as it's safe, she doesn't care. She says she tried a lot of new things when she was younger."

I can't help but wonder if one of the new things she tried fifteen years ago was Hurley.

"One of Mom's favorite sayings is how are you going to know if you like something unless you try it?"

Hurley smiles and shakes his head. "You are right about that. I remember her saying exactly that to me on several occasions."

"See?" Emily says. "She would be all about letting me go to Mattie's office. I've always loved science and that's what this CSI stuff is all about. It'll be educational."

"Whoa," I say. "I don't want you to get the wrong idea about what to expect over there. It's not like the *CSI* shows on TV. For one thing, we don't have sexy lighting and a high-tech, glitzy, state-of-the-art facility. Nor do we have gorgeously handsome people working there who get back DNA results faster than you can say, well, DNA."

This is a gross understatement. We have Izzy, who looks like an aging, short, balding teddy bear; Arnie, who oftentimes looks and behaves like an escapee from the nearest mental hospital; and Cass—not the other half of the Johnson Funeral Home twins, but rather our part-time receptionist-slash-secretary-slash-file clerk—who could look like anyone on any given day since she likes to dress up as characters in the thespian group she belongs to. In fact, I'm not sure I'd recognize the real Cass if I ran into her on the street.

"I'm not stupid," Emily says, casting me an impatient look. "I know that TV and real life aren't the same. I'm really interested in that kind of stuff, that's all. If you guys think I'm too naïve, or too young to see hard realities, let me tell you about the weeks that my mother and I spent living on the streets of Chicago after we lost our house."

If she's trying to make me feel guilty, it's working. Judging from the pained expression on Hurley's face, it's working on him, too. We share a look and a silent communication.

Hurley says, "Are you sure you don't mind taking her?"

Emily shoots me a hopeful look and I smile back at her. I like the kid. There's something about her that appeals to me. "Not at all," I say honestly. "I think it will be fun."

"Thank you!" Emily says, dancing in her seat. "I promise you I'll be fine."

While I do think showing Emily around the office will be fun, I also have an ulterior motive. If Emily is like most teenagers she'll want to talk. And I have a particular topic in mind.

I want to know exactly what's been going on at Hurley's house since she and her mom arrived.

Chapter 11

Hurley drives us to the ME's office and despite Emily's assurances about her ability to handle the rough stuff—something I'm inclined to believe based on what I've seen and heard from her so far—we take her to the library, where I figure there are enough books filled with gory pictures and the grim details of death and dismemberment to keep her occupied for a good while. If she truly has an interest in this stuff, there will be plenty of time to expose her to the real thing later on, assuming her mom is okay with it. Hurley buys Emily a soda from the vending machine and we leave her at the library table with a stack of books to keep her busy. Then Hurley and I head for the autopsy suite.

The door to the autopsy suite is closed, but we can see inside through the window in the top half. Bernie Chase is laid out on the autopsy table, naked from head to toe, his chest and abdominal cavity already flayed open with the standard Y-incision. Izzy is up by Chase's head, his back to us, doing something we can't see, though sewing up Chase's scalp is a definite likelihood since I can see an already dissected brain sitting on a side tray. Arnie is there, too, assisting from the other side of the table, currently engrossed in whatever Izzy is doing.

Hurley grabs my arm and stops me just as I'm about to open the door, making my back muscles yelp again, though the day's earlier activities seem to have loosened me up a little. "See what an effect you have on men?" he whispers in my ear.

I have no idea what he's talking about and my expression shows it. He nods toward the autopsy table and I turn to look, momentarily confused. Then I see the tumescence in Bernard Chase's penis.

"Oh, for Pete's sake, Hurley," I whisper back. "You've seen enough autopsies to know that a lot of men develop an engorged penis when they die." While this is true, I have to admit that Bernie's is impressive.

"I have one in life," Hurley whispers, wiggling his eyebrows at me.

His breath on my ear is making me feel hot all over. I push him off to one side, out of view of the autopsy room. "Really, Hurley?" I hiss at him. "You're going to do that here? It's bad enough you're doing it at all, but here?"

"I can't help myself. You make me crazy, Mattie Winston."

"You were crazy long before I met you. Now get yourself together and start acting like a professional. I don't want to give Izzy any reason to suspect there is anything between us."

"Is there?"

"No! Maybe. I don't know. It doesn't matter. We

can't act on it, Hurley. Now stop it and behave. I'll be damned if I'm going to lose my job again."

I turn away, open the door, and enter the autopsy room before Hurley can mess with my mind—or body—anymore.

"Hey Mattie, Hurley," Arnie says. "I hope you don't mind me offering to jump in on what would have been your first case since you came back, Mattie. I've been assisting a lot since Jonas took your job. Every time the poor guy came in here he swelled up like a puffer fish and started wheezing."

"So I heard. I don't mind at all. I've cut open enough people in my time, both dead and alive, that I don't mind sharing the fun. I'm sure I'll have plenty of other opportunities."

"Have I mentioned how glad we are to have you back here?" Arnie says.

"You have," I say with a smile. "But it never hurts to hear it. Thanks, again. I'm glad to be back."

I'm flattered by Arnie's enthusiasm and realize just how much I missed him during my hiatus even if he is a bit of a nutcase. I think *nutcase* might be too strong a term. After my session with Dr. Maggie, I'm more sensitive to labels like that, so I mentally correct myself and label Arnie as a conspiracy theorist with a very active imagination. The last time I spoke with him he tried to convince me that the electronic eyes built into the sinks and paper towel dispensers in public washrooms are really cameras put in there by the government to monitor the activities of people who use the washrooms. Apparently, Arnie thinks the elimination and hygiene habits of the public contain secret information that might someday save the world. Arnie also informed me that the reason some species of animals are either in danger of becoming extinct, or already are extinct, is because a secret group of people who believe the apocalypse is nigh are running a Noah's Ark–type zoo where they are protecting and breeding certain animals who will repopulate the earth after Armageddon. The dodo isn't gone, according to Arnie. The last of its kind are stashed away in the Ark zoo, waiting for some post-apocalyptic rebirth. When I asked him why these remaining dodos couldn't be used to repopulate their species now, Arnie babbled a bunch of stuff about changing ecosystems and maintaining a plant-animal balance.

Even though I suspect Arnie wears a tinfoil hat during some of his off hours, I can't help but like the guy. He's whip smart and a definite asset to the ME's office, though just how he came to be here is a bit of a mystery to me. I know that he worked for the LA coroner's office for several years, but left it and somehow ended up in Sorensen, Wisconsin. Izzy has always been vague and mostly mum on the topic, and Arnie cleverly changes the subject whenever I've tried to bring it up. I suspect his conspiracy theories might have been a bit too much for a coroner's office that tends to get a lot of PR attention, but for us here in Wisconsin, where wearing a giant cheese wedge on your head is considered normal, tinfoil hats barely raise an eyebrow.

Hurley walks over and peers inside Bernie's body cavity from a polite distance. "Got anything for me yet?"

"I do and I don't," Izzy says cryptically. "It turns out the isolyser powder wasn't a contributing cause of death after all. The powder got into his mouth, but he was essentially dead when it happened. He didn't swallow any of it and while there was a small amount mixed in with saliva and mucus in his airway, it wasn't enough to block it entirely. There was no trace of the stuff deeper in his lungs, so it appears he stopped breathing before the stuff made it into his mouth."

"That's good news for Bjorn," I say.

"So what killed him?" Hurley asks. "Did he have a heart attack?"

Izzy shakes his head. "No, he didn't. There's the rub. I haven't been able to find any cause of death. So for now, I'm listing the cause as undetermined, but I feel pretty certain that the manner is homicide. His heart muscle is in perfect health. In fact, his arteries are some of the best I've seen. There's no evidence of heart disease or a heart attack. I haven't found any blood clots or hemorrhages, and when I examined his brain, there was no evidence of a stroke. The only findings of any significance are his lungs, which are quite congested, and some cell death I found in some of his tissues. He was in shock for some reason and his body wasn't getting enough oxygen, but I can't tell you why. I don't see any evidence of a severe allergic reaction with anaphylaxis, so at this point I'm leaning toward a poison of some sort. What I can tell you is something we already know from Bjorn—Bernie didn't die easily. I did find skin and blood under his fingernails and I can't find any evidence that he scratched himself, so we should have some DNA, but we already know whose it will be."

Hurley, Izzy, and I all say the same thing at once. "Bjorn."

Arnie looks around the room at each of us, his brows drawn down with curiosity. "You guys know something I don't?"

We fill Arnie in on what we know about Bjorn and Bernie in the bathroom.

"It's ridiculous to suspect Bjorn anyway," Arnie says. "What possible motive would he have?"

Hurley says, "There's a rumor afoot at the Twilight Home that Chase was killing off the patients who became more expensive to care for. A number of the patients there seem to think there's some legitimacy to the idea."

"Do you?" Arnie asks, sounding excited at the prospect of a real, live conspiracy.

"It would be difficult for him to do," I say. "But not impossible. Patients in nursing homes are expected to die, particularly the ones who experience health setbacks. Of course, those are the very patients the others think Chase was getting rid of. But even if it's true, I don't see Bjorn as the great avenger here. Hell, half the time he can't remember where he is or what day it is, much less some wild conspiracy. His senility has worsened rapidly over the past few months."

"Not only that," Hurley says, "Bjorn is in his eighties. Physically, he manages for the most part, but I don't think he has the strength or the agility to overpower a man of Bernard's age."

"I don't know," Arnie says. "My cousin's mother had Alzheimer's and most of the time she was weak and pliable as a baby. But occasionally she had these fits of intense rage and anger, and when that happened the woman was strong as an ox."

"Of course, none of this is relevant given our findings so far," Izzy says. "It doesn't take brute strength to poison someone."

"That's true," Hurley says. "If any of the patients at the Twilight Home believe the conspiracy about Chase killing patients, we have a lot of potential suspects, including Bjorn." There is a moment of silence and then he adds, "Especially Bjorn, since he was probably the last person to see Bernie alive. He already told us there was something wrong with Bernie when he entered that bathroom, so if we're looking at who had access to Bernie, Bjorn is it."

"But Bjorn's proximity was accidental," I say. "If Bernie was in the building, anyone else who was there could have had access to him. Depending on how fast-acting whatever he was poisoned with is, he might not have even been in the nursing home when the poison was delivered. That means his wife could be a suspect, too, at least until we can narrow down the time line a little better. Do you have any idea what the poison might have been, Izzy?"

"I have lots of ideas, too many, in fact. We'll run a tox screen to see if anything shows up. If it doesn't, at least we can rule out some things."

"Do you think he might have been sedated somehow?" Hurley asks.

"It's possible," Izzy says. "An overdose is one scenario, though his behavior in the bathroom doesn't really fit with that. Until I get the tox screen results back and look at some more tissue samples on a microscopic level, I'm just guessing."

"How long?" Hurley asks.

Arnie says, "I can do some preliminary tests for the more common drugs—basic prescription drugs like opiates, benzos, and tricyclics, and the more common street drugs like marijuana, meth, and cocaine. Anything more exotic than that, like GHB or fancier prescription drug levels, will have to get sent to Madison's lab. Those results will likely take anywhere from a day or two, to a week, depending on what we're looking for. It would help if we knew what we were looking for. There are hundreds of tests we have the capability of doing, but obviously it doesn't make sense to do them all. We need to narrow the focus."

Hurley scrunches his face up in thought. "If a prescription drug was involved, that would imply a staff member rather than a patient, wouldn't it?"

"Not necessarily," I say. "Most nursing home patients are on long lists of medications that include any number of potential suspects. While it's true that the nursing staff generally doles out the drugs, it wouldn't be that hard for a patient to build up a stash, or even obtain a prescription from a doctor that they then fill elsewhere without the nursing staff knowing about it. That would tend to implicate one of the more independent patients, but I think the nature of this crime leans that way, anyhow."

"What sort of time frame are we looking at for the onset of action for the majority of the causative poisons?" Hurley asks.

Izzy thinks about it for a moment. "I'd say you're looking at a two to three hour window at the most. There are some poisons that are much faster-acting than that, but anything slower-acting that had to build up over time, like arsenic or thallium, would have caused long-term disability and illness prior to death. I think we can safely rule those out since we have no indications that Bernie was sick at all prior to today. The delivery method of whatever killed him might impact the time, too. Something injected would act faster than something ingested. I found no evidence of any injection sites on his skin anywhere, but I'll take another look just to be sure."

"Can you give me a time of death?"

"I can," Izzy says. "Based on lividity, rigor, and

body temp, he died somewhere between ten and eleven this morning."

"So maybe we can narrow down our suspects by figuring out who had access to Bernie between the hours of seven and eleven this morning," I say.

Hurley scoffs. "Yeah, that narrows it down to all of the nursing home patients, Irene, Bjorn, Chase's wife, and all of the nursing home staff who were on duty."

"We should search all of the patient rooms," I say. "Maybe we can find a stash of pills somewhere. And we should talk to the patients, too. They all love to gossip and someone might know if someone else has a little stash of something they keep on the side."

"I'll have to get a search warrant," Hurley says. "There are sixty rooms in that place, plus the ancillary areas like the cafeteria, the administrative offices, the therapy rooms. . . ." He shakes his head and sighs, then takes out his cell phone and punches in some numbers. "I'm going to have to call in some extra manpower. Between the patients, the room searches, and the staff at that place, we have a lot of interviews and territory to cover."

He steps outside into the hallway and I can hear the murmur of his voice as he talks into the phone. A minute or so later, he reenters the autopsy room and looks directly at me.

"I've got extra people coming in to assist with the search and the interviews, but I still have to call to get a warrant. I'm hoping that won't take more than an hour. Mattie, I want you to be involved with this. Your nursing experience will come in handy if we do come across any pills, and I think you can help us with the interviews, too."

"No problem. I'm happy to help." I cast a glance at Izzy, who nods in agreement.

Hurley glances at his watch. "I'll schedule a planning session over at the police station for an hour from now. Let's say three-thirty. We'll have the extra help there and we can divvy up the tasks to make sure we get it all done. I'll work on the search warrant in the meantime. Izzy, let me know if you come across any other good information that might be helpful."

"I will, but I'm essentially done with the autopsy at this point so I don't anticipate anything more here. We'll let you know when we get the results of the tox screen back."

I follow Hurley out of the autopsy suite, and as we pass the men's bathroom in the hallway, he grabs my arm and drags me inside before I know what he's doing. Then he pulls me to him so that we are in full frontal contact.

"Hurley, are you crazy? I thought we agreed we weren't going to do this."

"Do what?" Hurley whispers and then his lips descend upon mine before I have a chance to answer.

I give in to the sensations for several delicious seconds before reality brings me back to earth. "This is too public," I gasp. "Someone could come in. If we get caught, it will ruin everything."

"I can't help it. I miss you. I want you," he says, his voice deep and exciting.

"We shouldn't."

Hurley lays down a line of light butterfly kisses along the side of my neck. His hand snakes its way under my shirt and suddenly I'm very certain we should. "I think I want to create my own nipple incident since you won't tell me about the first one," he says.

I try one last protest. "It's not safe. Someone will catch us." Even as I say this, the idea of getting caught ramps up my hormones.

"Who's going to come in?" Hurley whispers. "Izzy and Arnie are tied up in the autopsy suite, Emily is occupied in the library, and the only other employee who might be here is Cass, and I don't think she'll use the men's room no matter what disguise she might happen to be in today."

I struggle to come up with another objection to Hurley's advances, but the sensations coursing through my body muddle my mind. Once again, I'm a goner.

Chapter 12

Ten very hectic but satisfying minutes later, Hurley and I exit the men's room. Hurley goes first to make sure no one is in the hallway outside the bathroom, and as soon as he determines the coast is clear, he signals for me to come out. We pull ourselves together, straighten our clothing and hair, and mutter something about never doing that again. After a quick discussion, Hurley heads for the police station while I make my way to the library and Emily, who I had temporarily forgotten about. I find her seated at the table where we left her, engrossed in a book. She looks up and smiles at me when I enter.

"What are you reading?" I ask.

She lifts the book and lets me see the cover. I'm a little surprised by her choice. While I expected her to be more drawn to the medicolegal textbooks that discuss and depict dead bodies and the steps necessary to determine how they got that way, she has chosen a book on facial recognition. She has it open to a page highlighting clay sculpture.

"Does that interest you?" I ask.

"It does. I had no idea how scientific this was. I saw a show on TV once that talked about how a scientist identified a body using clay sculpture, but I thought her primary expertise was artistic. Now I see that it's as much science as it is art."

"Very much so. Researchers spent a lot of time, study, and years figuring out the various skin and tissue depths as it relates to bone structure for different races of people. They have compiled all that data, and the artists who do facial recognition, whether it be through clay sculpture, drawing, or computer graphics, have to know how to apply it."

"I like to draw," Emily says. "I made a little money last year at school drawing portraits of some of my classmates and selling them. I was hoping to make enough to help Mom be able to keep the house, but that didn't happen. Maybe if I'd gone to school with a bunch of rich kids it would have been different. But most of the kids at that school weren't any better off than I was. So even though I was able to sell the pictures, I didn't sell them for much."

"If you were able to sell the pictures at all you must be quite good. In fact, if you were able to sell to people who didn't have much money, you must be really good."

Emily shrugs. "My mom thinks I'm good. She wanted to send me to art school but we couldn't afford it."

"Are you taking any art classes at school here?"

"Yeah, but it's pretty basic stuff."

"Maybe once you and your mom get back on your feet, art school can be an option for you again."

"I doubt it," Emily says with a weary smile. She sounds defeated and depressed and I find myself wondering just how awful her life was in Chicago.

"Hurley and I need to head up a strategy session over at the police station. He's calling in recruits to help because we have a lot of territory to cover and a lot of suspects to work through in the case we have."

"So was your victim murdered?"

"It appears so."

"Is the victim a man or a woman?"

"Man."

"How did he die?"

"We're not sure yet. Some kind of poison or medication we think."

"Why do you have so many suspects? Did a lot of people hate the guy?"

"Possibly." I don't want to say too much more given that it's an ongoing investigation. I could always tell Emily to keep what I tell her a secret, but if there is one thing I've learned from living in a small town, it's that the only secret you can guarantee will stay that way is the one you never share. "Would you like Hurley to take you home?"

"If it's okay with you, I'd like to stay here and finish reading this. It's kind of fun."

"I think that will be okay. Can I get you a snack of some sort?"

"No thanks. I'm fine."

"We should be done with our meeting around four I think. Do you know Hurley's cell number?"

She shakes her head, so I look it up on my cell and write it down for her. "If you need anything, just use the phone in here to call Hurley."

"Is that what you call him all the time?"

"Who? What? You mean Hurley?"

She nods.

"Yeah, I guess I do, though I'm not sure why."

"You like him, don't you?"

"Sure. He's a great guy and a good detective."

"No, I mean you *like* him. In a lovey-dovey way."

I hesitate to answer her, because I'm not sure how honest I should be. I know I can't be totally honest. The little sessions Hurley and I had today must stay secret if I'm to keep my job. In a way it's a shame since I'm pretty sure they'd count toward my exercise totals in the diary Gunther wants me to keep. But I also don't want to lie too openly to Emily. She already knows Hurley and I had something going on when she and her mom showed up. So I decide to go with half-truths for now.

"I had feelings for Hurley, yes," I say. "And maybe if things had worked out differently, it could have led to something. But it seems it wasn't meant to be. Everything has worked against the two of us ending up together. My office has been assigned oversight duties with the police department, and they've been assigned the same thing with us. That means each of us is policing the other to make sure everything is done right. In order for us to work together, we can't have a conflict of interest that might keep either of us from being totally honest in our scrutiny of the other. A romantic relationship qualifies as a conflict of interest."

"So quit your job," Emily says with a shrug, as if the answer is so obvious any idiot could figure it out. I envy her naïveté.

"I did. But the new job I thought I had fell through, and you and your mom showed up, and it just seemed like it wasn't meant to be. So now I'm back at this job, which I love by the way. And Hurley and I are partners and nothing more."

"Things don't always work out the way we want them to, do they?" Her tone is one of resigned acceptance.

"No, they don't. It must be hard for you, all this change."

She shrugs again, her expression an attempt at indifference that I don't buy. "You go with the flow."

I reach over and give her arm a gentle squeeze. The gesture seems to embarrass her and she suddenly becomes engrossed in her book again.

"I'll be back in a little while. Call if you need anything." I leave her in the library and head back to the autopsy suite. Bernie has been sewn back up and Arnie and Izzy are cleaning the room. I poke my head in and even though I know the answer, I ask, "Anything new?"

Izzy, as expected, shakes his head.

Arnie, however, surprises me. "Yeah, I had a thought. We should get a list of all the recent deaths at that nursing home and look at their records to see if there is anything suspicious. Just to see if maybe this guy really was killing people off." His face lights up as he speaks. This is what Arnie lives for, a real live conspiracy right here at home. "We might need to do some exhumations and autopsy any of the ones that look suspicious."

Izzy says, "That's assuming the bodies are still available. These days people are as likely to be cremated as they are buried. Plus I'm not sure the DA would be willing to spend the money necessary to do all that, especially if the perpetrator is already dead."

"Besides, the autopsies might not help," I say. "Irene told me she thought Bernard was varying his methods to avoid anyone catching on."

Arnie isn't going to give up that easily. I know he's hoping to uncover some sort of plot here, because being able to verify even one real conspiracy lends a level of validation to all the others. "We should at least look at the death rates and compare them to other facilities. If the Twilight Home's numbers are way out of line, that would mean something, wouldn't it?"

"I don't know," Izzy says. "It sounds like a lot of overwrought paranoia to me. I think we'll be looking for something that isn't there."

"But what does it hurt to look?" Arnie argues.

I think Izzy senses that Arnie is too excited to let the matter go, so he tries changing the subject. "How did it go with Bernard's wife? Did you get a sense that she might have wanted him dead?"

"Oh, I don't think she'll miss him. They were in the process of splitting up from what she told us. But Hurley doesn't think she would have killed him and I'm inclined to agree with him. The woman is a bit of a whack job, but she doesn't strike me as a killer."

"If you're right, that narrows it down to a few dozen patients and employees as suspects," Izzy jokes. "It sounds like you're going to have a busy weekend."

"I don't mind." Truth is, I'm delighted. I'm hoping that staying busy will help keep my mind off the casino. "It will probably be a late night tonight and an early start tomorrow. Do you want me to check in with you tomorrow morning before I hook up with Hurley?"

"I wouldn't mind an update," Izzy says. "But it

doesn't have to be in the morning. If you hit on something big let me know, otherwise just check in with me at some point tomorrow. At this point, the main focus has to be on the investigation and narrowing down suspects, so the best use of your time will be to assist Hurley in the investigation."

I wonder if he would still feel that way if he knew what Hurley and I had just done in the men's room. I promise myself to be stronger, and to draw a line with Hurley. But first I have to figure out a way to keep him from ever touching me again, because that touch does evil things to me.

Izzy throws Arnie a bone. "Arnie, you can assist Mattie and Hurley if you want. Given the amount of work that's involved with this case, and the fact that Jonas's last allergy attack was so severe he's still in the hospital, I imagine the police could use some help with the evidence collection, searches, and interviews."

"Seriously?" Arnie says, his eyes big with excitement.

"Why not?" Izzy says. "If you want, I can start the tox screen for you and process our samples here. It's been awhile, but I think I remember how to do it. That way you can spend some time in the field."

"Thanks, Izzy." Arnie looks over at me. "If it's okay with you, Mattie."

"Of course it is. I'm happy to have you."

"Just keep track of your hours for comp time," Izzy tells us.

Arnie and I mumble agreements even though we know the whole comp time thing is a joke. Our positions are salaried, based on an eight-to-five schedule with an hour taken out for lunch. We get paid for eight hours a day, forty hours a week, no matter how many hours we work. Because we have to put in call time and frequently end up working in the evenings, the middle of the night, or on the weekends, we are supposed to keep track of these off hours and then compensate for them by taking time off during our regular eight-hour day. The theory is that we never end up working more than those paid forty hours. The reality is we always seem to end up working way more than those forty hours and our schedules rarely resemble that eight-to-five ideal. Trying to make up comp time is a Sisyphean task. When I quit my job two months ago, I had almost a hundred hours of comp time banked, and I'd only been on the job for three months. I imagine Arnie and Izzy would both have thousands of comp time hours if it wasn't for the fact that it resets to zero every year. It wouldn't be too bad if we could cash that comp time in somehow, but it's a use-it-or-lose-it proposition.

It's easy to see how the time builds up. I started back at my job on Thursday so I've been at it for three days. I put in my eight hours on Thursday and Friday, and by the time the weekend is over, I will probably have twelve to sixteen more hours of time in. If I can find a way to use it during the week and work some short days, or even take a whole day off, it would help. But that rarely happens. There's always something that needs to be done: autopsies, results follow-ups, investigations, research, studying, and paperwork . . . tons and tons of paperwork.

Still, a day off during the week would allow me to hit up the casino, assuming I wasn't on call. Dr. Maggie pops into my head with a *tsk-tsk*, and I can see her writing *addict* on that damned notepad of hers. I mentally gag her and tie her down, a process that apparently puts a smile on my face.

"What's so funny?" Izzy asks me.

"Nothing," I say. "I'm just so happy to be back on the job."

Chapter 13

The police station is only a block away from the ME's office, so it doesn't take me very long to walk there. I find Hurley seated in the station's conference room, which does double duty as an interrogation room, albeit a cushier one than you'd expect to find in most police stations. In the room with him is Junior Feller, Bob Richmond, another detective named Larry Johnson, and three officers who are typically uniform cops but are currently in street clothes. I guess they were enticed with the promise of overtime and came in on their time off to help with the investigation.

As I enter the room, Hurley greets me with a smile. "Pull up a chair, Mattie. I just finished sharing the results of the autopsy and we're planning what our next steps should be."

Hurley's phone rings and as he answers it I walk to the end of the table and pull out a chair. A tiny moan escapes me as I drop into it, triggered by my still screaming muscles.

Bob Richmond is seated next to me and he leans over to whisper in my ear. "A little sore?"

"That's the understatement of the year," I whisper back. "I feel like I spent a day getting tossed around inside a cement mixer."

"It was like that for me at first, too. But it gets easier over time if you keep at it."

People always say that about exercise . . . that it gets easier with time . . . but I've not found this to be true. I can't even begin to understand those exercise junkies who claim some endorphin high that leaves them in a state of panting, sweating ecstasy. First of all, you have to endure pain for the endorphins to kick in, so by my way of figuring I could just sit in a room and pinch myself for thirty minutes and get the same result. And I could do it while watching TV, or eating bonbons, or watching TV *and* eating bonbons. Second of all, I loathe exercise for the sake of exercise. It's cruel, especially at a gym where the only machines I've ever mastered were always in the vending area.

Hurley ends his call and announces, "We have the search warrants. They're faxing them as we speak so we're good to go. Chase's wife's alibi clears her until ten or so, so we can't eliminate her, but I don't think she did it. We'll need to search the house at some point, but I want to focus on the nursing home for now. I need a group to conduct the room searches, a group to interview the patients, and a group to interview the staff and board members. I plan on doing the latter and I'll have Mattie with me, but if whoever is doing the room searches finds any medication of any kind, I want you to let Mattie have a look at it. Okay?"

Everyone at the table nods their understanding.

Hurley looks over at Larry Johnson. "Why don't you take two of the uniforms and start working on the room searches."

"Can do," Larry says.

"Record any ancillary dialogue that takes place during the searches. Make sure you document everything and take as many pictures as you need to. Use your phones, or buy some disposable cameras and turn the receipts in for reimbursement. If you find anything that looks like medication in any of the patient rooms, bag it, tag it, and let Mattie take a look at it."

Larry nods and addresses two of the uniformed cops at the table. "Connor and Fred, you two can come with me."

Hurley shifts his attention to Richmond. "Bob, I want you and Junior to start conducting the patient interviews. Mattie and I will help you once we're finished with the employees and board members. I don't think they'll take long."

"Will do."

"What about me?" asks Brenda Joiner, the only unassigned uniform cop in the room.

"I need you to start processing the crime scene for evidence. We'll need to dust for fingerprints in the bathroom where the body was found, in the hallway outside the bathroom, both exits to the hallway, Bernard Chase's office, and at a minimum the doors to the other offices in that wing. If any of them are unlocked, we'll need to take a look around inside, too."

"I thought Jonas was back on board to do that stuff," Brenda says.

"He will be, but he's still out on sick leave for now. So we're going to have to do it."

"There's going to be fingerprints all over the place," Brenda says.

"I expect to find prints from the board members and perhaps some other staff members back there, but I don't imagine patients go back there often, so if we find any patient prints in the administration area, that will be telling. Of course, it means we will need to print all of the patients."

Brenda groans.

"Izzy said we can use Arnie to help with evidence collection," I tell her. "Izzy's going to run the lab tests himself so Arnie's free to assist you with this. I'll help, too, when I can."

"Junior and Richmond can help in a way, too," Hurley says, then he turns to Richmond. "You and Junior get a ten set on each patient you guys talk to."

Richmond nods.

"Does anyone have any questions?" Hurley asks. "Okay then, let's get to it."

As everyone gets up and heads out of the room, Hurley turns to me and says, "I should probably take Emily home before we head out. Do you think she'll be okay at my place by herself?"

"She's old enough, she seems like a pretty bright girl, and she has a good head on her shoulders. I think she'll be fine. You can ask her just to make sure she's comfortable with it, but I don't see why it would be a problem."

"I suppose I need to feed her, too," Hurley says, scratching his head and glancing at his watch again. "Damn, this day has flown by. It's almost dinnertime already."

I realize just how complicated his life is likely to be

with Kate gone. Having responsibility for another person, particularly a child, demands a whole new way of thinking. And it gives me an idea.

"Tell you what. I promised my sister I would stop by and talk to her sometime tonight. Why don't you let me take care of Emily? I'll go get her and take her with me to Desi's house. I think she and Erika will get along well and she'll be somewhere safe where she can get a hot cooked meal. When we're done eating, I'll drive her to your place and make sure she's locked in tight before I leave. Then I'll head over to the nursing home and join you. You can start your interviews and I'll join you when I get there."

"But we're supposed to have someone from your office present. The whole oversight thing, remember?"

"Arnie's going over there to help. He's all excited about the possibility of a real conspiracy going on, so I'm sure he'll be willing to do whatever you need him to. Trust me, he won't mind."

Hurley considers this for a moment and then says, "Are you sure *you* don't mind?"

"Not at all. I like Emily."

"Yeah, she seems like a great kid." He smiles, but turns serious again. "I don't want her to think I'm trying to pawn her off."

"She won't. I'll tell her it was my idea."

Hurley runs a hand through his hair and sighs. "I'm not used to having someone else to look out for. I'm used to being on my own, and with the crazy hours I'm sometimes forced to work, a kid is not a good fit in my life right now. I shouldn't have let Kate leave."

"It'll work out, Hurley. Trust me. I need a ride back to my place so I can get my car, but after that you can leave Emily with me. I promise I'll take care of her."

"I'd love to take you back to your place," Hurley says, a wicked gleam in his eye.

"I don't think we have time for that. Besides, we agreed we weren't going to do that again."

"We did?"

"Yes, we did."

Hurley sighs. "Fine. I'll behave."

"Promise?"

"Promise."

He's true to his word, and fifteen minutes later, I have an eager Arnie en route to the Twilight Home, and I've called Desi and made arrangements for me and Emily to drop by for dinner, though all I tell Desi about Emily is that she's the daughter of a friend and that I think she will hit it off with Erika. I feed Hoover and pat him on the head, pour food for and say hi to the cats, who barely acknowledge my existence, and then I'm in my hearse headed back to my office.

Emily is still in the library, but she's no longer seated at the table. She is standing in front of a skeleton that hangs from a metal frame in the back corner of the library. In one of Emily's hands is a clipboard with paper on it, in the other a pencil.

At first, I think she is writing something, but as I draw closer I see that she is drawing. A face is emerging on the paper and when I get a good look at it, I'm stunned. "What are you doing?"

"I'm completing this skull. I'm playing with some of that information from the book I was reading and using it to draw a face."

What Emily doesn't know is that the skeleton belongs to a woman named Bertha whose husband

Herman was a doctor and coroner in the area up until about twenty years ago. They had a child who died of osteogenesis imperfecta, better known as brittle bone disease, and Herman dedicated most of his spare time to researching the disorder. When Bertha was diagnosed with terminal cancer, she donated her body to science so her husband could examine her bones in search of evidence that would indicate an inherited tendency toward the disease. Herman never found any, but he had Bertha's skeleton wired together and kept it in his office because he said it made him feel close to her. Quite a few people thought it was macabre, but over time people got used to Bertha's bones hanging around Herman's office, even to the point of a standing joke that circulated around town. More than once while I was growing up, someone in a café or at the grocery store would give someone else a sly wink, or an elbow in the ribs, and say, "I hear Herman has a boner in his office, thanks to Bertha."

When Izzy took over the office after Herman retired, Bertha stayed on. In the hallway outside Izzy's office, where Emily has never been, is a picture of Bertha taken about five years before she died. The reason Emily's drawing is stunning is because it bears a startling resemblance to that picture. It's a much younger-looking Bertha, minus the jowls and the gray hair, but the basic facial characteristics are the same.

Emily is focused on what she's doing and oblivious to my amazement, so I study her face as she draws. She is very focused, her blue eyes—Hurley's eyes—moving from the skull to the picture, skull to picture, not looking away even when she speaks to me. There is no doubt that Emily takes after her father when it comes to her looks. Kate's features are delicate and feminine whereas Emily's features are a bit more *there*—a patrician nose, a chin that is full and slightly jutting, cheekbones that are high and sharp. It's Hurley's face, just a slightly softer, more feminine version.

"You're staring at me," she says.

"Sorry." I look away, embarrassed. "It's just that you look so much like your father."

She turns to look at me finally and smiles. "It must have been hard for you having us show up like this."

I nod and shrug. I can tell she is a smart kid, and I don't want to bullshit her. "It definitely made for an awkward moment. I'm not sure there's a good time for something like your arrival to happen, but in terms of my relationship with Hurley it came at a pretty bad time. Though as it turns out, it was probably for the best."

"Are you sure you and Steve aren't still serious?"

If doing it like rabbits every time we see each other is serious, then yes, I guess we are. But no one can know that. And it has to stop.

"I'm sure," I tell her.

"That's too bad. You two seem to get along so well."

You have no idea.

"He and my mom fight all the time. She says that's the way it was when they first met, too. That's why they split up." There's the tiniest hint of angst in her voice when she says this and I suspect she is angry with her mother for keeping her father from her all these years. There's a lot she's missed out on.

It's a feeling I understand all too well. "My dad left my mom and me when I was only four years old. No warning, no explanation, no return. Just one day gone, never to be seen again."

"That sucks." She says this without looking at me, her focus back on her drawing.

"Yes, it kind of did. Sometimes it still does. I often wonder where he is, what he's doing, if he's even still alive." *Why he couldn't love me enough to stick around.* "Did you know you had a father out there somewhere?"

She shakes her head. "Mom told me he was dead, that he died in a car accident before I was born. She had a picture of him, and that's the closest thing to a father I've had all these years. It wasn't until we lost the house that she told me the truth."

"Do you like him?"

She shrugs. "He's okay. We're both adjusting to this new relationship and Steve's pretty good at giving me time and space to figure things out."

"Is that what you call him all the time? Steve?"

She smiles, acknowledging her awareness that I'm flipping her own question back at her. "What else would I call him? I wouldn't feel right calling him Dad. It's still awkward. We don't know each other very well and I don't feel any strong emotion toward him. Basically, he's nothing more than a sperm donor."

"Yikes. That's a bit harsh."

"Well, it's true."

"Does your mom still have feelings for him?"

"I don't know," Emily says, scrunching her face. "Sometimes I think she still has a thing for him. But other times I think she's just caught up in memories, recalling whatever attraction brought the two of them together in the beginning. She always said he was the only man she ever loved."

"Then why did she let him go when she was pregnant with you?"

"She said it was because she knew he didn't feel the same way toward her. I guess by the time she found out she was pregnant, they were already talking divorce. She said Steve always told her he didn't want to be tied down, that it was a mistake to get married, and he was really angry when a friend of his got trapped into marrying someone because she got pregnant. She was afraid he'd think she got pregnant on purpose to trap him into staying. If he said he wanted her to have an abortion, or give me away, she knew she couldn't do that. So she kept it all a secret."

"Why didn't she go through with the divorce?"

"I don't know. I've asked her that several times lately but she never gives me an answer."

"Hurley said he's finalizing the divorce now. How's your mom taking that?"

"I think she was hoping something would happen between the two of them when they got back together. But it clearly hasn't." Emily pauses and shrugs. "I think Mom feels lonely. She's been sick a lot lately, and even though I tried to take care of her the best I could, I still had to go to school, and do my homework, and I couldn't do things like drive to the grocery store, or drive her to the doctor's. She had to ask friends and neighbors for help with stuff like that and she hates to do that. Plus, I think she realizes at times like that how alone she is."

I feel bad for Emily. It's clear that she has shouldered much more responsibility than a girl of her age should have to. "How is your mom's health now?"

Emily shrugs. "She hasn't been to a doctor since we left Chicago so I guess she's doing okay. But I don't think the doctors were ever able to figure out what was wrong with her."

"That must have been frustrating."

Emily nodded.

"I'm sorry things have been so rough for you lately. Are you sorry you came here?"

"No. Besides, it's not like we had any choice. Mom lost her job because of all the sick time she had to take, and when she lost her job she also lost her insurance. It's because of all the doctor bills that we lost our house. I guess this is a chance for us to start over."

"What was she sick with?"

Emily shrugs. "I'm not sure. I know she had some really heavy periods and bled a lot and that made her anemic."

"Did you have a lot of friends where you were before?"

"Some. Most of them ignored me when my mom got sick. Some of the snobby ones wouldn't talk to me when they heard we were losing our house. I had one good friend who stuck by me and she and I still talk on the phone from time to time. But I don't think we'll be going back to Chicago anytime soon and I don't know if our friendship will survive the distance."

"I'm sure you'll make some new friends here."

"Yeah, I suppose. But it's hard when you're the new kid. There're all these cliques and stuff. It can be hard to break in."

I make a mental note to talk to Erika about Emily. Erika is thirteen and still has one more year to go in middle school before she gets into high school, but a lot of her friends have older brothers and sisters in high school. Maybe she can smooth the way for Emily to make some new friends.

"That picture that you've drawn there is pretty amazing," I say, deciding Emily could use a morale boost.

"It's nothing special," she says dismissively. "I'm just experimenting with some of that stuff I read in the book about skin depth and features."

"Actually, it is special and if you'll follow me, I'll show you why."

She stops drawing and I lead her out of the library, still carrying her clipboard, and down the hall past Izzy's office. We stop in front of the picture of Bertha hanging on the wall where it's been for the past two decades. I nod toward the portrait. "This woman is Bertha. Do you notice the strong resemblance between her and your drawing?"

Emily cocks her head, a quizzical smile on her face as she looks at the picture. Then she looks at her drawing. "Huh."

"It's not a coincidence that the two look alike. That skeleton hanging in the library is also Bertha." I pause and let that information sink in.

I can tell when Emily has registered the significance of what she has done. Again, she looks at the drawing in her hands and then at the portrait, her expression wide-eyed and amazed rather than just amused. She looks at me. "For real?"

"For real. I daresay you have a pretty cool talent there, young lady. With a little bit of training you might be able to pursue an interesting career. There's a huge need for artists who can render something like this from nothing more than bones."

"Sweet." Emily studies the photo of Bertha for a

few seconds more, then she looks at me and asks, "Where's Steve?"

"He got kind of busy with our murder case. He and some of the other cops are executing search warrants and interviewing people over at the nursing home. I'm going to join them later, but for now I want to get something to eat and I thought you and I could do that together, if that's okay with you."

"Sure. Are you going to cook or are we going to eat out?"

I laugh. "Neither as it turns out. And trust me, the news that I'm not going to cook is probably the best news you'll get today. The only thing I'm good at making when it comes to food is reservations."

Chapter 14

I fill Emily in on our dinner plans and despite my efforts to make it sound like a fun, relaxing time, she
seems understandably anxious. I feel bad for her. It
can't be easy having your life kicked out from under
you the way she has, and the one thing in her life
that has been a constant—her mother—is now gone.
Some strange woman who may or may not be in competition with her mother for the affections of her
newfound father is hauling her off to some strange
house to meet a whole new group of people. So far
Emily has adapted easily to new situations and people, so I cross my fingers that this encounter will be
no different.

My suspicion that Emily and Erika will have a lot in
common is supported by Emily's reaction to my car.
My niece has long had a fascination with things related to death, and her reaction the first time she saw
me drive up in the hearse was one of pure delight.
She climbed into the back and lay down where the

coffins used to go and pretended she was dead. I have to confess, it was a little creepy, but given that Erika is otherwise a normal happy teenager, I'm not too concerned. Neither is Desi, who has always been the type of mother who lets her children be who they want to be no matter how strange. I have to give the woman credit. There aren't many other mothers I know who would let their young son keep a tarantula and a three-inch cockroach as house pets.

Emily's reaction to my hearse is reminiscent of Erika's. She stares at it with her mouth agape for a few seconds, then says, "This is your car?"

"Yep," I say glibly. "It comes in handy given my line of work."

Emily's eyebrows scrunch together and after a few seconds of weighing my last statement, she narrows her eyes at me and smiles. "You don't really haul bodies around in here, do you?"

"No, I don't. A few months ago, I had a bad car accident and totaled my old car. I was going through a divorce at the time and didn't have very much money. Plus the insurance on the car was in my husband's name. I went shopping for a replacement with what little money I had and this was the only thing I could afford that promised to be reliable."

"It's the bomb," Emily says. She walks the length of the passenger side, running her hand along the dark midnight blue finish.

"My dog Hoover likes it a lot," I tell her. "I think it's all the strange smells inside."

"You have a dog?"

I nod.

"Can I see him?"

"Maybe after dinner. My sister is expecting us and I don't want to be too late. I also need to get to the nursing home to help your father and the other cops with their investigation."

"Okay," Emily says, clearly disappointed. She climbs into the passenger seat of the hearse and our trip, which only takes a few minutes, is made in silence, though Emily spends the duration craning around so she can see the back area of the car.

As I pull up and park beside the curb in front of my sister's house, a small groan escapes me. There is another car parked in front of mine and it's one I recognize—my mother's. This is not a good thing. My mother is difficult to deal with when things are going well and I'm pretty sure I'm at the top of her fecal roster at the moment, a dubious status that promises difficult conversations ahead.

Desi meets us at the front door before we have a chance to knock. She reaches up and hugs me; I hug her back, hard.

"I'm so sorry, Desi," I whisper. "I had no idea you and Lucien were having problems."

"We can discuss that later," she says. "I should warn you, Mom is here."

"Yeah," I say, releasing her. "I saw the car out front. Is William here with her?"

Desi nods. From behind her I see Erika walk up and I'm surprised. The dark Goth look she had the last time I saw her has been softened. The black dye she used on her hair is gone, and in its place is her natural dark chestnut brown. Her clothes are pretty ordinary-looking as well: blue jeans, a plain green T-shirt, and sneakers. Though I'm too far away to tell for sure, I don't think she's wearing any makeup. It's a stark contrast to the dark eyeliner she was wearing the last time I saw her. I can't help but wonder how much of this change is due to the breakup of her parents. I wonder if I've made a miscalculation by bringing Emily here.

I quickly make introductions, forgoing any detailed explanations, and before anything else can be said or done my mother appears in the foyer.

"Mattie! It's about time you made a public appearance. We've all been very worried about you. Desi and I even came by your place a week or so ago. That horrible car you drive was there so we assumed you were home, but no one answered the door."

"I know, Mom, and I'm sorry. I've been going through a lot lately and I—"

"*You've* been going through a lot," Mom interrupts. "Let me tell you the problems *I've* been having. All this worry about you has stressed me out so much that I think I must have an ulcer. I'm pretty sure I have that H. pylori bacteria in my gut. You know I'm anemic already. If I have an ulcer and it starts to bleed, I'm a goner."

My mother's words are spoken in a very dramatic tone, one I know well because I've been listening to it my entire life. She's been a major hypochondriac for as long as I can remember. That, along with her OCD, has led to her being banned from all of the local doctors' offices, not because of her disorders per se, but because of the scenes she makes whenever she has an appointment. Nothing is ever diagnosed right, nothing is ever cleaned well enough, and heaven forbid if you try to make her sit in the waiting room with all the sneezing, coughing, germ-blowing sick people. Because of her estrangement with all of her past medical caregivers, my marriage to a surgeon was probably the one moment in my life when I made my mother proud. She still has trouble understanding why I would let something as nitpicky as infidelity ruin a perfectly good marriage, especially to a doctor.

"I don't know, Mom," I say, looking her over. "Maybe it's the lighting in here, but your color looks better than I've seen it in a long time. I'm sure you're fine."

This last bit is a line I've uttered numerous times to her, and each time I'm painfully aware of the fact that eventually, one day, she will have something truly wrong. But like the boy who cries wolf, it's hard to take any of her complaints seriously when they've been coming at me more regularly than sniffles during flu season and thus far not a one of them has actually panned out. The day my mother tells me she's feeling fine and has no complaints is the day I'll start to worry; it will be a sure sign that Armageddon is nigh.

Seeming to realize that I'm not going to play, Mom shifts her attention to Emily. "And who do we have here?"

"This is Emily—" I stop suddenly, and look over at her. "I just realized I don't know what your last name is."

"It's Houston," Emily says. "Like the city in Texas."

"Ah, good to know. Let me start again. This is Emily Houston. She is Steve Hurley's daughter."

I watch my mother's eyes grow large, as do my sister's. That's when I realize that neither one of them knew about Kate and Emily, or at least not about their relationship to Hurley. It makes me wonder what the current gossip has been. Then again, Desi has likely been distracted by her own problems and therefore not tuned in to the town gossip. And my mother gets most of her gossip from me and Desi, so . . .

Erika saves the day. She takes Emily's hand and hauls her off into the living room, where she is trying to do some kind of dance moves with a Wii. I follow my sister out to the kitchen, my mother trailing behind us. I find William—or William-Not-Bill as he is more fondly known to me because that's what he kept telling me the first time I met him—sitting on a barstool in the kitchen. I'm a little surprised to find him there. The first time he sat on one of my sister's barstools he fainted at the sight of my nephew's three-inch Madagascar hissing cockroach and ended up with an ambulance ride to the hospital and a bunch of stitches in his scalp.

I give him a hug, genuinely glad to see him. I met William for the first time back around Halloween when Izzy set us up as a blind date. To say that our date didn't work out is a gross understatement, but all was not lost. I introduced William-not-Bill to my mother, who is currently divorced from husband number four, and they've been a happy couple ever since, despite the fact that Mom is a dozen years his senior. Turns out they both have OCD, and since they're living together, I'd bet money that their house is the cleanest one in the town of Sorenson, maybe in the entire state of Wisconsin.

We manage to get through dinner—a delicious pot roast that my sister had cooking in the Crock-Pot all day—without any contentious conversation. I had hoped Erika would be able to assist Emily with the teenage social landscape in Sorenson but ironically, it is Emily who ends up offering to help Erika negotiate certain social travails when she starts high school. I'm relieved the two of them seem to be getting on well, and when I hear them discussing plans for possibly getting together for spring break, I'm glad I decided to bring Emily along.

I discuss my return to my old job during the meal and the news is met with glee by all, though for different reasons. In my mother's case, it's because my job gives me access to lots of health department and disease information, which she expects me to use to keep her updated on all the latest disease trends. This perk is offset some, however, by her fears about the contagions I might expose her to while I'm "playing around with those dead people." Erika's glad to hear I have my job back because she thinks it's cool that I work with dead people all the time. Her brother Ethan is happy about it because he has connections with an entomologist from Madison, thanks to me, and he's scheduled to go to a special bug camp this summer where he'll be functioning as a paid advisor rather than as a camper.

As soon as we're done eating, I grab Desi and haul her into the laundry room, shutting the door behind us. "Look, Des, we need to talk, but I'm in a bit of a bind time-wise. There's been a murder over at the Twilight Home. The cops are there now conducting an investigation and I need to go help them with the interviews, interrogations, and evidence collection."

"Okay, but first tell me what's going on with you and Hurley? And what's with this daughter? Is that why you two broke up?"

"Yeah, that had a lot to do with it. Emily comes with a mother who, it turns out, is still married to Hurley."

Desi gasps and clamps a hand over her mouth. "Oh crap, Mattie. That's horrible. He's been married all this time and didn't tell you?"

"He didn't tell me because he didn't know. Apparently he thought Kate—that's Emily's mother—had filed divorce papers years ago. She didn't, for reasons only she knows and she never told him. Nor did she tell him that she was pregnant. Apparently, she and Emily have had a rough time of things lately and they ended up homeless. They showed up on Hurley's doorstep a couple months ago looking for help."

"How awful for you," Desi says, shaking her head. "We heard there was a woman living with him, but the assumption around town has been that she was either a relative or a new girlfriend who has a teenage daughter. To find out he has a wife . . ." She shakes her head again. "I'm so sorry that happened to you, Mattie. I know how it feels to be duped by a man you love."

"First of all, Hurley didn't dupe me and what happened between me and him is okay. The timing wasn't right for us. Maybe that will change somewhere down the road, but for now I'm happy just to be working with him again. I'm sure it's been one heck of an adjustment for him, too. Fortunately, Emily seems to be a great kid.

"And second of all, Lucien didn't dupe you on purpose. He was embarrassed and he didn't want to let you down. That's the only reason he didn't tell you what was going on. He was hoping he could fix it before you found out."

"You don't know what you're talking about," Desi snaps, crossing her arms over her chest. "Lucien betrayed my trust in him. He thinks that since I thought he was having an affair and he wasn't that everything should be hunky dory. Well it's not. He may not have had an affair, but he clearly has no compunctions about lying to me since he took it upon himself to wipe out our entire savings account without so much as a word to me."

"Look Desi, I know that what Lucien did with your money was stupid, but he didn't do it with any menace in his heart. In fact, if anything, it was the kindness in his heart that got him into trouble. He didn't want to disappoint his clients and friends and truly thought it was a temporary setback, that he would eventually be able to climb his way out of the hole he dug himself into."

"I don't know," Desi says, shaking her head and wringing her hands.

"Do you love him, Des?"

"Of course I do, but I can't trust him anymore." Tears well in her eyes and she snorts back a sniffle. "He humiliated me and the kids. And he lied to me, Mattie. That's what I'm having the hardest time with. I thought our relationship was one of mutual respect and trust, but now I just don't know."

"I get that. And you're right. He betrayed your trust. But he did so because he couldn't bear the thought of letting you down, of seeing the disappointment on your face when you look at him. He couldn't bear the thought of you thinking poorly of him. He made a mistake, several in fact. He knows that. He's working night and day to try to make up for the money he lost. I don't know how he can make up for the lying thing other than to never do it again, and based on what I saw and heard from him today, I'd bet money he won't."

In my mind's eye, I see Dr. Maggie arch an eyebrow at this statement, more proof in her mind that I'm a gambling addict. I shove her out of my head and continue.

"Lucien will survive the money thing. What he won't survive is losing you and the kids. You guys are everything to him. This separation is killing him. He looks awful. He's got big circles under his eyes, he's all slumped over, and he didn't come at me with a single double entendre, sexual innuendo, or suggestive comment during the entire time I was with him today. I'm telling you the man is broken. He needs you. Give him another chance."

Tears track down Desi's face and she swipes irritably at them. "I need some time to think about things, but thank you for talking with me." A short but almost hysterical laugh escapes her. "And for talking to Lucien. I know he hasn't always been easy for you to deal with."

I dismiss her statement with a little *pfft.* "I've always known Lucien's crap is just an act. A darned good act at times, but an act nonetheless."

Desi spends a minute or so getting her face together. "I don't want to upset the kids or Mom. How do I look? Can you tell I've been crying?"

"Not at all."

"You never were a very good liar."

"Are the kids doing okay?"

"Ethan is taking everything in stride. He lives in a world all his own most of the time, anyway. Erika is having a hard time of it. At first, she was really angry at Lucien, but now she seems just sad."

"Has he been in touch with them?"

"No, I wouldn't let him."

"Don't do that to him, Desi. Don't take his kids away, even if the two of you can't work things out. You'll destroy him. No matter how awful you think he's been, he doesn't deserve that."

Desi sighs heavily. "I suppose you're right."

"How's Mom been dealing with it all?"

Desi laughs. "She thinks you and I are the devil's spawn and off our rockers, though she thinks you're crazier than I am. She doesn't understand how any woman could cast aside a lawyer or a doctor husband simply because of a few silly little mistakes. She even came up with an eleventh rule in her official Rules for Wives."

"I shudder to think."

"You're going to love it. It's a twist on an old saying, kind of like one of those fractured fairy tales we watched when we were kids. Except this one isn't suitable for kids. It's rated R."

"Do tell."

"A rich man in your pocket is worth two plays in someone's bush."

I stare at my sister, wondering if I heard her right.

She laughs again. "I swear. That's what she told me. She was going on about how you were so quick to dump David because he screwed around on you, and she was upset that I was doing the same thing after one silly infraction on Lucien's part. 'You should always give them a second chance,' she told me. 'If they make it to three strikes, then they're out.' She got that real serious look on her face that she gets when she's convinced she has some terminal disease. And out it came. 'Always remember this,' she said. 'A rich man in your pocket is worth two plays in someone's bush.' "

I start giggling and that gets Desi going, too. It builds, becoming contagious, each of us feeding off the other and off our shared, twisted history with our mother. Within seconds, we have tears rolling down our faces. In Desi's case, I'm pretty sure the tears are a byproduct of her laughter, but for me they are a byproduct of the pain in my gut muscles that the laughing has triggered.

When we finally get ourselves under control, I walk over, wrap her in my arms, and give her a long tight hug that triggers even more pain. Clearly my ibuprofen has worn off. "I have to go," I say when I release her. "But we'll talk again soon."

We exit the laundry room and before I fetch Emily to leave, I go to my purse and take out my check-book. I write out a check to my sister in the amount of ten thousand dollars. Desi is at the sink doing dishes so I fold the check up and stick it in her pants pocket. "This is just a little something to tide you and the kids over for now." She opens her mouth to object, but before she can, I add, "I want to help you guys. And I'm in a position where I can. I gave some money to Lucien, too. You're my family, and I love you. So let me do this for you, okay?"

Desi hesitates a few seconds before answering. Finally she nods. "I won't say no because I need the money right now. But I insist that it be a loan."

I shake my head. "I'm considering it a gift, at least the money I'm giving to you. But if it makes you feel better to think of it as a loan, that's fine." I lean over and give her a quick kiss on the cheek and then head for the living room to get Emily.

A couple awkward good-byes later, Emily and I are back in my car and headed for Hurley's house. I pull into his driveway and leave the car running while I walk with Emily to the front door. She looks at me, but makes no effort to enter the house.

"Something wrong?" I ask her.

"You have the key, don't you?"

"Me? No. I don't have a key. Are you saying you don't have one either?"

She shakes her head. I mentally slap myself for not

figuring out this problem sooner. On the off chance that Hurley or Kate might've left the place unlocked, I give the front doorknob a try, but it doesn't budge.

"Okay," I say, hands on my hips as I think. "Plan B. How would you feel about staying at my place for a few hours? I have cable TV and you can play with Hoover."

"Can't I just go with you to the nursing home?"

"I don't think it would be appropriate, Emily. Besides, it's not going to be that exciting. Yes, it's technically a crime scene, but all we're going to do is talk to a bunch of old people."

"Fine," Emily says with a shrug, but I can tell it isn't.

We get back in the hearse and a few minutes later pull up in front of my cottage. "Who lives in the big house?" she asks as we get out of the car.

"My boss Izzy and his partner Dom."

"Partner? As in gay?"

"Yes."

"Izzy is gay?"

I nod.

"Huh."

I'm not sure what her comment means so I ignore it. I unlock the door and Hoover greets us with his usual wagging tail. He gives me a cursory sniff and then shifts all his attention to the newcomer. Emily squats down and starts massaging Hoover behind both ears at once, sending him to doggie heaven.

"There are two cats here, too," I tell her. "Tux and Rubbish."

She smiles at this. "Rubbish?"

"I found him in a garbage Dumpster. I didn't

name Tux, but it's fitting. You'll understand as soon as you see him. Do you like cats?"

"I like all animals."

"Well, the cats may not bother to introduce themselves. They tend to ignore people who like cats and make pests of themselves to those who don't. There's some pop in the fridge. Help yourself. I'm sorry I don't have any food. I was on my way to go grocery shopping when I got called to the crime scene."

"That's okay. I'm not hungry anyway."

"If you need anything, just go to the main house. I'll let Dom and Izzy know you're here."

I take out my cell phone and call Dom, who informs me that Izzy isn't home yet, but he is more than happy to keep an eye out and help Emily if she needs anything. After I hang up, I relay this information to Emily and ask her if she has a cell phone.

"All we had is a throwaway phone, and my mom has it with her."

The cottage doesn't have a landline so I dig out my own throwaway phone, the one I bought a couple months ago when I quit my job with Izzy and had to give that cell phone back. It's a basic flip phone and when I open it I see that the battery is almost dead so I plug it in to its charger. I look up Hurley's and Dom's numbers in my work phone and write them down for her. I also write down my work cell number after Emily helps me figure out what it is.

"The phone should charge up pretty fast," I tell her. "Don't hesitate to call if you need anything."

"Okay."

She looks a little frightened and I feel bad leaving her there, but I don't see any other choice. I get back into the hearse and head for the Twilight Home, a trip that takes four minutes—one of the perks of living in a small town. As I park and get out of my car, I remember my diary, which I left sitting on the kitchen table. It's there . . . with a teenager who's all alone in my house.

Crap.

Chapter 15

A changing of the guard has occurred at the front desk of the Twilight Home. No doubt Connie has gone home and spread the news about her boss's demise and how his fortune cookie predicted it with its lack of a fortune. In her place is a nursing assistant by the name of Penny, an overweight, red-faced young woman who looks like she just got lambasted. Standing at her side with her jacket on is Dorothy Granger, who I'm willing to bet was the lambaster.

"Hey, Dorothy," I say as I approach. "How are things going?"

"How do you think they're going?" she asks with ill-disguised reproach.

Penny slides the sign-in clipboard toward me and sets a pen down on top of it.

I look at it and then at her. "I'm not here to visit. I'm here in an official capacity."

"You have to sign in either way," Dorothy says. "It's not a visitor roster. It's a way of keeping track of who comes in and out of this building. It's a safety measure and a licensure requirement."

"I see," I say, sliding the clipboard toward me and looking at the empty pages beneath the top one. "Do you keep the old copies of these on file somewhere?"

"We do. The cops already have the sheets in question."

"I see. Have they talked to you yet?"

"No, and they aren't going to any time soon. Right now, I'm the administrator in charge and as such I have a responsibility to the facility so I won't be speaking to any authorities without our lawyers in attendance." There is no malice in her voice when she says this; it's merely a recitation of duty.

"Are the lawyers here?"

"Not yet. They're based in Milwaukee. They're sending a team to deal with this mess, and they should be here any minute." Dorothy sounds sad.

"I'm sorry this happened, Dorothy. I know you run a tight and professional ship so this must be very difficult for you."

"The others are set up in the dayroom talking to patients. I believe you know the way."

I realize I'm being dismissed and I head for the dayroom, pondering the enigma that is Dorothy. I wonder again how old she is and how close she is to retirement. She's had the same gray-streaked hair, the same lived-in face, and the same level of energy ever since I've known her. To be honest, I would've guessed she was close to retirement age back when I first met her, just based on her personality and her old-school way of doing things. More than a decade later, she doesn't look or act much different. Based on her personality, I wouldn't be surprised if she never retired. Dorothy is the kind of woman who will work right up until the day she drops dead, and I'm guessing the odds of that happening while she's on the job are even money.

Dr. Maggie pops into my head again and after I tell her it's just a cliché for cripes sake, I shove her back out.

As I approach the intersection and the nurse's station, I see three employees huddled behind the desk. They are speaking in low, almost whispery voices—not loud enough for me to hear what they're saying—but they stop speaking altogether as soon as they see me.

A quick scan of their name tags tells me they are all nursing assistants. I smile at them, turn the corner, and swear I can feel their eyes boring into my back as I make my way down the hallway to the dayroom. Some of the patient rooms I pass are empty, but others have collections of patients in them who are also huddled and speaking in low, whispery voices. One of the rooms has two elderly men standing in the doorway. Inside, Larry and the off-duty police officers who are helping him are searching the room. The elderly men glare at me as I walk by and I assume they have determined me guilty merely by association.

When I reach the dayroom, I see a group of a dozen or so patients at one end, and Bob Richmond is seated at a table at the other end talking to an elderly gent who is bald, arthritic, and so stooped over, the waist of his pants are nearly at his nipple line. If it wasn't for a pair of snappy electric blue suspenders I suspect those pants would be in a pool at his feet. Apparently, Richmond is done with Mr. Suspenders because the gentleman is shuffling his way across the room. I don't see Hurley anywhere so I head over to Richmond.

"How's it going?" I ask.

He shakes his head. "This is one scary place," he says in a low voice. "Some of these people are so old I suspect the candles on their birthday cakes might be the cause of global warming. And some of them are so decrepit. It's sad."

"Getting old ain't pretty," I agree. "But it beats the alternative."

"I don't know," Richmond says, shaking his head woefully. "It seems like getting old is just one loss after another. You lose your teeth, your sight, your hearing, your muscle, your sphincter control, and if you're really unlucky, your mind. Or maybe they're the lucky ones because they don't know what's happening to them. I don't know." He sighs and runs a hand through his hair, leaving it standing up like a Mohawk.

"So many of these people are just struggling to hang on to whatever dignity they have left. One guy I talked to has had three heart surgeries, both hips and one knee replaced, he wears hearing aids, couldn't read my name tag, and wasn't sure what day it was or where he was. He told me he takes thirty-some medications and that his diabetes makes him prone to blackouts. Since he can't remember where his room is, who knows if that's true? You know what the really scary part is? He still has a driver's license that he uses on occasion! And you know what? I get it. That would be me, hanging on to whatever bit of independence I had left. I should probably report the guy to the DMV, but I don't think I have the heart to do it."

"It's a crapshoot," I tell him. "Not everyone's

golden years are the same. You're seeing the bad luck end of the spectrum in here. Some people age well and stay relatively healthy. Part of it is genetics, part of it is luck, and part of it is how well you take care of yourself. I have to say, you seem to be well on that road these days. You really look great, Bob."

"Thanks. I'm trying. The gym has helped. Do you want to meet me there in the morning early? I usually go around six and work out for forty-five minutes, sometimes an hour. That gives me time enough to shower and hit the station by eight when I'm working."

I consider this for a nanosecond and then shake my head. "I'm not a morning person. I sicced my cats on the last bird that had the nerve to start tweeting outside my bedroom window at dawn. There was nothing left but feathers. Lord knows what I'd do to Gunther at that hour."

Richmond smiles tentatively and I can tell he is unsure how serious I am. "Okay," he says after a few seconds. "How about tomorrow evening then? I can be flexible."

My kneejerk reaction is to say no, even as the thought of the word *kneejerk* makes my leg muscles flinch. But Richmond really does look good compared to what he was before he got shot and yesterday he showed me up at the gym. I can also see muscle definition in his arms that wasn't there before, and overall he just looks better. Plus I need to do something to get my mind off the gambling.

"Okay. What time?"

"Why don't we shoot for six and see how the day goes? It's hard to know how busy we'll be with this investigation tomorrow, but I suspect it could be a long day."

"Okay. If I don't see you tomorrow, let me know if the time changes and I'll do the same if I can't get away from whatever I'm doing. Speaking of which, where's Hurley?"

"He's over in the administration wing looking through the offices. The board members told the staff they weren't to talk to any of us until the lawyers get here and if they did, they'd risk losing their jobs. For now we're limited to the search detail, evidence collection, and patient interviews. We did rock-paper-scissors to see who would do what."

I ponder this for a moment. "Who won?"

"I did," Richmond says. He pushes a computer tablet type thing toward me. "I wanted to play with the new toy. We just got this fingerprint scanner. It does a full ten card without the messy ink and uploads it to the AFIS database automatically. I figured it was worth the trade-off of having to talk to all these old folks. Though I didn't count on the fact that I'd have to repeat everything for half the people I talked to because they're so hard of hearing, or because they can't remember the question two seconds after I ask it. Lesson learned."

"Have any of the patients refused to be interviewed or printed?"

"Not yet. Some of them have acted a little outraged, but I think it's an act. To be honest, I think they're enjoying it. It's a little excitement in their otherwise dull worlds."

"How many have you done?"

Richmond flips through his notebook and takes out a piece of paper with a list of names on it, some of which are crossed off, and some of which have a blue star next to them. He counts the ones that are crossed off. "Twenty-two so far."

"Why do some of the names have stars next to them?"

"They're patients who are more or less bedbound, so they're basically eliminated from suspicion. That's a third of the patients, so when you take that into account, I'm more than halfway done."

"Anyone stand out?"

"Yes and no. Everyone I've talked to so far has heard the rumor about Chase bumping off his more costly patients and they haven't hesitated to say so. That's one thing I've found rather refreshing so far. These folks aren't afraid to be honest and tell it like it is, though no one has confessed to killing the guy yet." Richmond pauses and juts his chin toward the exit to the outside garden area. "There is a group of folks who seem to be avoiding me, however. They've been hanging outside in that garden area the entire time. At first, I thought they were out there because they're smokers, but they haven't come inside at all, which surprises me. Granted it was a sunny, warm day, but now the sun has set and it's chilly out there."

I remember the smoking group I encountered earlier when Irene first brought me here and suspect I know why they are avoiding the cops. "Let me talk to them."

Richmond glances at his watch. "Have at it. Let me know if you catch the killer." With that, he calls the next name on his list and a yellow-haired old lady with a walker gets up from the table across the room and starts toward us.

I get up from my chair and head outside. Over by a raised planter area sprouting daffodils and crocuses is the small group of folks Richmond was referring to: three men and two women. They are huddled together, whether out of secrecy, cold, or both I can't tell, and talking in low voices.

I know all five of them through different means. The one I know the best is Betty Young, a retired hairdresser who used to own a local salon. Betty hasn't lost her desire to always be seen with perfect hair, nails, and makeup, but she has lost her eyesight to a large degree. Either that or she thinks a beehive hairdo shellacked into chaotic submission that a tornado couldn't move is the fashion bomb. As I close in on the group, I see that Betty's makeup is also looking a bit dicey. Aside from the wrinkles filled with face powder, and a mix of teal green and sky blue eye shadow that's straight out of the seventies, her ruby red lipstick is applied far beyond the edges of her mouth and her eyeliner is crooked and smeared. The end result is rather garish and sad. I wonder if it's because she's been wearing it all day, or if it looked like that when she first put it on.

I say hi to Betty and then acknowledge the others in the group. There's Tom Watson, a retired CPA and part-time inventor who never invented anything anyone wanted to buy or use, though he did manage to lose his wife to the patent attorney who also took most of Tom's money. I also recognize Barry "Bubba" Hildreth, who used to run the Streets Department in town until someone discovered he was hiding the fact that he was legally blind. Unfortunately, that discovery came after Bubba buried three citizens in a snowbank and took out the corner section of a downtown pharmacy while driving the city snowplow. Judging from the white cane he is now carrying and the fact that he is living at Twilight Home, I gather he has finally accepted his handicap.

The third gentleman in the group is Randolph Pettigrew, who at one time was a highly successful insurance salesman and the main reason behind most of the divorces in Sorenson. Not only was he a very handsome man, something that is still evident even at his current advanced age, but he apparently felt the need to live up to his nickname, Randy. Personally, I'm amazed that he's managed to make it to eighty-whatever because rumor has it he was shot once, stabbed twice, and beaten at least a half dozen times by jealous, cuckolded husbands. Several times, he required blood transfusions and as a result developed chronic hepatitis. That's how I got to know him. His health problems led to several trips to the ER back when I worked there.

The other woman in the group is Aileen Cavanaugh, who used to own and run the local florist shop. It's now run by her son and daughter-in-law who do an adequate job but lack Aileen's talent. Aileen has a natural ability to pull together unusual combinations of flowers, greenery, and colors, resulting in some stunningly beautiful arrangements that built her a reputation. It will be interesting to see if the store survives now that she is no longer associated with it. Her talent built and maintained the business for more than three decades. I figure they'll be safe if no one else comes to town and opens shop, but if any competition arises, it's anyone's guess what will happen.

I don't know if there are any romantic liaisons going on in this group but I figure Randolph is safe. Betty and Aileen are widows so there are no husbands to worry about. Tom is about half Randolph's size and arthritic enough that Randolph could easily outrun him, even though Randolph's fastest pace these days is a slow shuffle. And Bubba can't see well enough to shoot, stab, or beat Randolph even if he wanted to.

"What a terrible thing," Betty says to me. "Do the cops know who did it?"

"Did what?"

The group all look at one another, except for Bubba who simply chuckles.

"Someone killed Bernard Chase," Randolph says. "We all know what happened. What we don't know is who did it."

"How about *why* someone did it?" I ask. "Do any of you know the answer to that?"

Once again they exchange looks, except for Bubba. After several long seconds, Bubba says, "Bernard wasn't a nice man. He was killing off patients who cost him too much."

Richmond was right. No one is holding back. "Why do you think that?"

Bubba shrugs. "It happened too regularly and too consistently to be a coincidence. One day you're bed-bound and a week later you're dead. No one questions nursing home deaths. We're old, we're feeble, and no one cares. Good riddance."

"That's a bit harsh," I say.

"Well, it's true," Randolph says. "We're the last pariahs in modern society. If we start costing too much, people think we should just be put down like a dog."

Though no one in the group is smoking at the moment, there's a lingering scent of spicy smoke in the air and I wave my hand in front of my face and lower my voice. "What are you guys smoking?"

Bubba coughs, Betty and Randolph exchange

wary looks, Tom starts chewing on a fingernail, and Aileen chuckles.

Randolph says, "What? You think we made up the thing about Chase killing off patients? Do you think the idea is nothing more than a figment of our drug-addled imaginations?"

"You're not going to turn us in, are you?" Tom asks.

"I don't care what you do unless it relates to Bernard's murder. And no, I don't think the idea about Chase killing off patients is some drug-induced paranoia, though I'm not sure I believe it's true, either. As to what you're smoking, I'm just curious."

Randolph extends an arm toward me and says, "Mattie, would you walk with me for a minute. I need to ask you something."

Though I'm certain I'm being handled, I decide to *go with the flow* as Emily said, and see where it leads me. I take Randolph's arm and let him steer me down a small walkway to a bench on the far side of the garden. The bench, which is metal, feels icy cold against my legs when I sit, despite my pants.

"Here's the deal, Mattie," Randolph says. "As you might imagine, life in this place can be pretty boring. All of us here are in the twilight of our lives, which makes the name of the place quite fitting, don't you think?" I start to answer, but he doesn't pause long enough for me to get a word out. "Our time is limited and our years are numbered. We are stricken with infirmities and indignities that remind us of that ever-ticking clock. When you get right down to it, there isn't a lot left for us to look forward to. So sometimes we create our own fun."

"By smoking pot?"

Randolph chuckles. "There isn't any pot here. That stuff they're smoking is a mix of herbal tea and oregano with a hint of dried mint. I grow the oregano and mint right here in my room."

"Seriously?"

"I swear. I mix it myself. Then I sell it to them at a price so reasonable they feel like they're getting a steal of a deal. Betty's grandson buys the real stuff and he's told her what it costs, so they know."

"You're selling it to them?" I ask, wondering who I'm more in shock over, Randolph for duping the others, or the others for being so gullible.

"I'm not breaking any laws, and neither are they. Nothing in that stuff is illegal."

"They have no idea?"

Randolph smirks. "I don't think so. They think it's the real stuff."

"So why do it?"

"Because it gives them an edge. It makes them feel like they're doing something a little naughty. It's an illusion that makes them feel alive. Where's the harm in that?"

I think about it for a few seconds and then shrug. "Is it safe to smoke that stuff?"

"It hasn't hurt anyone yet. Besides, most of them don't even inhale. I think Aileen suspects it isn't real, but she's having so much fun playing into it that she won't say anything. No one wants to burst the bubble. Life here is boring and stagnant. Anything that counters that is something they will embrace. To be honest, I think Bernard's murder is going to be the most exciting thing that's ever happened for most of the folks here. That's why everyone is so eager to talk to the cops while the employees and board members are all busy covering their asses. The patients want to be involved. They want to help you solve the case if they can, and do their own investigations. Some of them have already started asking questions and grilling one another. They all look more alive right now than they have in months, maybe years."

Death does have a way of making one feel alive. "One of them might have killed Chase," I remind him.

His ethereal smile disappears and after a moment he nods slowly. "I doubt it, but I suppose it's possible."

"If you were to pick someone here, a resident, who you think is capable of something like that, who would it be?"

Randolph ponders this a moment, his eyes narrowed in thought. Finally he says, "I don't know how Bernard died, but I would say Frank Dudley. Or Ruth Waldheim."

I commit the two names to memory. "Why them?"

Randolph flashes a brief, sly smile that suggests he knows something juicy. "Frank hates this place. His family dumped him here after he got the sugar diabetes and ended up having his left leg amputated below the knee. He was a farmer and the leg thing made it impossible for him to run the place anymore. No one in his family was interested in running the farm. All they wanted was the money it might bring in if they could sell it. So they tricked Frank into coming here to live by saying they'd run the farm. Then they sold the place and took off with the money. Frank is pretty bitter about it and blames Bernard for helping his family with what he calls 'duping me into becoming a prisoner here.' "

"Would Frank have the strength to overpower someone else?"

"Oh, yeah," Randolph says with a roll of his eyes. "The guy is built like a Mack truck. And I've seen him swing that prosthetic leg of his. Let me tell you, one good whack with that thing and you're going down. If Bernard has a dent in his head that looks like a heel or a toe, I'd be looking at Frank as the culprit."

I make a mental note to ask Izzy about any bruises, though I'm certain if he had found anything critical he would have told us. "Why Ruth Waldheim?"

"She's a small woman, but she has three boys who are all well over six feet tall, drunk much of the time, and always looking for a fight."

This is nothing new; most people in town know about the Waldheim family. "But why would Ruth want Bernard dead?"

"Technically, it's not Bernard she wants dead, but Ruth is senile as all get out and doesn't know who or where she is most of the time. She was sexually abused by a cousin when she was a teenager and in her confusion, she relives that on a regular basis. Apparently, Bernard bears a physical resemblance to the cousin so every time Ruth sees him, she starts to cry and accuse him of molesting her. The sons know about the past abuse, but are more testosterone and muscle than brains. They tend to want to lash out and protect their mother, even though the staff here is constantly reminding them that Ruth is confused."

"Interesting." I know the Waldheim boys. They look like backwoods hillbillies with long, scraggly hair and beards that look like they should be trimmed with a weed whacker. I've heard rumors about them in town from time to time, and the owner of the local hardware store swears the boys have the best recipes for squirrel and possum this side of the Rockies. None of them finished high school and I'd wager their combined IQ is probably lower than their mother's body weight.

Dr. Maggie suddenly pops into my head, wagging a finger at my use of the word *wager*. I shake off the image and tune in to what Randolph is saying.

"You should probably focus on the A, B, and C wing patients," Randolph says. I give him a questioning look and he explains further. "This facility is set up as two squares. The first one is where you came in. It houses the administrative offices, a laundry, a hair salon, a gym that serves as the PT and OT area, the dining room, and a few other rooms. The patient rooms make up the second square. The top of that square, which is the hallway you see straight ahead when you turn left at the entrance, is called the A wing. I don't know if it's intentional or not but it's where most of the Alzheimer and other dementia patients are roomed if they are relatively stable physically. The first hall to the right is B wing and the hallway that goes left at the entrance to the dayroom is C wing. B and C wings house the patients who are relatively stable and somewhat independent. It's also home to the temporary rehab patients, the ones who need to come here for a couple months after their hip or knee replacement because they can't manage on their own yet and don't have anyone at home to help them. I'm pretty sure those are . . . *were* Chase's favorite type of patient. I heard him say once that the reimbursement for acute rehab is better. That leaves the D wing. That's where all the severely disabled people live and I don't think it's a coincidence that they are stashed away in the hall farthest from the main door and the public areas."

I nod my understanding.

"I also don't think it's a coincidence that that's

where all the deaths have been lately," he adds in an ominous but hushed tone. "Out of sight, out of mind."

He's starting to sound like Arnie.

"Thanks for your insight," I tell him. "Anything else?"

"Not that I can think of, but if something comes to me I'll let you know." Randolph gets up from the bench and offers me a hand.

I take it, smiling at his womanizing ways. I have to admit, the guy is a charmer.

"You won't squeal to the others, will you?" he asks me.

"You mean about the fake pot?"

He nods. "They're just looking for a few final thrills to enjoy before their life journeys come to an end. Where's the harm?"

"Your secret is safe with me," I assure him.

"Thanks. Shall we?" He makes a sweeping gesture with his hand back toward the rest of his group.

"You go ahead. I want to talk to that guy over there." The guy I'm referring to is Arnie, who I've spied over the fence in the side parking lot standing next to a shiny blue BMW, dusting the driver's side door for prints. He sees me and waves me over.

Randolph returns to his group of clandestine smokers and I head for Arnie. I start to go through the same gate I used earlier, but it is locked on the other side. Fortunately, my baboon arms leave me well equipped for such a problem. I stand on tiptoe and reach way over the fence, and slide the bolt. I go through, lock the gate again, and make my way to Arnie. "How's it going?"

"Tedious, to be honest," he says. "All I've really done so far is lift prints and they're all over the place.

Brenda Joiner and I must have lifted a hundred or more in the men's room and then she went home. Now I'm out here checking Bernard's car. When I'm done, I'm supposed to go into Bernie's office and start dusting in there."

"Have you done any employee interviews?"

Arnie shakes his head. "Hurley spent an hour or so arguing with the board members about whether or not he could talk to the employees, but when he realized no one would speak to him out of fear of losing their jobs until they got the go ahead from administration, he gave in. I guess there's a bunch of lawyers on their way, and until they arrive, none of the employees are to talk to anyone. They tried to convince the patients to wait, too, but most of them are talking."

"So I heard from Richmond. Apparently, they've been quite forthcoming. Do you know where Hurley is now?"

"Last I saw him, he was inside snooping around in the mail room. He said he was going to get started searching the administrative offices, but the only one that is unlocked is Bernie's."

"Let me guess. The board isn't going to open them until the lawyers get here."

"You got it," Arnie says. "It's almost as if they're trying to hide something, isn't it?" There is a light in his eyes I know all too well. He gestures toward the administrative wing exit. "If you want to hook up with Hurley, I stuck a rock in that door over there so it wouldn't close all the way and lock."

"Oh, good."

Arnie beams. "I have my moments."

I leave him to his fingerprint dust and let myself into the administrative wing. The lights in the hallway are on, but the area is quiet and appears empty except for the police tape and barricades at the other end marking off the crime scene. I can see the entrance to the mail room at the far end of the hall and though the door is open, the lights are turned off. All the office doors are closed and the rooms are dark. The eerie quiet along with the darkened rooms spooks me. I stop just inside the exit door and holler, "Hurley?"

I get no response. I walk up to the door of Bernard Chase's office and lean into it to listen, to see if I can hear anyone on the other side. Just as my ear touches the door it's yanked open and someone charges out of the room, knocking me backward.

Chapter 16

I flail my arms and try to catch my balance just as I hit the back door. I jar it hard enough to knock the rock out of place and the door shuts. I lean against it, my arm in front of my face in a defensive gesture against whoever is there. Then I hear Hurley's voice say, "Mattie? What the hell are you doing?"

I lower my arms as I realize the person who mowed me down is Hurley. "I hollered for you and no one answered. I was spooked so I leaned in against the door to listen and you opened it just as I did." I try to look more dignified than I feel. "Why the hell were you in there in the dark? And what's the big hurry?" I add irritably.

Hurley reaches over, grabs my hand, and starts pulling me down the hallway. "I was using a black light to look for body secretions on that couch in there. And the big hurry is Emily. Why the hell is she at your place? And who's snooping around your place scaring the crap out of her?"

"Who? What? Wait!" I can't wrap my mind around all his questions that fast, and his tone of voice is irritating me. "First off, she's at my place because she doesn't have a house key and we couldn't get in to your place."

"Oh, right. Hell, I didn't even think—"

"As for the rest of it, I don't know what you're talking about."

"I didn't hear you yell. Sorry. I was on the phone with Dom. I'll explain as we go." Hurley turns and I stumble along behind him as we make a mad dash out of the administration wing and into the waiting room, then out into the parking lot. "Dom just called me and said that Emily is crying and scared. Some man was looking in the windows of your cottage at her. Apparently, Hoover started to growl and that's how she saw the guy. She called Dom, who called me."

We climb into Hurley's car and he sticks his police light on the roof. We make the trip to my place in just over three minutes and, when we pull up outside my cottage, all the outdoor lights are on, illuminating the backside of Izzy's house, the front and sides of my cottage, and a good portion of the woods surrounding us. All the indoor lights are on in both houses, too. As we get out of the car, the back door to Izzy's house opens.

Dom hollers out to us. "I have her over here."

I head that way, but Hurley hesitates, moving toward my cottage and taking a cursory look around the front porch and door area.

Emily bursts out of Izzy and Dom's house and runs over to Hurley. She flings her arms around him and hugs him tight. Her face is turned my way and I can see it clearly in the bright lights; it's tear-stained and terrified.

"I was so scared," she says, her voice breaking.

Hurley wraps one arm around her and strokes her head with the hand of the other. As I watch, I feel a pang of jealousy, but not the kind I usually feel when it comes to Hurley. This is different. It's that fatherly protector thing that has me jealous. That sort of attention is something I've never had and often yearned for.

Hurley looks over at Dom, who has been joined by Izzy. "What can you tell me?"

Izzy says, "Talk to Dom. I wasn't here when it happened. I just got home from the office."

Dom, whose big eyes, fair skin, and reddish-blond hair can make him look frightened to death on a normal day, has a hand splayed protectively over his heart. He sashays over to Hurley looking like he's just seen a ghost. "There was somebody there all right. Emily called me because Hoover started growling and wouldn't stop. It was making her nervous so I told her I'd come over and check things out. As soon as I flipped the lights on and stepped outside, I saw a man standing by the front window. He heard me and ran off into the woods, over that way." He points in the direction of my old house, the one I used to share with my ex-husband David. It burned nearly to the ground last November and as soon as the weather warms up enough to start construction, David plans to rebuild. Coincidentally, he's being helped in this endeavor by Patty Volker, our insurance agent and his new girlfriend.

"Could it have been David?" I ask Dom.

He shakes his head. "No, he was taller than David, and stocky. And the hair was dark."

Hurley takes Emily by the shoulders and pushes

her back, looking down at her. "Did you see this man's face?"

Emily nods. "Not for long, but when Dom turned the outside lights on it made me look over toward the window and for a second I saw him there. Then he was gone."

"What did he look like?"

"Dark, scruffy, older I think. Like I said, I only saw him for a second."

"You didn't see him until after you called Dom?"

Emily nods.

"What made you call Dom in the first place?"

"Hoover," Emily says, and my dog, who is sitting at her feet, thumps his tail when he hears his name. "I was on the couch watching TV and he was lying at my feet when all of a sudden he started growling. He got up and went into the bedroom so I figured he was just messing with the cats. I tried calling to him, but he stayed in there for several minutes and kept growling. He finally stopped and came out, but then he started walking around the house, whining and sniffing at the air. He went into the kitchen and started growling again, staring at the window. I still thought it might be the cats, but when I got up I saw both of them asleep in the bedroom on top of the bed. When Hoover came into the living room and started growling is when I called Dom."

Hurley leaves Emily to stand alone and walks over to the window, then around to the side and back of the cottage, shining his flashlight along the ground. "There are footprints that track around the house from the back. Whoever was out here was probably at the rear of the house first. That's why Hoover was growling in the bedroom." He looks over at me with a worried expression. "Who would be spying on you? And why?"

"I have no idea," I say, suppressing a chill.

"The obvious culprit would be David," Hurley says, "though he strikes me more as the in-your-face type, not the skulking type."

"What reason would he have to skulk in the first place?" I say.

Hurley takes out his cell phone and says, "I'm going to have some guys come over here and take a look around. Check out the woods and your old place."

As he makes his call, I start searching my mind, trying to think of someone who would want to spy on me. I have been avoiding people for the past couple months, but I can't think of anyone who would come to see me who fits the description.

Hurley ends his call and immediately places another. But this one gets no answer. When he disconnects, he stands there a moment, tapping his chin with the phone. Finally he says, "A couple guys will be out here shortly to see if they can find anything." He looks at Emily. "In the meantime, I suppose I should take you back to my place. Do you have stuff you need to get?"

She nods and heads inside my cottage to get her purse and jacket. To my amusement, Hoover goes with her.

With a nod, Hurley steers me over to where Izzy and Dom are standing and addresses us in a low voice. "I just tried to call Kate and she isn't answering. I have to consider that whoever was out here may have been spying on Emily rather than Mattie." He fills Izzy and Dom in on Kate and her brother and the situation there. "If these guys who are after Kate's brother somehow managed to track Kate to Sorenson in hopes of finding Brent, they could be watching Emily to see if he shows up."

"Then you can't take her to your place and leave her there alone," I say. "Not after this."

Hurley emits a sigh of exasperation and runs a hand through his hair. "I suppose not. But I can't stay with her, either. I need to keep working on this case."

"Why don't we just bring her along for tonight?" I suggest. "She wanted to come with me to the nursing home, anyway. She'll be fine in the dayroom with Richmond and the patients."

Hurley frowns at the suggestion, but before he can say anything, Emily rejoins our group, Hoover at her feet. She looks at the group of us and smiles. "What?"

"Are you comfortable with me leaving you alone at my place for a few hours tonight?" Hurley asks.

Emily squares her shoulders and after the briefest hesitation says, "Sure." But there is no conviction behind the word.

I give Hurley a look and he says, "Okay, you can come with Mattie and me for tonight, but just this once, okay?"

Emily smiles, looking immensely relieved. "Understood."

Two on-duty cops arrive to scour the area around my cottage and Hurley has us wait so he can check things out with them. Emily settles herself inside Hurley's car, and Hoover jumps in beside her. I shake my head and smile, and when Emily shoots me a pleading look, I say, "Fine. You can be the therapy dog trainer at the nursing home."

I leave the two of them and go inside my cottage

to make sure all the windows are latched. I also look at my diary, which appears undisturbed on the table where I left it, and tuck it away inside a drawer. The cats, who apparently could care less that someone was lurking about outside, are still asleep on my bed. I top off the food and water bowls, still pondering the night's events.

Why would a man be spying through my windows? I think about the casino and all the money I've lost there, recently. But since I don't owe anyone any money and the casino has made plenty from me, I can't imagine a reason they would want to spy on me. There were a few men at the casino who I'd flirted with casually from time to time. Had I perhaps attracted a stalker? I thought back to the men I'd befriended while playing the tables, but no one I could recall fit the descriptions Dom and Emily had provided.

I realize Hurley's theory might be right. Maybe it's Emily who is being watched. Had we been followed earlier tonight when I was driving her around? If so, why would they follow her rather than Kate? Then it hit me. Maybe they had followed Kate. Hurley said she hadn't answered her phone when he tried to call her earlier. Had something happened to her?

I'm feeling spooked and full of questions, so when Hurley comes in a few minutes later, I'm eager to hear what he and the cops outside might have determined. "Find anything significant?"

He shakes his head and sighs.

"How did this person come and go? He must have had a car somewhere. Were there any signs of one over at my old place?"

"Hard to tell," Hurley says. "The driveway is concrete and the roads are dry so there aren't any tire tracks to see. There isn't anywhere for a car to park along the road near here because it's too narrow. If someone had tried, I think we would have been called on it. I remember when someone broke down not far from here. We were flooded with complaint calls within minutes of the car being left at the side of the road.

"We didn't see any footprints in the woods, but the ground is pretty hard and covered with leaves. In fact, if it wasn't for those plant beds around your cottage, we wouldn't have any prints at all."

"Are the prints you do have of any help?"

Hurley shrugs. "Maybe. It's a large size and I think one or two of the prints have enough detail for us to identify the specific type of shoe. But unless we find a shoe to match it, that's about all we'll be able to know. I'm going to try to get a sketch artist to come in tonight to see if Dom can work on what he saw, although I don't know if I'll be able to find one this late."

"You might not need to." I tell him about Emily's drawing from earlier. "Let Emily be her own sketch artist."

"Can't hurt I suppose," he says, looking thoughtful. "It will give her something to do while we're at the nursing home."

"Have you tried to reach Kate again?"

Hurley nods and scowls. "I did. Still no answer. That worries me."

It worries me too, but I don't say so. A few minutes later, after locking the cottage up tight and some last-minute instructions Hurley gives to the officers on site, he, Emily, and I all head back to the nursing home.

It's close to nine o'clock by the time we get there

and we're all tired. The person seated at the sign-in desk is a nursing assistant by the name of Anne, who asks us to sign in.

Hurley grumbles, "We already did," and walks on past her toward the dayroom.

The assistant casts a wary eye at Hoover and looks like she wants to insist, but in the end her timidity wins out and she says nothing.

Hurley sets Emily up in the dayroom with some pencils and paper and gives her instructions on what to do. She appears eager to get to it, but several of the patients, intrigued by the young newcomer and happy to see Hoover again, start chatting with her.

Richmond is still here, and after we fill him in on Emily's presence and why she's here, he informs us that the lawyers still haven't arrived. He also tells us that the patient room searches are ongoing and haven't turned up anything of interest except some cigarette papers and some stuff the cops thought might be pot.

"It's not pot," I tell them. "It's a mix of oregano, mint, and tea."

The two men look at me with puzzled expressions.

"And you know this how?" Hurley asks.

"I had a little chat with the guy who's making it." I fill them in on my discussion with Randolph, including his theories about Frank Dudley and Ruth Waldheim's boys.

"Have you talked to this Dudley guy yet?" Hurley asks Richmond, who consults his list and then shakes his head. "All right, Mattie and I will do that next. What room is he in?"

Richmond finds the room number and tells us it's in the C wing. Hurley takes the fingerprint scanner, and he and I head for room number forty-four. We run into Larry Johnson and his helpers still conduct-ing room searches in room forty-three—one room away from Frank Dudley's and only five rooms away from being finished, with the exception of the D wing, which is where all the bedbound patients are housed. Hurley has Larry come with us to Mr. Dud-ley's room to conduct a search while we talk to the man.

We find Frank Dudley reclining in his bed watch-ing TV. His status as an amputee is glaringly obvious given that his right leg ends just above the knee, and an artificial leg, complete with sock and shoe, is propped up against the closet door on one side of his bed. He has the look of a lifelong farmer, with skin that appears to have a permanent tan, precancerous spots on his face and arms, and large calloused hands that look like they've hauled a lot of hay bales in their time.

"Mr. Dudley, my name is Steve Hurley and this is Larry Johnson. We are detectives with the Sorenson Police Department. This is Mattie Winston from the medical examiner's office. She's here to assist me. We're looking into the death of Bernard Chase and would like to ask you a few questions. We'd also like to take a look around your room."

"Why do you want to do that?" Dudley asks. "Do you think I killed the son of a bitch?"

"Did you?" Hurley asks.

"I would've been happy to, but I didn't. If I'm not mistaken, you can't search my room unless I give you permission, or you have a search warrant."

"As it turns out, we do have a search warrant," Hurley says. "Detective Johnson here will be happy to show it to you."

Larry takes a piece of paper out of his shirt pocket, unfolds it, and shows it to Frank Dudley.

Dudley looks at it for about two seconds and then shrugs. "Do whatever you have to," he says with irritable resignation.

Larry refolds the search warrant paper and tucks it back inside his pocket. Then he moves the artificial leg to one side, opens the closet door, and starts digging around inside.

"I didn't kill the guy," Dudley says, "but I can't say I'm sorry he's dead."

"Why is that?" Hurley asks.

"Because it's that bastard's fault that I'm even in this place," Dudley grumbles. "He and them damn kids of mine are all in cahoots together. They lied to me. When I lost my leg, the kids told me they would take over running the farm, and that taking care of me on top of that was going to be too much for them. So I let them talk me into coming here to stay for part of the year, so that they could have their time freed up to do the planting and harvesting. They were supposed to check me out of here in the wintertime and let me go back home. But that bastard Chase talked them into making this permanent. He convinced the kids that they deserve better than to be stuck on some old farm trying to eke out a living. Since I'd given the kids power of attorney so they could handle the farm business, they were able to sell the farm right out from under me. My kids took half the money and ran off with it, and that greedy bastard Chase got the rest." Dudley pauses and shakes his head wearily. "I'm glad Dora is dead. It would probably kill her if she knew what her kids had done."

"Have you ever been in Mr. Chase's office?" Hurley asks.

"Can't say that I have been," Dudley says.

"Then you won't object to us fingerprinting you to make sure your prints aren't found anywhere in that office."

"Actually, I do object. I have diabetes and those damned nursing assistants are in here poking my fingers all the time. The last thing I need is a bunch of dirty ink on my fingers that might give me an infection. Those of us with diabetes get infections really easy and we can't fight them off very well, you know."

Hurley looks at Dudley with a smug smile. "That won't be a problem. We have a new toy we're using now." He holds up the fingerprint scanner tablet. "No more ink. All you have to do is set your fingers on the screen here. Very clean and very painless."

Dudley frowns, but makes no further objections. As Hurley goes about getting Dudley's fingerprints scanned in, Larry Johnson starts going through Dudley's bedside table. In the bottom area he finds a plastic washbasin filled with rolled up socks. He pulls it out and sticks his hand into the pile of socks to root around, and then stops suddenly.

"Whoa. What's this?" He pulls out one of the sock rolls and squeezes it. Then he unrolls the socks and removes a small syringe with a capped needle attached to it. He starts to hand it to me, but I stop him.

"I'm not wearing gloves. Stick it in an evidence bag."

Larry doesn't have an evidence bag with him, so he leaves the room to go next door where his helpers do have some. He returns a minute later with the syringe safely bagged. He sets the bag down on top of the bedside stand and proceeds to label it. When he's done, he hands me the bag with the syringe inside.

"This is an insulin syringe," I say. "Don't the nurses administer all of your insulin, Mr. Dudley?"

Frank Dudley folds his arms over his chest and sets his jaw. He looks away toward the wall and I can tell he's not going to answer me.

I tap the side of the basin with the socks in it. "Check all of these," I tell Larry. "See if there's anything else in there."

He does so and it isn't long before he finds two more syringes and a vial of insulin. These are bagged and tagged like the first syringe.

"What are you doing with these in here?" I ask Dudley.

"I told you, I'm diabetic. Diabetics take insulin."

"The nurses are supposed to be in charge of administering your insulin."

"Yeah, somebody in this damned place is in charge of everything about me," Frank snaps. "I managed my own blood sugars for fifteen years at home and did a better job of it than they're doing here."

I look over at Hurley and give him a little head nod toward the hallway. The two of us leave the room and meet just outside the door. "An injection of insulin in someone who isn't a diabetic, or even too much insulin in someone who is, can cause what we call insulin shock. The symptoms of insulin shock are disorientation, hypotension, diaphoresis, and eventually death."

"Lay terms, Winston. I know what hypertension is but I don't know what di . . . dia . . ."

"Diaphoresis," I say. "It means a cold sweat. Insulin shock doesn't cause hypertension, or high blood pressure, it causes hy*po*tension, or low blood pressure. Based on what Bjorn told us about Bernie's behavior in the bathroom, it fits."

"Are you suggesting that Frank Dudley injected Bernard Chase with a dose of insulin?"

I think about this for a moment, with all the logistics that would be involved, and realize it would be very difficult. "It's possible, but I have to admit it wouldn't be easy. Even though the needles on those insulin syringes are very small, it would still be difficult to stick one in someone and have them not feel it. You would have to create some sort of a distraction, or some other reason for the pain."

"The guy does have motive," Hurley says. "Can Izzy tell if someone received an overdose of insulin?"

"I don't know, but I can find out." I take out my cell phone and call Izzy's number. I can tell when he answers that he was asleep. "Hey, Izzy, it's Mattie. Sorry to wake you. We've come across a situation here in our investigation and I need to ask you a question."

"Not a problem," Izzy says. "I hadn't gone to bed yet. I just dozed off on the couch watching TV. What's your question?"

"Could an injection of insulin have caused the symptoms that Bjorn reported in Bernie?"

"Hmm, interesting idea. And yes, it certainly could."

"Then my next question is can you test for it?"

"I can, but it's not a simple test and it's not one that we can do here. I'll have to send it off to Madison. The problem is, insulin is rapidly metabolized, so a postmortem level may not be helpful. Diabetics typically have anti-insulin antibodies, which is why they end up with the disease. Since Bernie wasn't a diabetic, if his serum and free insulin levels are elevated and there are no anti-insulin antibodies present it would certainly indicate that he received a dose of exogenous insulin. But even if I put a rush on the test, we probably won't have an answer for a couple days."

"What about a basic blood glucose level? Can we do that here to give us some idea of whether or not this theory is even viable?"

"We can, but we have to be careful where the blood came from. It's a known fact that people who go through what we refer to as death throes will have high glucose levels in blood taken from the right side of their heart due to glycogen breakdown in the liver. Of course, the other thing I can do is take another look for an injection site. If the needle used was the type that comes on an insulin syringe, it will be extremely small so I might've missed it when I looked earlier today."

"Which reminds me, I meant to ask you whether or not you found any bruises on Bernie's body."

"As a matter of fact, I did. It was on the back of his right arm and I assume it came from him hitting the edge of the sink when he collapsed in the bathroom. Of course, that would be a perfect injection site as well. I'll take another look first thing in the morning."

"Thanks, Izzy. I'll let Hurley know."

"You know, it may prove to be serendipitous that Bjorn was in the bathroom when he was today."

"Why is that?"

"Because if he hadn't been there, Bernie's body could have lain there all weekend before anyone found it. If that had happened, any traces of insulin would have probably disappeared."

"Interesting," I say. Hurley is giving me impatient

looks, eager to know what Izzy has told me. "Let me go so I can fill Hurley in on what you just told me. I'll let you know if anything else comes up. Otherwise, we'll check with you in the morning to see if you found anything that looks like an injection site."

"I'm curious. Is your suspect a patient or a staff member?"

"It's a patient. I'll fill you in on the details in the morning." I disconnect the call and then tell Hurley what Izzy has just told me.

"Damn," he says. "I hate waiting, but I don't suppose we have any choice. Since the insulin theory fits what we know about Bernie's death, we will definitely have to keep Frank Dudley on our list of suspects. It will be interesting to see if we can find his fingerprints anywhere in Chase's office. In the meantime, we need to continue with the investigation as planned."

"So what do we do next?"

"Since none of the employees are talking, we might as well finish up over in Bernie's office." Hurley takes a moment to give Larry a quick update, and tells him to let us know if they find anything else in the rest of their room searches.

On our way to the administrative wing, we check on Emily, who is seated at a table in the dayroom. Hoover is curled up under the table at her feet, sound asleep. Seated with her are half a dozen residents, all of whom appear to be very interested in her drawing. There is the vague shape of a face on the paper, but Emily has yet to give it any detail. Hurley tells her where we will be, listens as the residents at the table assure him that she is in good hands, and then he returns the fingerprint scanner to Richmond with instructions to upload Frank Dudley's prints ASAP.

With that done, he and I head for the administrative wing via the outdoor route. The exit door is locked, but Hurley raps on the door three times and a moment later a uniformed police officer opens it.

"Have any of the staff or board members tried to come back here?" Hurley asks the officer.

"No, the only person who was back here is that guy from the medical examiner's office." It's the new officer on the force, the one I don't know. According to his tag, his name is P. Foster.

I wonder what the P stands for and then ask, "You mean Arnie?"

"Yeah, that was it. He spent some time inside the victim's office dusting for fingerprints. He left about half an hour ago and said he'd be back in the morning to finish up."

Someone has left two boxes of gloves on the floor outside Bernie's office and Hurley is donning a pair when Officer Foster says, "Pardon me for saying so, Detective, but you threw me a bit of a curveball earlier. Was that some kind of test or initiation rite?"

Hurley gives him a puzzled look. "What are you talking about?"

"Earlier when I told you I was going to call for another on-duty officer to roll by because I needed to take a bathroom break, you were here in this office. You told me to go ahead and that you would keep an eye on things until I came back. But when I came out of the bathroom the person at the desk said she just saw you and the lady here go running out the front door of the place. I figured you must have had someone else come by to stand watch, but when I came back there was no one here."

"Damn!" Hurley says with a grimace. He gives himself a literal and a figurative slap on the head. "That was when I got that panicked phone call from Dom about Emily. I completely forgot that I was supposed to be covering for you. I'm sorry."

"No harm done," Foster says. "It was totally deserted when I came back. That Arnie guy showed up a minute later. He was ticked because someone took out the rock he had used to prop open the end door."

"That was me," I say, knowing I'll owe Arnie an apology tomorrow.

I put on a pair of gloves, flip on the light switch in Bernie's office, and step inside. Evidence of Arnie's presence is everywhere in the form of fingerprint dust on nearly every surface. The desk and the chair behind it are covered, as are all the items on top of the desk, including the coffee mug and the tax papers. I'm guessing Bernie's CPA won't be pleased.

Hurley walks over to a filing cabinet behind the meeting table. It has four drawers and Hurley opens the top one. "Might as well see what's in here although I don't expect to find any smoking guns."

I see Arnie has left his processing kit along with several empty boxes, packs of various-sized evidence bags, two large rolls of evidence tape, and several empty collection jars over by the couch. I turn to Hurley. "You said you were using an ultraviolet light on the couch earlier. Did anything light up?"

"Hell, yeah, the whole thing did. I wouldn't sit on it if I were you. It looked like a hotel bedspread."

"So Bernie was enjoying some hanky-panky in here?"

"So it would seem. The question is, was he alone or with someone?"

"Did you take any samples?"

"Didn't have time. You can do that if you want."

I don't particularly, and I don't know if Arnie already did, so I focus on collecting other items, instead. "We should probably bag up his entire coffee station since we're considering poisons," I say to Hurley.

"Yep," he says distractedly, flipping through hanging folders in the file cabinet drawer.

I bag and tag the coffee pot after pouring the coffee left in it into an evidence jar, and then I bag and tag the coffee maker, a box of sugar, a box of loose artificial sweetener, four clean spoons and one used one, a coffee grinder, a partial bag of coffee beans, and three coffee cups that appear to be clean. I stack everything in one of the empty boxes and go to work on the small refrigerator, where I find and bag a carton of half-and-half. When I'm done I have three boxes of evidence to take to the office.

I look over and see that Hurley is on drawer two of the filing cabinet, patiently looking through every page of every file. I look over at Bernie's desk and see his coffee cup sitting there. Knowing I need to bag it and collect its contents as well, I get the items I need to do so and head that way. But when I get to the desk, what I find there throws me. After staring at the coffee cup for several seconds, trying to decide if I'm losing my mind, I take out my cell phone and punch in Arnie's number.

He answers on the second ring and since I can tell he has food in his mouth, I at least know I didn't wake him.

"Hey, Arnie, it's Mattie. I'm in Bernie Chase's office with Hurley and I figured I'd pick up where you left off. I see you managed to lift prints everywhere. What else did you do?"

"Nothing else. There are more surfaces to dust if you feel so inclined."

"You didn't swab anything? Or collect any other evidence?"

"Nope."

"What about the coffee in the mug on the desk?"

"There was no coffee in the mug. It was empty."

"No it wasn't."

"It was when I was there."

"Hmm, maybe I'm mistaken," I say, though I'm pretty sure I'm not. After thanking him for his help, apologizing for the rock thing, and telling him we'll see him in the morning, I disconnect the call. I take out the camera I have in my pocket and scroll through the pictures I took earlier.

"Hey, Hurley, I think we have a problem," I say when I get to the picture of the coffee mug.

"What?"

"There was coffee in this mug when we were in here earlier, but now it's empty and it looks like it's been cleaned."

Chapter 17

Hurley appears extremely upset by my news. His lips are tight, his face is red, and the muscles in his jaw are jumping around like water dropped on a hot frying pan. "You're sure?"

I nod and show him the picture I took earlier. "I'll bag the mug anyway, but I suspect it won't be of much use." I do so while Hurley paces back and forth in front of the desk. I'm thinking things couldn't get much worse with this case when we hear a commotion out in the hall and Foster's frantic voice saying, "You can't go in there!"

A second later, a parade of people enter Bernard Chase's office. There are five people in all. Dorothy is in the lead, with three men and one woman behind her. The newcomers are dressed in suits, which gives me a pretty good idea who they are. Dorothy steps aside and lets the new woman take charge.

She does so by asking, "Who's in charge of this investigation?"

"I am. I'm Detective Steve Hurley with the Sorenson Police Department. Who are you?"

"Legal counsel for the Twilight Home," the woman says in a no-nonsense tone. She hands Hurley a business card that has LLOYD COLLINS & HUMMER LLP written on it, along with a Milwaukee address and phone number. I'm praying that the woman's last name is Hummer so I can at least make some crude jokes about her later, and then I wonder what Dr. Maggie would make of that thought. The woman is like a brain tumor, always in my head and causing me a lot of pain.

"I'm Trisha Collins," the woman says, dashing my hopes for her last name. "And these are my associates, John Hudson, Michael Finnegan, and Oscar Walden. I would ask that you immediately halt whatever you are doing until we've had a chance to examine your warrants and consult with the administrative group."

"Too late for that," Hurley says. "Our search is nearly finished. We've talked with the majority of the patients already, and I can assure you our paperwork is all in order. You're welcome to examine it all you want, but I'm not stopping anything we are doing to wait for you to do so. If you know anything about conducting a criminal investigation, you know the first hours are golden. You have already hampered our efforts and delayed things by threatening the employees with their jobs if they were to talk to us."

"We have done no such thing," Trisha says. "We just arrived here."

"Yes, of course. Plausible deniability," Hurley sneers. "You lawyers are pretty savvy when it comes to covering your own asses, but we know you told the board members to let the employees know what would hap-

pen if any of them spoke to us before you got here. I
don't much care how you made it happen, I just
know you did and you're interfering with my investigation of a murder. I don't much appreciate it."

I'm a little shocked by how in-your-face Hurley is
behaving. Judging from the tight lips and white
knuckles on the hand holding her briefcase, I'm
guessing Trisha Collins is surprised, too, despite the
stern bun in her blond hair and the stern tone in her
voice. I'm sure she isn't used to having people talk to
her this way. I suspect the reason Hurley is being so
confrontational is because he's tired, he's hungry,
and he's mad at himself for leaving our crime scene
unguarded, an action that has compromised some of
our evidence.

Trisha says, "I assure you we are quite familiar with
the investigative process, Detective. I apologize for
any inconvenience we may have caused you, but I'm
sure you understand that our primary concern here
is to make sure the facility continues to function and
to mitigate any liabilities that might be incurred by
the board of directors, the staff, or the residents. I assure you we have the best interests of the staff members and the residents in mind. I'm sorry that your
investigation was delayed, but it was unavoidable. We
are here now and you are welcome to talk to any of
the board members or employees who are willing to
talk to you. My only stipulation is that one of us must
be present at all times."

Hurley sighs and his shoulders sag. Whatever had
him ramped up is starting to fade away. "Fair
enough." He glances at his watch. "It's getting late
and I think the majority of what we have left to do
can wait until morning. However, I would like to interview the evening staff on duty now while we're

here, and I would also like to search the employee lockers. I'll talk to the day shift and your board members tomorrow morning. In the meantime, you and your people need to leave this wing. It's a crime scene and it's off-limits. I would appreciate it if you would leave and not touch anything on your way out."

"I'm sure your paperwork is in order, but I still need to look at it," Trisha says. "As for searching the employee lockers, I will leave that up to the individual employees."

Hurley cocks his head and gives her a weary look. "My warrant covers all the public areas in the building as well as any of the administrative offices, employee areas, and individual patient rooms. The only restrictions imposed on us are the patients' medical records, but if we have evidence that points to a suspect who is a resident here, and we believe the medical record might contain information that can assist us in our investigation, we can get a subpoena for that particular medical record."

Trisha makes a pointed look at the file cabinet and the open top drawer. "I doubt your warrant includes the confidential papers related to the facility."

Hurley hesitates with his comeback just long enough for me to know she's right. But when he finally answers, it seems like a good one. "We have reason to believe there might be some irregularities in the admissions and discharges of some residents here, so I'm looking for files that will help us determine that."

"What sort of irregularities?" Trisha asks.

"Cherry picking the admissions to create a favorable payor mix, for one. And there is reason to think someone might have been expediting the deaths of certain patients whose care became something of a financial burden."

Trisha arches her eyebrows at this. "That's a very serious accusation, Detective."

"It's not an accusation yet. It's only supposition at this point."

"Then I fail to see what relevance it has to your murder investigation."

"The relevance is that most of the patients in this place seem convinced that such shenanigans have been going on. And as such, they all have motive."

"Shenanigans?" Trisha says with a little laugh. "What a quaint word." She glances back at her trio of henchmen. "I do love these small-town folk, don't you?" She turns back to Hurley with a tolerant smile like one might use on an idiot cousin who's just said he thinks the earth is flat. "I believe any recent deaths that have occurred here are a matter of public record and as such you have no need to go through the facility's private files to find that information. Beyond that, if there is any specific information you want regarding the admission policies and procedures, or how those policies were applied to specific patients, you need only ask me for the information and I will provide it. Beyond that, you have no business going through our records."

Hurley's face muscles are twitching like the legs on my pithed frog in high school biology class. He's pissed, and at the moment he is also apparently at a loss for words. I'm guessing that's because the only ones he has in mind are not fit for polite company. Not that Trisha Collins would be considered polite in anyone's book. Miss Manners she ain't.

Trisha takes advantage of Hurley's stormy silence and says, "I believe you mentioned that you've already conducted the majority of the patient room searches and spoken with a number of the residents here. Have you come up with any suspects?"

"As a matter of fact we have several suspects," Hurley says, his jaw tight. "But at this point all we have on any of them is supposition, motive, and circumstantial evidence. I'm waiting on the results of certain tests from Mr. Chase's autopsy, and in the meantime our investigation is ongoing. It's quite possible that our suspect list will grow once we've had an opportunity to talk to your employees. In fact, I'm fairly certain it will."

I know this last comment is referring to the missing coffee. The likelihood that it was a patient who was able to sneak back here during the brief time that the administrative wing was unguarded is slight. But the fact that we have several suspects is news to me. Outside of the fact that the majority of the residents disliked Chase and believed he might have been bumping off troublesome patients, the only real suspect we've turned up so far is Frank Dudley.

"May I ask how Mr. Chase was killed?" Trisha says.

"You can ask anything you want but I'm not obligated to divulge the facts of my investigation to you," Hurley says, finally scoring a hit.

A long, awkward silence follows during which Trisha and Hurley stare one another down. The other three lawyers watch, intrigued, shifting in place nervously, waiting to see who's going to win this war of wills.

As entertaining as this battle of wits has been, I'm tired and my stomach is starting to feel a little queasy again. In the interest of moving things along, I decide to break things up. "Tick tock," I say, rubbing my hands together eagerly. "Which employee should we talk to first?"

Trisha breaks eye contact with Hurley, triggering a collective sigh in the room. That's quickly followed by a series of sharp inhalations as Trisha shifts her flinty glare to me. "And who, might I ask, are you?" she says in a snippy, condescending tone.

Despite the fact that she's only about five feet two inches tall and probably weighs as much as my right leg, I can tell Trisha Collins is the type of woman who likes to throw her weight around. But when it comes to throwing weight around, I clearly have her outmatched. I decide to accept the challenge and step up right in front of her, forcing her to look up to me. My boobs are practically in her face.

"My name is Mattie Winston, and I'm the medicolegal death investigator with the medical examiner's office." I unclip my newly reacquired badge from the waist of my pants and flash it in her face. "Sorry, I don't have any business cards with me. Now, if you don't mind, it's been a really long day for all of us and we'd like to get on with things."

Trisha doesn't say anything as I look down my nose at her.

After several seconds, I realize that even though I may have rendered her temporarily speechless, she is not going to back down in front of her coworkers. In the interest of moving things along I turn away from her and say, "Hurley, what employee would you like to talk to first?"

Hurley takes out the little notebook he always carries with him and flips it open. "Let's start with the evening charge nurse and work our way down the pecking order. I believe that would be Regan Simmons. Do you think you can track her down and bring her to the dining room, Mattie?"

"I sure can."

"Good." He turns back to Trisha. "Once again, I am telling you and your posse to leave this wing and be careful not to touch anything on your way out. If I have to tell you again, I will arrest all of you on an obstruction of justice charge."

Trisha scoffs at that. "That rap would never stick."

"Perhaps not," Hurley says, "but I'd still be able to lock you up long enough to get you out from under my feet. And you know how slow things can move in these cute little towns."

I swear I see sparks flying out of Trisha's ears. After another brief face-off with Hurley, she spins around and corrals her team out of the room, down the hall, and into the main front hallway. Hurley and I follow and watch as Trisha and her honchos enter and stake out a table in the dining room and then form a huddle, speaking in low voices. For all I know they may be plotting our demise.

I tell Hurley I'll be back in a jiff and then I head for the main reception desk. I walk up to Anne and introduce myself.

"I know who you are. We all know who you guys are," Anne says with a frown.

"I apologize for not signing in with you before, but the detective and I had signed in earlier. We had to leave in a hurry and we never signed out. Technically we were still on the books. I forgot about the young girl who came back with us. She wasn't here earlier so I'll sign her in now. Do you want me to sign my dog in, too?"

Anne thinks about this a moment and then shakes her head. "Is that girl who came with you some kind of cop, too?" she asks, looking doubtful.

I shake my head and smile to get her to relax. "No, she's not. She's Detective Hurley's daughter. I'm not a cop, either. I'm with the medical examiner's office. I just assist the cops with their investigation."

"Some investigation," she says sourly. "It looks like everyone is a suspect."

"It does seem that way at first, but all we're really doing is gathering information. We like to talk to everyone who has any remote connection to the victim even if there's nothing obvious that would seem of interest. Sometimes we find answers in places where we least expect to. You'd be surprised at some of the little tidbits of information that come in handy."

"You mean like Mr. Chase's girlfriend?"

Whoa! "Mr. Chase had a girlfriend?"

Anne bites her lip. "Crap. No one told you guys yet?"

"I don't know," I tell her honestly. "We're only beginning to talk to the employees."

"Most of the residents know, too. It's not like they were very good at hiding it."

"They who? Who was Mr. Chase seeing?"

Anne bites her lip and shakes her head. She leans back in her seat, physically and mentally withdrawing from me. "I shouldn't have said anything. We're supposed to wait for the lawyers before we talk to any of you cops. I could lose my job."

"I told you, I'm not a cop. I'm an assistant investigator with the medical examiner's office. I'm just here to help the cops out." This isn't the whole truth, but I'm counting on Anne not to know that.

"So anything I say to you now won't be part of my official statement?"

"Not unless you say it again later when there's a cop present. I promise that if you tell me who Bernard's girlfriend is, it will stay between us."

Anne looks hesitant, but she leans forward and glances both ways along the hall. I'm guessing it's to make sure no one else is within hearing distance.

Finally she caves. "It's Regan Simmons," she whispers, "the evening charge nurse."

Chapter 18

Since Regan Simmons is the person Hurley wanted me to bring to him, this bit of information segues well with my plans. "Do you know where Regan is right now?" I ask Anne.

"She's over in the D wing passing meds."

I thank her and turn to head that way, but she stops me. "Are you going to tell her I told you about her and Mr. Chase?" Anne looks genuinely frightened at the prospect.

"I don't see any reason to tell anyone who gave me the information. From what you've told me, other members of the staff and many of the residents know, so I don't think you have anything to worry about. There will be plenty of likely culprits."

She nods, but she's gnawing at her thumbnail and still looks frightened.

"Trust me, you'll be fine." I reach over and give her arm a reassuring squeeze, then head for the D wing, leaving her there to fret about her future.

It's my first time in this part of the building and I can't help but notice that the smell of stale urine that permeates the air seems to grow stronger as I get closer to the D wing. When I turn the corner into the D hallway, I see a woman I presume is Regan Simmons standing beside a medication cart at the far end of the wing. She's wearing a white uniform, which I'm guessing pegs her as either an LPN or an RN. While a lot of places these days allow their professionals to wear various forms of scrubs, I know that Dorothy is old school when it comes to dress codes. It was one of the things she and Molinaro butted heads over back in the day, so it comes as no surprise to me that she makes her nurses wear white uniforms.

The woman turns and watches me approach, sizing me up, her expression impassive. She is reasonably attractive with dark red hair pulled back into a twist, green eyes, and finely freckled skin. Her lips are full, her nose is pert, and her build is slender. I peg her to be around my age, somewhere in her thirties. As I get closer, I can see from her name tag that she is, indeed, Regan Simmons and an RN.

"Hi, I'm Mattie Winston, with the medical examiner's office."

"Yes, I know you. Hard not to if you read the paper."

She's right about that. Thanks to Alison Miller, Sorenson's star reporter and photographer, and at one time my competition for Hurley, I've been the main feature in the local paper several times over the past six months, and not in a good way. The only reason Alison isn't here now is because an aunt of hers passed away and she's out of town visiting the family.

"I'm here with the police helping with the investigation into Bernard Chase's murder. Detective Hurley and I would like to speak to you."

"We're supposed to wait for the lawyers to get here."

"They're here. They will be present."

"Okay, just let me finish passing my medications. I have two patients left and I'm behind schedule because of all this stuff that's going on."

"That's fine. I'll wait."

Her expression grows pinched, and I'm guessing she doesn't like the idea of me standing by waiting and watching, but she doesn't object. She goes about her job, opening a drawer in the cart with a name that corresponds to the medication administration record she has in front of her. She removes several pills, checks them against the paper schedule, and places the pills in a mortar, where she grinds them into small pieces with a pestle. Then she dumps the pieces into a plastic medicine cup and carries it into the room on her right.

I follow her and see a body curled up in the bed in a fetal position. The blankets hide all but the body's shape and the person's head. Based on the hair I can see, I assume it's a woman.

"Caroline, I have your medications." Regan walks over and burrows under the covers with one hand, extracting Caroline's arm. She looks at the armband there, and then puts the arm back down on the bed. I'm guessing this gesture is done for my benefit. Technically, it's standard procedure to always check the ID band on a patient before administering a medication, but in a setting such as this one, the nurses rarely do so once they get to know the patients.

Regan sets the medication on the nightstand, and reaches over and pushes a button on the rail that raises the upper part of the bed. Caroline's body slowly rises, her eyes darting about. One side of her face, the downward side, is slack, her lower eyelid drooping, the corner of her mouth trailing a long line of drool.

"Stroke?" I ask.

Regan nods. "She had a massive hemorrhagic stroke at the age of forty-eight. It left her with total right-sided paralysis and severe expressive aphasia. She can't talk, can't walk, can't move much on her own, and has no control of her bowels or bladder, but she is aware and understands what's going on."

Caroline's eyes shift from Regan to me and I am struck with the horror of the woman's situation. She is trapped inside her traitor of a body, unable to function, unable to communicate, unable to have any independence. Or dignity, I imagine, and at such a young age. For one second, the idea of helping someone like Caroline out of this world doesn't seem like such a horrible thing to do. But the decision should be Caroline's alone. Doing it because Caroline wants to be released from this hellish life she has is one thing. Doing it because her care is too expensive is another. Maybe Caroline has a reason to live, even a life as horrific as the one she has now.

As if she read my thought, Regan says, "Caroline has four kids, ages ten to seventeen. They visit her quite often."

There it is, I think, *a reason to live.* But how awful it must be for her and her family. Caroline's eyes are still on me, watching my face, gauging my reaction. It makes me uncomfortable, but my nursing background kicks in to help. I place a hand on Caroline's shoulder and give it a gentle squeeze. "My name is Mattie. It's a pleasure to meet you, Caroline. I'm sorry it's under these circumstances. And I'm so sorry this happened to you."

Caroline blinks at me and finally turns her gaze away. It's all I can do not to sigh with relief. I can't imagine being in her situation, with a quality of life that must suck on the best of days. I'm sure it's the love she feels for her family that keeps her going, her desire to see her kids grow up.

I watch as Regan turns back the covers and lifts Caroline's gown to get access to a feeding tube snaking out of Caroline's stomach. She uses a large syringe and some water to force the pill fragments down the tube.

When she is done, Regan flushes the feeding tube and clamps it off. Caroline's arms and legs are severely retracted, frozen into bent positions that make her fetal posturing permanent. It also makes what comes next a little easier for one person to do. Regan grabs the draw sheet beneath Caroline's withered body and with a practiced tug-and-flip maneuver, turns her tortured body over onto its other side. She then adjusts the pads and pillows to minimize the pressure on Caroline's bony prominences, giving Caroline a back rub in the process.

When we're done, I follow Regan back out into the hall and she tells me about the next patient before we go in, letting me know that he is blind and a triple amputee: both legs just above the knee, and his left arm just below the elbow. All of this is the result of years of poorly controlled and managed diabetes. His name is Charles Dresden and Regan announces herself as she passes through the door since Charles isn't able to see her. At least he is out of bed. He's strapped into what amounts to a highchair for adults, a giant chair with a tray that folds down over the front of it.

Parked nearby is a Hoyer lift, a mechanical device used to move patients from a bed to a chair and back again without hurting them or the staff. It's a good thing to have in this case since Charles is a huge man even without most of his limbs.

Charles takes his meds—there are a lot of them in the cup, somewhere around ten different pills—and asks when someone can come and put him back to bed. Regan explains that the staff is a little off schedule because of the mishap but that someone will be in soon.

I'm struck by Regan's use of the word *mishap* to refer to Bernie's murder. It makes me wonder if the staff has told all of the patients what has happened, or if they're trying to whitewash things for some of them. The truth is sure to get to everyone sooner or later. Enough of the patients know already and they're bound to gossip. That's one of the reasons it's so important to interview people as soon as possible. The hearsay and gossip often colors people's memories and they start remembering things they never actually experienced.

When we are done with Charles, I follow Regan to the intersection by the nurse's station and watch as she parks the medication cart in a locked room at the back of it. Then I lead her over to the dining room, where we find Hurley seated at a table with Trisha Collins.

As I approach the table I ask, "Where did the rest of your crew go?"

"They are looking into the other areas of your investigative efforts," Trisha says in vague lawyer-speak.

Since I'm pretty sure Trisha isn't going to elaborate any more than that, I shrug it off and do the basic introductions. "This is Regan Simmons, the evening charge nurse. Regan, this is Detective Steve Hurley with the Sorenson Police Department and Trisha Collins, one of the Twilight Home lawyers."

"Regan, please have a seat," Hurley says, gesturing to a chair across the table from him. "I would like to ask you a few questions regarding your boss's murder."

Trisha jumps in with her own set of instructions. "Ms. Simmons, you should understand that my presence here is to represent the facility. I am not your personal lawyer, nor am I here to protect your individual rights or interests. If you desire to have counsel present for yourself you will need to let Detective Hurley know that and obtain a lawyer. If you opt to move ahead at this time with any questions the detective might have, I would ask that any questions regarding the administrative aspects of the hospital be answered only by myself, one of my colleagues, or one of the board members. You may address questions about day-to-day functions you perform in the course of your duties. And of course, patient confidentiality is to be maintained at all times. Do you understand?"

Regan nods and then looks at Hurley. "Do I need a lawyer?"

"That's up to you. You are not under arrest and I'm not doing any sort of official interrogation at this point. We intend to speak to all the staff members as part of a general information gathering and you are the first. If you aren't guilty, you don't have anything to be concerned about. If at some point you reveal information that I think makes you a suspect, I will read you your rights."

"Why did you pick me first?" Regan asks. She looks nervous, and at the moment, I'm the only one in the room who fully understands why.

"No particular reason," Hurley says. "We had to wait for the lawyers to arrive, and when they did, I decided to start with the person or persons currently in charge and work my way down the pecking order. That's all."

"So I'm not a suspect at this point?" she asks.

"That's correct," Hurley says. "It's my understanding that you work the evening shift from four to midnight and that you are typically the person in charge of the facility once the administrative people have left for the day. Is that correct?"

"Yes."

"Are there any other nurses on duty with you?"

"Nurses? You mean registered nurses or LPNs?"

"Yes."

"I typically work with a staff of just nursing assistants."

"Who in the building has access to the patients' medications?"

"Once the administrative people leave, I'm the only one who has that access. Our medications are kept in a locked room at the nurse's station and there is one set of keys that is passed from nurse to nurse at the change of shift."

"I see," Hurley says. "Do any of the patients ever have access to, or administer their own medications?"

"They're not supposed to, but it's happened from time to time. Well-meaning family members sometimes bring things in, or the patients themselves will visit an urgent care clinic outside of their regular one during a day leave and get a doctor to prescribe something that they then fill and bring back with them. For some, it's a matter of wanting to maintain a level of control over their own health management, for others, it's a fear of embarrassment, or a desire to be secretive about their true health condition. It's a dangerous practice because even simple over-the-counter medications like acetaminophen can cause problems serious enough to be life threatening if we don't know someone is taking them."

"How well did you know Mr. Chase?" Hurley asks, switching gears.

I watch Regan closely as she answers. Her face remains impassive, but I notice she is fiddling with her wedding ring.

"I knew him to say hello to him when I saw him." There is the faintest quaver to her voice, so subtle that it could just be her normal manner of speech. "Our hours tend to run opposite one another so I didn't see him that often. Usually it was at the start of my shift, when he was leaving for the day."

"So he was a basic Monday through Friday, nine-to-five kind of guy?"

Regan shrugs. "I guess so."

"You never saw him here in the evenings or on the weekends?"

"Maybe once in a while. Several of the administrative people have come in during off hours at times. It may be more often than I'm aware of because that administrative wing is locked in the evenings and on weekends. I imagine anyone coming in during those hours would use the back outside entrance since it's closer to the employee parking lot."

"Are you aware of anyone who had a grudge against Mr. Chase?" Hurley continues.

Regan lets out a nervous little giggle. "Well, there

is that silly rumor the patients bounce around from time to time."

"What rumor is that?"

"Some of them seem to think that certain patient deaths have been suspicious."

"I'm sorry," Trisha jumps in, "but I'm not comfortable with that line of questioning."

Hurley gives her a ticked-off look and then says to Regan, "Without stating what the rumor is, tell me if you think there is any credence to it."

Trisha objects again with a frantic, "Detective!" but she's a hair too late. Even though Regan doesn't say anything, she shakes her head almost immediately.

Not one to be deterred, Hurley asks Regan, "Are you aware of any patients who believe this rumor strongly enough to want to exact revenge on Mr. Chase?"

Surprisingly, Trisha doesn't object this time.

"Not really," Regan says. "I mean, I've heard lots of them discuss it, but only in a speculative manner. I don't think anyone seriously believes it, at least not enough to act on it in a manner such as this."

"Okay," Hurley says. "I think that's all I need to ask for now. Is there anything you want to add?"

Regan shakes her head quickly and starts to rise from her chair, but I have a question that stops her cold.

"Is it okay if we fingerprint you and get a sample of your DNA?"

Hurley gives me a puzzled look. I'm guessing because of the DNA question.

Regan gives me a panicked look. "Why do you need those things?"

"Well, we're dusting Mr. Chase's office for fingerprints and if you rarely saw him and had little to no contact with him, we wouldn't expect to find your fingerprints in there."

Regan looks to the side for a heartbeat and I can tell her wheels are spinning. "I've been in his office," she says. "As the shift supervisor, I have keys to the administrative offices when I work. Our admission files on all the patients are in those offices, as are certain other papers we need to access from time to time."

"What papers would those be?" I ask.

"Um . . . you know . . . licenses and stuff like that."

"Those are kept in Mr. Chase's office, not in Dorothy Granger's office?"

"The facility licenses are in Mr. Chase's office," Regan says quickly. "Nursing licenses are kept in Ms. Granger's office."

"When is the last time you had to access the facility licenses?" I ask her.

"I don't know. It was some time ago. I'd have to look at the records. But the point is, you might find my fingerprints in that office." She flashes a nervous little smile, apparently relieved that she has dodged my bullet.

But she hasn't. I'm far from done.

Chapter 19

"Tell me, Regan," I say, "would we find your finger-prints on the couch in Bernie's office? Oh, heck, forget about the fingerprints, what about your DNA? Would we find that on the couch? Because somebody's DNA was all over that thing and we've got samples of it."

Hurley shoots me a surprised but admiring look.

Regan shoots me one that is lethal. "What are you implying?" she says, all indignant.

"Come on, Regan. I know you and Bernie Chase were having an affair."

"I'm a married woman and I love my husband."

"Maybe it was your husband who killed Bernie," I suggest.

"No," Regan shoots back in a tone that suggests I'm being ridiculous.

"He seems like a good suspect to me," I say, prod-ding her a little harder. "Does he know about the af-fair?"

"Of course not," Regan snaps. Then, realizing what she's just said, she tries to fix it. "What I mean is there is nothing for him to know about."

Hurley and I stare at Regan, waiting patiently. We have her and she knows it. It's just a matter of how long it's going to take her to cave.

Regan glances at Trisha, who doesn't say a word. "I have nothing to admit to," Regan maintains. "And if you insist on perpetuating this misinformation about an affair, I will have no choice but to sue you for libel."

She's good; her vehement denial is quite convincing.

I decide to prod a little harder. "Technically you would have to sue us for slander."

"What?" Regan snaps, looking at me like I'm a tick on her dog's ass.

"Mattie is correct," Trisha says. "If someone says something that damages your reputation, it's considered slander not libel, assuming you can prove actual damages. Libel has to be in writing. In either case, it's only a problem if what is said or written can't be backed up by the truth."

Regan glares at us, her eyes moving from me to Trisha to Hurley and back to me again. Her lips are tight with anger and she's twisting her wedding ring so hard I wouldn't be surprised to see her finger come off. Her next words come out clear and taut. "I will not discuss or tolerate any suggestion that Bernie and I had a romantic relationship. If you would like to discuss other matters, that's fine. Otherwise I need to get back to work." Her complexion is flushed and I can tell we have her rattled. That and the fact that she slipped by using the more familiar name for Chase.

"Think very carefully, Regan," I say. "This is a small town. People see things, people talk. So if you and *Bernie* were having an affair, people will know. Odds are we will be able to prove it, if through no other means than through that DNA sampling I mentioned. Believe me, I know. I've been there."

"Mattie is absolutely right," Hurley says, leaning forward and closing the gap between him and Regan. "Let me ask you one more time, and please think very carefully before you answer. Were you and Bernard Chase having an affair?"

Regan's eyes dart back and forth and tears are starting to well in them. I can tell she's hesitant to admit the truth. She's gauging the veracity of what we just said, weighing her options.

"Yes," she says finally with a little sigh of resignation. Her entire body sags. "Bernie and I were having an affair."

Everyone sits back in their seats and now that the truth is out, it's as if someone opened a window and let all the tension rush out of the room.

"How long has it been going on?" Hurley asks.

Regan drops her gaze to her lap, and I sense she's no longer willing to look us straight in the eye now that we've caught her in a lie. "Six, maybe seven months. Dorothy hired me a little over a year ago. I met Bernard during the interview process and the attraction has been there from the beginning, but it took a while before we acted on it. Both of our marriages were falling apart, and we commiserated about it over lunch a few times. Then we went to a conference together and met up in the bar after the sessions were over. One thing led to another and here we are."

"Did you kill Bernard?" Hurley asks her.

"Of course not," she says in a tone of disbelief. She shakes her head in misery and the tears are free-falling now. "I genuinely cared for Bernie. I had no reason to kill him."

"Do you think your husband might have?" Hurley asks.

"N-no, of course not," she stammers. "I'm sure he doesn't know." But there is a fearful look on her face, a hint of doubt that tells me she believes it's a possibility. The revelation about Regan and Bernie's little affair has widened our suspect list considerably. We now have Regan herself if Bernie decided to break things off and Regan didn't like it, and Regan's husband if he knew about the affair and flew into a jealous rage. This also adds motive for Bernie's wife Vonda, though I somehow think she wouldn't have cared that he was having an affair.

"Who do you think killed him?" Hurley asks Regan.

"How would I know? Maybe it was his wife, or a patient. Some of them can get pretty crazy, particularly the ones with the mental disorders."

"I thought you said none of the patients really believed that rumor," Hurley says.

"Well, how can I know for sure? No one jumps out to me as a suspect, but who knows what secrets these patients may be hiding?" No one says anything so Regan jumps in to fill the void. "How did he die? Was he beaten? Stabbed? Maybe I could give you a more educated guess if I knew."

Hurley and I look at each other and smile. Regan Simmons is no dummy and I don't believe for one minute that she hasn't heard all the gossip going around about where and how Bernie was found. Too many people knew about it, including Irene and whoever else might have peeked in that men's room before I got there. And I know everyone in the building has been talking all day long.

"Let's switch from who and how to why," Hurley says, avoiding Regan's question. "What do *you* think about this rumor that Bernard was killing off his more expensive patients?"

"Detective!" Trisha interrupts.

"It's absurd," Regan says at the same time. Then, ignoring Trisha's objection, she turns to me and says, "Mattie, you just met two of our most disabled patients. Both of them have been here for several years, so if Bernie was trying to get rid of the patients who were costing him money, those two should have been at the top of the list."

"I respectfully ask that you change the subject," Trisha says.

Hurley ignores her. "So you don't believe the rumors?" he asks Regan.

"Of course not," Regan snaps. "It's an utterly ridiculous idea. But that doesn't mean some of those patients out there don't believe it. And if they do, who's to say one or more of them didn't decide to kill Bernard?"

Regan's tune is changing pretty quickly now that she's trying to shift our focus away from her lies, as well as her own and her husband's motives.

"When is the last time you saw Bernie?" I ask her.

"Last night after my shift finished. Bernie often came by here at night and he and I would meet up in his office at the end of my shift. He'd let himself in through the back door to the administration wing and wait for me. I'd call him when I was done and he would let me in through the same door."

"Were you supposed to meet with him tonight?"

She shakes her head. "This afternoon. Before my shift started. Obviously that didn't happen."

Hurley switches gears and asks about some of the day-to-day operations of the facility. "When does the administration wing get locked up?"

"Between five and six PM on most weekdays," Regan says. "On the weekends it's locked all the time. We open it up again at seven on Monday morning."

"Whose responsibility is it to make sure it's locked?"

"The on-duty nurse supervisor is responsible for making sure the inside entrance is locked. The rear exit door is locked at all times. Anyone can go out, but no one is supposed to be able to get in without a key."

"Who has keys to these doors?"

"Each of the board members has a set of keys that opens pretty much every door here. I believe the medical director, Dr. Zimmerman, has a key to the front and back doors since he sometimes has to come here during off hours, but I don't know that he has keys to anywhere else. There is a master key set that we on-duty nurse supervisors hand off at shift change."

"There are two parking lots here?"

"Yes," Regan says, and now that the questions have veered away from her personally, she has relaxed considerably. "The side parking lot is for all employees and board members except for the night shift. They can park out front. Other than that, the lot out front is reserved for visitors and vendors."

"Vendors?"

"Salesmen and such."

"Do you get a lot of those?"

"Not on my shift, but I've heard the day nurses say they see some occasionally."

"Is the front desk with the sign-in book manned twenty-four-seven?"

"No, we have someone there during our open hours, which are from six in the morning until ten at night. Between ten PM and six AM the entire facility is locked. The evening nurse supervisor on duty has to man the front door to let the night shift staff in between eleven-thirty and midnight." Regan makes a pointed look at her watch. "In fact, I need to be heading that way soon."

"Okay. I have just one more question for you," Hurley says, and she smiles with relief. "How free are the patients here to come and go?"

"Well, with the exception of the ones who wear ankle monitors, they are all basically free to come and go as they please during the open hours. It's expected that everyone will be here by the time we lock up at night, although some of our patients have had overnight furloughs, especially around the holidays. Those have to be arranged ahead of time, though. It's rare for anyone to leave during the day for anything other than church, or a doctor's appointment, or an occasional family event because most of them don't have the means to go anywhere. They're dependent upon a friend or family member to come and take them somewhere."

"Okay, Regan, I think that wraps it up for now, but I would like you to go to the dayroom and get fingerprinted before you leave for the night. I would also like to search your employee locker."

I expect Regan to object, but she doesn't. She nods and then asks, "Are you going to talk to my husband?"

"More than likely," Hurley says. "At this point, he's a suspect with motive."

"He doesn't know about Bernie and me. I'm sure of it."

"Then you might want to tell him," I say to her. "He'd probably prefer finding out from you rather than us."

Hurley calls Bob Richmond on his cell phone and arranges for him to print Regan and search her locker. "And see what other employees you can get to agree to prints and a locker search."

Over the next hour we talk to five more staff members, all of them nursing assistants, and all of them with Trisha present. Two of them—one of which is Anne—are brave enough to mention the relationship between Regan and Bernard. The other three don't, but judging from their body language and their evasive answers, I'm pretty sure they all know. It's moot at this point since Regan confessed, but it's still disheartening to see how many people aren't telling us the whole truth.

Just before midnight, the night shift staff starts coming in, and we talk to and fingerprint an LPN named Lucinda and three more nursing assistants. Other than Lucinda telling us about Regan and Bernard's affair, we don't get any useful information from anyone. Nor do the locker searches turn up anything of interest.

It's nearly one AM when Hurley closes his notebook and stuffs it into his pocket. "Let's call it a night. I would like to talk with your administrative group in the morning," he says to Trisha. "What time works best for you?"

"Give me a few minutes to check with my associates and I'll let you know," Trisha says, taking out her cell phone. "I'll find you in the dayroom."

Hurley and I head to the dayroom where we find

Emily curled up on a couch sound asleep. Once again, Hoover is stretched out nearby, and I marvel at how quickly he has taken to her. He appears to be sleeping, too, but when we enter the room he lifts his head and looks at us, before dropping it again and closing his eyes.

On the table beside Emily is the drawing she did of the face she saw in the window earlier. I pick it up and study it, thinking it looks vaguely familiar somehow. But I can't come up with any definitive identification and after a minute or so I hand it to Hurley.

Bob Richmond is sitting at a table on the other side of the room writing on a tablet. Dozens of pages that have been torn from that tablet are scattered about the tabletop, each of them covered with writing. Hurley walks over and sifts through the pages, scanning what's written there.

"Come up with anything?" he asks Richmond.

Richmond shakes his head. "Larry said that aside from that Dudley guy you talked to, the room searches didn't reveal anything of interest other than a hunting knife they found under one man's mattress and some cigarette papers and baggies filled with dried plants in the bedside stands of several people. They opened and smelled each one and said it wasn't pot. Larry said he thought he smelled oregano and maybe some mint."

"Told ya," I say.

"Are Larry and his guys done with the search?" Hurley asks.

"Yeah, they finished up about an hour ago and I sent them home. As soon as I finish these notes I'm heading that way myself. There are about a dozen employees who aren't here who we still need to print and whose lockers need to be searched. I also have eight of the forty patients to talk to yet, but they're all in bed now. I was hoping to get through this whole list for the A, B, and C wing patients, but these people tend to ramble on and on and half the time you have to say everything two or three times before they hear you right. And that's assuming they actually remember your question two seconds after you've asked it. Plus that dog of yours didn't help. They all wanted to pet him. He was a huge distraction."

"Sorry."

"Nah, don't be. He brought these folks some joy and affection, and believe me, most of them need both those things in spades. But I think all the petting and attention has worn poor Hoover out."

I look at Richmond's list and tell him, "I chatted with several of those names you have left on your list when I was outside earlier. They're the ones who are smoking the oregano. I don't think they have anything useful to offer other than the same conspiracy theory everyone else is spouting, but I can talk to them a little more at some point."

Hurley lets out an irritated sigh and runs a hand through his hair. "Man this case sucks. I feel like we've wasted hours and come up with nothing." He challenges the Fates yet again by asking, "Can this day get any worse?"

In the next instant we find out that indeed it can.

Chapter 20

Trisha Collins and two of her three cohorts march into the dayroom. Judging from the smug expressions on their faces and their overall demeanor, I suspect we won't like hearing whatever they're about to say.

Trisha hands some papers to Hurley and says, "This is an injunction to stop you from searching the administrative offices of the Twilight Home until we have a chance to preview any paperwork you want to see. And just so you know, we will not be available tomorrow."

Hurley takes a few seconds to flip through the papers and then glares at Trisha. "Let me guess. You guys bill by the page?"

"We are simply looking out for the best interests of our clients. There are some potentially sensitive items listed in the injunction that we want to review first to determine their relevance, if any."

"Well, since you're not conducting the investigation and don't know what evidence we have so far, how the hell would you know what's relevant?" Hurley snaps. He's madder than I've seen him in a long time and he isn't done yet. "No matter what else you think might be detrimental to this facility's future and reputation, I can assure you the public won't take kindly to the knowledge that you value your"—he pauses and refers to the papers she handed him—"meeting minutes and admitting policies more than you do the safety of the staff and residents here."

"I assure you we are concerned over much weightier issues than those," Trisha says in a haughty tone. "I can see why you might think we are ignoring patient safety, but I assure you we are not. Perhaps if you had a law degree you might have a better appreciation for our position and our concerns. But since I'm sure none of you do, I don't expect you to understand."

"Geez, lady, don't be such a witch." The voice belongs to Emily, who has apparently been awakened by all the excitement and has decided to pipe in with her opinion on the matter.

Trisha gapes across the room at her and then looks at Hurley. "Did that child just call me a bitch?" she asks askance.

"Actually she said *witch*," I tell her.

"Same difference," Trisha says. "There is no need for name-calling, especially from some . . . . some . . . insolent child."

"Hey, if the broom fits," I mutter with a shrug.

One of the male lawyers bites back a smile, but Trisha shoots me a look that says she wants me as dead as Bernie Chase. I find myself backing up a step and sidling a little closer to Hurley for protection, just in case. I'm thinking Emily should do the same.

Hurley says, "Okay, lady, as it turns out I have a pretty full schedule tomorrow that does not include going through your administrative records. We can plan on doing that first thing Monday morning. However, I am going to continue to process evidence in Mr. Chase's office and any other office I think might be necessary. If you don't trust my word that I won't go through your files, you best have someone here to watch. Since I don't trust you not to mess up my crime scene, I will have an officer posted here at all times to make sure that no one enters those offices and nothing leaves them until we conduct our search. That said, I do want to meet with the administrative group of the facility tomorrow morning so if you aren't going to be available, I guess I'll have to talk to them without you."

Trisha narrows her eyes at this challenge and her knuckles whiten again. "They won't talk to you if we're not present," she counters.

"Fine," Hurley says. "I'll just see to it that all of you are brought up on obstruction of justice charges."

"Don't be ridiculous."

"I'm not," Hurley says, closing the gap between them and pinning her down with eyes the color of cold, blue steel. "But like I said, this is a small town. And in small towns we sometimes get away with stuff that folks in the big city can't because we dumb hicks just don't know any better. Sure, you'll be able to show us the error of our ways eventually, but I promise you that we can lock up every one of you long enough to piss off your fancy law firm and cost you a lot of valuable time and money. Now I'm tired, I'm pissed off, I've got a murder to solve, and I'm not going to put up with any more of your crap. So if you want to test me, go ahead. It's your call."

Trisha's face twitches a couple times before she says, "Fine. We will plan on being here at ten o'clock tomorrow morning if that suits you." With that, she spins on her heel and leaves the room with her two cronies trailing behind her, letting us know that she doesn't really care if it suits us.

"God, I hate lawyers," Hurley grumbles.

"I think we're all tired," I say. "Let's go home and get some sleep so we can start again in the morning."

"Let's plan on meeting at the station at nine and we'll map out the day," Hurley says. He takes out his cell phone, punches up a number, and walks off toward the hall.

I help Richmond gather up his papers and then head out. As I pass Hurley in the hallway, he is disconnecting his call. "Kate still isn't answering her phone," he says in a low voice so Emily, who is walking a few feet ahead, can't hear.

"Maybe her battery is dead. Or maybe she's in a spot with no service. Those throwaway phones can be very unreliable."

"It worked fine when she was here." He runs a hand through his hair, looking worried. "I have a bad feeling about this. I never should have let her go."

"Give her until the morning and then try again. If you still can't get ahold of her we'll figure something out."

He nods, but not convincingly.

"Take Emily home and get some sleep. Things will look better in the morning."

I turn to leave, but Hurley grabs my arm. "Wait. After what happened earlier, I want to follow you home to make sure you get in okay."

"I'm not going home yet," I tell him. "I need to take all the evidence I collected in Bernie's office back to our lab so I can log it in."

Hurley frowns. "Normally I would say it could wait until tomorrow since we have an officer to make sure nothing else is tampered with. But clearly someone tampered with that coffee cup already, so you're right. We need to take it back tonight. I'll help you get it all checked in."

Emily comes with us and despite the fact that she looks exhausted, she perks up when we take her into the administrative wing and down the hall to Bernie's office. She can tell from all the police tape that this is where the murder occurred and she checks out every detail.

A little over an hour later, the evidence is all secure inside Arnie's lab and I'm at home. Hurley has just finished checking out the woods around my cottage and Emily is outside waiting in the car. Hurley and I are standing just inside my door.

"I don't want to leave you," Hurley says, tucking a strand of hair behind my ear. "Come and stay at my place tonight."

"We don't seem to handle the temptation very well so I don't think that would be a good idea."

Hurley flashes a guilty smile. "No, I suppose not." He leans over and gives me a kiss on my forehead. It's nothing more than a peck and yet it zings through my body like an electric shock.

"You need to go," I say, a little breathless.

"Okay. Keep your phone with you and leave the outside lights on. I'll have whoever's on duty drive by here a few times during the night to keep an eye on things. If anything happens, you call me."

"I will."

I'm relieved and sad once he's finally out the door. Hoover looks disappointed, too. "That man definitely has a hold on us, doesn't he, boy?" I say to Hoover, giving him a scratch behind the ears. He whimpers in agreement.

After a brief shower, I drop into bed, wondering if I'll be able to go to sleep since I'm usually still up at this time of night holding down a blackjack table. I toss and turn, and when Hoover raises his head once and stares at my bedroom window, I start to wonder if my spy has returned. After an hour, I get up, go out to the kitchen and look for a snack, forgetting that my cupboards are bare. Instead, I take out my diary and settle in at the table with a glass of water.

Sunday, March 2
Dear Diary,

It's been an interesting and long day. I ended up at the scene of my first official death since returning to my job and it's a puzzler with a list of suspects longer than my arms, which are always longer than any long-sleeved clothing item I've worn. The good news is I like puzzles and this one is keeping me busy and distracted enough that I haven't thought about going to the casino more than about a hundred times today. I know Dr. Naggy thinks I have a problem when it comes to gambling, but I think I've proven that I am fine with not going for a day or two.

Seeing Hurley didn't go as well as I thought it would. My first sight of him was gut-wrenching. I underestimated the emotional pain I might feel at being around him. That pain was mitigated somewhat by the fact that we had sex. Three times. I should probably feel guilty or ashamed or embarrassed or worried that we indulged in this forbidden behavior, but oddly enough the very fact that it was forbidden made it that much better. And it was good. How can something that feels so good and right be so bad and wrong? What am I going to do about it?

Hurley has implied that we can have a working relationship and a romantic one as long as we're careful, but I have my doubts about keeping something like that secret from Izzy. He seems to be able to smell when I'm lying to him and he knows me too well. Irene could tell something was going on between me and Hurley, too, and even young Emily, Hurley's daughter, has picked up on the attraction. And that's another issue, the whole Kate and Emily thing. Hurley says he's finalizing his divorce from Kate, but it became apparent to me today that even if he does that, they are going to be a permanent and frequent part of his life from here on. I don't know if there's room for me in there, too.

Relationships shouldn't be this difficult. I always thought the people I love would be the anchors in my life, the people who would keep me from going adrift. But sometimes anchors just drag you down. Look at what happened to my marriage to David. I believed in marriage, I believed in my marriage, and I believed in him. And yet he betrayed me in the most horrible way. I'm not sure what makes me madder, the fact that he did what he did, or the fact that he seems so unaffected by it all. How can something that devastated me and flipped my life upside down be so easy for him? And the bastard wasn't happy ruining my life once, he's still doing it by interfering with my ability to get a job. Not that that matters anymore, but it's the principle of the thing. It leaves me wary of any future relationship with Hurley. Will it fall apart eventually? Do all relationships fall apart eventually?

It has happened to my sister and her husband Lucien. They are having big problems now and they always seemed so stable to me. Then there's my mother, who four marriages later, is living with a man I once dated. All these complicated emotions and issues make it seem like it's not worth it. But the alternative, being alone, or even being without Hurley, is harder for me to imagine. Can I be content to simply spend time working with Hurley, socializing with him, and being at his side on a regular basis?

Maybe my expectations are unrealistic. Maybe it's enough to take what I can get, the way the stroke patient at the nursing home is doing. Clearly she can't interact with her children and husband on a regular basis, nor can she enjoy a normal life. I can't imagine how hard it must be for her, to be mentally alert and aware, yet unable to hug, or talk, or even smile. She is a prisoner in her own body and yet she is content, so it seems, so she can spend whatever time she manages to eke out with her children.

Children. Another thing I always thought I'd

have, but now I'm not so sure. I had imagined that
David and I would eventually start a family. Little
did I know he was starting one, however unintention-
ally, with someone else while we were still married.
And Hurley has found himself the instant father of a
teenager. I think it's sad that he missed all those
early years with Emily, but I also think it's going to
complicate his life a lot now that he knows her.

I'm tired now and I think I can finally go to sleep.
I have to admit to Dr. Maggie that this diary thing
isn't such a bad idea. Well, at least her part isn't. I'm
not sure how Gunther's going to react when he learns
that the only exercise I indulged in today was sex.
He said he wanted me to write down everything that
went into my mouth . . . does Hurley's tongue count?

Chapter 21

I wake to the alarm the next morning and it takes me a few seconds to figure out what the noise is. For the past two months I've slept for as long as I wanted each day, often not getting up until noon or later since I didn't get to bed until four or five in the morning. I stumble out to the kitchen and set up the coffee pot while the cats do their best to make me trip by winding in and around my feet. I give them some food to get them out of the way and then let Hoover outside. Once Hoover's back in and fed, I pour myself a much-needed cup of coffee and drink half of it before I call Izzy to check in. Even though it's a Sunday, I know Izzy is a morning person and will be up, and I want to bounce all that happened yesterday off him. He's a smart man who often thinks just enough outside the box to be enlightening.

"Whatcha doing?" I ask when he answers.

"Eating breakfast. You're welcome to come over

and join me if you want. Dom made his blueberry pancakes."

"Thanks, but I think I'm going to have to pass. Maybe another time. It was a very late night last night and my stomach isn't awake yet."

This is only a half-truth, because whatever was bothering my stomach yesterday is still lingering this morning and the thought of breakfast isn't very appealing, but I'm also trying to avoid any relaxed, friendly time with Izzy. I'm afraid he'll sense the truth about me and Hurley, somehow. For now, the less time I spend with him the better.

"No problem," Izzy says. "That's all the more pancakes for me. What's on your agenda for the day?"

"I have to meet up with Hurley in a little while and head back to the Twilight Home so we can talk with the administrative group and the lawyers at ten o'clock."

"They won't want to give you anything."

"Oh, I know. They've made their lack of cooperation quite clear already."

"Well, don't let them bamboozle you. Our office has the right to review any of the records of those patients who have died recently if we suspect anything out of the ordinary, and given what you've told me about the rumor surrounding Chase, I'd say we have cause. If you need me to come over there and throw my weight around, let me know."

"I think I've got enough weight on my own even without the pancakes," I say, and we both chuckle. Weight issues, along with a fondness for men, are two things Izzy and I have in common.

Izzy says, "Arnie is going to go into the office first thing to check on some of the test results I ran last night before he goes back out to the nursing home."

"I'll meet him there. Do you know when he's going in?"

"He said between eight and eight-thirty."

I look over at the clock on my kitchen wall. It's a little before seven-thirty so I've got some time.

"I'll probably be there around the same time," Izzy says. "I'll take a second, closer look at Bernard's body to see if I can find any puncture or injection sites."

"I'll meet you there and give you a hand before I go to the police station."

We arrange to hook up around eight-thirty and no sooner have I disconnected the call when my phone rings again.

"Hello?"

"Hi, Mattie, it's Desi."

"Hey, Des, is everything okay?"

"Yeah, we're fine, at least mostly. That's why I'm calling. I've been thinking that with all the money problems I've had, and with everything that's been going on between me and Lucien, the kids have been under a lot of stress. Thanks to your loan, the money issues have eased up a little and while I know it's kind of a splurge, I was thinking of taking the kids to the Dells and spending the day at an indoor water park. They could use some fun, and frankly, so could I. I was hoping you might come along?"

"I'd love to," I lie. I'd rather be quartered and drawn than spend a day feeling self-conscious in a bathing suit. "But I've got a ton of work to do with this nursing home case. Can I take a rain check?"

"Of course, you can. I promise I'll spend the rest of the money wisely. I just feel like the kids need something fun in their lives right now, at least one day to forget all the crap."

"I think it's a great idea. And the money is a gift, Desi. Spend it however you want. I'm glad I'm able to help."

"You have, and I can't thank you enough, although Mom says we're both going to end up in the poorhouse if we don't stop throwing away perfectly good, financially stable husbands."

"That sounds like classic Mom."

"Yes, it does," Desi says with a chuckle, and it does my heart good to hear a little happiness in her tone. "Listen, there's another reason I called. Erika wanted me to see if Emily might like to go with us for the day. I thought about calling Hurley and asking him, but I don't have his number."

"Let me check with her and Hurley and I'll call you right back." I hang up and dial Hurley's number.

He answers before the first ring is done.

"Wow, you must be up and at it already," I say.

"Technically I never went to bed. I slept on the couch and I've been awake since five o'clock, trying to get hold of Kate."

"Still no luck?"

"No. I was just about to call the Cincinnati PD."

"Kate was pretty adamant that she didn't want you to do that."

"I know, but if she's not answering my calls all bets are off. How do I know she's not in trouble?"

"Maybe she's outside a service area." I'm mentally cursing Kate for doing whatever it is she's doing. Her actions are distracting Hurley and he's got too much on his mind already between our current case and caring for Emily. "Give it a little more time," I tell him. To get his mind running along a different track I ask, "What are you going to do with Emily today?"

"She's going to stay here. I can have an officer

drive by every hour or so and she can use the house phone to call me on my cell if she needs anything. My place isn't as isolated as yours so I'm not too worried about someone trying to spy on her during the day. How was your night?"

"Slept like a baby." This is true if I only consider the four or so hours I actually slept. "If anyone was peeping in my windows, I wasn't aware of it. I might have a better idea for Emily." I tell him about Desi's invitation.

"That would be a huge load off my mind. Hold on while I ask her if she wants to go. I just heard her come out of the bathroom so I know she's awake, but she hasn't come downstairs yet."

I listen as he walks upstairs and knocks on a door. I can hear him offer her the trip and then I hear Emily's, "Yeah that sounds like fun . . . except I don't have a bathing suit."

Several phone calls later, we've arranged for Hurley to drop Emily off at Desi's and for Erika to loan Emily a bathing suit. With that out of the way, I get dressed, throw on a little makeup, and try to fix my hair. As I look at my roots and shaggy ends, I realize Irene is right. I'm long overdue for a trip to Barbara, my stylist for eternity. I make a mental note to call and set up an appointment tomorrow, and then I head out.

When I arrive at the office, I head upstairs to Arnie's lab area first. I find him standing in front of some machine that's spitting out paper.

"Good morning, Arnie. Got any news for me?"

He gives me a disappointed look. "Normally, they say no news is good news, but in this case I don't think that's true."

"Let me guess, nothing showed up on the tox screen?"

"You got it. We tested for opiates, benzos, tricyclics, and your basic street drugs like cocaine, marijuana, and meth. I also did a rapid test for cyanide. All of them came back negative. His blood alcohol was zero. The microscopic tissue slides didn't reveal anything helpful, either."

I frown at this news, knowing it's not going to make anyone happy. "How long before we get results back from Madison?"

"A few days, maybe a week," he says with a shrug.

I tell him about Frank Dudley and the insulin suspicion.

"Do you think this Dudley guy did it?" he asks.

I think about it seriously for a moment. "No," I admit. "I don't. An overdose of insulin fits with Bernie's behavior before he died, but insulin has to be injected. You can't take it orally because the stomach enzymes destroy it. And that whole thing with the coffee cup would seem to suggest something and someone else."

"Speaking of which, I see you were busy last night." He gestures toward the boxes of evidence I left stacked in one corner. "Are you going back out there today?"

"Yeah, we're supposed to meet with the board members and lawyers at ten this morning. But after that I know there are some people outside the home we need to talk to, including the cuckolded husband of one of the staff members who was sleeping with the victim, and the sons of one of the nursing home patients."

"The lawyers are here?" Arnie says, making a face.

"They're not only here, they're already making life difficult."

"You and Hurley can handle them," Arnie says with a dismissive wave. "You guys make a great team."

This comment makes my heart squeeze.

"I'll come by and finish dusting for prints and help with whatever other evidence collection we need to do as soon as I'm done processing this stuff," he adds.

"Okay, see you there." I head downstairs and poke my head into Izzy's office, but it's empty so I head for the autopsy suite. He's there, with Bernie's body on the table. He has on a headpiece with magnifying lenses in it and he's bent down close to Bernie's left arm, studying it.

"Hey, Izzy," I say.

He looks up at me and I have to bite back a smile. His eyes appear huge behind the lenses; he looks like a bug, or Mr. Magoo.

"Good morning," he greets as I approach the table. He picks up Bernie's arm and scrutinizes the back side of it. "You're just in time," he says, setting the arm back down when he's done. "I need to turn Bernie over so I can examine his backside. Can you give me a hand?"

"Sure." I don a pair of gloves and then help him flip Bernie's body up onto its side. It's quite stiff, making the process easy. As Izzy gets up close and personal with Bernie's backside with his magnifying glasses, I say, "I take it you haven't found anything yet?"

"Not so far. There are no puncture or injection sites in the front side of his limbs or torso that I can find. I suppose the scalp is a potential site, but I've looked pretty closely there and while it might be easy to hide a puncture site, as vascular as the scalp is, I would expect to find some signs of hemorrhage, or at least some minor bruising. There's nothing there." After fifteen minutes of intense inspection, Izzy determines that there are no injection sites on the backside of Bernie's body, either.

"I'm sorry, Mattie," he says, taking off his magnifiers. "The whole insulin theory isn't holding up very well. We'll wait and see what the blood analysis shows, but I doubt that insulin was the cause of death unless the perpetrator figured out a unique way to deliver the drug."

"To be honest, I think we're leaning in a different direction now, anyway." I fill him in on the mystery of the missing coffee in the cup that was on Bernard's desk.

"Well," Izzy says, nodding his head thoughtfully, "that certainly is suspicious. Who had access to that area during the time that it wasn't being guarded?"

"That's the problem. Pretty much anybody in the facility had access between when Hurley and I left and the police officer returned. We're not even sure exactly how much time there was."

Izzy's expression brightens. "Well, there was coffee in Bernard's stomach contents, so that gives us something more specific to focus on. I'll run a couple tests on it myself today since Arnie is going to be at the nursing home most of the day working on evidence collection. I'll also give the Madison lab a heads-up so they can broaden their testing and focus more on the gastric contents. Any more news on last night's Peeping Tom?"

"No, and Hurley hasn't been able to reach Emily's mother yet, either. He's quite worried."

"I can't blame him." Izzy scrunches his face in thought. "It has to be distracting for him. You should probably stick close and keep an eye on him through this investigation at least until Kate returns."

If Izzy had any idea just how close I've been to Hurley so far, I doubt he would say that. But since he has, I can't help but flush with guilt. I turn away quickly so he won't see it; Izzy has an uncanny ability to read me. "I'll keep an eye on him," I say, heading for the door. "And I'll check back with you later to see if you turn up anything with the gastric contents, or to let you know if we find out anything else."

I manage to escape without any probing questions from Izzy and I make my way to the police station. Hurley isn't in yet, but I find Junior Feller sitting in the conference/interrogation room. He looks like I feel—tired and a little logy.

"Hi, Mattie," Junior says when he sees me. "There's coffee in the break room."

"Thanks, but I think I'll pass." Police station coffee is notoriously bad. In fact, rumor has it it's often used during interrogations as a form of torture.

"I have addresses for Regan Simmons's husband and for the Waldheim boys," Junior tells me. "I didn't call them to tell them we're coming. I'll leave that decision up to Hurley but if you ask me, I think it's better to surprise them, especially the Waldheim boys. They're not likely to be friendly and I doubt they're bright enough to come up with any good lies on short notice, so why give them a chance to develop one."

"Sounds good to me," I say.

Hurley walks in then. "What sounds good to you?" He is carrying a stack of folders stuffed with papers. He, too, looks weary and like he's aged ten years overnight.

I have a nearly irresistible urge to walk over and hug him.

Junior repeats his theory about the Waldheim boys.

"I agree," Hurley says, "though to be honest I'm not nearly as concerned about them as I am these damned lawyers at the Twilight Home." He drops his stack of folders on the conference room table and sets a hand on top of the pile. "These are all the notes and findings from yesterday's searches and interviews. Aside from our Mr. Dudley, no one seemed to think there was anything significant in here."

"I think we can rule out Mr. Dudley at this point." I share with them Izzy's findings from this morning, or rather his lack of findings. I also explain to them how the missing coffee from the coffee cup pretty much rules out insulin as a poison. "There is some good news though," I add. "Given that someone made an effort to dispose of that coffee, I think it's safe to say that whatever did Bernie in was in that coffee. Izzy said there was coffee in his gastric contents, so that will give us a better focus in looking for a poison. It will also make it easier to test for substances because most of the poisons or drugs he might have ingested will be more concentrated and in their original form if they are still in the stomach, whereas by the time most of them hit the bloodstream they've been filtered by the liver and broken down. That can make it difficult to identify them or detect significant amounts. In a way, it's a good thing. The bad news is that the tox screen we ran on Bernard's blood and gastric contents came back negative. That means the most common drugs and poisons are ruled out, so we're still going to end up on a bit of a hunting expedition."

"I think that missing coffee helps us in another way," Hurley says. "I was thinking about it last night when I got home, and anyone who has an alibi for the period of time when the coffee went missing basically has an alibi for the murder. Under the circumstances, I can't imagine anyone dumping the coffee for someone else because everyone there knew it was a crime scene. Going after that coffee was a risky, desperate move, so I'm thinking whoever did it is most likely our killer. Unfortunately, that doesn't bode well for anyone who was at the nursing home at the time."

"So where do we go from here?" I ask.

"For now, we continue with the staff interviews at the nursing home, including the board members. I don't plan on spending a ton of time with them because I haven't found a motive amongst any of them yet. We do, however, have plenty of potential motives with Mr. Simmons and the Waldheim boys."

Junior gives Hurley a wary look. "Those Waldheim boys may have motive, but from what I know of them I rather doubt they have enough sense between the three of them to coordinate something this sophisticated."

"I have my money on Regan Simmons or her husband," I say. An instant later, I mentally wince at my use of yet another gambling term.

"And though my gut doesn't like her for it, there is still Vonda," Hurley adds. "We can't rule her out." He looks over at Junior. "Did Monica give you any information?"

"She did," he says.

Junior's girlfriend Monica works at a local bank. In addition to being a bank officer, she's also a badge bunny who has previously dated at least three other cops in town. So far, things seem to be working out with her and Junior, but time will tell.

"She said Bernie and Vonda bank where she works and both have plenty of money of their own. Vonda does quite well with her art sales and she's financially independent, whereas Bernie comes from family money and plenty of it. There doesn't appear to be any strong financial motive on the wife's part. That's all unofficial, of course."

"Of course," Hurley says with a nod. He pats the stack of files on the table. "If we don't uncover something today to point us in any one direction, we should come back to these notes and go through them. Maybe there's something in here we missed. Or maybe there's something in here that's significant and we just don't know it yet." He pauses and stares at the files with a frown.

"What is it?" I ask him.

"There's something about this whole scene that still bothers me."

"How so?"

"That powder that ended up in Bernie's mouth. Bjorn said he dropped the bottle and then ran out of the bathroom because Bernie was clawing at him. Yet that stuff ended up inside Bernie's mouth as if someone poured it in there. And you said you found the empty container under Bernie's leg, right?"

I nod.

"That container was completely empty. If Bjorn had simply dropped the bottle the way he described, I'd think some of the powder would still be in it."

I suddenly see where Hurley's thoughts are headed. "You think someone else entered that bathroom in between the time that Bjorn left and Irene appeared, don't you?"

Hurley nods. He has a far-off look in his eyes and I can tell he's visualizing a scene in his mind. "Maybe there was someone with Bernard in his office, some-one who had a reason to want him dead. Maybe they struggled and Bernard was able to get away. But then the person caught up to him in the bathroom, saw that powder, and used it."

"That would imply someone who knows what that powder does," I say. "But if Bernie got away, why run into the bathroom? Why wouldn't he just run out-side, or to the front reception area where there were other people around?"

"He saw Bjorn walk by and thought he could get him to help, so he went after him. I suspect he did that after finding out his cell phone was dead. I'm not sure what happened with the land line. I imagine he either tried to call out on the desk phone and stopped when he saw Bjorn, thinking that would be faster help, or he was too confused in his deteriorat-ing state to use the phone. Plus, from what Bjorn said, Bernie wasn't talking much. If he was too weak to talk, the phone wouldn't have done him much good."

"That makes sense," I say.

Hurley glances at his watch. "Let's go back to Twi-light and meet with the administrative group and the lawyers. I have some questions regarding the finan-cial operations and I'm thinking we should get a list of recent deaths so Mattie can at least review those charts. If necessary, we'll look into exhumations and autopsies, but for now we'll follow the paper trail to see if there's any credence to this crazy idea about Chase killing off his more expensive patients. Assum-ing, of course, that the lawyers give us what we want."

"I wouldn't count on that," I say, remembering Trisha's behavior from last night.

"I don't have a good feeling, either, but we have to

try. I also want to interview the day staff on duty and maybe we can get a list of names, addresses, and phone numbers for the off-duty employees we haven't been able to talk to yet. Once we're done there, we'll go talk to the Waldheim boys and Regan Simmons's husband. Then we regroup and see what we've got." He turns to Junior and asks, "I see you're in uniform. Are you on the books today?"

Junior shakes his head. "Nope, it's supposed to be my day off, but Monica's birthday is coming up and she's been hinting not so subtly about a pair of diamond earrings she likes. So I can use the overtime and the chief said he'll okay as much overtime as we want for the next two days to help you with this case. After that, he said he has to reevaluate. I'm all yours for the day. I wasn't sure what you'd want me to do, so I wore the uniform."

"I'm glad you did and I can definitely use you. I think it will make our presence more official, and by that I mean intimidating. I think you should bring a patrol car along, too."

"Works for me," Junior says.

Hurley glances at his watch again. "We have time to grab a quick bite to eat before we head for our meeting with the lawyers and the board."

"I already ate," Junior says. "You two go ahead. I'll meet you at the Twilight Home at ten." With that, he heads out.

"Hungry?" Hurley says to me.

My stomach feels more settled than it did earlier so I nod. "I haven't eaten yet."

"I have some leftover ham I need to use up and neither Emily nor Kate will eat the stuff."

"Speaking of Kate, have you been able to talk to her yet?"

Hurley shakes his head, his expression worried. "If I don't reach her today, I'm calling the Cincinnati police tomorrow no matter what. In the meantime, let's zip over to my place and I'll cook for you. I make a mean ham and cheese omelet."

"If you twist my arm you could probably talk me into it." Ten minutes later, Hurley and I are in his bed and, after he mumbles something about my prior nipple incident, I discover it wasn't my arm he wanted to twist at all.

Chapter 22

"This has got to stop," I say to Hurley as I climb out of bed and start putting my pants back on.

"I didn't hear you say stop at any point," he says with a devilish grin.

"You got me over here by telling me you were going to cook for me."

"And now that we've got things all heated up, all I need to do is crack a few eggs."

"Dammit, Hurley, you're too good and too sneaky. By the time I realize what you're doing, I'm too far gone."

"I like it when you're gone."

"Gone is what we need to be. Let's get going."

"We still have time for breakfast," Hurley says, glancing at his watch. "I promise I'm a fast cook and if need be we can eat it on the way." He's already dressed, whereas I'm still in the process of trying to find my bra. "I'll meet you downstairs in ten. Would you like white toast or rye?"

"Rye, please."

Hurley takes off at a half run down the hall and the stairs. There is a small half bath off the master bedroom, and I head in there to do a quick cleanup before I finish getting dressed.

A few minutes later, I come back out and start looking for my bra again. It's nowhere in sight, and I pause for a moment to remember back to our frantic arrival in the bedroom. Though it isn't there now, I vaguely recall seeing it hit the bedside stand when Hurley tossed it off to one side after a speedy removal. Sure enough, when I walk around the bed to look, I see it on the floor between the bedside stand and the bed frame. When I bend down to pick it up, I find a white envelope lying beneath it. The face of it is blank except for the name *Steve* written in a feminine-looking hand. It isn't sealed so after a brief moment of indecision, I open it and take out the letter inside. It's one sheet of unlined paper that looks like it was probably pulled from a printer. It's folded into thirds and when I unfold the first portion of it, I see the closing signature at the bottom, written in the same tiny, neat handwriting as the rest of it. *Love, Kate.*

Those two little words trigger a gamut of emotions in a period of a few seconds—jealousy, anger, sadness, and self-pity. After arguing with myself about what I want to do and know I shouldn't, I give in to curiosity and start to unfold the rest of the letter.

A voice behind me makes me stop. "Hey, what's taking you so long?"

It's Hurley and his voice sounds so close it makes me jump. My hand crunches the page I'm holding and I slap it to my chest along with my bra. I turn halfway around pretending that I'm covering my bare breasts when in reality I'm trying to hide what

I'm holding. Hurley has managed to sneak up the stairs and he's standing at the top of them at the end of the hallway, looking at me.

"I'm sorry," I tell him. "I'll be right down. I took a few minutes to clean up and then I couldn't find my bra."

"Hurry up," he says. And then much to my relief, he turns and heads back down the stairs, but not before delivering one final shot over his shoulder. "There's nothing worse than a cold omelet."

I pull my hand away from my chest and look at the crumpled paper I'm holding. I'm dying to read it, but I don't have time. If I take it, Kate will know when she comes back and asks Hurley what he thought about whatever the letter says. Will she know that I found it? And if she does, will she tell Hurley? And if she does will he be mad that I snooped? The whole thing is a big can of worms, and I can already imagine the expression on Dr. Maggie's face when I tell her what I've done.

I quickly put my bra and blouse back on, and then I fold the letter as neatly as I can, put it back in the envelope, and stuff it in my pants pocket. It will need to wait until later. Maybe then I can figure out how to get it back into Hurley's house in a way that doesn't make it obvious that I read it. Hoping I don't look too guilty, I head downstairs.

Hurley wasn't lying when he said he can make a killer omelet. Because of the time constraints, we eat quickly and wash it all down with cups of coffee in to-go mugs so we can take our java with us.

Ten minutes later we head out, arriving at the Twilight Home with plenty of time left. The front parking lot is nearly full, and for a moment, it looks like

we're going to have to drive around and park in the
side lot used by the employees. At the last minute, we
see a car back out of a space and we take it as soon as
the car leaves.

By the time we get out of the car, we have at least
fifteen minutes before our appointed meeting time,
and it wouldn't surprise me if we ended up with
more than that. From listening to Lucien, I know
that lawyers like to show up late. It's a tactic they use
to put their adversaries on edge. In this case, it's a
tactic that may well backfire on them. I have something particular in mind that I want to do and it's
something I suspect the lawyers would prevent me
from doing if I were to ask. I've always been a be-
liever in the philosophy that it's easier to ask for for-
giveness than permission, and since what I want to
do won't interfere with any actual evidence, I decide
to go ahead.

Hurley leaves his unfinished coffee in the car, but
I bring my to-go mug along with me. As we enter the
front door, I start to think I might not get away with
what I want to do after all. I forgot to take into account the fact that the board members would also be
here. Some of them, I suspect, won't show up until
the meeting time, but Dorothy is here already, settled
in at the front check-in desk. She doesn't look any
happier than she did last night, so I smile at her and
greet her with a cheery, "Good morning, Dorothy,"
in hopes of bettering her mood.

"That remains to be seen," she says dryly, making
me suspect my efforts are wasted. "The lawyers told
me to tell you we can meet in the dining room. I believe you know the way."

"We'll be there when the time comes," Hurley

says. "Right now, I'm going back to the administrative wing to talk to the officer on duty. Is there any problem with that?"

Judging from the expression on Dorothy's face, she does have a problem with it, but she keeps it to herself. She shoves the logbook toward us and curtly instructs us to sign in.

"The parking lot is full this morning," I say, signing my name and then handing the pen to Hurley. "Judging from all the names in this book, it's been a busy morning."

"It's Sunday," Dorothy says. "A lot of people go to church." There is a subtle tone in her voice, one that suggests perhaps we should all be there as well.

Hurley and I head for the administrative wing and when we step through the door we see Brenda Joiner, the uniformed officer on duty. She is seated in a chair in the hallway a few feet down from the bathroom. Like me, she has a cup of coffee in one hand. Unlike me, she has the morning paper in the other.

"Good morning, Brenda," Hurley says. "Anyone try to come through here last night or this morning?"

"Not on my watch," she says. "I came on at two and I'm supposed to be done at ten, but my relief hasn't shown up yet."

Hurley walks over and pushes open the door to the bathroom. The crime scene tape is still up and the bathroom doesn't look any different than it did yesterday with the exception of the fact that Bernie's body is gone. As crime scenes go, it's a tidy one with no blood, no bullet holes, and, at the moment, no body.

"Listen, Hurley, I want to go sneak a peek at a couple patient charts. I'm going to make my way to the nurse's station via the outside route so I don't attract Dorothy's attention. I don't want to upset her."

Hurley gives me a curious look. "What are you looking for?"

"I want to check on an idea that I had. It's just a hunch and it may turn out to be nothing. I'll let you know."

Hurley glances at his watch. "Okay, just be careful. Do you think you'll be done and in the dining room by ten o'clock?"

"I should be. What I need to check won't take long." I head down the hall and out the exit. Apparently it's too early in the morning for the fake pot smokers to be out, or perhaps it's too cold. There's a damp chill in the air that makes me huddle inside my jacket as I make my way through the gate and across the garden area to the dayroom. There are a dozen or so others in the room, most of whom look over at me and then go back to whatever they're doing. At one end of the room, the wall-mounted TV is airing a Sunday morning religious show that's keeping several people occupied . . . several hard-of-hearing people if the volume level is any indication.

I head across the dayroom and glance down the C wing hall. It's clearly a busy time of day. Both the B and C wing halls have a lot of activity going on. There are residents dressed in their Sunday best making their way toward the front entrance with family members who are presumably picking them up and taking them to church. Down the C wing hallway, I also see a medication cart with a white-uniformed person standing beside it. A second later, the person turns, exposing her profile to me, and I see that it's Connie. Relieved that she is occupied elsewhere, I hurry down the B wing hallway.

When I reach the nurse's station, I'm delighted to see it's vacant. I slip inside, walk over to one of four large wall racks that hold patient charts, and set my coffee cup down on the counter below them. I'm after two charts in particular, and it doesn't take me long to find them since the charts are organized by wing and room number. The first one I grab is that of Caroline Masters, the forty-eight-year-old stroke patient I met last night when Regan was giving out medications. I flip the chart open, quickly read the tabs that separate it into sections, and open to the area that has her demographics. Thirty seconds later, I flip to the social service section and several minutes later, I have my answer. I return her chart and grab the one for Charles, the triple amputee. After a few more minutes of digging, I have everything I need and put his chart back in the rack. I'm just in time, too, because I hear voices and footsteps approaching from the B wing and the main front hallway. I don't want to step out into either hallway and make it obvious that I was in the nurse's station, so instead, I go to the B wing entrance of the nurse's station and lean against the wall as if I've been waiting awhile. Seconds later, several staff members, family members, and patients appear, coming from the direction of the cafeteria. I smile at them and a moment later, a second group of people appear from the B wing. Among them, pushing her medication cart, is Connie. When she sees me she looks startled for a moment, then she eyes me suspiciously.

"Thank goodness," I say, pushing myself away from the wall. It's then that I see my coffee mug sitting on the counter beneath the chart racks. It's too late to get it, so I have to hope that anyone who sees it assumes it belongs to a staff member. "I was beginning to think no one was going to show up. Dorothy told me she thought you'd be here at the nurse's station."

Connie pushes her cart past me toward the medication room. As she unlocks the door and shoves her cart inside, she says, "Normally I would've been, but it always takes a little longer to pass meds on Sunday mornings because of all the church comings and goings." She pulls the door to the medication room closed, and gives the knob a little jiggle to make sure it's locked. Then she slips the keys into the pocket of her uniform. "Is there something I can help you with, Mattie?"

"As a matter of fact there is. I need a list of all the residents who have died here in the past two years." I'm pretty sure Connie doesn't have this information at her fingertips, nor is she someone who would be privy to it. But it was all I could think of on the spur of the moment to explain my presence.

As expected, Connie says, "I don't have that information. Did Dorothy tell you I would?"

"No, she didn't. But I didn't tell her why I was asking for you, only that I wanted to talk to you." Connie still looks very suspicious, so in an effort to put her at ease I try a little flattery. "You seemed like someone who has a good feel for the pulse of this place, so I sort of assumed this was information you could provide for me."

"Well I can't," she says, but my flattery has worked because she straightens up and squares her shoulders. "I do know quite a bit about what goes on around here, but that information is something I don't have access to. Even if I did, I wouldn't give it to you until I talked to the lawyers."

"The lawyers wouldn't be necessary. It's a matter of public record," I tell her dismissively. "I could get the information elsewhere, but it will take longer. That's why I was hoping to get it from here, but I understand your hesitance. I'm not here to get anyone in trouble. Thanks anyway."

I push away from the wall and head back toward the dayroom, intending to retrace my steps back to the administrative wing. I've only taken a few steps when I hear a noise behind me. I turn and see two men closing in on me in their scooters. One is on either side of the hall and, as I stand there, they zip past me heading for the dayroom.

When I reach the dayroom, I see the two men parked in front of the exit door looking at me expectantly.

"I can give you that list of names you want," one of them says to me. "I keep a diary, and I've written down the name of every person who's been admitted, discharged, or died since I've been here, and that's been six years now."

"That's good to know." *Score another point for diaries.* "I'm hoping to get the information I need from Dorothy or the lawyers, but if I have any problems I'll come back to you."

"Okay. My name is George. George Watson."

I step past him and head outside, making my way back to the administrative wing. When I reach the door, I check it just to make sure it's locked. It is, and I make a fist and pound on it. I must've hit it harder than I realized, because when Hurley opens it a few seconds later, he has a panicked look on his face.

"What's wrong?" he asks. "Are you okay?"

"I'm fine."

"I was beginning to think you weren't going to get back here in time. Did you get what you need?"

"I did." I tell him about my findings.

"Good to know. We'll keep that in mind when we talk to the lawyers. It may or may not prove to be significant."

We walk past Bernard's office and when I glance inside, I see Arnie wearing a head visor with an ultraviolet light on it, hard at work swabbing samples from the couch. "Hey, Arnie," I say.

He waves in our general direction, but says nothing; he's totally focused on his job at the moment. Outside the men's room, Brenda Joiner has been relieved and another uniformed police officer has taken her place. We exchange polite greetings with him and continue on to the dining room. The board members are assembled inside—Dorothy Granger, Al Hubbard, and Jeanette Throckmorton. There's a fourth person with the group and it's someone I know—Joe Zimmerman, an internal medicine doctor and the medical director for the Twilight Home. Not surprisingly, Trisha and her little band of helpers are nowhere in sight.

Hurley starts to walk in, but I grab his arm and stop him. "My coffee has run right through me and I need to make a pit stop at the bathroom in the main hallway. Since the lawyers aren't here yet, I don't see any need to rush."

"Okay," Hurley says with a shrug. "I'll wait."

Inside the bathroom, I settle in on a toilet, take the letter I found in Hurley's bedroom out of my pocket, and read it.

It takes me a minute or two because the handwriting is very small and precise, and Kate managed to fit a lot of words on one page. I also find myself rereading several lines, wanting to make sure I read them right the first time.

When I'm done, I sit there stunned for a moment, trying to digest what I just read. I carefully refold the letter and slip it back into my pocket, knowing I will be keenly aware of its presence until I give it to Hurley. And give it to him I will. I must. The question is when.

For now, the letter resides in my pocket, making me feel like a suicide bomber who knows she will alter several lives forever once she makes the fateful decision to deliver her payload.

Chapter 23

By the time Hurley and I join the others in the dining room, it's a couple minutes after ten. We settle in at the long table where the others are already seated, and after a few perfunctory greetings followed by introductions between Hurley and Dr. Zimmerman, we all sit there bathed in awkward silence. At twelve minutes past the hour, Trisha and her trio of yes-men finally enter the dining room, confirming my suspicion about their late arrival.

"Good morning, everyone," Trisha says, with clearly forced cheerfulness. Her gaze doesn't linger on us long. "I trust you haven't been snooping inside any of the offices prior to our arrival?" Her tone of voice suggests she thinks we did exactly that.

"Snooping?" Hurley says with surprising patience. "No, we haven't been snooping. We have, however, been collecting evidence in the bathroom where Mr. Chase was found, and in his office."

Trisha narrows her eyes at Hurley. "Exactly what evidence have you collected so far?"

"A lot of fingerprints," Hurley says. "We have taken pictures of everything, including the tax documents Mr. Chase left on top of his desk." This gets an arched brow from Trisha. "We also collected a lot of miscellaneous items, including the coffee cup that was sitting on his desk, all the items in Mr. Chase's coffee station, and some swabs of stains we found on his couch."

I scan the faces of the others closely when he mentions the coffee cup, but no one seems to react to it.

"Beyond that, we haven't looked at any documents, opened any drawers, or sifted through any files other than the ones you knew about last night. Nor have we been in any of the other offices."

"You couldn't have gone through the file cabinets or the desk drawers if you wanted to," Trisha says with a hint of smugness in her voice. "I made sure they were locked before we left last night and I have the only key."

Hurley lets out a hearty laugh, which makes Trisha's smile falter ever so slightly. "Your efforts to keep me honest are laughable," he says. "The locks on that desk and those cabinets can be picked by an amateur in about two minutes."

Trisha's smile is gone completely. This is Hurley at his best, and I wince, knowing that sometime today I will have to divulge the letter to him. Its contents will undoubtedly put him off his game.

"Were you honest, Detective?" Trisha asks.

"Of course I was."

She and Hurley lock eyes for several seconds, each of them weighing the other. It's a battle of wills and I'm curious to see who will back down first.

"Okay then," Trisha says, looking around the table at the others. "What questions do you have for us, Detective?"

"My first question is about the ownership structure of the Twilight Home. My understanding is that Bernard Chase is the owner, but I would like to know if he is the sole proprietor, or if the facility is structured as a corporation or partnership of some type."

Al Hubbard glances over at Trisha, who gives him a nod. "Bernard is . . . was . . . the majority owner, but he did structure his ownership as a partnership."

"Who are the other partners?" Hurley asks.

"There's only one," Al says. "And it's a secret partner. None of us knows who that person is. The actual structure of the partnership agreement dictates that Bernard gets sixty percent of any profits and the secret partner gets forty."

"Is this secret partner also an investor?" Hurley asks.

"That's been my understanding," Al says. "Though to be honest, I'm not privy to the actual contractual arrangements. As the CFO, my responsibility is managing the inflow and outflow of money related to the day-to-day functions of the facility. As for the ownership structure, I've nothing to do with that."

Hurley looks over at Trisha with a questioning expression.

She shrugs and shakes her head. "Our firm was not involved in the establishment of the partnership. We are aware of the terms of the partnership contract, but we don't know who the secret partner is, either. I assume Bernard had another lawyer draw up the agreement."

"What happens to the partnership now that Bernard is dead?" Hurley asks her.

"The partnership automatically dissolves," Oscar Walden says. "However, Mr. Chase did tell me once that the terms of this specific partnership allow for either partner to buy out the other if one wants to sell, or if one of them is incapacitated in some way. If that doesn't happen, the business is put up for sale."

Trisha says, "Our function is to make sure that the facility continues to run and that the patients are properly cared for until the disposition of the business is determined and finalized."

"Do you know where Bernard's money comes from?" Hurley asks. We already have a pretty good idea what the answer is, thanks to the information that Monica revealed to Junior, but it never hurts to verify things.

"It's family money," Trisha says, confirming what we've already heard. "He inherited a good chunk from his parents, both of whom are dead. I believe he invested in some other businesses that didn't do so well for him, so he decided to try some aspect of healthcare, thinking it would be a business with more longevity and opportunities for profitability."

"What about a will?" Hurley asks. "Does your firm have one on file?"

"No," Trisha says. "I'm guessing that's with the same lawyer who drafted the partnership agreement."

Jeanette Throckmorton says, "I know Bernard had a file containing legal documents. It's possible his will and the partnership agreement are in it."

"And where might that file be?" Hurley asks.

"In his safe."

"And where is the safe?"

"In his office."

Hurley and I exchange puzzled looks. If there was a safe in Bernie's office, neither of us saw it.

"Where in his office?" Hurley asks. "I don't recall seeing one anywhere."

Jeanette explains why. "It's hidden. The wall between the two narrow cabinets hanging on either side of his sink is a false one. If you push on it, it opens, revealing a safe."

"Do you know the combination for it?"

Jeanette shakes her head.

Hurley lets out a perturbed sigh and rolls his eyes. "I don't suppose any of you know the combination?" he asks the others in the room.

There is a collective shaking of heads as they all exchange looks.

"Great," Hurley says. "I'll have to get a locksmith to drill it open." He looks over at Trisha. "Do you have any objections to that?"

"What? You can't pick that one with your handy little Boy Scout lock pick set?" Trisha says with a sarcastic grin.

Hurley glares at her and I mentally award a grudging point to Trisha.

"Whenever you get around to opening it," Trisha continues, "I or one of my colleagues needs to be there. Since none of us know what documents Bernard might have kept in that safe, it's imperative that we have a first look at anything that comes out of it."

"That's fine with me," Hurley says.

"Good, then let's move on."

"I would like to see a current copy of the Twilight Home financial records, and a list of all the admissions and deaths since Bernard bought the place."

"Those are all a matter of public record," Trisha says.

"Yes, I know that, but it will save me a lot of time if you can provide them for me. Call it a gesture of good will, a demonstration of your intent to cooperate. I'm interested in going a little deeper in the financial records than what is required to file with the state. I want to see the payor mix for all the patients here."

"I don't see the relevance of the payor mix information," Trisha says.

"The relevance is this rumor going around about Bernard Chase bumping off patients that don't pay well."

"I thought we resolved that issue last night," Trisha says irritably. "Mrs. Simmons pointed out two very needy and costly patients who have been here for a long time. Certainly if that rumor was true, those two patients would have been 'bumped off' long ago," she says, making little air quotes with her fingers for the words *bumped off.*

"It's far from resolved," I say. "The two patients that Mrs. Simmons mentioned are both private pay patients. Caroline Masters won several large malpractice settlements against her physician, a Milwaukee hospital, and a drug manufacturer. It seems her stroke wasn't a hemorrhagic one as I was told initially. Originally, she had a blood clot and her doctor used a new drug to try to break up that clot. That drug was still being trialed and the doctor didn't obtain the appropriate consents before using it. It caused a massive hemorrhage in Caroline's brain, which is what left her in the condition she's in now. She has millions to pay for her care, so when it comes to footing the cost, Bernard wasn't limited to any capped Medicare or Medicaid payments. The Twilight Home can charge whatever it wants and get it.

"Charles Dresden has his own money, too, though his comes from his wealthy family. So you see, they don't really fit the mold of 'costly patients.' " I couch my last two words in finger quotes for Trisha's benefit.

Before anyone else can say a word, Hurley jumps in. "Besides, it doesn't really matter if the rumor is true or not. The fact that people here believe it to be true is all that's important. At this point, I have no evidence to prove the rumor untrue. That's why I need the list of deaths I requested."

Trisha was looking at Hurley while he spoke, but as soon as he finishes she shifts her steely glare toward me. "May I ask how you obtained this information about these two patients?"

"We have our own sources," I say vaguely.

Trisha narrows her eyes at me and I know she suspects me of looking at the charts of these two patients. If she happens to talk to Connie at any point, I will surely be busted. But if that happens, I'm hoping it will occur late enough in the process that it won't matter.

Just when I'm about to think that Trisha's icy stare is putting a freeze on my heart, Hurley distracts her with his next demand. "I also want to have a look at the other offices in the administrative wing."

Trisha lets out a little sigh. "I will be happy to escort you into each of the other offices, but I'm going to limit you to whatever is clearly visible. There will be no opening of drawers, examining of files, or any other invasive searches unless I okay it. Is that understood?"

Hurley nods. "A walk-through is all I need for now. But only one lawyer is to go with me. The rest of you will need to find somewhere else to wait until we're done. Or if you prefer, you can leave."

"And Ms. Winston will need to be with us," Trisha says. "I don't want her wandering off on her own."

Before either Hurley or I can respond to this demand, Arnie enters the dining room carrying a small kit bag.

"Perfect timing," Hurley says, turning back to the others in the room. "This is Arnie Toffer with the medical examiner's office. He is going to fingerprint all of you."

Joe Zimmerman looks at Trisha. "Can they do that?"

"At this point, only with your permission," Trisha says. "However, their main objective is to rule out those prints one would expect to find in the crime scene area, meaning the administrative offices. So unless your fingerprints will be found somewhere where they shouldn't be, there's no reason for you to refuse. I'm sure each and every one of you has been in all of these offices at one time or another."

"Mr. Toffer is also going to ask each of you for your whereabouts between the hours of nine and noon yesterday morning, and between seven and nine o'clock last night."

Trisha shoots Hurley a confused look. "I get the morning hours, but why the evening ones?"

"I'm not at liberty to divulge that at this time," he says, and I mentally add another hatch mark in his column. Hurley then asks, "Which one of you lawyers is going to accompany me to the other offices?"

While Trisha and her cohorts decide who's going to do what, I sidle over to Arnie for a chat. He's unloading his supplies from the bag he brought with him, including a stack of blank ten cards, a black ink pad and roller, and a package of baby wipes.

"What's up with the black ink and the ten cards?" I ask him in a low voice. "Didn't you see that nifty new scanning tablet they were using last night?"

"I did," Arnie says. "But I had a little chat with Hurley this morning while you were elsewhere doing whatever you were doing, and he told me he specifically wanted me to use the ink pad on this group. I think he's doing it to piss them off."

I smile at that. Once again, it's Hurley in classic form. And once again, I remember the letter in my pocket and the devastating information it contains. I'm dreading giving it to Hurley and I wish I had someone to talk to, someone to get advice from about how to do it. I briefly consider talking to Arnie, but quickly discard the idea. I would have to explain how I found the letter in the first place, and doing so would shed an unwanted light on my current relationship with Hurley. That means Izzy is ruled out as well and that makes me sad. Izzy is a smart man who understands human nature and emotions better than most. I value his judgment and opinions highly and would love to bounce this situation off him before I do anything. But I can't. For this one, I'm afraid I'm on my own.

"Well," Arnie says, "I best get to it. It looks like I have a lot of fingers to roll."

After some discussion, the lawyers agree that Trisha will accompany us to Bernie's office to have a look at the safe while the others remain and get finger-printed. Once the fingerprinting is done, the board members are free to leave after Hurley and I have toured their respective offices. As Arnie commences

with the fingerprinting, Trisha, Hurley, and I all
head for Bernard's office.

Once inside the office, Hurley puts on a pair of
gloves, walks over to the sink area, and probes the
wall that Jeanette mentioned. A few seconds later,
the wall pops open, swinging on hidden hinges. Behind it is a wall safe with a combination lock.

"Well, you were right, Trisha," Hurley says. "I
won't be picking this thing open."

"Hold on a sec," I say. I walk over to the desk and
look at the day calendar. One of the days is circled in
red and has a special notation on it. I do a quick
mental calculation in my head using Bernie's age, a
fact I recall from the paperwork I saw at the office.
"Try this combination—three, thirty, sixty-eight."

Hurley dials the numbers in and opens the door.
"How did you know that?"

"It's his birthday."

"Oh for heaven's sake," Trisha says. "He used his
birthday for the combination? How stupid is that?"
She steps up quickly to see and commandeer whatever is in the safe. She starts to reach inside, but Hurley grabs her arm and stops her.

"You don't touch anything in there until you put
some gloves on," he says.

Trisha pulls her arm loose. "Fine. Where are
they?"

I grab a pair of gloves and hand them to her.
While she's pulling them on, Hurley is looking inside
the safe. "I think we're going to find the contents a
bit disappointing. I see a passport, some cash, a few
loose pills, and some letters."

Now that she's gloved, Trisha walks over and starts
pulling things out of the safe. The first thing she
grabs is the passport, which is Bernard's. It's been

well used. There are stamps from several European countries, a couple South American countries, China, and Japan. Next, she removes the cash, which turns out to be four stacks of fifty dollar bills. We don't take the time to count it all, but it appears that there are close to one hundred bills in each stack. I do some quick math in my head and realize there is somewhere around twenty thousand dollars in total. It's a large amount of money to have lying around in cash, and it makes me wonder why Bernard felt he needed to have it.

Next, Trisha removes the pills from the safe and hands them to me. There are seven of them in total and they are all the same: pear-shaped, beige-colored pills with a script letter *C* inscribed on them along with the number twenty.

"Do you know what those are?" Hurley asks.

I shake my head. "No, I don't. I'll have to look them up using our pill identifier software. But I'm pretty sure they aren't narcotics or any type of street drug." I drop the pills into an evidence bag, seal it, and then label it. While I'm doing this, Trisha removes the stack of letters from the safe, and after a quick glance, she hands them to Hurley. "What are those?" I ask after he's looked at a couple of them.

"They appear to be love letters from Regan to Bernie."

"Interesting," I say.

Hurley nods his agreement. "I'm guessing Bernie didn't want these or the cash found if he and Vonda moved forward with the divorce."

"Bernard and his wife are getting a divorce?" Trisha says.

"If what his wife told us is true, then yeah, they are," Hurley explains. "According to her they've been separated for some time. They even divided the house into separate wings so that they wouldn't have to cross paths."

"If he had a lover and there was that much animosity between the wife and Bernie, maybe his wife killed him," Trisha proposes.

"Maybe," Hurley says. "But I'm not seeing a strong motive there. His wife is very well-off financially on her own. She doesn't need Bernard's money, and given their living arrangements, I don't see his affair as being that important, either. We plan to visit her again today and conduct a search of the house, so we'll see if anything else turns up."

Chapter 24

Dr. Zimmerman is the first board member we talk to. Because he doesn't have an office of his own at the nursing home, we question him off to one side of the cafeteria. It's a short interview as he has a strong alibi that is quickly and easily verified. He was at the hospital making rounds on his patients Saturday morning between the hours of nine and twelve.

Next, we invite Al Hubbard into his office. Al is in his forties, overweight, balding, and wears thick glasses. He blinks all the time, though I can't tell if it's an attempt to adjust his vision or a nervous tic, and his features are coarse and kind of blubbery. He is wearing khaki pants that are too short, possibly because they are being held up with a pair of blue suspenders. His shirt is a lightweight cotton blend button-down in a blue and green plaid with two breast pockets. His socks are basic white cotton, and his shoes are a pair of black penny loafers that are so scuffed and creased I suspect he's probably had them for a decade or more. Despite their worn condition, each one bears a shiny copper coin in the penny slot. All Al lacks to be the poster boy for middle-aged nerds is a pocket protector.

As he unlocks his office, Hurley asks him who else has a key to it.

"All the board members have keys to the offices back here," Al says. "And I believe there are office keys on the master set that the nursing supervisors have. As far as I know, that's it."

His office is less than half the size of Bernie's and it lacks any warmth or personalization. There are no pictures on the wall, there are no family pictures on the desk, and other than a coffee mug that says FI-NANCE GUYS MAKE MORE CENTS, there is no evidence that a human being with a personality ever occupied the room.

When Hurley asks Al where he was yesterday morning, he says, "I was home, watching TV."

"Was anyone with you?"

"No, I live alone."

"Did anyone see you at home? Like a neighbor or a friend?"

Al shakes his head. I get the sense that he's very much a loner, though whether that's by choice or not, I can't tell.

Nothing in the office jumps out at us and when Hurley asks Al for the financial information he said he wanted earlier, Trisha says she'll have Al pull it together and send a copy to the police department by the end of the day.

We go back to the dining room to get Jeanette Throckmorton, a thin, mousy woman with brown hair who I guess to be in her late thirties. A bit of discussion clarifies the fact that Jeanette is not actually a member of the board of directors, but rather the administrative assistant or secretary. However, in this role she is privy to much of the same information that the board members have because she attends and types minutes for all their meetings, and processes nearly all the paperwork that comes through the facility. She also has a key to each of the administrative offices, just as the board members do.

As we are walking down the hall of the administrative wing toward her office, which is right next to Bernie's, Hurley asks her if she knew about the affair between Bernard and Regan Simmons.

"Yes, I did," she says very tight-lipped, making it apparent she did not approve. "Neither she nor Mr. Chase were very good at being sneaky. There were mornings when I would come in and find condoms in the trash, and articles of clothing lying on the floor by the couch in his office. And Regan was calling him all the time."

It's clear by the way she wrinkles her face when she says the word *condom*, as if she just touched something gross, dirty, and nasty, that Jeanette is disgusted.

As we enter her office, Hurley asks, "Are you married, Ms. Throckmorton?"

"No."

"Any love interests?"

She hesitates a beat before answering and I see her eyes dart toward her desk. "Not at the moment," she says finally.

"Where were you yesterday morning between the hours of nine and noon?"

"I didn't get up until after nine. I went out around ten to get something to eat. After that, I drove around for a while since it was such a nice day."

"Can anyone verify that?"

"I got my food at the McDonald's drive-through, so I guess they can vouch for that part of the time. But beyond that, I don't think so."

"Do you know of anyone who would want Mr. Chase dead?" I ask.

"No, of course not," she answers quickly.

"What about this rumor the patients have been talking about, that Mr. Chase was killing off the patients who became too expensive?"

"That is utterly ridiculous," she says angrily. "Mr. Chase is a thoughtful and kindhearted man. He would never do anything like that."

I walk around behind the desk, scanning the items on top of it. Like Bernie's desk, Jeanette's is covered with neat stacks of papers, most of which appear to be dealing with official nursing home business. "Jeanette, would you mind just opening the drawers of your desk for us?"

"I don't see why that's necessary," Trisha jumps in. "As Mr. Chase's secretary, Jeanette may have proprietary documents in there. I reserve the right to look through the desk first."

"I'm not interested in reading any papers that might be in the drawers. I would just like Jeanette to open them so I can take a quick look inside."

"To what end?" Trisha asks.

"To satisfy my curiosity," I say vaguely. I shift my gaze from Trisha to Jeanette. "You don't have anything to hide, do you?"

Jeanette shakes her head, but she looks frightened. She defers to Trisha, who after a moment's hesitation says, "Go ahead and open the drawers."

Jeanette unlocks her desk and proceeds to open

the drawers, beginning on the top left. There are three drawers on either side—two regular drawers atop a larger one made to hold hanging files—and a shallow one spanning the middle. The top drawer on the left contains typical office items such as boxes of extra staples, paper clips, pens, and pencils. The drawer beneath that contains two packages of printer paper and some sticky notes. The bottom drawer is filled to capacity with hanging files. A quick glance at the tabs indicate they are all work-related. The center desk drawer is filled with loose paper clips, pens, pencils, binder clips, and more sticky notes. The top two right drawers are filled with files—manila folders stuffed with papers. When Jeanette opens the bottom right drawer, my hunch is finally confirmed. Inside, I see a coffee mug, the back side of some greeting cards, and a bouquet of dried roses. I glance at Trisha and ask, "Any objections to me taking a closer look at the coffee mug?"

Trisha looks inside the drawer and shrugs. "Be my guest."

Jeanette, however, looks anything but indifferent. I reach down and pick up the mug, reading what it says on the side. At the top are the words, WORLD'S GREATEST, and below that the crossed-out word SECRE-TARY. Below that are the crossed-out words ADMINI-STRATIVE ASSISTANT, and at the bottom is the word LIFESAVER.

"A gift from Bernie?" I ask Jeanette, holding the mug aloft.

She nods, her face flushing a bright, flaming red. "He gave it to me for National Secretaries Day."

"Were the flowers from him, too?"

"Yes."

I return the mug to the drawer, and then give Jeanette my best sympathetic look. "You were in love with him, weren't you?" I say softly.

Jeanette stares at me for several seconds as tears well in her eyes. When the tears flood over and run down her face, she swipes at them with shaking hands. She opens her mouth as if to speak several times, but all that comes out are sobs. Finally she just nods.

Hurley turns to Trisha and says, "I believe we have motive and opportunity here. I intend to search this entire office. Now."

Jeanette finally finds her voice. "You think I killed Bernie?" she asks, her voice quivering. "That's ridiculous! I could never hurt Bernie."

Trisha sighs heavily, gives Hurley and me the go ahead and we spend the next twenty minutes searching through Jeanette's thankfully small office. With Trisha looming over us the entire time, we do no more than fan through the pages inside the manila file folders, and finger our way through the tabs on the hanging files. We're not looking for anything that would be on paperwork; we're looking for something that could be used as a poison. We come up empty-handed, and when we leave the office Hurley makes Jeanette turn over her key. We then have the police officer who is currently guarding the wing cordon off the office with police tape to keep anyone else from entering.

Jeanette continues her vociferous denials the entire time, and when Hurley asks her if it would be okay for us to search her house, she readily agrees. I can tell her adamant denials along with her willingness to let us go through her house have left Hurley feeling skeptical about her possible guilt. After giving it some thought, he gets on his cell phone and calls Bob Richmond in, asking him if he would be willing to take Jeanette home and search her house with the help of one or two other off-duty officers who might be looking for overtime. Bob agrees, and Jeanette is returned to the dining room where she is to remain under the watchful eye of Trisha's cohorts until Richmond comes to get her.

Next up is Dorothy Granger, and I can tell from the way she's watching what's going on with Jeanette that she's very curious about what has just happened. To her credit, she doesn't ask. As we're walking down the hallway of the administrative wing toward Dorothy's office, Hurley asks her where she was yesterday morning between the hours of nine and noon.

"I was home until about ten or so, and then I was out running some errands," she says.

"Such as?" Hurley prompts.

"I had to gas up my car, and then I took it through the self-serve car wash. After that, I walked around downtown window shopping. I have a niece with a birthday coming up and I was hoping to see something that might make a nice gift."

"Do you have any receipts?"

She looks over at Hurley, brow drawn down in thought. After a moment she says, "You know, I don't believe I do. I paid cash for the gas and I have a stash of tokens that I keep in my car for the car wash. And I never actually bought anything downtown. I was just looking."

We are at the door of her office and she reaches into her pants pocket and removes her key ring. As she pulls the keys out, a small brown bottle falls out onto the floor. It rolls toward me and I recognize it right away as a bottle of nitroglycerin tablets. I pick it up and look at the pharmacy label as Dorothy busies herself unlocking the door. The pills were dispensed only a week earlier, but the bottle is nearly empty. If Dorothy is taking these for a heart problem, it must be a severe case for her to have used this many of the pills already.

I hand her back the bottle as we head inside, and then I lean over and whisper into Hurley's ear. "Go easy on her. She has a bad heart."

Dorothy's office is a mirror image of Al's, but despite the similarities they are worlds apart. Her office is filled with personal touches. Framed certificates hang on the wall, interspersed with tasteful artwork. A dozen plants, including two blooming African violets, are thriving atop a small credenza in front of the single window. The desk chair has a crocheted cushion in the seat, and on top of the desk are framed photographs of three smiling, blond-haired children. Even the lighting in the room is warm, thanks to lamps with arts-and-crafts style, stained-glass shades sitting atop two small corner tables. One of those tables has a small coffee maker—one of those single cup brewing systems—and a selection of teas and hot chocolates to go with it.

"Are those your grandchildren?" Hurley asks, pointing to the pictures on the desk.

Dorothy smiles warmly at the pictures. "No, that's my grandniece and my two grandnephews. They're my brother's daughter's children. I was never blessed with any children of my own."

"Who do you think killed Bernard Chase?" Hurley asks.

Dorothy gives him a funny look. "I have no idea."

"Did you know about his affair with Regan Simmons?"

Dorothy nods and sighs. "Yes, I heard the rumors and I saw enough evidence on my own to believe them. But it was harmless, really, at least as far as the Twilight Home is concerned. I knew they were both married, but I also knew from talking with Bernard that his marriage had been over for a long time. He just hadn't formalized it yet. As for Regan, I don't know what shape her marriage is in, but as long as she did her job while she was on duty here and didn't let her affair get in the way of that, who am I to say what she should or shouldn't do?"

"What about this rumor the patients mentioned?" I ask. "I mean the one about Bernie getting rid of his expensive patients."

"That's just poppycock," Dorothy says with a laugh and a sad little shake of her head. "It's nothing more than a fantasy that some of the patients dreamed up in an effort to make their day-to-day lives more interesting. It's something exciting for them to focus on. It gives them the impression that they're living on the edge. Take a look at most of the books on the book cart in the dayroom. The selection on that cart is by request and it's almost entirely made up of thrillers and mysteries. When those aren't enough, the patients make up their own thrillers and mysteries. That's all this silly rumor is. Believe me, there's absolutely no truth to it. If there was, I would be one of the first to know."

Dorothy is more than willing to let us look through any part of her office that we want. At one point, when Trisha tries to object, Dorothy cuts her off with a look and an impatient, "Hush, woman. We have nothing to hide here and all you're doing with your ridiculous limitations is delaying their investigation."

It doesn't take us long to finish Dorothy's office, and once it's locked and Trisha and Dorothy have left, it's just past noon. Arnie has finished printing the board members and he's back in Bernie's office, so Hurley and I meet him there to strategize and figure out where we go from here.

Arnie is nearly done printing the office, though Hurley tells him to make sure he dusts the safe door before he leaves. We discuss the need to have him process prints or other evidence in Jeanette's office, but in the end Hurley decides not to. I can tell he doesn't think she had anything to do with the death and since we have Richmond searching the woman's house, it makes sense to wait and see what, if anything turns up.

Hurley excuses himself and steps outside the office to make a phone call. I try to eavesdrop, but I can't hear a thing. When he returns a minute later with a worried frown on his face, I know he was trying to call Kate again. I feel a twinge of guilt knowing I could stop those phone calls any time, but I'm not ready to do it yet. Something about this case is starting to feel better to me, like we're making some progress. I'm not sure why I feel that way given that we don't have a clear suspect yet, but I also know that once I share the contents of Kate's letter with Hurley, that progress is likely to stop dead in its tracks.

Chapter 25

It's lunchtime and the patients are walking and wheeling their way to the dining room. Since everyone is likely to be otherwise occupied and we need to eat, too, Hurley and I decide to make a quick run out for lunch ourselves. We ask Arnie if he wants anything, and when he says yes, we also ask the guard officer on duty. With a list of requests, we decide to stop at a local sub shop and get sandwiches to go, which we then take back to the nursing home and eat in the hallway outside Bernie's office.

By the time we're done, most of the patients have finished eating their lunch and are either back in their rooms taking a nap, or congregating in the dayroom and the garden area behind it.

After a brief discussion, Hurley and I decide to divvy up the duties. He heads for the dayroom with the list of patients that Bob Richmond wasn't able to speak to last night, and I take the list of employees on duty. I spend some time with Linda, the nursing assistant who is manning the front desk, and the three other nursing assistants on duty. None of them have much to offer, and the threat of losing their jobs has all of them pretty tight-lipped. I also talk to Connie, and while I half expect her to accuse me of sneaking a peek at patient charts earlier this morning, she doesn't say a word about it. She also has little to offer, which comes as no surprise given her behavior the day before. In between these interviews, I walk past the nurse's station and see that my coffee cup has disappeared.

When I'm done talking with the employees, I head for the dayroom to see how Hurley is doing with his interviews. Along the way, I take out my cell phone and place a call to Izzy.

He answers on the second ring. "What's up?"

"Did you find a medical record for Bernard Chase?"

"I did, but there wasn't much in it. The guy was healthy and had no major problems of any sort. His only visits to the doctor were for physicals and the occasional flu bug or cold."

"Did he take any medications of any kind?"

"None at all. Why?"

"Because we found a handful of pills locked up in a safe in his office."

"What do they look like?" I describe the pills to Izzy and he chuckles. "I can tell you what those are. They're Cialis."

I thank him, and disconnect the call, pondering how Izzy was able to identify erectile dysfunction pills so quickly. Then I decide I don't want to go there.

I find Hurley surrounded by a bunch of white, gray, and blue-haired ladies, and if the tittering giggles, bashful hand gestures, and sideways eye flutters are any indication, they are all gaga over him. I can't say I blame them. After one look at Hurley's black hair, blue eyes, chiseled jaw, and lanky legs, it's hard to keep the hormones in check, and apparently, despite being well past menopause, these ladies have plenty of hormones left.

I venture over toward the group and ask Hurley if I can speak to him a moment. This earns me several looks of contempt, and one of the women goes so far as to voice her objection.

"Hey, wait your turn, missy!" she says. The woman is well built and attractive for her age with carefully coifed, snow-white hair, hooker-red fingernails, and a carefully made-up face. She is dressed in tight black slacks, a low-cut red blouse, and shiny red pumps, which strike me as inappropriate for a woman her age until I see that she is sitting in a motorized wheelchair. Hell, the woman could wear six-inch stilettos if she wanted to because she doesn't have to walk anywhere in them.

"I'll give him back to you," I say. "We work together and I just need to speak to him for a minute."

Clearly she is not satisfied with my answer because she motors toward me, grabs my arm, and pulls me aside. "You need to make it quick, darling, because I'm working my best magic on this guy and right now he's the only man in this facility who looks like he's capable of sustaining a stiffy for any length of time. Hell, half these guys can't even *get* a stiffy, much less maintain one. I once tried to talk Bernie Chase into salting the food with Viagra, arguing that it would help him with his safety record because it would keep some of these old fools from rolling out of bed. But he wouldn't go for it and now I'm stuck with a bunch of limp noodles. Don't let this wheelchair fool you.

I'm not dead in that part of my body yet, and while I'm not saying it's been a long time since I last had sex, I do vaguely recall seeing a T-Rex thunder by during my post-coital haze, so I'm in need here, understand?"

"And you think you can score with that detective?" I say, barely suppressing a smile.

She then does something so shocking it makes me back up a step. First, she turns her wheelchair away from the others so that only I can see her face. She contorts her lips and pops both an upper and lower denture loose, letting them stick partway out of her mouth for a second before she sucks them back in. Then she leans in closer to me and wiggles her carefully drawn eyebrows. "Play a skin flute once without the teeth and you got 'em for life," she whispers.

It takes a lot to shock me. If you work as a nurse in an ER for any length of time you see and hear things that would mortify most people. Despite that, Snow White's comment makes me gasp and clamp a hand over my mouth.

Hurley hears it and looks over at us. "Did Gwen just confess?" he asks with half a grin.

"Not to murder," I say.

Gwen gives me a smug smile and motors back over to Hurley. "I'll share everything I know with you," she says, stroking his arm. "You come and find me when you're done talking to the big-boned blonde."

I see Hurley's mouth twitch and know he's trying to suppress a smile.

"Will do," he says, and then the two of us leave the dayroom and head down the hall. There are still a lot of people milling about in the halls: patients, family, and staff. When we glance inside the employee break room and see that it's empty, we head inside for privacy.

"Mystery solved on the pills we found in Bernie's safe," I tell him. "They're Cialis. Apparently Bernie needed a little help from time to time in obtaining and maintaining an erection."

"That's a problem I never have when you're around," Hurley says, wiggling his eyebrows salaciously. "You have this funny way of getting me all hot and bothered, Winston."

His words make my insides go all squishy. When he reaches over and takes my arm, I think he's going to hug me but instead, he turns and hauls me into the locker room that's off to one side of the break room. He pulls me to him and before I can utter a word, he kisses me. For a nanosecond, I consider stopping him, but the physical sensations pulsing through my body prevent me. For the next two minutes, our hands, our lips, our entire bodies are stroking, touching, caressing. . . .

The break room door opens and we hear women's voices out in the main room. Hurley and I split apart so fast I'm surprised it doesn't cause an explosion, particularly given all the heat between us. We spend a few seconds smoothing our clothes and hair, wiping our lips, and trying to look as innocent and professional as possible. I'm not sure we succeed before two of the nursing assistants I talked to earlier, Debbie and Miriam, enter the locker room nibbling on chocolate chip cookies. They stop short at the sight of us.

Several long seconds of silence follow and I wonder if I'm the only one who can hear my heart pounding in my chest.

"I'm sorry, ladies, do you need to get to your lockers?" Hurley says. "That would be great because I don't believe we've had the opportunity to search yours yet."

Neither of the women answers for several long seconds. Then Miriam says, "Have at it. I've got nothing to hide unless you're looking for lip balm and tampons." She sticks the remainder of her cookie in her mouth, walks over to unlock her locker, and flings the door open wide. Debbie shrugs and follows suit.

We find no smoking guns hiding inside either locker and after Hurley says, "Thanks. We appreciate your cooperation," the two of us leave the room. There is a container of chocolate chip cookies sitting on the table in the main part of the break room and before we exit, I grab two of them.

Out in the hallway I offer one of the cookies to Hurley, but he turns it down, leaving me to wonder if I should confess my consumption to Gunther.

"You know what?" Hurley says, leaning up against the wall and speaking in a low voice so others navigating the hall won't hear. "I don't think we're going to find anything helpful here by talking to any more of these patients. None of them have an alibi because they were all here at the time of the murder, but as far as we know, none of them would have had access to the administrative wing on Saturday, either. Nor can I see any of them exacting some sort of vigilante revenge on Bernard Chase because they believe that rumor that's been going around. None of the employees look good for anything except maybe Regan Simmons and Jeanette Throckmorton. As for the rest of the board members, only one of them, the doctor, has a solid alibi, but I'm not seeing a motive for any of them. I think we need to look outside the facility more. I'm going to give Junior a call and think we should head out to interview the Waldheim boys, Vonda Lincoln, and Mr. Simmons."

"There's one thing that bothers me about looking outside, though," I say, taking a small bite of cookie. "Access. The front door is manned all the time so if anyone gained access to the administrative wing via the front entrance, they would have been seen. Even if they hadn't signed in, the person on duty would have known about it and that was Connie. She swears no one got in through there and she's a bit of a sign-in Nazi. I can't see her letting anyone slide. That leaves the back door, the one to the outside. But it's locked all the time. Even if you come in that way with a key, the door remains locked once it closes. So how would any of these outside people get in?"

"Chase would have had to let them in," Hurley says. "Maybe he arranged to meet with someone and met them at the door at the agreed upon time. Or maybe he made a copy of his key for Regan Simmons so she could sneak in to meet him for their trysts. Maybe her husband followed her, or spied on her and saw her go in that way and then borrowed her key to pay a surprise visit to Chase."

"Okay, but how would he know that Bernie would be here on a Saturday morning?"

"Maybe he was following Chase, too."

"That seems like a lot of maybes. There is another possibility. Bjorn let himself in using Irene's key. What if someone came in with him and he just doesn't remember it?"

"If that were true, then whatever drug or poison was given to Chase would have to be very fast acting, almost instantaneous. Any ideas what that might be?"

I think about that for a moment. "Cyanide is the

only thing I can think of. But we already tested for that and it came back negative."

Our hallway tête-à-tête is interrupted by the mechanical hum of a motor as Gwen, aka Snow White, comes cruising up to us. "Hey there, handsome," she says to Hurley. "I'm tired of waiting. If you and the cookie monster here don't have a thing going, you might want to give me a try. We mature women have our perks, you know." She leans forward in her chair, giving Hurley a bird's eye view of her cleavage.

It also gives me a bird's eye view of the waist of her underclothes. Before she can shock Hurley with her teeth trick, I say, "You mature women also have some things that can be a bit off-putting."

"Such as?" Gwen says with a scowl.

"Depends."

"Depends on what?" she snaps.

"Just Depends."

Gwen narrows her eyes at me and I wouldn't be surprised to see steam come out her ears. She toggles her wheelchair around, nearly hitting me in the process, and motors off toward the dayroom.

"This case is making me crazy," Hurley says, running a hand through his hair. "And all these old people are making me crazy. Let's go interview some outsiders."

I nod, and give him a halfhearted smile knowing that I'm going to give him a whole new definition for crazy when I finally hand over Kate's letter.

Chapter 26

A light rain begins to fall as we head out to talk to the Waldheim boys, who live on a sprawling farm a mile or so out of town. It's a working farm, complete with cows, pigs, and the requisite faded red barn with a fieldstone foundation. Ironically, the barn is in better condition than the original farmhouse, a two-story boxy structure that looks as if a strong wind could blow it down. Spaced out around the main house are three mobile homes, six pickups of various ages, and a number of rusted car and tractor bodies.

If it was a few weeks later in the year, the odds of catching the Waldheim boys anywhere near the barn or the trailers would be long ones because they would be out tilling the fields, readying for their spring planting. Despite the warm weather we've had recently, the ground hasn't thawed much yet. Apparently it's not too early to fertilize the soil however, because the smell of manure is strong in the air. It's a smell any Wisconsinite gets to know, and normally it doesn't bother me. But for some reason today it's making my stomach lurch.

Hurley parks his car and the two of us get out. Junior is behind us in his patrol car, and because the Waldheim boys have something of a reputation and we're technically outside Hurley's jurisdiction, we have also notified the county sheriff and deputies are on standby should we need them.

The Waldheim farm has been family run for four generations. Ruth's husband inherited the farm from his father at the tender age of twenty after a tragic combine accident, and running it kept him busy and single well into his forties. He met Ruth, who was also in her forties and willing to take on the role of farm wife. Everyone thought they were too old to have kids, but the couple proved otherwise when Ruth spit out three boys in as many years.

As we pull up and park alongside the old farmhouse, the Waldheim boys come out of the barn to see who has arrived. All three of them are huge men standing six and a half feet tall and weighing well over three hundred pounds. They have always been huge. Even in grade school, they towered above the rest of the kids, including me. If the oldest boy, Jordy, had made it to high school, he might've saved me from being the tallest person in my class my freshman, sophomore, and junior years. But old man Waldheim died when Jordy was in the sixth grade for the third time, and when that happened, Ruth pulled all three of them out of school so they could help with the farm. Supposedly she homeschooled the boys, but I've met and interacted with them enough times to know that if Sorenson is ever invaded by brain-eating zombies, the Waldheim boys will be safe.

At first glance, one might assume the boys are triplets, but upon closer inspection you begin to notice subtle differences. This triplet effect is enhanced by the fact that they are all wearing the same clothes: denim overalls with long-sleeved, plaid flannel shirts, and knee-high, "muck-rucking" rubber boots. Their heads are bare; the only things protecting them from the rain are dark tonsorial rings, earmuffs, and a rather pronounced brow ridge. They make up for the lack of hair on their heads with thick winter beards that will likely require weed whackers and hedge trimmers when it comes time to trim them, assuming that's ever done.

"Can I help you?" one of the brothers asks as we approach. I'm pretty sure it's Jordy, but I haven't seen them in a few years so I'm not certain.

Hurley makes the introductions and then asks the boys for their names. I discover I'm right in thinking the one who spoke is Jordy. Jerome and Jethro flank him on either side, and all three of them are staring at me in a way that makes me squirm. I suspect they are undressing me with their eyes, but I can't tell if it's because they want to have sex with me, or if it's because they want to skin me alive, tan my hide, and boil up the rest for dinner.

Junior has his hand hovering close to his gun, but if Hurley is at all intimidated, he doesn't show it. "We're here to talk to you about the death of Bernard Chase."

Jordy arches his brow. "That creep is dead?"

"He is," Hurley says. "Murdered, in fact. Know anything about it?"

"No," Jerome says with a snort. "But I'd like to buy a beer for whoever did it."

"Why is that?" Hurley asks.

"Because that asshole was molesting our mother," Jethro says with a sneer.

"What proof do you have of that?" Hurley asks.

"Momma said so," Jethro yells. "What more proof do you need?"

I step up, trying to make eye contact with Jordy since he seems to be the one in charge. "I don't mean any disrespect, Jordy," I say, using my best calming nurse voice, "but we all know that your mama is pretty confused these days. What happened to her when she was younger was a terrible, terrible thing, but then she found your daddy and everything was good. Now that her mind is starting to go, she's living in the past. I remember when you brought her into the ER seven, eight years ago. Even then, she was pretty confused, and I've heard that Bernard Chase looked like the guy who attacked your momma when she was younger. Is that true?"

"It is," Jordy says. "But that doesn't mean he didn't do what she said."

"If you truly believe Bernard Chase molested your mother, why haven't you filed a police complaint about it?" Hurley asks.

All three boys narrow their eyes at Hurley, their feet shuffling nervously, their fists opening and closing, opening and closing.

"Yeah, right," Jethro says. "Like that would do any good. All you snobby, smarty-pants, rich people hang together and protect the perverts."

"I need to know where the three of you were yesterday morning between the hours of nine and noon," Hurley says, clearly growing impatient.

The brothers look at one another and then Jordy smiles. "Seems we got us an alley-by. We drove up to Green Bay yesterday to buy seed. Left here around seven-thirty in the morning and didn't get back until after five last night."

Hurley looks quite bummed at this news, particularly after he asks for addresses and the brothers provide them without hesitation, along with the names of people who saw them there. After jotting down all this information, Hurley asks the brothers when they were last at the Twilight Home.

"We take Momma breakfast from McDonald's every Monday, Wednesday, and Friday morning," Jordy says. "So, the last time we were up there was Friday morning. We usually stay . . . what . . . a couple hours?" He looks over at his brothers for affirmation and both nod.

As Hurley finishes writing down all the details the brothers have provided, he sighs and sticks his notebook back in his pocket. "I'll check out what you said. If what you say is true, then we won't be back. But if it's not . . ."

"Man, you cops never quit, do you?" Jerome says. "You just love to harass people."

Jordy says, "Let it go, Jerome."

"He's right, Jordy," Jethro says. "First that asshole cop from yesterday, and now these yahoos. I'm tired of being treated like we don't matter."

"What cop from yesterday?" I ask.

"That deer was gonna die, anyway," Jethro says. "They had no right to take my gun away."

"What deer?" I say.

"What gun?" Hurley says at the same time.

Junior steps up, his hand poised over his gun. "Everybody settle down. We're not here to harass you."

"The hell you ain't." Jethro spits on the ground and then spins on his heel and heads for the barn. I watch him disappear inside it, wondering if he's in there to sulk or to dig out the rifle they probably have stashed in there somewhere.

"Jerome! Go look after your brother!" Jordy's loud command to the remaining brother makes it clear who is in charge and that he will brook no objections.

Jerome shoots us a dirty look and then follows his brother's footsteps into the barn.

"I apologize for my brothers," Jordy says. "They tend to get worked up pretty easily, although they get picked on enough that it's justified."

"What's the story with the cop and the gun Jethro was talking about?" Hurley asks.

"We had what the sheriff called a little incident yesterday," Jordy says. "We was almost to Green Bay when some guy in front of us hit a deer. He didn't die but he was pretty messed up, so we stopped and Jethro got out of the truck and shot him to put him out of his misery."

"I hope you mean the deer," I say, swallowing hard.

"Of course I mean the deer," Jordy says. "You think I'd shoot some guy for no reason?"

I kind of do, but I don't say so.

"You can't just shoot a deer like that," Hurley says.

"Yeah, well we know that *now,*" Jordy says, his eyes big. "But we didn't know it yesterday. Farming is hard work. We don't make a lot of money and that there deer was enough food to feed the three of us for a good long while so we decided to load the carcass in the truck."

"You can't just take the carcass like that," Hurley says.

"Yeah, we know that, too, *now,*" Jordy says, clearly

frustrated. "At the time, it seemed like a smart thing to do, you know? All that good meat . . . why just leave it to rot on the side of the road? But then the guy who hit the thing comes backing up along the shoulder and gets out of his truck and says the deer is his. We said it was ours because we were the ones what actually killed it, you know? But this guy didn't see it that way and afore you know it, we was all arguing pretty loud and Jethro started waving his gun around. He wouldn't a shot the guy. He was just trying to put the fear of God in him, you know? But I guess someone driving by called the cops and the next thing you know some sheriff shows up and wants to take away our deer and Jethro's gun."

"I can see where that might not have gone well," I say.

"You can say that," Jordy scoffs. "I thought we was going to have to get Jethro out of jail, but after I got him calmed down, the sheriff was willing to let us go with a warning."

"What time of day was this?" Hurley asks.

"I think it was right around nine o'clock in the morning," Jordy says. "Maybe ten?"

"Did the sheriff let you take the deer?" I ask.

"Um, no," Jordy says, his eyes shifting nervously.

Hurley shoots me a funny look, one I can't quite interpret. Then he says, "Let me guess. The sheriff told you to leave the carcass on the side of the road so it could be tagged and picked up later. Then he made you leave. And I'm guessing you came back sometime later, saw that deer was still lying on the side of the road, and figured no one would be the wiser if you took it."

"You can't prove that," Jordy snaps. "That meat in our freezer could have come from anywhere."

"Whatever," Hurley says. Then he turns to me. "Come on, let's go."

Junior gets back into his squad car, turns around, and heads down the driveway. Hurley and I get into his car and do the same.

"Well, that was entertaining, but a total bust," Hurley says. "If what Jordy just told us is true, they couldn't have been anywhere near the Twilight Home when Bernard was killed. And it will be easy enough to verify their story with the sheriff's department because the call should be on record."

"So what's next?" I ask.

"Vonda Lincoln and Regan Simmons's husband. If they don't look good for this, we're stuck going through all those files back at the station." Hurley takes out his cell phone and makes a call. I can hear the distant ring of the other phone as he holds his own up to his ear, but that's all I hear. There is no answer, no voice mail, no nothing. After a minute, he disconnects the call, tosses the phone on the seat between us, and swears under his breath.

"Let's go to the Simmons place next. I don't know how long it will take to search Chase's house so I want to save it for last." He picks up his cell phone again and punches in another number. "Junior," he says after one ring, "what did you find when you ran Mitchell Simmons?"

He listens for a minute, and I struggle to overhear what Junior is telling him, but I can only make out a few words. Finally Hurley says, "Interesting," then disconnects the call.

"What?" I ask.

"Maybe we're finally on to something. It turns out that Regan Simmons's husband has a prior battery offense and a restraining order. His victim's name was Ron Hildebrand. Apparently this isn't Regan's first affair and Mr. Simmons is a very jealous man. Want to guess the name of Regan's last paramour?"

"Ron Hildebrand?" I guess.

"Bingo!"

Chapter 27

The Simmons home is in a newer development on the east side of town. Hurley's phone rings as we pull up and park and he grabs it eagerly. I suspect he thinks it might be Kate, but it's only Junior Feller calling to let us know the sheriff's department has verified the "incident" and, subsequently, the alibi of the Waldheim boys.

As we sit in the car listening to Junior's update, the Simmons's two-car garage door opens and a Mazda SUV backs out into the street. The car zips by us and I see Regan Simmons behind the wheel. She shoots us a dirty look as she passes, which comes as no surprise to me since she must know that we are about to reveal things to her husband that she would rather keep hidden. She's in a tough position with plenty of contentious days ahead given that she has a murdered lover on one hand and a husband who's about to find out he's been cuckolded on the other. Given her husband's history regarding her last affair, I'm not surprised that Regan is making a run for it.

When Hurley disconnects his call, we get out of the car and head for the front door of the Simmons house. Mitchell Simmons answers, and I'm surprised to see that he is a tall, handsome, blond-haired, blue-eyed man with a deep, sexy voice. Maybe I'm just shallow, but when I look at someone like Mitchell Simmons and compare him to Bernard Chase, I can't help but wonder what made Regan's eye ever wander in the first place. Then again, looks certainly aren't everything. Maybe Mitchell Simmons is a wife beater. Or maybe he's terrible in the sack. Or maybe he's a psychotic nut job. Was his one violent episode an anomaly triggered by jealousy? Or is he a cleverly disguised violent psychotic all the time?

If it's the latter, he hides it well. He is polite and cordial when he answers the door, and even though he seems surprised to see us and puzzled as to why we are here, he doesn't hesitate to invite us inside. What we can see of the house is neat and clean, and the living room is furnished with an eclectic combination of traditional and transitional mismatched pieces that go together surprisingly well. Mitchell invites us to sit on the couch, which is plush and covered with a soft, textured, plum-colored fabric. As I sink into it, I take in the warm, café au lait color of the walls and the dark stained wood of the floors, both providing a pleasing contrast to the wide, white trim. There is a funky coffee table that appears to be some sort of reclaimed factory warehouse cart complete with large, metal wheels and worn wooden planks. Across from the couch are two chairs: one in sage green, the other in chocolate brown leather, both of them wide, cushy-looking, and inviting. At the end of the room to the sides of the chairs and couch is a large fireplace trimmed in the same wide, white wood as the rest of the room and topped with a large, flat-screen TV. I get the sense that each piece of furniture in the room was chosen for its individual attributes rather than because it would fit into some coordinated display. The room should look like a hodgepodge mess, but it doesn't, thanks in part to a Persian area rug that nicely ties in the plum, sage, and brown colors and feels like heaven beneath my feet. I can't help but wonder how much of the room is Regan and how much of it is Mitchell. I get a sense that it's a mix of both, that the eclectic nature of the room is representative of their mutual respect for one another's desires and tastes. It's too bad Regan's desires went beyond the furnishings and the marital bed. I like this room, and I think that under different circumstances, I might have liked the Simmonses as well.

Hurley takes the lead with Mitchell, who has settled onto the leather chair across from us. "Mr. Simmons, I'm sure you're aware of the death of Bernard Chase at the nursing home where your wife works?"

"Yes, Regan mentioned something about him collapsing. It's sad when people so young develop serious health problems."

"What did she tell you he died from?" I ask.

"She didn't know for sure, but she said it was probably a heart attack. It really shook her up." He looks at me suspiciously. "Why are you talking to me about this?"

"How's your marriage?" Hurley asks, deftly ignoring Mitchell's own question. "Are you and Regan getting along okay?"

Mitchell frowns. "I imagine we're like any other couple. We have our ups and downs, but overall our relationship is a solid one. Why do you care?"

His tone of voice has changed; Mr. Nice Guy seems to have left the building. At this point, I'm pretty sure Mitchell has no idea his wife has been having an affair. I'm curious to see how he's going to react to the news, whether it will be with anger or despair.

"The two of you have no children?" I ask.

Mitchell shakes his head. "Regan says she isn't ready yet."

"Are you?" I ask.

"Am I what? Ready to have children?"

I nod.

He shrugs. "I've always wanted children, but we've got time yet, and obviously Regan and I need to be on the same page with that regard."

"Did you know Bernard Chase?" Hurley asks.

"I met him a time or two," Mitchell says. "Once at a Christmas party, once at an employee picnic, and I've seen him around town on occasion. I know who he is, but we're not what I would call friends. More like acquaintances."

"It seems your wife knew him very well," I say.

Mitchell smiles, looking a little baffled by the statement. "Of course she did. He was her boss."

"He was more than that," Hurley says.

"What do you mean? What are you implying?"

Up until now, Hurley and me taking turns with the questions and comments has forced Mitchell's focus to shift slowly back and forth between us. It's a technique that has evolved between us naturally over time as we've worked together. It turns out it's an effective tool, as it keeps people a little on edge, a little unsettled. It appears to have worked on Mitchell, who is more than a little unsettled. Instead of a baffled expression and a slow shift of his attention, he looks panicked and his gaze is bouncing rapidly between the two of us, unsure just who he should settle on. Hurley gives me a subtle nod, and I deliver the coup de grace.

"Your wife was having an affair with Bernard Chase."

Mitchell practically explodes with nervous laughter. "That's utterly ridiculous!" he scoffs. "Regan wouldn't do that to me."

In my gentlest, kindest voice I say, "You truly didn't know, did you?"

"I don't know what you're talking about. There's nothing to know."

"Think about it," Hurley says. "I'm guessing Regan has had a lot of reasons to be gone from the house lately. Based on what we've learned, I'm also guessing she was frequently late getting home from work, or had some explanation for why she needed to go in early."

Mitchell opens his mouth to object yet again, but something in what Hurley has said finally drives the truth home. It's painful to watch the reality hit him, and when it does, it's apparent. His entire body sags with the weight of this newfound knowledge. I imagine the self-doubt, self-recriminations, and anger will come later. They always do. I feel a little sorry for Mitchell, given that I've been in his position myself, and it appears that this is the second time for him. His marriage may have survived the first betrayal, but I seriously doubt it will survive this one. Part of me wants to take him off to one side and have a private chat with him, to prepare him for what's to come, to let him know the despair doesn't last forever. But I don't. I doubt it would help, anyway. I think this type of pain is something people have to experience and learn to deal with on their own. It's an agonizing but necessary part of the healing process.

I feel certain that Mr. Simmons had no idea of his wife's affair prior to our arrival and as such, he is an unlikely candidate for Bernie's murderer. I suspect Hurley feels the same way, but we still need to take care of the basics.

"Mr. Simmons, can you tell me where you were between the hours of nine and noon yesterday morning?" Hurley asks.

Mitchell stares at him and blinks hard several times, as if he's seeing him for the first time and can't quite believe his eyes. "I was here at home," he says finally. "I had work I brought home with me and I didn't leave the house all day. It's a very busy time of year for me."

"What is it you do?" I ask.

"I'm a CPA. And it's tax season."

"Was your wife here at home with you?" Hurley asks.

Mitchell stares at the floor, still wearing his stunned expression of disbelief. "Part of the time," he says with a frown. "She said she had some errands to run and she left around nine-thirty. I think it was around noon or so when she came back. She brought me lunch." He looks at me when he says this, his tone suggesting that his wife wouldn't have done such a sweet, thoughtful thing if she was sleeping around on him. Would she?

"I think she was home after that until she left for work at a little after two-thirty."

"You think she was?" Hurley says.

"I never came out of my office, but I heard the TV

going, so I assumed she was here. She told me she had to leave a little early for work because she still had some errands to—" The reality hits him and he squeezes his eyes closed.

"Have you ever been to Bernard Chase's office?" Hurley asks.

"His office?" Mitchell scrunches up his face with the effort of his thinking. "No, I don't think so."

"So we shouldn't expect to find your fingerprints or DNA anywhere in that office?"

He shakes his head. "Nope, I've been to the nursing home before, but I'm pretty sure I've never been in any office there."

Hurley gets up and I follow suit. I think we are both satisfied that Mitchell Simmons had nothing to do with Bernard Chase's death. And now that we have ruined Mitchell's life—however temporarily—we thank him for his time and depart, knowing we are leaving a trail of emotional devastation in our wake.

It's not a pleasant feeling.

Outside in the car, Hurley says, "Damn, I had high hopes for that one, but I don't think he had any idea his wife was stepping out on him again."

"Neither do I. In fact I'd bet money on it." I wince as soon as the words are out of my mouth. Had I always used so many betting clichés, or were they new to my vocabulary now that I was a regular at the casino?

Hurley's phone rings and he answers it. I can hear the voice on the other end well enough to know it's not Kate. But lest I have any doubt, the sagging disappointment in Hurley's face would clue me in. Not that I think Kate will be calling if what her letter said holds true. But maybe she'll have second thoughts.

I hear Hurley say, "No, just leave her there for now. But tell her not to leave town. And have the officers who helped you meet me at the Chase house." He sighs and disconnects the call. "That was Bob Richmond. The search of Jeanette's apartment didn't turn up anything more than a two-year-old prescription for some codeine that she had left over from a dental procedure. No drugs, no potential poisons, no nothing."

"So what are we left with?"

"Not much," Hurley says. "Let's hope my initial impression of Vonda was wrong and we can find something significant at her house, like a signed confession letter." He glances at his watch. "When do you think Emily will be back?"

"I don't know, but the last time my sister took the kids to The Dells, they didn't get home until after eleven that night. That wasn't a school night, though."

"Neither is tonight," Hurley says. "When I dropped Em off, Desi told me the kids don't have school tomorrow because of some teacher workshop day."

"Well in that case, I wouldn't expect them anytime soon."

"Okay then, what do you say we take on the Green Fiend?"

"Let me at her," I say with a smile.

Chapter 28

Hurley makes a phone call to arrange for some help with our search. When we arrive at Vonda Lincoln's house for the second time, it takes her so long to answer the door that we start to think she isn't home. Then, when she finally does answer, it makes me suspicious. Was she hiding something?

Her demeanor when she greets us is anything but friendly. "What is it now, Detective?" she asks in a tired, put-upon voice.

"I have that search warrant I promised you," Hurley says, handing her the paperwork. He pushes past her and waves for me and the other officers to follow.

"Hold on, hold on!" Vonda yells, running to put herself in front of Hurley. "You can't just come barging in here like this. I'm going to call our lawyer."

"I can come barging in here like this," Hurley says. "That paper you're holding says so."

Vonda's objections make me think of something, so I walk over and take her by the arm, pulling her off to one side as the officers make their way into the living room. As soon as I hear Hurley start to give them instructions, I turn to Vonda and say in a very concerned and serious voice, "You absolutely should call a lawyer. I hope you know someone good."

Vonda looks momentarily confused, but she takes to my concerned, helpful tone immediately. "We have a lawyer we use for legal stuff like contracts and business deals, but Malcolm wouldn't deal with something like this, would he?"

"Oh, I'm sure he would," I say, though I don't think it's true.

I make a mental note of the name and tell her, "I think he probably would handle something like this, but what are the odds you can get ahold of him at this time on a Sunday?"

"I have his home number!" Vonda says excitedly.

I had hoped as much, given that Bernard and Vonda were quite well off financially. The rich tend to get certain privileges the rest of us don't, like their lawyer's home phone number.

"We should go and call him right away," I say, and when Vonda turns and heads deeper into the house, I follow.

The house is a sprawling ranch with a central section that contains the kitchen, dining, and living areas, and two wings that branch off at angles on either side. She leads me into the right wing of the house and straight ahead I can see an open door and what appears to be a sitting area that I'm guessing is part of her bedroom. We stop at two open doors, one of which leads to what appears to be a guest room, complete with its own bathroom. The other is a much smaller room that is being used as a home office. While it may not be as big as the bedroom, it's large enough to house a massive and scarred old oak desk that I'm sure Vonda has recycled, two big bookcases, some ancient-looking metal cabinets replete with dents and dings, and a mini forest of green plants that includes two rubber trees and a small lemon tree that is actually bearing fruit.

It's an ugly mess of used and recycled stuff and yet I find I'm a little envious given that my work space at the medical examiner's office is the library, which is hardly private and doesn't even have a desk. Given Vonda's propensity for recycling and reusing items, I'm curious to see if there is a home office on the other side of the house that Bernie uses, and if so, what it looks like given his taste for the somewhat ostentatious.

Vonda walks over behind her desk, opens a drawer, takes out a small address book, and flips through the pages until she finds what she wants. She picks up a phone on the desk and punches in a number. I walk over as casually as I can and glance down at the address book to see the name and the number of the lawyer she's calling. My hope is that her lawyer is also Bernie's lawyer, and that this person will lead us to the documents we seek, including Bernie's will if he has one, and the partnership agreement for the Twilight Home. Maybe we can find out the identity of the silent secret partner in the business.

I try to commit what I see in the book to memory, but there are two phone numbers and I feel like I should get them both since I don't know which one is the home, and likely unlisted, number. Not wanting to trust my memory, I take out my cell phone and proceed to punch the numbers into it, saving each one as a contact under Malcolm, the lawyer's first name. I can't quite make out the last name, but I can see that Vonda is in the W section of her address book. She seems oblivious to what I'm doing. Malcolm has apparently answered the phone and she is ranting to him about Hurley's activities and the search warrant. But she does reach down and casually close the book just as I'm punching in the last number. I'm bummed that I don't have the lawyer's full last name, but figure I have enough information to make a contact. I back out of the office and head for the main portion of the house, where I find Hurley and the other officers calmly searching through the kitchen cabinets.

I pull Hurley off to one side and tell him about my conversation with Vonda, and the information I just obtained. I bring up the numbers in my phone and he writes them down in his little notebook along with the first name of the lawyer.

"Good job, Winston," he says. "You do have a knack for digging up dirt."

I smile, but a part of me winces inside as I recall the dirt I dug up from next to his bed.

We continue our search until Vonda reappears from her office. She looks very unhappy. Her arms are folded tightly across her chest, her lips thinly set, and her jaw muscles twitching irritably. But she says nothing, leading us to believe that her lawyer told her there was little she could do about the search warrant except stay out of our way.

Over the next two and a half hours, we painstakingly search through the half of the house that belonged to Bernie, the common shared area, and then Vonda's wing, including all the bathrooms, her office, her massive bedroom, and a small studio that extends off the southeast corner of her bedroom. Several of her pieces are on display in the studio, propped on easels positioned close to the windows. I have to walk around the easels to see them, and at first glance I take them to be abstract acrylic paintings filled with violent, spiked splashes of blood red, bile green, and cyanotic blue. Up close, it all appears chaotic and random, and yet I sense an underlying order. I back up to give myself a different perspective, and when I do I see it. Each of the pictures takes on the shape of a human form: one reclining, one standing and reaching as if for a book on a high shelf, and another sitting pensively as if deep in thought. They are quite clever and engaging, and it's easy for me to see how Vonda has achieved such success with her works.

While Bernie Chase's house is a fascinating example of how two completely different people and lifestyles can merge into one, it is useless in providing us with any clues or help in understanding exactly how Bernie died and who might've killed him. Hurley had hoped to find paperwork somewhere that would reveal the will and the partnership contract, but that didn't turn up, either.

Junior Feller calls during our search and informs Hurley that he has verified Vonda's alibi at the grocery store on Saturday morning, but she left there somewhere between nine-thirty and ten, giving her plenty of time to have done in her husband. Without any other evidence, we have nothing on her. At the moment, we have nothing on anybody, and I can tell Hurley is frustrated.

It's almost seven o'clock by the time we're done and Hurley and I are hungry. Since we haven't heard from Desi and the kids yet, I suggest we grab a bite to eat somewhere and go over our findings so far, though I have another agenda in mind. After a bit of discussion, we decide to eat at Pesto Change-o, our favorite combination restaurant and magic show in town.

No sooner have we settled in at our table when my phone rings. It's Bob Richmond calling. "Hey, Mattie, I was wondering if you're still going to meet me here at the gym tonight?"

"Geez, Bob, I'm sorry. I forgot and anyway, I can't. Hurley and I are just now sitting down to eat and it's been a very long day. Maybe tomorrow?"

"No problem. Want to go first thing in the morning?"

"I can barely go to the bathroom first thing in the morning, much less a gym," I tell him, making Hurley chuckle. "Evening is a better time for me."

"Evening it is then. How many calories does Gunther have you burning each session?"

"I don't know. He didn't say anything about calories, just about building muscle."

"I'm up to a thousand calories burned each session now. It's amazing how much better I feel."

"That's great."

"How's the case going? Have you and Hurley made any progress?"

"So far all we have are a lot of potential suspects and dead ends."

"I'm sure it will come together at some point. Some cases just take longer than others. Tell Hurley to let me know if there's anything else he needs me to do. I'll see you tomorrow evening, if not sooner."

We say our good-byes and I pass his message along to Hurley. Then we place our orders: a totally forbidden big-assed plate of alfredo pasta for me, and a small pizza for Hurley. While I enjoy a few minutes of feeling virtuous while we eat our salads, I know that after the stuffed mushroom appetizer, the garlic bread, and the main meal, Gunther will be lecturing me sternly tomorrow. And that's assuming that I don't go for dessert. At the moment, everything tastes and smells much too good for me to care.

I wait until our entrees are nearly finished and the proprietor, Giorgio, has been to our table to perform some magic tricks before I broach the subject of Kate's letter.

"Hurley, I have something to tell you and it isn't going to be easy. I want you to understand that I thought long and hard about how and when to do this. I even thought about not doing it, but I know that would be wrong and I've already done something wrong enough that I don't want to make it worse."

He chews on a bite of pizza and smiles quizzically at me. "What have you done now, Winston?"

"This morning after our little rendezvous in your bedroom, it took me a while to find my bra. I remembered you tossing it to one side and seeing it briefly hit your bedside table. I eventually found it on the floor between the table and the bed, and with it I also found this." I take the folded letter from my pocket and set it on the table, sliding it toward him, but I leave my hand on top of it so I can explain myself further. "It's a letter from Kate."

Hurley puts down the slice of pizza he is holding and swallows hard, his expression curious and confused.

"It was inside an unsealed envelope with your name on it and even though I knew I shouldn't, I took the letter out, intending to read it. I thought it was a love letter of some sort and I was feeling jealous and insecure. Just as I was about to unfold it and read it, you startled me when you came up the stairs and hollered to me to come down for breakfast. I crumpled the note in an effort to hide it, feeling guilty that I'd even removed it from the envelope. I didn't feel like I could just put it back where I found it because it had obviously been tampered with. So I stuck it in my pocket, thinking I would read it later. I finally got around to doing that this morning and maybe I should've shown it to you then, but I didn't want to distract you from the case and I don't think the timing will make a significant difference."

Hurley leans forward, his expression serious. I reach across the table and lay my other hand over one of his arms in an affectionate gesture before launching into the speech I've been rehearsing inside my head all day long.

"Kate isn't calling you or answering her cell because she never intended to. The story she told you about her brother was a lie. She made the whole thing up. He's dead, and she's dying, Hurley. She has acute lymphoblastic leukemia, a very bad and advanced type, and the doctors have given her only a few months to live. That's why she came here with Emily when she did. She has no family left to take care of Emily, so she brought her here to make sure you could do it. Once she felt certain you two would be okay, she left. She's checking into a hospice program and giving them strict instructions not to tell anyone she's there. She doesn't want Emily to watch her die."

In the minute or two that it has taken me to say all of this, I've watched a bevy of emotions race across Hurley's face: disbelief, suspicion, anger, pain, and acceptance. At one point, he looks as if he thinks I'm trying to punk him. Then he simply looks dumbfounded. I take one hand off the note, take the other hand off his arm, and sit back. He looks at me, his face a mosaic of emotion, and then his eyes settle on the note. After a few seconds, he picks it up and starts to read.

I watch the emotions play over his face as he reads through the letter. It's relatively straightforward and unemotional, yet the overall message is such a devastating one that it can't help but have a hard-hitting effect.

When he's done reading, Hurley looks at me and says, "How could I have not seen this?"

"I've asked myself that same question," I admitted. "The signs were there, I saw it, but I didn't put it all together. As a nurse, I should have. But I was too wrapped up in my own emotions and my own life to see what was right in front of my face."

They say hindsight is twenty-twenty, and in this case that certainly is true. Now that I know the truth, when I look back at my thoughts about Kate's pale, mousy appearance, I realize that I should've known something was wrong. She had dark circles under her eyes, her energy level seemed low, and her appetite was off.

"Emily knows nothing about this yet?" Hurley says.

I'm not sure if he's making a statement or asking me a question. "She knows her mother was sick. She told me her mother's illness was the reason she lost her job and her medical insurance. The medical bills were the reason they lost their home. But when I asked Emily if her mother was okay now, she said she thought she was because she wasn't seeing any doctors anymore."

"Damn," Hurley mutters. He flicks a finger at the letter. "Kate says in here that she sent Emily a letter of her own. I don't know when she mailed it, but it could arrive as soon as tomorrow. I'm going to have to tell her either tonight or tomorrow. And then I'm going to try to find Kate."

"She made it pretty clear in her letter that she doesn't want to be found," I say.

"I don't give a damn what she wants," Hurley says, raking a hand through his hair. "I can't believe she did this. It's not fair to Emily, it's not fair to me, it's not fair to anybody. The last thing I need right now is full-time responsibility for a kid. If I'd wanted to be a father, I would've had kids of my own." He drops the letter on the table as if it just burned his fingers. He leans back in his chair, wipes both hands down the side of his face, and sighs heavily. "This is so typical of Kate," he says, clearly ticked. "She's always been so self-centered, thinking only of herself."

"I think you're being a little harsh on her," I say. "She's dying, Hurley. Her primary concern seems to be for Emily, not for herself. Whatever relationship the two of them have built over the years is what she seems determined to have Emily remember her by, rather than some deathbed scenario."

Hurley lunges forward so fast it makes me lurch back. He stabs a finger on the letter lying on the table. "Where did you say you found this?"

"It was underneath my bra on the floor between your bedside table and the bed. I'm pretty sure Kate must've left it on your bedside table, thinking you'd see it when you got home last night and went to bed."

"Except I never went to bed. I slept on the couch all night."

"When you and I were in the bedroom earlier

today, you tossed my bra over your shoulder and it hit the table. It must have also hit the letter and they fell to the floor."

"It's a pretty crappy way to handle this," Hurley says, his anger clearly not abating. "Why couldn't she have just sat down and talked to me face-to-face? Why couldn't she have sat down with Emily and done the same thing?" He grabs the letter up in his hand, scrunching it beneath his fingers and shaking it. "This is how she says good-bye? I hope to hell she does a better job in her letter to Emily." He opens his hand and lets the letter drop back to the table. "Dammit!"

Clearly there will be no dessert tonight, at least not here. Hurley pays the check for our meal, stuffs the letter in his pocket, and drives me back to the police station.

"Let's call it a night," he says as he parks. "I need to do some paperwork and I think I'll just stay here until I hear from Desi and can pick up Emily."

"Do you want me to help you talk to Emily about her mother?"

Hurley thinks about this for a moment and then says, "No, I think it will be easier for her coming from me alone. Since I've basically been hoodwinked and duped into fatherhood, I might as well figure out how to do it. I'll probably screw it up, but at least Emily is old enough that most of her psyche is already formed. If she turns out to be a mess, I can always blame it on Kate."

"I'm sure you'll do fine with her."

"Thanks for the vote of confidence, but I just don't think I'm cut out to be a father, Winston. Between the crazy hours I keep with my job and the number of years I've been on my own, I don't have the time or the patience to be a father. Or the desire for that matter."

"You said Emily was a great kid."

"She is. She's smart, funny, polite, down-to-earth, all the things you want to see in a teenager . . . someone else's teenager."

He looks genuinely upset and it tears me up to see the hurt and worry on his face. I lean over and give him a kiss on the cheek. "I have faith in you, Steven Hurley. I know you can do this."

He turns and gives me a wan smile. "I guess I'll have to. The kid doesn't have anyone else so I don't really have a choice, do I?"

"Let me know if I can help in any way."

"I will."

"Do you have anything planned for tomorrow work-wise? Or should I just plan on spending the day in the office?"

"Our case is going nowhere so you might as well hang in the office until we hear something back from Madison and have a better idea of exactly what poison was used on Chase. I'm probably going to take a personal day tomorrow since I'll have to tell Emily about her mother and I don't know how she's going to take it."

"Call me after you've told her and let me know how it goes. I bonded with Emily a little and I might be able to help. If I can't, I bet Hoover can."

"Are you suggesting a little pet therapy?"

"It can't hurt."

He leans over and gives me a kiss on the cheek. "Thanks, Winston. I'll keep you posted."

We get out of his car and head our separate ways,

him into the police station, me to my hearse parked under the ME's office. Driving home, I'm struck by a terrible sadness and an odd sense of loneliness. When I get home, I'm glad Hoover is there to greet me because I can use a little pet therapy of my own.

Chapter 29

Sunday, March 2 (still)
Dear Diary,

What a day this has been, filled with confusing thoughts, events, and emotions. Our current murder case is nothing but one frustration after another. We have tons of suspects with a variety of motives, but no hard evidence. We don't even know yet what killed the victim. Trying to solve this case is like trying to nail Jell-O to a tree.

My commitment to keeping my relationship with Hurley on a strictly platonic, business level has been a miserable failure. Well, not totally miserable. The man can make me feel better than anyone else ever has, but guilt and a renewed sense of determination always follow. He seems to think we can have a sexual relationship and keep it under wraps so no one else knows. I have my doubts. The man makes me glow on the inside and I imagine that someone, sooner or later, will see that glow on the outside. It will probably be Izzy or Dom, and then I'll need to have an explanation for it. I need a lover double, like the actors and actresses who have body doubles. In my case, it needs to be someone who will pretend to be my lover so that I can have a plausible excuse for my after sex glow. I'll have to think about who I know that might fit the bill. It will have to be someone believable, someone people can imagine me sleeping with, and someone who won't be hurt by the rumors.

Speaking of rumors, there is one going around about a nasty gastric virus that's sickening lots of people in town. Some of the folks in the nursing home where we've been investigating have had it and I fear I'm coming down with it myself. I'm exhausted and my body is aching in odd places, plus I've been fighting nausea off and on all day long. If what I heard about this virus is true, I'll soon be converting to a religion that worships a porcelain god.

Speaking of gods, there is poor Hurley. I feel so bad for him and for Emily, whose mother is apparently dying of leukemia. Emily doesn't know this yet and Hurley just found out. That's because Emily's mother has decided to run off and die alone in some hospice somewhere. Part of me understands why she's doing this, but another part can't imagine how she can pass up those last precious days and hours with her daughter. It's hard for me to comprehend a mother who doesn't want to be with her children as often as possible.

I take that back. How foolish of me not to remember my own childhood. My mother is the antithesis of what a loving parent should be. It's not that she didn't try; she made an effort to do what she knew she was supposed to do. But her problems always came before ours. With her severe hypochondria and OCD, life was a series of threats and pressures, obstacles and setbacks that she was never quite able to overcome. When it came to caregiving and nurturing, our roles were reversed most of the time. Desi and I nurtured our mother more than she ever nurtured us. Thank goodness Desi and I had each other.

Still, I find it hard to understand how Kate can do what she has and I feel bad for Emily because I know how much it's going to hurt. I'm not sure how Hurley feels about Kate's condition, but he made it pretty clear how he feels about his sudden status as a single father. He feels trapped, coerced, forced into something he doesn't want to do and doesn't feel he is fit to do.

And speaking of fit, my muscles are still sore from my first session with Gunther, and Richmond is nagging me to return to the gym for a second round. Gunther told me there's a thin person inside me who is screaming to come out. I think I can probably shut her up with a pint of Ben & Jerry's, but I agreed to go to the gym tomorrow evening anyway after begging off for today. I have to confess there is a tiny part of me that almost wishes for a GI bug so I can cancel. Plus a little vomiting and diarrhea might accomplish the same thing weight-wise. Richmond says his trainer has him burning off a thousand calories during each workout session. Hell, the last time I burned a thousand calories at one time was when I set a frozen pizza on fire because I didn't clean the oven. I'm not sure this whole exercise thing is going to work out. Ha, ha. Work out. Get it? I crack myself up.

Chapter 30

Monday morning dawns warmer than the previous days and despite feeling exhausted, I wake up at six-thirty and can't go back to sleep. After making a cup of coffee, I throw on a robe and take Hoover outside. He is sniffing around, and on a whim I take him to the base of the window where the Peeping Tom was the other night. I point to the ground, then squat down and pat it, and he sniffs around eagerly and then looks at me, unsure what I want him to do. Next, I walk him around to the back of the house where the footprints can still be seen and repeat the same actions. He sniffs again and this time he starts tracking, nose to the ground. He heads around the house and back to the front window where we started.

"Good boy! Go find it!" I say.

He seems to understand and he starts tracking across the yard and into the woods, his nose to the ground. I follow him and we go all the way through the woods and come out on the other side. We end up at the base of the driveway of my old, burned-up house where he walks around in circles for a minute before he sits down, looks at me, and whines. Apparently, this is where the guy parked.

"Good boy!" I say, and he thumps his tail and jumps up on me. We head back to the house, Hoover trotting along with pride, and after rewarding him with a treat, I put in a call to Izzy.

"Good morning," I say. "Anything on your agenda for the day?"

"At the moment, my agenda is to eat the omelet Dom is fixing for me. Want some breakfast?"

"I'll be right over."

Five minutes later, I'm seated at the dining room table with Izzy, still in my robe. Dom is in the kitchen and the intoxicating smells of bacon, coffee, and onions fill the air.

"How did the rest of your day go yesterday?" Izzy asks me.

"It was interesting." I tell him about the note that Kate left for Hurley and his reaction to it, leaving out the part about me finding the note and how that happened. As we're discussing the implications of it all, Dom delivers his cooked-to-perfection cheese and onion omelets, rye toast, crisp bacon, and hash browns. I'm hungry and plowing through it, grateful my nausea seems to be gone. Hopefully, I nipped the virus in the bud, although that means I'll have to go to the gym tonight.

"Is today the day you're seeing Maggie again?" Izzy asks.

I nod. "This afternoon. You know, I have to say that the whole counseling thing wasn't as bad as I thought it would be."

"Good. Has it helped?"

"It has, I think."

"Glad to hear it. What's on your agenda for today? You're welcome to take some time off if you want to make up for all the hours you put in over the weekend."

"Arnie collected a lot of evidence yesterday so I thought I'd go in and help him process it. Hurley said he was probably going to take a personal day today to be with Emily, so after I get done with Arnie I think I'll go over to the police station and go through the files we have on all the interviews we did at Twilight. See if anything jumps out at me."

"Sounds reasonable, but don't hesitate to cut out early if you need to."

"Maybe I'll go in a little late this morning, say around ten?"

"That will work if nothing else comes in."

"My appointment with Maggie is at four, so I'll probably stay in the office or at the police station until then. After that, I told Bob Richmond I'd meet him at the gym."

"Two visits in less than a week? That's a record, isn't it?"

"It is," I say with a laugh.

When I'm done eating, I thank Dom and head back to the cottage and take a leisurely shower. I try to call Hurley, but it flips straight over to voice mail so I get dressed and head to the grocery store, leaving Hoover home.

I'm able to get my food without interruption and I even manage to get mostly healthy food, including some salad makings, lots of fresh fruits and veggies, and some whole grain cereals. When I get to the frozen foods section, my willpower weakens and I succumb to the lure of some Chunky Monkey and Cookie Dough ice creams.

After taking my groceries home and sampling the ice creams to make sure they are adequate, I head for the office. I find Arnie in his lab with a stack of bagged evidence samples next to him. "Can I help you out with any of this stuff?" I ask.

"Thanks, but I'm doing okay with it. All the fingerprint data has been uploaded to AFIS and I sent the DNA stuff off to Madison. Now I'm just going through the various samples we collected from the coffee station to split them out for testing and do a microscopic exam to see if there is anything obvious in any of them."

"If you change your mind, give me a call. I'm going to go over to the police station and wade through the interview notes from the other night."

"That sounds exciting—not. Have fun."

I head for the police station, a small part of me hoping that I'll find Hurley there. When I walk in the front, the dispatcher on duty is Stephanie.

"Hey, Mattie," she says.

"Hi, Steph. Are Detectives Hurley or Richmond here?"

She shakes her head. "Neither. Hurley took a personal day and I think Bob Richmond is on call. Larry Johnson is on duty. Do you need me to call him?"

"No, thanks. I want to look through the interview files on the Bernard Chase case that Hurley had yesterday. Do you know where they are?"

"Hurley's desk maybe? You're welcome to go in the back and look around." She buzzes me through and hands me a stack of papers she takes off the fax. "You can put these on Hurley's desk for me if you don't mind. They came in last night." Her phone rings then and as she takes the call I head back toward the break room.

There are four offices along the main hallway that I have to pass, one of which belongs to Chief Hanson. The other three are shared by the detectives and I know which one Hurley uses. When I pass Chief Hanson's office I see him sitting behind his desk.

"Hey, Chief. How are things?"

"Doing good. I hear you're on at the ME's office again. Welcome back."

"Thanks."

"You and Hurley make a good team."

"Yeah, we work well together." *We do other things well together, too.* "I'm here to look through the interview files Hurley had on this Bernie Chase case. Is it okay if I use Hurley's desk since he isn't coming in today?"

"Sure. Have at it."

"I have a question for you. Irene Keller says she talked to you some time back about how she and some others thought Bernie Chase was killing off patients at the home who were too expensive to care for."

"Yeah, she did, but if you ask me it was nothing but some bored, paranoid folks looking for something to make their lives more interesting."

"You looked into it?"

He shrugs. "Irene mentioned a couple recent deaths that she thought were suspicious and I looked into those, but I didn't find anything. One was a lady who had a massive stroke that left her bedbound and three weeks after she went to Twilight she died. I talked to her doctor and told him what sort of symptoms the staff at the home said the old lady had with sweating, low blood pressure, and a fast heart beat and he said it sounded like she either had a heart attack or something called neurological shock."

"Neurogenic shock."

"Whatever. Anyway, her doctor said she had very bad heart disease and he wasn't surprised by the death."

"But no one looked into it officially?"

"No, no real need."

"Who else did you look into?"

"A man who had been wasting away for a while and finally became bedbound. He died a few weeks later, but his doctor said it was a natural progression of things."

"There wasn't anything strange about his death?"

"He went the same way as the lady, sweaty, fast heart rate, dropping blood pressure. The doctor said those symptoms are classic for heart failure and that the guy's heart just finally gave out."

"Any others?"

"There might have been. I don't recall now. But I found no evidence of anything unusual and I did talk to the doctors of these patients."

"I see."

He narrows his eyes at me, trying, no doubt, to determine if I'm annoyed with him and the situation. "Do you feel like I missed something?"

"I don't know. Probably not," I say. "But I might take a second look at things just to be thorough."

"I'm sure you'll be wasting your time, but have at it if you want."

I leave him, sensing that I've worn out my welcome. The break room is surprisingly clean, the table crumbless, the countertops clear, the coffee pot cleaned and drying next to the sink. I start a pot of coffee and then head for Hurley's office.

On the corner of his desk is the pile of folders. I settle into his chair and Hurley's smell wafts up from it. And just like that I'm hit by a wave of nausea.

I sit there for a few seconds convincing myself that it's an anomaly, and eventually my stomach settles down.

I glance at the papers Steph gave me from the fax machine and see that they're financial statements for the Twilight Home. Since I doubt I'll be able to understand them, I set them aside and grab the first file off the pile.

Bob Richmond's notes are well organized, precise, and surprisingly easy to read. He has nice penmanship. He also has a flair for the narrative and reading some of the notes is like reading a short story. It also reveals what a Peyton Place the Twilight Home is. He has dug up scandals and rumors of unrequited love, late-night trysts, contraband food, and the whole pot thing I heard about from Randolph. But based on Richmond's notes, Randolph wasn't totally honest with me. Fake pot isn't the only thing he's dealing according to one patient. Randolph also had a secret stash of Cialis and Viagra that he got from his doctor and was selling to other residents. Since they didn't find the pills when they searched his room, he either had them on him somewhere, or he was out of them. I remember the pills we found in Bernie's safe and wonder if that's where he got his from. Maybe he found Randolph's stash and took them away from him and locked them up for safekeeping. Maybe they weren't Bernie's pills at all.

My cell phone rings and I grab it, thinking it's Hurley. But it's Arnie.

"I found something weird in the stuff we collected

from the coffee area in Bernie's office," he says excitedly.

"What?"

"Well, I figured if the coffee was the delivery system for the poison, then anything that went into the coffee was a candidate, too. So just for grins, I decided to look at the sugar substitute under the microscope. That fake sweetener has a very characteristic appearance, sort of a lacy look, and while I saw plenty of that, I also saw some other stuff. It looked like there was a mixture of two different things in there. Just to be sure, I got some of the same sugar substitute from Izzy's office and compared it with what came out of the box in Bernie's office. There's definitely something mixed in Bernie's that doesn't belong. I'm not sure what it is, but I'm isolating it and running some tests."

"Okay, let me know if you come up with anything."

As I disconnect the call, Stephanie walks in wearing her headset. "This just came over the fax," she says, tossing a sheet of paper on the desk and then leaving.

It's a list of patients who have died at Twilight in the past two years. There are twenty-two of them, nearly one for every month. It seems high given the number of beds in the facility, but I'll have to compare it to the national and regional rates. I set the sheet off to one side and see Hurley's little notebook, the one he always carries in his pocket, sitting by his desk phone. I pick it up and flip through the pages to the most recent notes and see he has a small to-do list. The last item on it is to call Vonda Lincoln's lawyer.

I grab my phone, pull up my list of contacts, and find the numbers for the lawyer that I put in last night when I was with Vonda. I strike pay dirt with the first number.

A secretary answers with, "Wentworth Law, may I help you?"

"Is Malcolm in?"

"Which one, Junior or Senior?"

Figures. I decide to take a gamble. "The one who serves Mr. Bernard Chase."

"That would be Malcolm Sr. May I ask who's calling?"

"My name is Mattie Winston. I'm a medicolegal investigator with the medical examiner's office in Sorenson and I'm investigating Mr. Chase's death."

"Malcolm Sr. isn't in now. Can I take a message?"

"Yes, please ask him to call me and tell him it's urgent." I give her my phone number and hang up.

Since I'm in wait mode, I go back to skimming through the interview notes. Forty minutes later, I reach the last page in the file. It's the drawing Emily did of the man who was peeking in my window at her the other night. I realize that with the new information we have about Kate and her real reason for leaving, odds are that man wasn't there to spy on Emily. That means he was there to spy on me. I study the picture, still nagged by the feeling that something about it is vaguely familiar. I take it up front to Stephanie and have her make me a copy of it along with the lists containing the names of the staff and patients at the Twilight Home. I stuff all the lists in my purse and after straightening up Hurley's desk, I head for the Twilight Home. Most of the names on the lists have been crossed off, but there are a few remaining and I figure it can't hurt to talk with them.

Chapter 31

When I arrive at the Twilight Home, Dorothy is once again ensconced at the sign-in desk. I wonder if she sits there often, or if she's here so much because her own office is off-limits.

"Good morning, Dorothy. How are things today?"

"They'd be better if I could get some work done. Any idea when they're going to release our offices back to us?"

"I'm not sure. That's up to the police, but I can try to find out for you. Is there something in particular you want from your office? Maybe I can arrange for permission to escort you back there and get it."

"I'm okay for today, but if we're going to be locked out much longer, I will need to get in there. What brings you back here today?" She taps a finger on the sign-in book and holds a pen out for me.

"There are a few more patients and employees we need to talk to."

"The lawyers said they wanted to be present for

any employee interviews, so if you want to speak to an employee, I'll have to call them. They're not here, but they said they'd be staying at the Sorenson Motel for a day or two."

"That's okay. I'll focus on the patients for now."

"How many of them do you need to speak to?"

"Not many. I think there were five or six left on the list. Plus I need to talk to Randolph Pettigrew again. Did you know about his little side business selling fake pot and erectile dysfunction medications to patients?"

Dorothy looks genuinely surprised.

"I'll take that as a no," I say.

"Fake pot?" she says.

"Yeah, it's some mix of oregano, tea, and mint. The patients he sells it to think it's the real stuff and they're rolling their own and smoking it out back."

"You're sure it's fake?"

"The cops said so. And to be honest, the patients seem to enjoy being a little naughty, so perhaps there's no harm done."

"Somehow I don't think the licensing inspectors will think so." Dorothy shakes her head. "Thanks for letting me know."

I head down the hall to the dayroom feeling a little guilty for busting Randolph. But while the fake pot is probably not a big problem, the pills could be dangerous to the patients if the people who take them don't know about the contraindications that might come into play with other meds they may be on. With this thought, something niggles at my brain, but before I can figure out what it is, I hear a whirring sound closing in behind me and someone hollers out, "Hey!"

I turn and see Gwen approaching in her scooter.

"Where's that gorgeous hunk of policeman you had with you before?"

Today Gwen is wearing brown dress slacks, a pale blue silk blouse, and a pair of navy blue pumps. Her hair is perfectly coiffed, her makeup is on, and there is a hungry, eager look in her eyes that makes me leery of answering her honestly. Something tells me she'd turn that scooter around and hunt Hurley down if she knew where he was.

"Detective Hurley isn't here today and I don't think he'll be here anytime soon."

"Oh, I didn't mean Detective Hurley," Gwen says. "He's a little too young for me, a bit out of my league. I was referring to that other detective, Bob Richmond."

I stare at her dumbstruck for a moment. The idea of Bob Richmond as a romantic interest had never entered my mind. I think about it and realize some women might consider him a decent catch. He's not bad looking for his age, and now that he's lost so much weight I can see where he might be appealing to some. The thought of fixing him up with Gwen makes me smile.

"I'm not sure if Detective Richmond will be here today, either," I tell her. "But I'm sure I'll be talking to him soon. I'll be happy to give him a message for you if you like."

"Why will you be talking to him?" Gwen says irritably "You don't have your eye on him, do you? I thought you had your claws in that Hurley fellow. Can't you leave one of them for me?"

"I have no romantic interest in Bob Richmond," I tell her. Then, remembering my job restrictions, I add, "I have no romantic interest in anyone at the moment." I can tell from the expression on Gwen's face that she smells bullshit, so before she has a chance to subject me to an inquisition, I take my leave. "I'd love to chat more, but I have something I need to do and I'm in a bit of a time crunch." I turn and continue my way to the dayroom.

"When you see Detective Richmond, tell him I would like to see him," Gwen says to my retreating back.

"I will."

When I reach the dayroom, I look around for Randolph but don't see him. I walk over to the back door and look outside and see him with his little band of smokers hanging out by the back garden area. I head outside and approach the group.

"Randolph, I need to talk to you for a minute," I say.

"What's up?"

"Can we go somewhere private?"

The others in the group exchange worried looks but Randolph smiles and says, "Sure." He leads the way over to the same bench area we sat at the other day and he settles in, patting the space beside him.

"My apologies, but your little fake pot ring is probably going to be busted. Dorothy knows."

"That's okay. We'll get a lecture and she'll watch us close for a while and then eventually everyone will forget and we'll be able to start again."

"Some of the patients we talked to said you've been selling more than just fake pot."

"You mean the Cialis and Viagra?"

I nod.

"I only sold those to two people. Then I got busted and they took the rest of the pills away."

"Just as well," I say, thinking that this explained the pills we found in Bernie's safe. "That stuff can be very dangerous if it's mixed with the wrong medications."

"Yeah, I knew that," Randolph says. "I wasn't being reckless. I asked both of the guys about other meds first."

My cell phone rings and when I look at the caller ID I see that it's the attorney's office calling. "Excuse me, Randolph, I need to take this call." I get up and walk over toward the administrative wing as I answer.

"This is Malcolm Wentworth, returning your call."

"Yes sir, thank you for getting back to me. I'm investigating the murder of Bernard Chase and we've been trying to track down his private lawyer to get a copy of his will and his partnership agreement for the Twilight Home. Would that be you?"

"It would."

"We'll need copies of the will and the partnership agreement sent to the police department."

"I'll have my secretary fax them over right away if you give me the number."

I don't know the fax number for the police station, so I give him the one for the ME's office. "I appreciate it," I tell him. "I'm not at the station now, but I'm curious. Who is the primary beneficiary on his will?"

"Interesting that you ask since he just changed it last year. He left everything to his three nephews. His brother has two boys, and his sister has one."

"Where are they?"

"The brother lives in California, although I think one of his kids is in college in Arizona somewhere. The sister and her son live in Florida."

"Is his brother or sister the secret partner who went in with him on the Twilight Home?"

"Nope, that's someone local," he says. And then

he tells me who it is and the specifics of the agreement that will come into play now that Bernie is
dead.

I disconnect the call and try to call Hurley again,
but it flips over to voice mail immediately, making
me suspect he's on his phone with someone. I briefly
consider leaving a voice mail, but decide against it. If
he really is taking a personal day, I should call someone else, anyway. Then I remember that I have someone here I can talk to: whatever officer is currently
guarding the administrative wing.

I head for the outside door to the wing and pound
on it. After waiting for a minute or so with no response, I pound again. When I still get no response, I
realize I'll have to get in from the inside. I debate
going back in through the dayroom, but realize it
will be quicker to go around the building through
the side employee parking lot and go in through the
main front door.

When I come in through the front door, I expect
to see Dorothy at the sign-in desk, but instead, the
nursing assistant named Linda is there. "Where's
Dorothy?" I ask.

Linda shrugs, sliding the sign-in book toward me.
"She said she was going to run some errands."

"I already signed in," I tell her. "I just came around
the building from out back."

She looks like she wants to argue the point with
me so I decide not to give her the chance. I head
straight for the door to the administrative wing.

The hallway in front of me is empty, but I see
lights on inside Bernie's office so I hurry toward it.
I'm a few feet away when I see the blood. Another
few feet and I see the head, and then the prostrate
body of Brenda Joiner, who is out cold, face down on

the floor just inside the doorway to Bernie's office. A large pool of blood is beneath her head and I see what appears to be a gash on the back of her scalp. Nearby on the floor is a golf trophy I remember seeing on the bookshelves. It has a thick, heavy base that is currently covered with blood.

I rush over to Brenda and feel along her neck for a pulse. To my relief there is one, and it's strong and steady. I reach for my cell phone to call 911, but as I hit the nine button the world explodes in a bright white light of pain. Then it all goes dark.

Chapter 32

My head feels like I've been banging it against a wall for the past four hours and the rest of my body feels weighted down, as if some giant hand from above is holding me down. Beneath me is hardness and when I try to shift my position to make the pain in my back and hips ease up, I find I can barely move. Someone cradles my head, lifting it gently, and then a comforting female voice says, "Here, drink this. The doctor said it will make you feel better."

I do as instructed, swallowing down a warm drink that tastes like super sweet chocolate. It burns a little and my entire mouth starts to tingle. The fierce pounding in my head is making it hard for me to think.

"A little more," the voice soothes, nudging the cup at me.

The liquid is coming too fast and after a few more swallows I clamp my lips shut against the cup. I try to push it away, but my arms feel leaden and I can't get them to move. The voice speaking to me sounds familiar and I try to open my eyes to see who it is, but there is a blinding white light that prevents me. The mention of a doctor makes me think I must be in the hospital, perhaps in the ER, recovering from whatever made me pass out. But something about that voice is telling me I'm in trouble. The cup nudges my lips again and I turn my head away, spitting out what is still in my mouth.

"Now, now," the voice says.

My skin breaks out in a cold sweat and my head starts to spin. I sense myself fading away and I struggle to hang on. I realize that the pressure I felt is someone straddling my torso, and I start writhing, bucking, and thrashing. I have the satisfaction of feeling my cheek connect with the cup, and feeling the warm liquid it contains sloshing over my face and neck. I also feel my leg connect with something hard and thin, like a vertical bar. As I hear a loud crash and the sound of breaking glass, the bright light I sensed beyond my shuttered eyelids disappears.

"That wasn't very nice," the voice says, all the sweetness gone from it. A hand grips my chin and brings my face straight up. I open my eyes and see the face hovering above mine.

"Dorothy." I'm frightened at how weak my voice sounds and in a flash, my thoughts just before I lost consciousness come back to me. "It was you. You killed Bernie, didn't you?"

"Why would I do such a thing?" Dorothy asks. The tone in her voice makes the question sound more like a challenge than a denial.

"I haven't quite figured that part out yet," I say, struggling to sort my thoughts. I look around and realize I'm on the floor inside Bernie's office over by the couch. "The rumor that was going around, that the patients were dying off before their time, was true wasn't it? Except the patients had it wrong. It wasn't Bernie killing them off. It was you. It all made sense when I heard about the symptoms the dying people experienced. It kept nagging at me that such very different causes of death would bring on such similar symptoms."

"You always were one of the smart ones," Dorothy says. "I knew that back when I first met you, back when you worked in the ER. You should've stayed there. You were a good ER nurse."

My head is still spinning and I can't get rid of the sensation that I'm slowly fading away, like the Cheshire cat. "That nitroglycerin you had in your pocket, you don't really need it, do you?"

"My doctor would say otherwise," she says. "But then he tends to believe anything I tell him."

"You mixed them together, the Cialis and the nitroglycerin pills."

She shakes her head at me and clucks. "Now, why would I do that?"

"Because you know the combination of the two can be extremely dangerous. That's why we ask patients who come to the ER with a complaint of chest pain if they've used any Viagra or Cialis in the last 24 hours. It's because we might have to give them nitroglycerin to relieve their chest pain. I'm guessing you used more than one tablet on Bernie and the others, didn't you?"

She sighs and drops the pretense. "I wanted things to be quick and merciful."

"You made their blood pressures plummet down to nothing, throwing them into shock. Their bodies couldn't compensate for the rapid vasodilation caused by the nitroglycerin because the Cialis does the same thing and for much longer."

"It isn't painful," she says, as if this should make it all acceptable. "Is it?"

Her question terrifies me. I understand now why my head is pounding so hard and why I feel so weak. I thought it was because she coldcocked me with something, but it's much more than that. Dorothy has poisoned me with the same drugs she used on the others. My blood pressure is probably so low it can barely sustain consciousness, and it's only doing so because I'm lying down. When I try to get up, my dilated vessels won't be able to compensate for the change in position and the extra pumping power needed to get blood to my brain. "You gave me the same thing? You gave me what you gave Bernie and those patients?"

"Well, not exactly. Bernie confiscated the Cialis I had in my desk here at work, but he didn't know that I also had several tablets at home from the stash I took from Randolph. Sadly, I used all of it on Bernie so I have none left for you. It's a shame, but I had to be sure. And it's a good thing I didn't scrimp because he almost didn't die. It's much easier with the older folks. Their systems are so weakened already that it doesn't take much. With the comorbid conditions they have, no one expects any other cause. Even if they did, who would think to look for an erectile dys-function drug in someone who is bedbound in a nursing home?"

"You put it in Bernie's coffee?" I ask weakly.

"Humph," she says, looking troubled. "I didn't think you'd find it that fast, though technically it wasn't in the coffee."

"It was in the sugar substitute," I say.

"Very good," Dorothy says, bestowing me with a begrudging smile of admiration. "Bernie used a ton of that stuff in his coffee all the time."

"You were here when he drank it?"

"Of course I was. I try to never leave things to chance. I called him Saturday morning and told him I wanted to go over the financials because I had uncovered some irregularities in the tax filings. The Saturday timing was intentional, of course. None of the other admin staff comes in on the weekends so we had the wing all to ourselves. I got here early, parked two streets over, and came in through the back door so no one would know I was here. I unplugged Bernie's desk phone and mixed up the crushed drugs with the sweetener. Then I brewed a pot of coffee and waited for him to get here. I know he typically uses the back door so odds were no one was going to know either of us was in the building.

"Everything went according to plan at first. Bernie got out the tax papers and we each poured ourselves a cup of coffee. Same routine we'd gone through a hundred times before. That's how I knew he put a lot of that fake sweetener into his coffee. Apparently, I didn't make the mixture strong enough because while it did weaken him, it didn't do it fast enough to kill or even disable him right away."

I remember Hurley commenting on the tumescence in Bernie's penis during his autopsy. The evidence of what was used on him—short and long acting vasodilators—was there all along, but we didn't realize it. "Coldhearted," I mutter, knowing I shouldn't, but unable to help myself.

"I didn't mean it to be. Honestly, I thought it would be quicker. I never stuck around with the others, so Bernie was the first one I was able to witness." She pauses a moment and looks off into space with a reverent little smile. "I have to admit, it was intriguing to watch it all unfold. While all the close calls seemed a bother at first, I found the whole thing kind of exciting."

"Close calls?" I asked, confused.

"Oh, yes. Several of them. When Bernie felt himself going, he asked me to help him, but I just sat there. He looked for his cell phone, but he'd set it on the desk when he first arrived and I picked it up with a loose glove and slipped it into my pocket while he was busy pouring his coffee. Then he tried to use the desk phone, but of course that didn't work. I'd unplugged it."

"We were wondering about that phone. Figured Bernie was too weak to use it. Or dropped it when he saw Bjorn."

"Ah, yes, Bjorn. When that fool came in the back door and headed for the restroom, I didn't know who it was at first because I had my back to the hall, and I thought my plan was going to fall apart. But no one came into the office and then Bernie lurched out of his chair and into the hallway. I'm sure he saw Bjorn and followed him, thinking Bjorn would help him. Everything in me told me to run, but I stayed in the office because I didn't want to be seen and I didn't know who had come in. Those moments were quite a rush, I tell you! I heard the bathroom door squeak the way it always does and I knew where they were."

"You got lucky."

"Not luck," she says, looking offended. "Smarts." She taps her temple a few times. "If you're smart and you plan well, things go your way."

I'm stalling for time and know Dorothy is smart

enough to figure that out, but her reaction to my luck comment makes me think I might be able to get away with it a little longer if I go after her ego. I shake my head weakly and say, "No, just dumb luck."

Dorothy frowns, but rather than broaching any further objections, she continues with her story. "I decided to go ahead as originally planned and I put on the gloves I had in my pocket and plugged the desk phone back in. I swapped the dead battery from my cell with Bernie's and put his phone back on his desk. They're company phones and the same make and model, so that part was easy. After that, I decided I was going to sneak out the back way and let whatever happened happen, but just as I reached the door to Bernie's office, I heard the bathroom door open and saw Bjorn come shuffling out of there in a panic. He had his head bowed down so he didn't see me as I ducked back inside the office. He went right by me, mumbling and muttering to himself.

"Again, dumb luck," I say.

Dorothy's jaw tightens. For a second, she looks like she wants to hit me, but she visibly gathers herself together, getting her emotions in check, and continues on as if I hadn't said a thing. "Once Bjorn was out the door, I went down the hall to the bathroom and found Bernie on the floor, unconscious but not dead. I knew it wouldn't be long before someone else arrived and I didn't have much time. I'm not sure what I would've done if Bjorn hadn't been kind enough to leave behind that isolyser powder. It provided the perfect finish and someone else to blame for Bernie's death."

"Bernie was already dead by then."

"Was he? Hmm. I must be losing my touch." She pauses, looking thoughtful for a moment, and then shakes it off. "Anyway, after dumping the powder down his throat, I hurried back down the hall and cleaned up my coffee cup so it would look like only one person had been there. I was going to empty Bernie's cup and refill it with fresh coffee, and take the altered sweetener with me, but before I could, I heard voices and the back door opened again. That's when Irene came in. That was a shocker. I didn't know she had a key."

"She's had it for years," I say, fighting the faintness. I'm still trying to stall for time because I know that if Dorothy gave me nitroglycerin only, the effects will be short-lived. If I can wait her out, I might have a chance. "The previous owner gave it to her," I say. "They used to take the bodies out through the administrative wing."

"Whatever," Dorothy says, dismissing my side story with an irritated wave of her hand. "The point is, she got in. Fortunately, she went past the office straight to the men's room and didn't see me. I thought there might be others outside the door so I didn't want to risk going out that way and being seen, and I couldn't go out the front way. Not only was it likely Irene would see me, but whoever was at the front desk would, too. Plus I thought Irene would call the police right away, so I couldn't stay and hide in Bernie's office." Dorothy pauses and sighs. "I have to say, that was my lowest moment in this whole thing. But I kept my cool and used my head. That's when I saw the windows."

"Windows?" I say, looking confused.

"Yes, those windows over there that open onto the side of the building near the end of the parking lot. They're close enough to the ground that it was easy to unlock one and climb out."

My challenges to Dorothy's ego have bought me precious time. I can feel my strength starting to return, and the dizziness starting to recede, but I sense Dorothy's growing impatience. I decide to switch it up and stroke her ego a little. To make her think I'm growing weaker, I talk in shorter gasps as if I'm fading. "Taking the coffee . . . that was . . . brilliant."

"Yes, it was, and it wasn't easy," she says with a smile. "When the cops started talking about poisons and posted a guard back here, I thought my goose was cooked." She pauses and frowns. "I still don't understand how you were cued in that there was another cause of death. I figured suffocation from the powder would be obvious enough and would point the finger at Bjorn."

"Might have," I say in a breathless whisper. "But you were . . . too thorough . . . too neat."

My cold sweat has dried and I can feel my strength returning bit by bit. I realize this means Dorothy was telling the truth when she said she didn't give me the entire cocktail she gave the others. I can tell my blood pressure is slowly rising back to normal, but I know that she will soon realize this as well. If luck is with me, I might have one chance to escape from her clutches, but I will have to be careful to time any move I make with Dorothy's awareness and my body's recovery. If I get up too fast or too soon, I'll simply pass out again. I need to keep her distracted a little longer.

Dorothy gives me an odd little smile and for a moment I fear the jig is up. But then she says, "I was too thorough? What do you mean by that?"

"Bjorn said he dropped . . . the container of isolyser powder . . . and some of it spilled on Bernie's face." I say this in short, halting phrases as if I'm too weak to speak an entire sentence at once. "But when we found Bernie . . . the bottle was empty . . . the powder all poured into his mouth." I pause and moan for effect before continuing. "That, plus . . . massive pulmonary edema . . . we realized something and . . . someone else . . . was involved with his death."

"Yes, I see that now," Dorothy says. "Very clever." She is still straddling me, her knees pinning down my arms. She's not a particularly heavy woman, but she is tall and solid. Getting her off me won't be easy and my arms are starting to go numb from her weight on them. Hoping for a little more time, I go back to Dorothy's coffee coup, and toy with her ego a little more.

"You were lucky . . . a chance . . . to get rid of . . . the coffee."

"Okay, I'll give you that one," she says. "That *was* a stroke of luck. When I saw you and that detective go running out like the place was on fire, I saw my chance. I knew the guard officer on duty had just gone down the front hallway to use the public bathrooms, and he had a magazine with him so I figured I might have a minute or two to do what I needed. I went outside, climbed back through the same window I'd gone out earlier, dumped the coffee down the sink, rinsed the cup, and put it back on the desk. After the guard yelled out, 'I'm back,' there was a silence so loud I could hear my heart pounding. Then he started mumbling something and I could tell he was walking down the hall toward Bernie's office. I thought for sure he was going to find me, but I heard the door at the end of the hall open again and heard the cop ask, '*Who are you?*' "

"It was Arnie," I say, recalling Officer Foster's recounting of the events that night.

"Yes, how did you know?"

I don't answer her. Instead, I let my eyes drift closed, feigning a barely retained consciousness.

"Doesn't matter," Dorothy says. "Anyway, I knew I had to get out of there because this Arnie fellow said he wanted to go into Bernie's office to dust for prints. That's when I realized that I hadn't been wearing gloves when I rinsed out Bernie's coffee cup. I pulled the sleeve of my sweater down over my hand, picked up the cup, and wiped it off with the front of my sweater. I set it back down and made a mad dash for the window. It was quite a rush!" she says, her voice excited. "Just as I slid that window back into place, the two men walked into the room."

"Surprised we didn't . . . notice window unlocked," I say weakly, keeping my eyes closed.

"Remember when I paraded into Bernie's office with the lawyers that first time?" she says with a smug tone. She doesn't wait for me to answer or nod. "I locked the window while you and that detective were exchanging barbs with Trisha. It was the perfect distraction. I would have liked to get the sweetener then, too. I was prepared to grab it and hide it under my sweater, but it was already gone."

I open my eyes and risk a look. The dizziness is better, but not gone. Dorothy is staring down at me and as soon as she sees me look at her, the smug smile on her face evaporates. I know my time is up unless I can find a way to keep her talking. I switch gears again and try to put her on the defensive.

"You weren't . . . clever enough," I say. "Bernie figured it out . . . didn't he? That's why you . . . killed him. He knew . . . what you were doing."

"No way," she says irritably. "Bernie was an idiot. He found those Cialis pills in my desk drawer, but he didn't know what they were. He thought they were some kind of street drug or narcotic and told me I would have to be drug tested." She rolls her eyes and scoffs. "Can you imagine someone suspecting *me* of drug abuse? I'm much too professional to do something like that."

Clearly the irony of that statement, given that she has just admitted to committing cold-blooded murder on several people, is lost on her. "I'm confused," I say, slurring my words on purpose. "Then why . . . kill Bernie?"

"Because he had no idea how to run a business for profit," she says with a sneer. "He'd already run several other businesses into the ground and this place would have sunk months after he bought it if I hadn't managed our patient population the way I did. Bernie didn't care. He had family money to fall back on. But I put everything I had into this place. I never married and I have no children, so this place is the only mark I can leave behind. It's my legacy."

Probably not the sort of legacy you had in mind.

"The partnership agreement specifies a buyout option in the event that either partner is incapacitated or dies," she goes on. "With Bernie out of the way, I can buy his portion of the business and become the sole proprietor. I intend to change the name of the place to the Granger Home."

"Can you . . . afford that?" I ask, stunned that she is talking like she's still going to be able to go ahead with her plan.

"I can now. I've saved quite a bit since I became a partner, and my mother died last year, leaving me a moderate inheritance. I've been trying to convince Bernie to let me buy him out for the past year, but he kept refusing. When he found those pills and started talking about drug testing, I saw the writing on the wall. He was going to flip things around and try to get rid of me so he could buy out my portion. I couldn't let that happen, not after everything I've put into this place."

Dorothy pauses and looks over at the spilled drink. "Enough of this talk. Clearly you don't have enough of the nitro in you since you're still conscious. And you got me talking long enough to weaken the effects of what you did get. Since you spilled the little cocktail I made for you, you've forced me to come up with a Plan B." She reaches into her pocket and removes a small brown bottle that I recognize immediately as nitroglycerin pills. "I'll just have to do this the old-fashioned way." She unscrews the lid from the bottle, grabs my chin in one hand, and squeezes my cheeks together hard, forcing my mouth open.

I realize she's about to dump the entire bottle of pills in my mouth, and I know how fast they work. Whether I'm ready or not, it's now or never.

My reaction time is a split second too slow. I feel the pills falling into my mouth and I struggle to spit them back out. I manage to rid myself of some of them, but a few are stuck under my tongue, to the sides of my inner cheeks, and to the roof of my mouth. At the same time I'm spitting, I lunge up as hard as I can with my legs and body in an attempt to throw Dorothy off me. I succeed in toppling her, but when I try to get on my hands and knees so I can get up from the floor, I discover my arms are half-asleep and not obeying me. Instead, I start to roll like a log, wanting to get as far away from her as I can. I roll until I hit something while I keep trying to spit out what's left of the pills. They're only pieces now, more than half dissolved. The medication is already in my system, absorbed through my oral mucosa. The question is how much.

I look over and see Dorothy struggling to get to her feet. She's not a young woman and that's working in my favor, but at the rate I'm going she's still going to beat me. My arms are gradually waking up, but my mouth is tingling again and I know it's the effects of the nitroglycerin pills. I feel something hard and cold at my back and I feel around with one hand trying to discern what it is. When I realize it's Arnie's scene-processing kit, I quickly roll back half a turn so I'm facing it, and I fumble with the latch. When I get it open, I try to raise the lid, but the kit is jammed against the wall and there is no room for the lid to swing.

Dorothy is on me then, and I roll onto my back to fight her off. The cold sweat has returned and I know that my moments of consciousness are numbered. I reach behind me for the evidence box again and manage to slide it away from the wall. As she grabs my chin with her iron grip, I think she must have more of the pills and I try to keep my mouth tightly shut. Instead of squeezing my cheeks together, she thrusts my chin upward, and I feel her hands close around my throat.

I fumble with the evidence box, getting the lid open. I visualize the layout in my mind as my hand grapples with what I can feel. I have what I need, a scalpel that's used, among other things, to scrape dried blood samples off surfaces. With the last bit of strength I have left, I take it in my fist and swing it around, jamming it as hard as I can into Dorothy Granger's neck, right where her jugular and carotid should be.

Everything goes dark again.

Chapter 33

Tuesday, March 4

Dear Diary,

I finally came home from the hospital today after nearly dying. I have to say that as far as near-death experiences go, this one was a disappointment. There was no feeling of calm, no disappointment when I realized I was still alive, and no beckoning bright lights. The only bright light I saw was the ophthalmoscope the ER doctor was shining into my eyes. Beyond that it was nothing more than an all-encompassing darkness.

I wanted to leave the hospital last night, but the doctor insisted I stay overnight to make sure there were no residual effects from the nitroglycerin and the precariously low blood pressure I had when the EMTs finally got to me. Izzy and Dom promised to take care of Hoover and the cats for me, so I agreed to stay and rest. In one way, Dorothy did me a favor. She got me out of my gym appointment and my session with Dr. Naggy. Plus, this crappy hospital food is bound to help me lose a pound or two, though I know that won't last.

It's a good thing that annoying lawyer, Trisha, came by when she did or it's quite possible Dorothy Granger and I would both be dead. That nursing assistant stationed at the desk ratted on me by calling Trisha, who then hurried over to make sure I wasn't looking at things she had said were off-limits. As a result, both Dorothy and I survived, though I dare say Dorothy probably wishes she hadn't. I managed to grab a scalpel from a scene-processing kit that Arnie had left behind, and apparently I nicked her carotid artery. Had I hit the artery square on, she'd be toast now. But I didn't, and after some quick surgery to fix her up, she is sitting in jail. I was unconscious when Trisha found me and the EMTs were able to figure out what the problem was when they took my blood pressure and saw the empty nitroglycerin bottle on the floor along with the pills and pieces of pills I had spit out. They got two IVs into me and ran fluids wide open to bring my pressure back up, and then they rushed me to the hospital.

By the time I got to the ER, I was conscious and my pressure was up, but not a lot. And it didn't want to stay up when they slowed down the IV fluids. I also had a gash in the back of my head where Dorothy had initially hit me with what I later learned was the base of one of her fancy office lamps.

I'm lucky she didn't hit me hard enough to kill me. Fortunately, the crack on the head she gave Brenda Joiner wasn't a fatal one, either, though she did end up with a slight skull fracture that will earn her a month or two off duty. I've been told it will be with pay. Heck of a way to get a paid vacation.

Ironically, David was on duty and in the ER when I arrived because they thought I might be a surgical candidate, and they knew Dorothy would be. Fortunately, I didn't have to let the bastard touch me and I told the staff on duty that I didn't want him to have anything to do with my care. That left him free to fix up Dorothy. I figure they deserve one another.

Arnie called earlier today and told me that after he cued the Madison lab on what to look for they found traces of nitroglycerin and Cialis in Bernie's stomach contents and in the artificial sweetener. I have to admit, it was a brilliant way to kill someone and we may never know for sure just how many patients Dorothy did in with this little drug cocktail over the years. She was right. No one would have thought to look for those two drugs in the average, bedbound nursing home patient.

I suppose I should be glad Bernie Chase's murder has been solved and that my friend, Bjorn, has been absolved of any crime associated with the death. Solving this case meant answering a lot of questions, but it also left a lot of things unresolved. I think the thing that saddens me the most is that the only peo-

ple who are likely to be hurt by Dorothy Granger's actions—other than her murder victims, of course—are the patients who live in the Twilight Home.

Trisha Collins and her band of greedy lawyers will be raking in the dough for years to come, by charging Bernie's estate for the day-to-day management required to keep the Twilight Home open and functioning, and by defending against all the lawsuits that are bound to come from the family members of the patients Dorothy Granger killed.

Now that the partnership between Dorothy and Bernard is irrevocably broken, the place will be put up for sale (another revenue stream for Trisha, no doubt). I can't help but wonder what will happen to the place. Will it continue to function in the capacity it is now? Or will it be closed down and reopened as a different business altogether, forcing its residents to find new homes? No one knows at this point, but for now the residents will be allowed to remain there. No doubt the uncertainty will have some of them feeling out of sorts, but I imagine they will continue on with what's left of their lives, finding that little bit of joie de vivre wherever and however they can. I imagine they'll continue to smoke their fake pot in the garden, have their motorized wheelchair races down the halls, and escape from time to time by going to church, taking a Sunday drive, or simply walking out a door they're not supposed to. I wish all of them lots of joy, the best of luck, and happiness for whatever is left of their lives.

I received several shocks during my stay at the hospital. No, not shock therapy, Dr. Maggie. They were shocks to my psyche.

The first came Monday night when I was lying in my hospital bed and my mother appeared along with William-not-Bill. For the woman to leave the house for any reason was surprising enough, but for her to leave the house and enter a building known to be a source of deadly infections was nothing short of a miracle. Granted, she did wear a mask and gloves the entire time—I suspect she put them on before she ever left her house—and she avoided touching any surfaces or sitting in any of the chairs. She said she came because she was concerned about me and felt like maybe she hadn't been the best of mothers over the years. She said she wanted to try to make up for it.

I couldn't help but suspect an ulterior motive, but I didn't figure out what it was until she told me I needed to primp a little because, after all, I was in the hospital and there were lots of cute and potentially available doctors running around. Maybe I could find one to replace David. I laughed off her efforts and told her I would never marry another doctor. She ignored me and went digging through my purse looking for makeup. What she found instead was the copy of Emily's drawing.

Mother took it out of my purse and stared at it for a long time before she asked me what it was. When I told her it was a drawing of a man who had been lurking outside my cottage and peeking in through my windows she broke into a huge smile. Needless to say, that wasn't what I was expecting so I asked her what was going on. She came back at me with a question of her own, asking me if I didn't recognize the face in the picture. I told her I didn't although I had thought the face looked vaguely familiar when I first saw it. She said she wasn't surprised I couldn't remember because it had been a long time and I was very young the last time I saw him. According to my mother, the face is that of my father.

I have no idea why my father would suddenly reappear, or why he would be spying on me through the windows of my house. Since I haven't seen him again, I realize I may never know. Part of me wonders if my mother is mistaken in her identity of the face in the picture, but my gut tells me it's true. I guess all I can do now is wait to see if he shows himself again.

Desi came to see me this morning, and she told me she and Lucien talked and she has decided to let him move back home. They are taking things one day at a time, but I feel good about their chances. They clearly love one another and belong together. I'm glad I was able to provide a little financial help for them and at least relieve some of the pressure. I have to say, family relationships can be so complicated!

Hurley and Emily came to see me last night right after my mother and William left, but it was a very brief visit. I could tell from Emily's face that she had been crying, so I assumed Hurley had told her the news, but I wasn't sure if the letter from her mother had arrived. I didn't want to ask. I was feeling a lit-

tle embarrassed that I knew such a private thing
about Emily in the first place, not to mention the circumstances under which I came to know it. I finally
learned where things were just as they were about to
leave. Emily needed to use the restroom so a nurse
directed her to a public one, leaving Hurley and me
alone for a few minutes so we could talk.

Hurley kissed me and stroked my head and told
me he was glad I was okay and that he couldn't bear
the thought of losing me. It wasn't an "I love you,"
but it was about as close as I'm probably going to get.
He told me that Kate's letter to Emily did come and
that she was taking things quite hard. He said he
planned to keep her out of school for a few days and
take time off to be with her, to help her get through
this.

I listened to him complain again about having to
learn this new dad role that "was forced on me," and
how he didn't want kids and didn't need this kind of
complication in his life. I reassured him that he'd do
fine, but he didn't seem convinced. He does seem resigned to being there for Emily, though. He told me
he even called in a few favors from a private detective he knows in Chicago to see if he can find Kate.

Hurley called me this morning to say he wouldn't
be up to visit me today. That's when he delivered my
second shock. Apparently, the PI has succeeded already and found the hospice where Kate is staying.
Hurley is going to take Emily there so she can be
with her mother during her final days. He told me he

wasn't sure how long he'll be gone. It doesn't matter. I miss him already.

The final shock of my hospital stay was also the biggest. When Doc Leonard, the hospitalist who was taking care of me today, asked how I was doing, I told him I felt good except for a continued battle with nausea. At first, he thought it might be an aftereffect from drinking the nitroglycerin-laced cocoa, but when I told him I'd had the nausea before that and thought it was a stomach bug of some sort, he ran some more tests. He said he thought I might have developed irritable bowel, or colitis, or some other bowel disorder that can be triggered and exacerbated by stress, because I'd certainly had plenty of that in my life. All but one of the tests came back negative. The one that was positive was my pregnancy test.

I spent the next ten minutes in complete and utter denial. I told him I couldn't be pregnant. I'm on the pill. While I did admit to a few sexual excursions with Hurley recently, they were mere days ago, too soon to register as a pregnancy. He asked me when my last period was and I couldn't remember. My days and nights, heck my entire life has been a blur of sleep, eat, and casino for the past two months. I admitted that I didn't always take my birth control pills at the same time every day and I might have missed one here or there when my sleep schedule got flip-flopped by the casino hours, but surely that wasn't enough for this to happen.

Doc Leonard looked at my medical record and

saw the bronchitis and sinusitis I had right before Christmas, which was treated with antibiotics. That was my weak point, he told me. Antibiotics can interfere with birth control pills. He did a little bedside ultrasound and even though all we could see was this little bleeping light that he said was a heartbeat, he told me I was likely at least eight weeks along. That means it happened that first night, the night that Emily and Kate arrived.

Once I accepted the fact that I was pregnant, I became worried about how my recent encounter with Dorothy might affect the fetus. Not only was I concerned about possible teratogenic effects of the nitroglycerin on the developing fetus, but also about the frighteningly low blood pressures I'd had. Had they affected my level of circulation enough to compromise oxygenation to my baby?

I discussed the ramifications with Dr. Leonard, who agreed there was some room for concern, though he didn't think it was a lot. Pregnant mothers with heart conditions take nitroglycerin all the time and he found some study that showed only one birth defect in all the mothers who were in the group. He felt the low blood pressure was more of a risk and since mine was low for such a short period of time, he again said he felt the risk was very, very small, not enough to be statistically significant. Still, there is a risk and he suggested that I have genetic and other early studies done if I am concerned. I might do that. There is always a risk of potential birth defects, even in a normal pregnancy. Unless the tests reveal something

truly horrific, I know that I will have, love, and care
for this child no matter what. It feels so right to me,
though I can't help but wonder what Hurley would
say or think if he knew.

My feelings about Hurley are mixed. Over the
past few days, I heard him tell me several times how
trapped he feels by his sudden forced fatherhood,
how he isn't fit for the role, how he doesn't want to be
tied down, and how he feels duped by Kate. How can
I tell him I've just doubled his trouble?

Plus, I just got my job back and at some point I'll
have to tell Izzy. I don't think I'm fat enough yet to
hide an entire pregnancy. The one thing I am sure of
in all this is that I want this child and I'm going to
keep it. I want it more than anything in the world, no
matter what happens between me and Hurley.

But I also have to face the reality that I might end
up being a single mom and I'll need a way to support
myself and my child. That means having a job. Here
in Sorenson, the only job I seem able to get that provides me a decent wage and some benefits is working
with Izzy. If he knows Hurley got me pregnant, it
might jeopardize my job, and if I lose my job I'll
probably have to go looking for another one outside of
town. But I don't want to leave Sorenson. All my
family support is here.

I suppose I can tell Izzy that the pregnancy is the
result of a one-night stand and leave it at that. I
don't have to tell him about the other episodes with
Hurley. Hell, I don't even have to tell him the one
episode was Hurley, but since that episode occurred

when I was no longer at my current job, it shouldn't be viewed as a problem. The problem is what will happen down the road.

Based on recent behavior, I think it's safe to assume that Hurley has feelings for me, but are they enough? Am I simply a fun roll in the sack? Will he be angry that he's been "trapped" once again into fatherhood? I'll have to tell him of course, at some point, but I may wait awhile and ease into it. Either way, I can't see myself ever marrying him, even if he asked. I'd never be able to convince myself that he wasn't doing it out of some sense of duty and obligation.

For now, I'll give him some time to get through the thing with Kate and Emily. He has enough on his plate and it won't be easy no matter how or when I tell him.

Still, I know that regardless of the outcome, my future is looking brighter than it has in a long, long time. Dr. Maggie would be delighted to know that my overwhelming emotion right now is happiness.

There is another upside to all this, one I can't wait to tell Gunther about. Now I can eat pretty much anything I want. Not only can I blame my appetite on the fickle hormonal surges of pregnancy, for the next seven months I'll be eating for two.

Life is grand.